ELEVATOR TO HELL

MATTHEW BENJAMIN

ELEVATOR TO HELL

A NOVEL

A BLACK AND BLUE BOOK PUBLISHING GROUP
LOS ANGELES

A Black and Blue Book
Copyright © 2012 by Matthew Benjamin
Cover Design Copyright © 2012 Kate Jones
All Rights Reserved
Published in the United States of America by A Black and Blue Book Publishing Group,
Los Angeles

ISBN 978-0-615-48926-1

Printed in the United States of America

Contact http://ablackandbluebookpublishinggroup.com for electronic
and other pertinent information regarding this publication.

This first novel is dedicated to Sasha and Bert—
two sides of the same coin

ACKNOWLEDGEMENTS

This independent work of fiction was in many ways a great learning experience. Looking back, I don't know how I ever reached the finish line. But I do know that I could not have done so without the following people: Megan Speer, Trudy Conchita-Joseph, Kate McCarthy, Micole Loeffler, Susan Han, Bill McCann, Patricia Locacciato, Alex Constantine, and the Orange County University of Chicago Alumni Book Club—eight or nine brave souls who had the willingness to read my first draft in between Shakespeare and Dante. I, of course, am responsible for all its flaws.

"Home is a place where, when you got to go there, they got to take you in."

—Robert Frost, *The Death of the Hired Man*

APRIL 23, 2005

My name is Nic Reilly. I'm thirty years old, going on thirty-one, and I'm writing this from an undisclosed location in the Mexican Sierras as I ponder my next move. I did not always live in hiding south of the border, and my transition was rather sudden and unexpected. Until about a year ago, I led a challenging but relatively stable life as the owner of an eclectic music shop in Detroit, struggling to survive in an industry that was experiencing seismic change with the onslaught of the digital-file-sharing revolution. Yet despite the daily uncertainty, my routine was ordinary, my intentions pure, and my conscience clear. Every morning I'd wake up in my rented house, make myself coffee, and drive over to my shop on Woodward near Grand where I spent most of the day selling and buying, bullshitting with clients and friends, and discussing strategies with my beautiful store manager, Karolina Torgustive. I was also sleeping with Karo whenever she allowed it. That was pretty much the core of it.

I mention this modus operandi not to put anyone to sleep, but to highlight the transformation that has occurred since. My metamorphosis was and is, by any measure, by any standard, quite remarkable. On one level, I changed from a caring and peace-loving musicologist—a man who adored Johann Sebastian Bach, Miles Davis and Marvin Gaye, to name a few—to an unflinching, cold-blooded, murderous saboteur; a person who would secretly journey seventeen hundred miles across a continent loaded with seditious materials to methodically and savagely execute his own brother. Yes, brother. Or, more precisely, half-brother. That was just one atrocity. There were others.

So what happened? How did I become so skewed? What caused the big 180? Well, these things are never simple, but for the sake of expediency I'll just say it began where it begins for all of us—with parents. And when I say parents, I'm referring to my mother and my biological father, not the man whom I always considered to be my father. That man's name was Barney Reilly, but more on him later. First, let us deal with the perpetrators, the scourges of my misfortune, the spermatocytal vagabonds, if you will: good old Marge and bio-Dad.

1
ROOFTOP ROMANCE

Marge is my mother. She is a good woman who has always been there for me throughout my life. I could not ask for a better guardian or teacher and I am not the least bit bashful to say to the world at large that I love her dearly and always will. I also believe that she is unique given her geographical heritage and cultural upbringing. Marge was born in the year 1951 of Irish and Polish decent and grew to an adult in the city of Detroit during the 1960s and 70s. Her teenage years coincided with the final stages of that city's great white flight to the suburbs and the dismal transmogrification of the once first-rate Detroit-based American automobile industry. No one, I believe, who lived at that time, under those circumstances, came out of that social and economic cement mixer unscathed. Yet, for me, two decades later, growing up in northwest Detroit, some of the things I remember most are the principles that Marge instilled in me and which categorically defied what I was presented with in the world outside my home. The first of these principles she promoted is tolerance, a priceless asset if you are to survive and prosper in any setting. The second is giving people the benefit of the doubt, even if it takes great imagination and causes consternation to do so. The third is forgiveness, which does not need explanation but is probably the most difficult to truly embrace on a daily basis, especially in a city torn apart by racial enmity and bitterness.

Now, as you will soon find out, I did not always adhere to Marge's borrowed teachings. In fact, I would say I made an absolute mockery of them when I was presented with certain inflammatory situations that begged me to apply these principles to my life and to whatever immediate decisions I was to make. Perhaps a more visible comparison would be that of a young son of a once chronic alcoholic who survives his ordeal and continuously warns and preaches about the evils of alcohol abuse to the son and then on the son's twenty-first birthday the son goes out on a ten year bender and drops dead of alcohol poisoning. Hence, my spectacular failures as an adult are entirely of my own making and have little or anything to do with my upbringing. I proved this to myself when I singled out Marge as the person I feared most when in the passions of my heretic obsession to destroy another human being for my own profit and then again afterwards when I was dodging my tenacious persecutors. Her eventual discovery (along with tens of millions of others) of my actions was probably more punishment than any criminal justice system could ever impose on me. So Marge, directly or indirectly, on a tangible level, is not responsible for any of this recent madness; in fact, it is quite possible that she has become one of its biggest victims.

I purposefully preface with the above attributes and brief character study of my mother and her innocence because I also painfully (and cynically because I can't help myself as much as I try) need to point out that Marge has her faults, or had them, and what I have to reveal is not pretty, yet it is essential to my story and must be told. My mother also has an adventurous personality. Adventure, of course, can be a very good thing and usually is but there are those times when a little less adventure may be the wiser course. This is typically acknowledged in retrospect. In Marge's case, one of those times happened somewhere between the ages of 21 and 23 when she decided to become a rock and roll groupie. Yes, my principled mother was a Detroit groupie. Now, to me, the word groupie doesn't sound all that horrible, but let's face it the specific job description details are rather crude. In her defense, though, this was in the early 1970s and not the best decade in American history in terms of morale and hygiene. Or, as my best friend Jonathon—who now teaches at Harvard—used to say: "There was no Martin Luther King, Jr. or Malcolm X in the Seventies, but there were Cheech and Chong and the Symbionese Liberation Army—the diaper rash unit of militant revolution." And apparently the well-documented drug experimentation of the previous decade, the 1960s, was no longer an experiment, but more like a way of life. So I have to allow Marge a little leeway here. She was a product of her time and that should not be forgotten. Although, having since become a musicologist, it is enough to make me hemorrhage to imagine my good mother bending over for some of the most untalented, ephemeral, two-chord pinheads ever to step foot on a chartered bus. Because along with the shooting stars of that period—such as David Bowie, Stevie Wonder (Motown had already moved out of Detroit to Los Angeles by this time), John McLaughlin and the jazz-fusion surge, Lou Reed, Duane Allman, to mention a few—there were some seriously defunct stray hacks calling themselves musicians roaming about the countryside with hollow sounding secondhand guitars and getting their tubes cleaned on a regular basis. This, remarkably, is the backstory to my genesis; this is the pasture in which my prize Arabian horses grazed, because it is a documented fact that my mother was impregnated by one of these so-called musical talents while practicing her chosen vocation.

I learned most of this information, mind you, not from Marge but from Stu Manowitz, a bushy-haired, slightly overweight, poorly dressed Detroit Tiger baseball-fanatic lawyer, who was and is my mother's oldest and best friend. Stu and Marge grew up a few blocks from one another in East Detroit, went to grade school and high school together, and, although this was never openly discussed, were romantically involved for a brief period in their teens. From what I pieced together she dumped him, but that did not affect their close and ongoing friendship which has lasted to this very day.

As told to me by Stu, who sequestered the information from Marge, my holy creation went as follows: I was conceived on the roof of the Riverbed Hotel on Fourth Street in downtown Detroit after a rock show at the Cobo during a mid-August heat wave. Evidently, the window air conditioner in the band's shared hotel room went on the fritz that night, which prompted Marge and her evening date to break away from the sweltering orgy and climb the fire escape to the roof for some fresh air. Once there, they proceeded to fornicate like wild boars in the wilderness, their course, guttural moans blending into the deep rumble of the internal-combustion city traffic below. (I told you I was cynical and it may not have happened exactly like that.) Regardless, and despite the imagery, I have tried to look at the bright side and have concluded that this hire-wire conception induced some major change, and not all bad, either. First and foremost, it forced Marge to temper her passions, forever ending that rather dubious phase of her mostly honorable life. Second, and perhaps more important, a little less than nine months later she became a loving and devoted mother—even if it is I who was born.

*

As I understand it, and I am by no means an authority, Marge's decision to go through with the pregnancy could be considered unusual. This was right around the time of Roe v. Wade, and most groupies in her circumstances, I assume, would have chosen an alternate path. My belief, however biased, is that Marge wanted out of that lifestyle and I was her exit. That's the storybook version, anyway. Whatever the true reasons (I never asked), it still took Marge a good six or seven weeks to fully comprehend the fact that she was pregnant—a mini-eternity in her walk of life—and thus was forced to do a little adding and subtracting in order to correctly pinpoint the other individual involved. Once that complex process was over, and having made her decision, she then attempted to notify the father and request that he participate on a financial level in the birth and upbringing of this baby. She expected no more and in my thinking a very reasonable request. After all, it takes two. Unfortunately that proved to be more difficult than anticipated because of my bio-Dad's musical obscurity at the time coupled with his gypsy lifestyle. Eventually she caught a break through her pipeline and tracked him down to a little club in West Berlin where he and his band members were performing as a third act. Not surprisingly, bio-Dad was quite surprised by the news, especially since he, according to Stu (according to Marge), barely remembered the incident. And who knows, maybe he was legitimately skeptical and did not believe he was responsible. She was, after all, a backstage groupie and he most certainly was not her only recent partner. The net result was that he was not interested in the offer and confirmed it by slamming down the phone and never taking her calls again.

To Marge's credit, she never gave up. She was quite certain about the identity of the father and she most assuredly needed his support and was reminded of it each day as she watched her body grow large. Finally, some seven months following her decision, and about three weeks after I was born (prematurely), bio-Dad had quietly returned to the United States and was discovered hibernating in an unheated log cabin in Northern California with his poet girlfriend and promptly subpoenaed. This sting could not have been accomplished without the assistance of Stu, who had recently passed the bar and was hired by a Detroit law firm in the Bricktown area downtown. With Marge urging him on, Stu utilized the firm's private detective services and cornered bio-Dad into taking a court-mandated blood test.

In those pre-DNA days, blood tests did not definitively prove the identity of the father, but they could establish a "probability of paternity" if the computation of the three blood types (mother, father, child—the As and Os and Bs, and negatives and positives, etc.) did not disprove the alliance, and if other circumstantial facts such as timing and mutual consent were in order. And that is exactly what happened. Bio-Dad was found to be my probable parent and ordered by the judge to pay child support. Or, another way of looking at it, there was no more mystery or doubt by anyone about who my co-creator was.

I'm sad to report, however, that after bio-Dad made his obligatory court appearance—the second and last time bio-Dad and Marge would ever set eyes on each other—he began his elusive touring again, and did not follow through with his commitment. Once this deadbeat pattern was firmly established, the burden to keep track of him became a liability and Marge finally had to accept her lot. She was on her own. She would receive no help from gypsy bio-Dad in the upbringing of her newly born child. To compensate, hair styling became her chosen profession, and she began cutting hair part-time at a discount until she earned her beautician license. She also turned her living room into a playpen and provided undocumented child care services for her many single mom friends. And from what I learned there were other small-time entrepreneurial gigs for small-time cash, such as doing people's laundry, sewing and similar tasks.

But as many of us know, this type of good, honest labor can be insufficient to cover the mounting expenses of modern daily life. As a single mom with limited resources, Marge struggled with uninsured doctor bills, baby formula, rent, living expenditures, and the fear and uncertainty that goes along with that struggle. This resulted, for Marge, in a terrible episode of the shingles and a deteriorating mental condition in the latter portion of my first year of life—a downward spiral heightened by an incident that, given its timing, might have seemed unduly cruel but miraculously turned out to be a huge blessing in disguise. (Doesn't it often seem to work that way? Just when you think you can't take another step, a miracle happens? Or is it just me?) The unexpected providential sequence went as follows:

The utility company turned off our electricity for lack of payment, and Marge had to scramble to borrow money to get the power restored—a nerve wracking experience for anyone with a small child in the house. The very evening of the day the electricity got turned back on, somehow my feisty nine-month-old frame climbed out of my crib and got tangled in the web of electrical wiring that converged under the kitchen table. Back then, in the Stone age, sparse kitchen outlets doubled as electrical grids for clumsy pre-digital machines such as the waffle iron, the fat toaster, and the noisy refrigerator. In my growing entanglement, which quickly worsened, like a cat in a snake pit, sparks flew, appliances went crashing, and I proceeded to almost decapitate myself, burn to a crisp, and blow up the apartment building for good measure. After Marge frantically untangled me, saving my life, the lights flickered a few last times before the entire building turned an ominous dark. This was, so to speak, the last straw. Marge completely broke down. Weeping uncontrollably in the blackness and the clutter, utterly desperate and forsaken, she found the strength to call Stu, her best friend. Stu in turn called an electrician buddy, and lo and behold, the darkness began to turn to light. A beautiful, bright and shining light it was— and his name was Barney Reilly.

2
THE LIFE AND DEATH OF BARNEY REILLY

It was about thirty minutes after I almost torched Marge's little garden apartment building that Barney arrived. He was inhaling a Kool menthol cigarette and carrying a hand-painted psychedelic toolbox that he designed himself. He swiftly took out his flashlight, perused the humble surroundings, the blown fuse box, the athletic kid in the now-fortified crib, the good-looking, shapely single mom who was still in tears, and that was pretty much that. He knew he was home. Everything else was just a matter of time and logistics. He was going to live with these two for the rest of his life and take care of them, which is exactly what he did.

The first sixteen years or so of my life I never thought for one second that Barney was not my biological father. True, we didn't look too much alike, but a lot of families didn't look alike. Similarly, we didn't look too unalike, either—enough, anyway, to draw attention to our separate genetic identities. So it never crossed my mind. I mean, why should it have? Barney was a part of my earliest memories and photographs and no one soul told me otherwise. It's only when I look back now, long after the fact, that I can spot clues that would make me question any of it. Not that it would have made a difference had I known as a child because Barney was a terrific father and I was blessed to have him in my life. My only complaints are petty and on par with what every kid has to deal with when coexisting with much larger beings on a daily basis. In Barney's case, he smoked too much, both cigarettes and the evil weed. He also talked aloud to himself quite often—running conversations in public places—as he debated, say, the pros and cons of purchasing a particular product. And perhaps his greatest flaw, as I saw it, he *abused* his live, bootleg Grateful Dead and Creedence Clearwater

Revival tapes by playing them to death. But that was about as bad as it got. In terms of the things that really matter: he was not a drunk or a pervert, he rarely lost his temper, he was a creative and entertaining teacher, and, above all, he stood as a good example of what a man should be like.

Given my recent history, it doesn't make me feel any better to confess that I had two relatively well balanced adult figures in my life and I still turned into a front page mess. I've known many others who had nightmare experiences growing up with abusive parents or none at all and they turned into model citizens. Nonetheless, Barney had one particular interest that needs to be highlighted because of its relevancy to my subsequent bio-journey: his great enthusiasm for fireworks. In truth, it was more of an obsession than an interest and he was a complete nutcase about anything that exploded above his six-foot frame and was continuously blowing things up. I absolutely loved it, but not so with our neighbors who would regularly call the police because Barney was regularly lighting up the neighborhood skies in the middle of the night, sometimes in midwinter. We lived in a house off McNichols next to a small park, and the infield of the baseball diamond was his launching pad. Back then, Barney knew all the cops and bribed them with free electrical service and devices. But even bribed cops from a remarkably corrupt metropolis like Detroit—a city known for its random gunfire, violence and arson—could not look the other way when the heavens were flashing and thundering all around them. After numerous warnings and pleadings, Barney was formally instructed by the police chief himself to cease with the flying gunpowder or he would be arrested for violating city ordinances.

Like any good addict, Barney found other ways to feed his habit. By far the most enjoyable for me was the periodic desert excursion. Every once in a great while, when the funds were liquid, Barney would pack up me and Marge and fly us all out to Las Vegas, rent a van, and drive about forty miles east of town to an Indian reservation where Barney was allowed to blow up anything he wanted. The Indians had their own patch of the Mojave, their own autonomy, and an unlimited supply of fireworks for sale of which Barney took full advantage. From what I remember, too, everyone—Barney, Marge, and the Indians (I wasn't allowed)—shared a healthy penchant for the evil weed and indulged accordingly. Those colorful, magical desert night skies in the middle of nowhere are some of my best memories, thanks to Barney. But all good things come to an end, and in this case, the end was Barney's.

I was sixteen-years-old at the time, and it was the first tragedy I had ever experienced. We were back in the desert, and a faulty fuse caused a missile to ignite prematurely and explode in Barney's face. Adding to this horrendous spectacle, the explosion sent a stray fireball whistling into the rental van where Barney stored his arsenal, detonating it, and causing the loaded vehicle to buck and dance across the black desert like a wild bull with a giant stick of dynamite stuck up its ass that wouldn't stop firing. When it finally did stop, some fifty yards later, all that remained was the chassis and axles. Everything else was gone. And I say this not to be disrespectful, but watching that van gallop and burst into mighty nothingness was one of the most remarkable things I've ever witnessed, and I am absolutely certain that Barney would have felt the same had he not already been scorched unconscious from the initial explosion and, thus, missed the whole thing.

Barney spent fifteen weeks in a Vegas hospital in a pseudo-vegetative state, his upper body severely burned and bandaged. He was then flown back to Detroit where Marge and I were allowed to wheel him home and tend to him ourselves.

As you can imagine, this was a challenging adjustment for everyone and took some getting used to. Interestingly, the logistical complications and restrictions attached to Barney's unsightly bodily deformation were not our biggest concern. Rather it was his mental condition. According to the physicians, the brain damage was restricted to the left cerebral hemisphere, causing paralysis to the right side of his body, and also some really goofy general behavior. It was goofy because he would at times act perfectly normal (bedridden, paralyzed, perfectly normal), but other times he would suddenly drift off into a semi-conscious state where he could not be "reached," yet would still be awake. His eyes were still open and blinking, and he would crush-out his cigarettes, if that helps any. Sometimes I would go on talking to him for quite some time before realizing his switch had turned off. I never quite figured it out, nor did I ever fathom how conscious he was of his semi-consciousness. It was, for me, complex, and I believe the same held true for the physicians. Eventually, I dealt with it the best I could, as did Marge, although it pained me even more to watch Marge cater to him. She never let on, of course, to either one of us, yet I knew it destroyed her to see Barney in that state, a fragment of the handsome, life-loving man she adored. No more wild nights frolicking in the desert or between the sheets. Those days were gone forever.

This was equally true for the revenue that Barney generated. Until the accident, Barney was responsible for all our living expenses and insurance premiums. The Blue Cross he paid into all those years covered the hospital visits and the proliferating pharmaceuticals, but it ended there. Marge had to drain their savings accounts to pay the mortgage and the other regular bills, as well as to fund the new semi-invalid incidentals, including a conversion of the downstairs den into Barney's bedroom and bathroom since he could not navigate the second floor. Unfortunately, again, the real victim of this new financial stress was not me or Marge, but Barney—his awareness of it. His unusual mental condition did not shield him from the harsh reality that he was unfairly stuck in time and could no longer provide for his family. Even worse, that he had become a burden. And no matter how much we lied to him, he knew better. In my opinion, this *awareness of helplessness* is what eventually did him in. That's what killed him.

To compensate, Marge returned to the salon and I was fortunate to find a part-time job at a very hip record store called *Sledge's Eclectic Emporium* on Woodward. The owner was, and still is, a tall, angular, bespectacled black man named Sledge Parker, who possessed an uncanny ability for dates. To pay the bills Sledge promoted the Detroit Motown sound and rock and roll, but his real love was jazz, and he had practically everything ever recorded in stock. I learned much from Sledge and eventually took over the shop, but I'm jumping. The point is this job helped to compensate for Barney's immobilization—a suffering that came to an end about three weeks prior to his fortieth birthday and nine months following the desert incident.

The cause of death was not brain seizure, stroke, blood clot or something brain-related as one might suspect, but lung cancer, of all things. Conveniently, we were planning a big birthday party for him, and the invitations were quickly revised to give notice of his death. To this day, I'm convinced that Barney chose the time and cause of his farewell (an instinct that was corroborated years later by a backwoods preacher). Both reflected his wry sense of humor, and his concerns for me and Marge. Over one hundred people attended his funeral, including neighbors, customers, many members of the Detroit Police Department, and a group of Hopi Indians who flew in from Nevada to perform a drum recital in his memory. As the drums beat and the chanting grew louder, I kept thinking about how much I loved Barney and yet how relieved I was to see him move on. He was not a happy camper in his new role as paraplegic, brain-damaged, burn victim, and I knew in my heart that it was time for him to leave this physical world and see what was next.

*

As Barney's son I learned many things. One of them was the inner workings of electricity—a magical and powerful force that few people understand. I don't really understand it either, not the way I understand baseball or even certain laws of physics, but I get the general idea: electricity never takes the long route. It always chooses the shortest path. It seeks its freedom in the most direct manner, and it will light, heat, fuse, fry, or sizzle anything that is too weak to resist it. This principle became important to me not only as a practical necessity, but also as a metaphysical law: be direct, know your limitations, and if someone gets in your way, push through them.

What follows is the heart-to-heart that Barney and I shared right before he died. I like to refer to this as Barney's "deathbed revelation." Because of this conversation, I later found myself forced to apply the electricity principle to its absolute fullest. This memorable and somber exchange took place in midwinter, and I distinctly remember it was snowing a unique, brownish Detroit slush. It could not have been more depressing if we were being pissed on by Satan himself.

But at least it blanketed the shit-stained, month-old sidewalk ice that I had just slipped on coming into the house. He called me into the den and asked me to sit down. "I got something to tell you," he said. I replied with the usual, "What is it, Dad?" And that's when it started:

"I'm not your dad," he blurted out.

Not sure of his mental condition at the moment, I remained calm and asked him to repeat himself, thinking he could very well be in some other universe.

"I'm not your dad," he repeated firmly without any signs of ambivalence.

"You're kidding?"

"Take a good look at me, son. Do I look like I'm kidding?"

I looked at his toasted, mangled body. He was not kidding and appeared to be in a lucid sate.

"Can you be a little more specific, then?" I asked politely, still thinking there might be a screw loose somewhere.

"I wasn't the guy who got your mom pregnant."

"What?"

"I said," he said, "I am not the man who impregnated your mom. There was someone before me."

"Who was before you?" I asked weakly.

"A musician."

"A musician?"

"His name is Ben Tyler."

This took a second. A long second. "Ben Tyler? You mean *the* Ben Tyler?"

"Yeah, the *Iron Horse* guy."

"You're kidding?"

"I thought we covered that, son. I'm not kidding."

This was incredible, surreal information if it was true. Ben Tyler was a well-known rock star who reached stardom in the 1970's with a band called *Iron Horse*. This was followed by a solo career with even more fame and success.

"This is a little hard for me to take, Dad. Ben Tyler is my biological father? Is that what you are telling me?"

"Yes. I know this must be weird to hear this. That's why I wanted to be the one to do it—tell you."

"Why didn't you tell me before?" I asked in disbelief.

"Well," he said, as if expecting this, "at first you were too young. Just a baby. And then as time went on we figured it was best to just leave things the way they were."

"Why?" I asked with a little bit more authority.

"Let's just say," he said slowly, "when I met your mom it was over between Ben and her and Ben wasn't doing too well as a musician. He didn't have any money at that time."

"So you mean like he wasn't able to help out or anything?"

"Yeah, yeah, that's exactly what I mean. So I kind of just took over."

"I see."

"Yeah," he mumbled, carefully monitoring my reaction.

"Well, what about later?"

"How much later?"

"After he became rich and famous."

"Well, actually, son, that wasn't too much later. I think it took him about another year or so to hit it big with that trashy album of his. The *Elevator* one."

"And?"

"And then I think, well, he was kind of busy, you know, being a rock star and all."

I was waiting to hear more but he stopped talking. And for a moment I thought he checked out, but he hadn't. He was just thinking about how best to proceed:

"You know, Nic," he said as he lit up and inhaled deeply, finding the strength, "I love you more than anything in the world and I tried my damnedest to be a good father to you."

"I know you did, Dad. You're a great father. The best!"

"Thanks. But there's something more I want you to understand. It's important."

"What?"

"I adopted you when you were almost a-year-old. That's why we all have the same last name."

I thought about it a moment. This was the first time I considered the technical aspect of Barney being my father given this new information. Yes, this was true, we had the same last name.

"And when I did that," he continued, "adopted you—Ben was no longer responsible for you. Legally and forever."

"Yeah?"

"Yeah. That's the law."

It took a few more seconds before it clicked: Ben Tyler was a wealthy man and I was not entitled because of the adoption.

"Oh, I see," I said slowly as the reality filtered through my blood stream like a giant thimble of whiskey.

"Trust me, son," he said, knowing I understood, "no one in a million years thought Ben would get lucky. And, well..."

"What?"

"—there was the temptation—for me anyway—to tell you about him so maybe you could develop a relationship with him but your mom was against it."

"Why?"

"She was afraid he wouldn't respond."

"Why?"

"After he suddenly got rich, Stu contacted him for past child support and he paid up, or his lawyers did, but he still made no effort to see you, and the door was wide open. I made sure of that. I wanted you to have every advantage. But he never did. I think some of it had to do with him getting married right afterwards. I imagine a lot was going on for Ben back then. I'll give him that. Although, that's no excuse."

Working at the record shop, at the time, I remembered reading in the music gossip columns that Ben Tyler married twice and had five kids from the two marriages. The first wife was a poet, and the second a performance artist.

"It was a tough decision not to tell you," he continued, "but we were trying to do the best thing for you. I swear."

"You did the right thing, Dad."

"I hope so. I thought about it every time one of his songs came on the radio, and they were always coming on. That's why I listened to those old Dead tapes all the time."

Finally his Dead and CCR fixation made sense.

"Thanks for telling me, Dad."

"Thanks for understanding, son. You sure you're okay?"

"Yeah, I'm okay."

Although, to be absolutely truthful, I wasn't okay at all. If anything I was stupefied. Later, after Barney checked out, I remember taking a long walk despite the winter hazard. This was more than a lot of information to synthesize. Barney was correct. It was indeed most strange to think, to accept, that after all those years someone other than Barney was my blood, my co-creator, and that Ben Tyler, a household name, was that person. At some point, I thought, I would have to talk to Stu. Not just then, but when the time was right. It's always a good idea to talk to a competent lawyer before venturing into the unknown.

3
DISCOVERY

About three weeks after Barney's funeral, the time had come to find out more about my estranged bio-Dad. So I jumped on a Grand River Avenue bus and rode downtown to talk to Stu. As noted, Stu was a baseball fanatic, and back then he shamelessly cluttered his office with corny Detroit Tigers memorabilia, particularly from the year 1968. That autumn the Tigers captured the World Series led by their star pitcher, Denny McClain—the last player in the majors to win thirty games in one season. Tragically for Stu, he later had a falling out with the city and the Tiger organization when the Tigers abandoned old Tiger Stadium in 2000 and moved into the new Comerica Park. That half-mile or so cross town transition, according to Stu, was a form of "esthetic and cultural urban genocide" with which Stu could never reconcile. A harsh assessment, perhaps, but if anyone had a basis to complain about municipal injustice, it was Stu. He was one of the very few in his economic class who did not join the white flight to the suburbs in the 1960s, and as of this writing he continues to make his home in Corktown, a progressive little Detroit neighborhood, no more than a few blocks away from what's left of his beloved Tiger Stadium.

When I approached him that one day after school seeking news about Ben Tyler, he patiently heard me out and agreed that I had the right to know the facts. He assumed that I would seek them out regardless, as kids do, and it would be better, for accuracy's sake, if most of the inflammatory information came from him. His one major concern was Marge. Well aware of her reticence (guilt) regarding the touchy subject matter, he did not want me going back and discussing my new found information. I assured him of my discretion, and soon after he entrusted me with everything he knew.

And he knew quite a bit which I will now convey. I must warn you, though, some of this information may seem extraordinary in terms of character, but as you'll soon find out that's precisely the point. So bear with me:

At the time of my high school discovery, which is our time reference here, both of Ben's parents (my blood grandparents) were deceased, but Ben had two siblings, both older and both still breathing. Of the two, however, Gertrude Tyler, the eldest, was to die tragically four years later. Gertrude started out a missionary nun in Bolivia in the early 1960s and was later expelled from her diocese for gross sexual misconduct, an obsession that I quickly found out runs in the family. She stayed in the general area nonetheless, joining radical lay missionary sisterhoods, a few of which she reportedly started herself. Her goals in life were to provide for the needy and the oppressed, to oppose ruthless governmental oligarchies and their punitive methods, and to satisfy her strong carnal desires.

Her death, according to two Chilean newspaper reports, was caused by her "slipping off" an edgy cliff high up in the Chilean Atacama Desert while attempting to organize local labor forces that were building sites for the new powerful telescopes that were beginning to pop up along the Andes for the Southern Hemispheric view. This accident was witnessed by more than two dozen people, including many scientists and engineers who were supervising the installation of a forty-meter telescope on this particularly mountainous sight. Because of the credentials of these individuals, there was never an official investigation beyond recording initial eyewitness statements, even though her body was never found. Yet everyone, friends and foes alike, was fairly certain that Gertrude was dead because she was never heard from again, and that alone was sufficient evidence. So Gertrude never figured into my story, but her personality should be noted, for it was this type of extremism that I would soon become accustomed to from all the Tylers.

Gertrude's other younger brother, Hank Tyler, is an entirely different story in that he plays prominently in my adventure and is still very much alive to this day. Much more will be devoted to him as events unfold. Suffice to say that at this time, not too long after Barney's death, Hank partnered with Ben in a record label called Prostitute Records based in Los Angeles. Because of Ben's copious industry connections and his brother's aggressive marketing campaign, it was not long before Prostitute Records stores began spreading like acne throughout the country and then Europe and elsewhere, although at this point in time they were just getting underway.

Ben's first marriage was to the poet Molly Sivad. Her claim to fame was a published collection of dark poems entitled *To Die Or Not To Die*, which explores the horrors of adolescent angst and indecisiveness. For a poetry book it was considered a rogue success and sold over 400,000 copies between 1972-75. Their first child, Megan Tyler, was born in North Hollywood five months after Ben and Molly were married in a graveyard ceremony (Molly's choice), and six months after I was born in Detroit. Thus, Megan was Ben's oldest legitimate child and six months my junior. Eleven months later, she was followed by her brother, Stan Tyler, Ben's oldest legitimate boy, and it was in between these two births, Megan's and Stan's, when Ben struck gold as a rock star with the sloppy and mediocre album, *Elevator to Hell*—which Barney made reference to in his death bed revelation. The story of how this occurred is rock and roll legend and worth repeating:

Ben and his struggling Iron Horse band members were especially hung over one afternoon (they always awoke, when they woke, in the afternoon) and were forced to buy two new amps because the bassist had thrown up on stage the previous night. Apparently, the puke was so fetid that no one would go near the two saturated amps, including the stage hands, which allowed the chunky, reeking liquid to filter and drip into the circuitry and ossify the boards. This forced Ben, the band leader, to drag his tired ass out of bed the following afternoon and go to Sears, the cheapest place he knew, with money he didn't have, to buy equipment for a gig that night. For spite, he woke the band and forced them to go along.

After they walked across town to save a few pennies, they entered the store and onto the small elevator. Just as the elevator door closed, someone farted. This provoked a heated argument among the members, but Ben had reached his limit. Trapped, suffocating, gassed, hung over, and broke, he allowed his temper to get the best of him and began repeatedly hitting his bass player over the head with his guitar, screaming "this is hell, this is hell..." Before he knew it, he had himself a nice little melody. Just to make sure, Ben whacked the bass player a few more times, and, yeah, he was sure, as were the others. Once the elevator door opened, they ran like hell down the stairs and over to the studio to record it before they forgot, adding lyrics and a chorus. Six weeks later, *Elevator to Hell* became an instant mega-hit, and Iron Horse went on to make three consecutive platinum albums before Ben went solo and continued the platinum streak.

It was following the beginning of this magnificent stardom that Ben married his second wife, the performance artist Isabella Vasquelez. His interest in her began when he attended one of her shows in a closed wing of the San Diego airport terminal that had been converted into an underground theater. That particular night, Isabella was dressed only in a white diaper and sat perched on a flimsy wooden highchair and stuffed large, shapely vegetables down her swollen throat which generated course, primal noises as the juices and pieces of skin and flesh from the dark herbaceous objects squirmed down her face, down her neck, across her breasts and into her soaked diaper. For Ben, this particular performance art was impressive on a number of levels and after the show he walked backstage and ran off with Isabella, as rock stars will do.

Ten weeks later, Isabella was pregnant. And there was a very good possibility that Ben would have attempted his typical legal sidestepping if not for Isabella's father, Marco Vasquelez, an extremely proud Mexican rancher and business man who bred race horses, grew and exported marijuana from his home state of Michoacán, Mexico, and operated a labor contract business that catered to California landowners and agribusiness managers who were in need of cheap, seasonal manpower to harvest big-money crops. Once Marco discovered that Isabella, his only child, was with child, he did nothing less than threaten to kill Ben if he did not do the responsible thing and divorce his poet wife and marry Isabella. Ben wisely did as he was told, divorced Molly (which cost him a fortune), and married the rancher's daughter. To Isabella's credit, though, Ben did not need much persuasion. She was, by most accounts, a strikingly beautiful and unique woman and you might even say that Ben fell in love for the first time in his life when he met her.

Isabella gave birth to three more of Ben's children in slightly over five years: Joseph, Jessica, and Josh. For some reason the letter J must have meant something to them. Ben now had two (three if you count me) sets of children, with both families residing in the Los Angeles area: Molly, Megan and Stan lived in Topanga Canyon; Isabella, Joseph, Jessica, Josh and Ben in the Hollywood Hills—although from what I understand, after Josh was born, Ben spent most of his time outside of California traveling the world.

*

Finding out about all this Tyler history was fascinating, slightly disturbing, and emotionally confusing because I realized rather quickly that I was alone with it. Marge, through Barney and Stu, was aware of my general knowledge, but her motherly pride would not allow her to open up with me, despite my many subtle references. I was not interested in the sordid details (I kept my promise to Stu), but I believed the circumstances of my birth should no longer be swept under the rug like it had for seventeen years. But it was to no avail. Marge would always find excuses to avoid the subject, and I eventually had no choice but to accept her position. As time went on I was hoping this would change.

I was equally disappointed with my friends. In sharing my new bio-story, I was seeking camaraderie and support and all I got was doubt, resistance and cross-examination. I then quickly realized that I might be compromising Marge and possibly the memory of Barney by answering their many nosy questions. So I stopped almost before I started and decided to keep my strange biology below the radar. This was Stu's advice as well because nothing had really changed (with the exception of Barney dying). Everything else, legally anyway, stayed the same. Of course, had I not been adopted, it would have been a much different story. According to the state of California I had "birth rights." Unfortunately those rights dissolved with a notarized, City Hall paperwork exchange some sixteen years prior.

One of the few people I did choose to talk to about bio-Dad was Sledge Parker, my employer and the owner and visionary of Eclectic Emporium. Sledge was a successful businessman and musicologist, and, at an earlier point, ran a profitable counterfeiting operation until one of his operatives got sloppy and made a swap for real cash with a planted federal agent. Fortunately for Sledge, he was not convicted of printing phony bank notes, just passing them on, so his stint was limited to a first-offense, plea-bargained, five-year federal prison rap tied to a lengthy parole. It was in prison where he was tagged with the nickname Sledgehammer, or Sledge for short. Usually a peaceful man, the incident that brought on the change was a violent one and tells us much of what Sledge was dealing with in his life at that particular period in American history.

One average prison day in 1966, a white supremacist cold-cocked Sledge from behind in the prison chow line for no apparent reason, other than, you know, Sledge was black, and the other guy was superior, or however that works. Sledge went down hard but was able to endure the blow and tripped up his attacker using his spidery arms. Once the bigot dropped, Sledge sprung up like a cartoon superhero and proceeded to pound the guy mercilessly using his two stick-like arms, which appeared to be smelted together into an iron rod. This imagery was enhanced by large, sharp-knuckled hands, and the combination of arms and hands swinging windmill-like, over and over, gave the impression to those who witnessed this punishment that Sledge was wielding a sledgehammer and literally pounding his opponent into the ground like a railroad spike. Luckily for both Sledge and the supremacist, three prison guards halted the carnage just in time, preventing a bloody death. Since there was no swollen corpse to deal with—just a bunch of broken bones and pierced organs—the warden coolly declared that Sledge had acted in self-defense and sent his attacker packing to a maximum-security joint in Florida to serve out the rest of his term.

When Sledge was released from prison in August 1969, he returned to Detroit and started up Eclectic Emporium on Woodward. Because he was out of circulation, he missed the 1967 riots and part of the city going up in flames, but he did witness the tail end of the great white flight out of the city and the hardening of the color lines. I understand these were not easy times for urban dwellers, and despite the abundant challenges, Sledge maintained a healthy profit from a multiracial clientele, many of whom would come back from the swelling suburbs and other parts of the state to purchase from his store. For Sledge, it was all about the music, and music was still what drew people together. His shop became an instant classic and was a quiet, insider Detroit landmark by the time I started working there years later.

Sledge became my only true confidant other than Stu regarding the facts of my birth until I went to college later that year. His age, detachment, empathy (he still did not know who fathered him), and especially his familiarity with musicians and the music business made him a good choice. Without his fatherly presence I don't know what I would have done. He kept emphasizing one thing, "You can handle it," although my actions somewhat deified his counsel. At one point I asked him if I could set up a separate area in the frowned-upon rock division to devote to Ben Tyler and Iron Horse. It was a spontaneous request, and perhaps a bit bold, but Sledge allowed it. "Blood is thick, and you're the proof," he kept telling me—an obvious reference to how little he cared for bio-Dad's music. Nonetheless, he was dead on. Blood is thick, especially when it comes to parent-child bonding. Despite my devastation from the loss of Barney Reilly, a good and honorable man who will always be my father, I was equally intrigued that I had Ben Tyler's blood pumping through my veins. I was to quickly learn, however, that fame is a peculiar phenomenon, not only for the touched one, but for the people connected to them as well.

4
BLOOD AND MORE BLOOD

Fortunately, I had two other obsessions to distract me from the bio-Dad mind drain. One was music. My tenure at Eclectic began shortly after Barney's accident and CDs were coming into vogue (even though they had been around for a while and more on that later). The second, and much more important obsession, was my awareness of the existence of siblings.

As someone who grew up his whole life thinking he was an only child, the news that I did, after all, have brothers and sisters was nothing less than exhilarating. I can't adequately express the joy this information brought me. Granted, they were my half brothers and sisters, but the same held true for most of them. Unlike any one of them, however, I had no full siblings and grew up alone as an only child. Nonetheless, I instantly felt a deep bond with these coastal strangers. Here, I fantasized, would be the beginning of a lifelong collaboration that was sanctioned by the Almighty through the mysterious earthly progenitive process—a sacred union that could never be undone. I also took a childish pride in the fact that I was the oldest, the firstborn. Not by much, mind you, only six months or so, but like a crowned prince, I owned that title by birth and would not shy away from it. Needless to say, I became extremely excited and hopeful.

The only question that remained was how I was going to approach them and share the good news. Stu suggested writing. So I wrote letters to the oldest sibling from each family, Megan (family #1) and Joseph (family #2). I purposively chose not to write to all of them because I didn't want it to appear like a barrage of Christmas mail from, say, a distant, obnoxious relative. I believed the exclusivity would have greater impact. I also decided to include a note to dear old bio-Dad, since he would naturally be approached by his children at some point. Obviously, I had many other good reasons to contact the man who caused my birth and then abandoned me, but I chose to link the initial bio-Dad correspondence to the siblings. Likewise, given his history, I made the logical assumption that no one in California knew of my existence except bio-Dad and possibly his first wife, Molly Sivad, who was pregnant with Megan when bio-Dad was ordered to pay child support to Marge. I kept this in mind when composing.

In my letters to Megan and Joseph, I briefly introduced myself, explained my adoption, and mentioned a few of the less morbid reasons why my parents chose to withhold the truth of my biology until recently. Specifically to Joseph, who was barely fourteen-years-old at that time, I added, "It will be interesting to see if you and I look alike." This was done as a tiny gesture of brotherly affection. And that was all. The shorter the better, I thought. I didn't want to overwhelm them with details.

Bio-Dad's correspondence was of a slightly different tone. With him, I did my best not to sound like a battered housewife but stuck to the business at hand and suggested the time had come for the two of us to meet. I emphasized his rock star status meant little to me (not true) and, for guilt, made sure to include, "I am now seventeen years old and will be graduating high school in a few months." I punctuated all three letters with my address and phone number and encouraged a speedy reply.

As far as where to send them, I had little trouble securing the poet Molly Sivad's address (Topanga Canyon area), but digging up celebrity bio-Dad's street address was not as easy, especially in the pre-Internet, unlisted land-line numbers days. When confronted with problems of this nature, I would always default to the public library on Woodward. Early in life, I learned I could always find answers in the library. That never changed and this time was no different. So I took the bus to the library and after forty minutes or so of viewing dusty microfiche, I ran across a print advertisement in a Los Angeles fan magazine for something called *Hollywood's Map to the Stars*. This was reference to an actual street map that pinpointed where the celebrities lived. Ben was not a movie star, but he was a rock star, and, hoping a star would still be a star, I called the toll-free 800-number and was pleased to hear that Ben Tyler's house was indeed listed. All I was required to do was buy the map. I did so by mailing in a money order to a Hollywood post office box. Three weeks later I had in my possession bio-Dad's home address. I was now, incredibly, within reach.

Not trusting the corner mail box, I walked over one mile in the bitter cold to a central post office and proudly mailed my carefully crafted bio-letters. Soon, I thought, I would be in communication with my California siblings. Soon I would no longer be an only child as I had been my whole life. On the walk back home, after posting the letters, I did not feel the freezing weather. I was on a mission.

*

Growing up in Detroit, I have experienced racism firsthand and have come to understand that this social ill is so deep-seeded and ancient and complex, that most of us are helpless when affronted by its slithery tentacles. Yet it has gotten better over the centuries, and I'm confident that somewhere down the line racism will cease to exist and people will find more interesting reasons to viciously hate and sometimes destroy one another. But here's the point: in the meantime, you can be a common denominator, run-of-the-mill, urban racist and still be polite and a good citizen. In fact, it happens all the time. If this were not one hundred percent true, there would be nonstop mayhem in most communities throughout the world. Thus, this civility, regardless of its inbred hypocrisy (that is a separate issue) can apply to any kind of bias, hatred or annoyance. And it usually does. That's life. When I wrote the bio-letters to my California siblings, I was expecting nothing more than bare-bones reciprocity—the kind I have just described. I was hoping for more, of course, but I would have settled for the basics. That did not happen. In fact, nothing happened at first, because there was no reply. I briefly entertained the possibility that my letters had never reached them. Maybe I had the addresses wrong or the letters were intercepted and screened by fan-mail agencies, something along those lines. But then, I reasoned, if the letters were interrupted or incorrect, they should have been returned to the sender as required by law. They were not. So I waited until the beginning of spring—April, a time of renewal and rebirth—before following up with another round of letters. With Megan and Joseph, simply: "Did you get my last letter? This is Nic, your half-brother from Detroit. Please write back." But with Ben, the gloves were finally off. "If by chance you received my previous letter and still have not found the time to write back, you should be ashamed of yourself. I'm your oldest son, your own flesh and blood. How can you be so cruel? Farewell! P.S. I agree with everyone who says you got lucky. Your music sucks the big one."

As it turned out, my half siblings did indeed get my letters, both sets. This was confirmed by a letter I received in the mail about ten days after mailing the second set. The letter was from Megan Tyler. I'll describe it—not to bore you with details but because it very much needs describing. The front (address) side of the puffy envelope was blank except for a big, light-reddish stain near the bottom that looked like spilt ink of some kind, perhaps Indian ink. I wasn't sure. The back side, the pasted side, had my name and address scribbled on it. The writing substance used was smudgy purple crayon, and the penmanship so ungainly that it could have been written by an adolescent cerebral palsy victim. And that's being generous. Upon viewing it, I immediately thought that it was nothing less than a miracle that it ever reached my doorstep.

After marveling over it for some time, I opened it carefully. I pulled out what I thought was wrapping tissue but was actually toilet tissue. There was quite a bit of it, too, and for a brief moment I thought perhaps there was a small gift wrapped inside, such as a ring. I was wrong. There was nothing but crumpled toilet tissue. Just as I was about to toss it, I noticed markings on the very end. Upon closer inspection, the smudges turned into crude letters and read as follows, in the same disturbed purple crayon: "Eat my sloppy ass you fucking horse gonad. Love 'sis.' P.S. Since we're all of communal blood I thought you might like some of mine."

I put down the toilet tissue and looked again at the red stain on the front of the cheap white envelope. It was not Indian ink, after all.

The next postmarked letter from Los Angeles arrived two days later. This one was from Joseph. His envelope was unique, too, in that it was homemade and constructed from what looked to be an old *Scientific American* magazine cover. My name and address were neatly hand-printed on the front of the envelope using an atypical, creepy mixture of upper and lowercase letters. I was not sure of the writing substance he used, but it was thicker and grainier than ink or magic marker, and it smartly contrasted with the existing colors and print of the magazine cover. If I were to guess, I'd say he used dirty motor oil and a fountain pen. Inside there was no separate letter but there was a message written on the inside portion of the envelope, in the same upper-lowercase style, using the same relief writing substance. I unhinged and flattened out the magazine paper, and read the following:

"DeaR PAathEtiC lOSeR wiTH THe stUpID sTaTIonARy: i UndeRSTanD DetRoiT is haRD BUT pLEaSe kEEp mE ouT oF yOuR DEluSIoNs. OBViOUslY YoU aRe GeneTICALly prEDeStiNEd fOr AN eArLy DEAtH sO i'M noT Too woRRiEd BUTT YoU muST stoP WRiTinG THose HEinoUs lEttErs iN THe meaN TiMe. pLEaSe hURry Up aND DiE—YouR lITTle BRO. pS. iF i Do LooK LiKE yoU i wilL kIll mYSelf or JoIN THe CirCUs.

Despite the 9.0 earthquake warning I received in the previous letter, I was jolted by the second one as well. And scared, too, because two out of two was not a coincidence. Two out of two was nothing less than a trend—a biological trend in this case. A fucking virus. What species would write letters such as these? Was it peculiar to Los Angeles or was it simply the poisoned family blood? Or was it a combination? Still, I was not ready to abandon ship yet. There could be an explanation of some kind. Maybe they did not believe who I said I was, and they were being purposefully cruel.

Once again, I needed feedback. I jumped on a downtown bus and checked back with Stu. "I want your opinion," I said as I handed him the letters. He read Joseph's first, and I watched his eyes freeze as he was about halfway through. It was that same pensive, focused stare that you see in the faces of actors playing explosives specialists defusing bombs in the middle of Times Square. That grimace stayed chiseled on his face until he finished the tissue letter from Megan. The last thing he did was re-examine the back of Megan's envelope, as I had done.

"Menstrual blood?"

"I think so."

He handed back the envelopes, took out his handkerchief, and wiped his hands. "I thought Detroit produced the angriest youth in the world," he said. "I was wrong."

"What should I do?"

"What's there to do?" he asked back with a confused look on his face.

"I should still try to do something," I insisted.

"Change your address. That's what I would do."

"You don't understand. I've never had brothers or sisters."

"I have. They're overrated. How much more evidence do you need?" he said, waving the toilet paper in the air. "Did you hear back from Ben?"

"No."

"It's just as well. He spawned these things."

"That's more of a reason."

"What can you possibly do, Nic?"

"I can go out there."

"To California?"

"Yes. To talk to them."

"But you're not a psychiatrist."

"I'm a brother."

"Apparently, that means absolutely nothing."

"I'm the oldest. I feel I should try to do something, if not for them, for me. I can't just walk away."

"Why not try writing the other ones? Maybe you'll get a better response."

"What if it doesn't get better?"

"That's my point."

"I want to see them before it can get worse."

"I don't recommend that."

"If I meet them face to face, it can make a difference."

"How?"

"Because maybe I look like them, or maybe Ben will be there. He couldn't deny me then. Face to face it would be different."

"It's a very bad idea," he said, stressing the word *very*.

"I wouldn't go right away."

"When would you go?"

"I'll wait until I graduate."

"That's right around the corner."

"I'll take a train out," I said. "I always wanted to take a train across the country."

"So head to New York. That's across the country."

I was getting nowhere with Stu, and it was probably a mistake to consult him. In truth, though, no rational person would go along with this. Yet inside I knew I could not simply write off my newly discovered kin just because they represented themselves as disturbed and dangerous. I needed to take this one step further. I would journey across country and reach out to my brothers and sisters. This wasn't about insults, after all. This was about something much more important. This was about family.

5
VIRGIN CALIFORNIA

Before I left for California, I found out I'd been accepted to all three colleges I applied to: University of Michigan, Michigan State, and UCLA. Originally, my three choices were the Berklee College of Music in Boston, NYU in Lower Manhattan, and UC Berkeley across the bay from San Francisco. I chose those schools for their academic programs but also for their locations. All three cities—San Francisco, New York, and Boston—seemed like a dream to me. I pictured bustling cafes, an exotic night life, and ubiquitous fornication amongst strangers. This delusion was harbored by traversing the frigid, torpid urban-prairie of a depopulating Detroit for over 17 years.

The reason for the changes had to do with Barney dying. I did not believe Marge could handle losing both of us in the span of a few months. So I swapped my first two out-of-state choices to the two Michigan schools, and I switched my third choice from one California school to another. UCLA was not any closer to Detroit than Berkeley, but it was in Los Angeles, the home of bio-Dad and my half siblings. Thus, in the hazy, decomposing moments of that strange early gnostic period (everything seemed to be happening around the same time), I reasoned that even though I would probably not attend UCLA if accepted, I still had family there. Eventually, I went with University of Michigan. Ann Arbor was just a couple of hours drive from Detroit and this would allow me to return home for holidays, weekends, or emergencies. Michigan was also noted for its history and music departments, the two areas that interested me most.

To celebrate my high school graduation, Marge and Stu took me out to dinner in Greektown. Marge was happy that I had graduated with honors but deeply skeptical about my upcoming journey. She understood my urge but was fearful that I may continue to be harshly disappointed in my earnest attempt to bridge the huge gap at this relatively late date. Stu told her about the odious sibling replies and Ben's no reply. She cautioned that this twisted exchange/ non-exchange could get worse in California, only this time I'd be "all alone in a strange city." She even broke her silence regarding her relationship with my co-creator and admitted that she "barely knew him." She did not go all the way and admit that she barely knew him for only a few lascivious hours, but it was a courageous acknowledgment and the beginning of a new openness that would continue as the years rolled on.

Nonetheless, I had no intention whatsoever of changing my plans. I was going to Los Angeles. To prepare for my journey I purchased a new Walkman and stacked up on CDs. At the time I was listening to Philip Glass, John Williams and other contemporary classical composers, but decided to include a few Iron Horse albums in the spirit of hope and conciliation. I also singled out a couple of worn out softcover John Steinbeck books, *The Grapes of Wrath* and *Cannery Row*. Steinbeck was a hero of mine, and I was finally going to visit his golden California. My destination would be farther south than his beloved Salinas and Monterey, but it was still California.

On the day of departure, I repeatedly told Marge not to worry and agreed to call her collect every day once I reached L.A. That was the only way she'd let me out the door. Stu drove me to the train station downtown, and I could tell he was happy for me. Despite his concerns, at heart he was another old hippie and any kind of traveling—you know, "tripping around"—whether it be physical or in the mind, was considered healthy.

The plan was simple: take a regional commuter train to Chicago and then switch to the cross-country *Zephyr*. Once in Los Angeles, use mass transportation to get around. I did not deviate from that plan and inwardly I was thrilled to be leaving.

*

Los Angeles, as with most other places on first visit, was not what

I expected. Because it was new to me, it could have been an open sewer and still possess some novelty. Unfortunately, that turned out to be more true than I would have liked.

After I checked my bags into a locker at this Union Station, a beautiful Spanish Colonial style fortress that appeared to be recently renovated, I began walking in no particular direction. What I found out rather quickly, especially in my high school graduation year of 1992, was that much of downtown Los Angeles was a virtual slum with the exception of a few tall office buildings, a patch of government officialdom, and a couple of manicured historic areas—the train station being part of that last group. Granted, it was not as forlorn and burned out as many parts of Detroit—nowhere was—but it did contain the largest homeless population that I'd seen before or since in this country. And all this in one of the wealthiest cities on the planet.

Stupefied, I limped back to Union Station, collected my belongings and gladly took a bus up Sunset Boulevard and away from downtown. This westerly direction, I realized, led me to the real Los Angeles, through and beyond the community of Hollywood—which appeared considerably indigent, itself—and into West Hollywood, where the Sunset Strip begins and the ambiance of Tinsel Town, as most of us know, takes over.

Consulting my map, I departed the bus at the corner of Crescent Heights and Sunset and walked west, looking for affordable lodgings. The first thing that caught my eye was the rugged Marlboro Man levitating above the Chateau Marmont, a hotel I could not afford, followed by a series of giant billboards of exotic and shapely women wearing naughty underwear, expensive jewelry, tight jeans, and other brand names that I failed to register because I was too focused on the body parts. Below the billboards were bars, clubs, restaurants, boutiques, hotels, and an occasional pizzeria or hamburger joint that would not rupture my guarded budget.

I decided on El Matador, an aging hotel quite a ways up the strip that was in need of renovation and maintenance. It still possessed a distinct Southern California charm with its tall palms (branches missing), outdoor patios (cracking), fountains (not working), and indoor-outdoor lounging and dining environment (picnic tables and vending machines). My room was on the third level and gave me a good view of the Sunset Strip below. I could also see beyond the strip into the greater Los Angeles basin going south, southwest, all the way to the Pacific Ocean, which I could barely make out through the dense smog. Overall, I was quite satisfied with my choice, and I felt properly positioned to get down to the real business at hand: connecting with the elusive and mercurial bio-clan.

My first attempt to make contact followed a simple military tactic of attacking the farthest enemy position first and then working backward to the enemy line. This meant that I would first venture out to Topanga, and approach the poet Molly Sivad and her menstruating daughter, Megan, and go from there.

After a sound sleep with the windows open, I gobbled the complimentary hotel breakfast in the lobby and climbed down the zigzag, overgrown, cobblestone path to a sun-sparkling Sunset Boulevard. There I boarded an express bus that took me over the mountains to Woodland Hills, a community in the west San Fernando Valley, that was still, somehow, technically part of the City of Los Angeles, despite its suburban esthetics, deep valley location, and lofty economic base. I then switched buses and rode back into the mountains, and ascended through the canyon until I reached the Topanga village, a *Sleepy Hallow* type community with one main thoroughfare and perhaps a dozen or so tributary streets that wiggled up the mountain sides.

After getting my bearings at the post office, I walked about three hundred yards and began climbing one of the tributaries and stopped when I saw the number twelve etched into a wooden mail post. I had reached Molly Sivad's address. There was no house or driveway connected to the post, but there was a trail that swirled northwest through the thickening brush. I followed the trail about thirty yards until I approached a tall, gray tent that was shaped like a teepee. I was not sure why the tent was there, but I assumed it was functional and not decorative because of its authentic ugliness. It looked like something you would have actually seen four hundred years ago around Jamestown if you just fell off a ship from England dying of gout. Beyond the tent stood a three-story, red-brick, cylindrical structure that could have been mistaken for a lighthouse had it not been located in the middle of a forest. This strange building was covered with spotty foliage and capped with a lazy white flag. The flag implied a military or municipal affiliation until I saw what was written on it. It read, I quote: "SURRENDER GOD—YOU PUSSY—FOR WE ARE MORE POWERFUL." When I saw this, I knew for sure that I had reached my destination. Who else but people related to the authors of those horrible bio-letters could be responsible for such blasphemy? This is where one of them was breast-fed and reared.

Pleased that I had reached my destination, but reminded of the huge, huge gamble I was taking, I concluded there would be no bio-connection established here in the Topanga forest. It was too risky. The outcome too dangerous. I would be crazy to go forward. I might be killed, spat on, and buried, and no one would ever know. The only question left for me at that particular moment was whether I should pee before I turned around and returned to the hotel. Since I was sort-of in the middle of the woods, I just whipped it out and aimed it at a sturdy oak. The initial release felt detoxifying, and as I continued to hose the rich brown bark, I began to wonder why men feel more secure peeing on an object, such as a tree or wall. Maybe it's a subconscious habit formed from childhood? Then again, dogs piss on things, too. If you notice, they go out of their way to pee on fire hydrants and telephone poles.

As I was reflecting on this puzzling phenomenon, I heard a throaty female voice boom out: "That's what the tent is for." Startled, I looked up and there was a woman staring at me no more than twelve feet away in front of the tent entrance. She looked to be about 45-years-old, with short black hair, strong facial features, and a slender, sinewy body. Her most salient feature was her almost hollow but penetrating green eyes zeroing in on my watering Johnson like a cruise missile.

Embarrassed, I turned away and zipped up, coming damn close to clipping it off in the process.

"You're on private property," she continued.

"I'm looking for Molly Sivad, the poet," I said nervously.

"Aren't we all," she mumbled, and began walking to the lighthouse.

"Please, let me explain," I pleaded.

She stopped, turned, and looked at me again. "Listen," she commanded, "if you're going to kill yourself or you're thinking about killing yourself or killing someone else, please do it elsewhere and not on my property. My job as a poet doesn't include adolescent counseling services. Don't read the poetry if you can't handle it."

"I don't want to kill myself," I replied.

"Sure you do, everybody does," she said, and meaning it. "Especially at your age."

"Okay, maybe, but that's not why I came here."

"I never talk about my poetry. So you might as well go."

"That's not why I came either."

"Then why did you come here?" she asked, trying to control her anger. "To piss on my property?"

"I'm Ben Tyler's son, and I want to meet my half brother and sister," I blurted out.

Her no-nonsense energy came to a complete halt, like shutting the window in a wind storm. She began to study my features, my body. She inched closer to me. And then, incredulously, she squatted, yanked my partially zipped pants to my knees, and looked at my cock up close. "Well, I'll be damned," she marveled.

And from that point on, everything was okay. It was like the return of the wayward son in the New Testament. She invited me into her strange house, cooked banana pancakes from scratch, and answered all my questions to the best of her ability. She also filled me in on a lot of missing Tyler history, most of which I've already stated. I was right, too, to guess that Molly knew about me. Ben told her about Marge's lawsuit in an attempt to avoid marriage, the logic being that he could not afford matrimony because he was obliged by the court to provide child support. It didn't really make sense back then, either, and Molly got her way using her own methods.

After breakfast, Molly poured herself a glass of red wine that one of her neighbors had made right there in the canyon. It was only 10:50 in the morning, according to my watch, but I quickly realized time of day was not a big deal around here. Molly was curious about my upbringing in such a raw city as Detroit, and I gave her an overview of the geography, the neighborhoods, and my situation, including a little bit about Barney and Marge and why they chose not to inform me about bio-Dad until recently. She was a good listener, at first, but somewhere after her second glass she began to do most of the talking and delved into the important subjects of philosophy and religion. She was not an atheist, she said, and the God she believed in was neither a punishing God nor a forgiving God, but rather a doesn't-keep-His-eye-on-the-ball kind of God. That is why the world is so screwed up with poverty, disease, war, cruelty, insanity, and so forth. We humans are a reflection of that flawed deity, and if we are to survive, we must be strong. Indeed, God's recklessness forces us to be fearless, and that is our challenge—hence the flag on top of the lighthouse. Furthermore, and keeping with this primal theme, Molly explained that she designed the lighthouse herself. The goal was for each family member to occupy his or her own floor and be self-sufficient. Personally, I did not know if I agreed or disagreed with Molly's philosophy because I was barely 18 years old, but I did find her discourse interesting, if just a bit lopsided. At some later point in the conversation, I sought to change the subject and tactfully asked her, as though it were an afterthought, "By the way, where are Megan and Stan?"

As it turned out, Megan and Stan were camping in Alaska for the summer, having departed no less than two days prior. According to Molly, the Alaskan peninsula would soon be nothing more than a refuge for rotting fish, oil spills, and fast-food joints that serve fake frozen fish (at this time, to Molly's credit, global warming was not universally accepted). And she wanted her children to see it before that happened.

"I guess my timing is off," I said, disappointed.

"Sorry."

She then guzzled the remaining wine in her glass and took off her shirt. I was mortified—but pleased. For most teenage boys, older women are merely a fantasy, but this was beyond my wildest imagination. She had such full, lively breasts and looking at them made me feel very happy. For a split second, I became bitterly confused because I thought I may be related to her in some way and was forced to quickly compute the data, you know, she used to sleep with my estranged blood father many years ago—a man whom I had never met—and I happened to be related to her children... but I quickly surmised there was no direct connection between the two of us and acted accordingly.

About an hour later, I left Topanga. It was a mixed stew. I got to have sex with Molly, but I failed to accomplish my mission. Molly was also pessimistic about my chances with Megan and Stan. "They despise the other ones," she said, referring to Joseph, Jessica, and Josh. "I don't see why it would be different for you."

6
BROTHER, SISTER AND... FATHER

That night, after returning from Topanga, I moseyed down to Sunset to check out the club scene. It was fun walking around on the strip, but I couldn't get into most of the clubs with all the tattooed gorillas chained to the entrances checking IDs. I did locate one place with no age restriction and saw a decent female scratch band followed by a couple of Kurt Cobain imitations but found myself getting bored rather quickly. I was beginning to see the downside of hanging out with a musical genius such as Sledge. I also felt a little insecure because everyone, except me, seemed to have tons of money, or at least that is how it appeared. Maybe it would have helped had I been significantly buzzed. Part, if not most, of this scene was pharmaceutical with the music being an important sideshow.

After about ninety minutes or so, I decided to return to the strip and visit the record stores. Back then there were quite a few sprinkled about, and I did my best to hit every one within walking distance. Of all of them, I liked Tower Records the best because of their inventory and floor design. They were also blessed with plenty of real estate and that, of course, made me deeply envious. Eclectic Emporium had stacks reaching up to the ceiling, and more than a few times I almost fell on my ass while engaging in acrobatic inventory on rolling ladders. I happily spent the rest of the evening inside West Hollywood and Hollywood record shops before calling it a night. It had been a long and interesting day.

The next morning, it was back to work on the bio-trail. Since my crude approach of cold-calling on family No. 1 went fairly well, despite the lack of concrete results, I decided to repeat the process on the slightly more important family No. 2 (four blood members opposed to two). They lived up the mountain off Coldwater Canyon, west of where I was located. This was much closer to my hotel than the Topanga address but there were no bus routes to take me up there. I was quickly discovering the inadequacy of convenient public transportation in Los Angeles. I called a few cab companies, and each one quoted me over fifty bucks round trip. I decided to walk. My funds were limited, and a good portion of my life I spent trudging through the most virulent and unforgiving Detroit winters imaginable, so how bad could this balmy Beverly Hills trail be? (It wasn't as if I'd be crawling over the Rockies in mid-January pulling a cart full of pots and pans.) It was a direct route, too: straight down Sunset, up Coldwater almost to the top, and then a zigzag through a few winding streets, according to my map.

I filled my backpack with little plastic bottles of water, put on my running shoes, and off I went. About two-thirds there, half-way up Coldwater, I once again observed a Los Angeles pattern where houses are built anywhere regardless of how impractical or dangerous the sloping or cliff-like landscape may be for construction. I first saw this trend when busing from downtown Los Angeles to West Hollywood. I saw much more of it on the ride to Topanga and in the Topanga area itself. And now I was seeing it again on a grander, more expensive scale. In a few instances, the structures appeared to be impossibly hanging off the hills, perpendicular to the foundation, with no apparent fortified center of gravity. It was no wonder many of them mud slide into the ocean when the rains fall heavy, or crumble to pieces when earthquakes strike. But they were original and tasteful, and I suppose people have a right to live the way they choose if they can afford to do so.

When I reached my destination, I felt strong, determined, and ready to take the next step and go face to face with my estranged celebrity bio-Dad and his defective offspring. This particular house was a sleek, two-story, Frank Lloyd Wright-type polygon design that meshed smartly with the sweeping landscape of thick underbrush and rising slopes. Its most distinguishing aspect was an expansive, second-level greenhouse, and it appeared that one had to walk through the greenhouse in order to get from one side of the house to the other on the upper level. With nothing or everything to lose—I couldn't figure which—I rang the doorbell and waited. I rang again and again waited. I did not panic because in planning I considered the high probability that no one would be home. It is a risk one takes when barging in on unsuspecting strangers without the slightest idea of their schedules or habits. I was more than prepared to hang around until someone showed, preferably somewhere out of sight, not wanting to be mistaken for a nutcase fan or a potential thief by the roaming private security patrol cars. Fortunately, the street dead-ended into a wooded recess about 25 yards away. I walked over to the modest brush and into the shaded interior. I found a patch of soft ground covered with freshly fallen leaves. This spot will do, I thought, and slid my backpack under my head and looked through the coppice into the smoggy sky. Then, just as I was getting comfortable, feeling the pleasant fatigue from the upward journey, an ugly thought came to mind: What if the entire family is out of town, like Megan and Stan? What then? I mean, it was summertime and even *I* was out of town, and I had virtually no means at my disposal. These people were rich and privileged. I must have been in idiot-mode not to have considered this while planning in Detroit. Thankfully, I fell asleep, and by doing so, forgot about it. When I awoke it was dark and I had no idea where I was or what I was doing. I could have fallen out of the space shuttle. It took quite a while to regain my compass in the unfamiliar darkness, and it was only after leaving the alien cove that I began to remember my mission: I'm in the famous Hollywood Hills waiting for bio-Dad and family No. 2 to return to the nest so I can attempt to bond with my kin after a lifetime of separation. I looked at my watch: 8:10 pm, which meant another marathon slumber, sleeping in the dirt under the smoggy sun and then the barely visible stars. I looked over at the chosen house and saw light coming from the windows on both floors. Someone was home, for sure. There was hope after all.

Numb from the excessive nap, which did not hurt my courage (like a boxer who is punch-drunk from a long fight and hears the bell for the final round), I walked to the door, rang the doorbell, and waited. This time someone answered. Again, it was not what I expected—a small, blockish, milky-white, red-haired woman who looked to be in her forties and could easily have passed for

42

a poster child for nineteenth century Irish immigration. When she saw me, her freckled faced revealed discomfort. Behind her, somewhere upstairs, I heard someone playing an electric guitar without accompaniment. I also heard the sound of banging dishes coming from the first floor, probably the kitchen.

"Can I help you?" she asked firmly.

"I'm here to see Ben Tyler."

"You are?" she moaned, her discomfort rising slightly.

"Yes, Ma'am."

"Are you a young fan of his, because he doesn't receive guests without an invitation."

"To be honest, I'm not a fan at all," I said.

"Who are you, then?"

"I'm his son—his biological son."

I saw her discomfort transform into despair, suggesting to me that my intrusion would not be a simple matter, and she may be forced to call the police or an ambulance, depending on how unbalanced I was.

"I will tell Mr. Tyler you stopped by," she said nervously. "Please go now, for your own sake."

I knew I had to respond to this misunderstanding forcefully and instantly, and blurted out the following without hesitation:

"I'm not crazy, lady. My name is Nic Reilly. I'm from Detroit. I'm Ben Tyler's oldest child, even older than Megan from his first marriage. Right after I was born, the court ordered Ben Tyler to pay my mother child support. Her name is Marge Reilly. It's public record. I wrote Joseph about it. He wrote me back, although I don't think he believed me."

Again, I hit a chord. Her eyes froze, similar to the way Molly reacted when she realized the truth, except this proper lady did not drop to her knees to inspect my cock.

"Jesus, God almighty—you act just like him," she moaned.

"That's because it's true."

"He's not here."

"When will he be back?"

"Who knows? He lives all over the world with his friends. He's only here a couple of weeks a year."

"What about Joseph, Jessica, and Josh?"

Again, she was confused. The guitar kept whining, and the kitchen noise kept banging. Some of them were there for sure.

"Mrs. Tyler isn't home right now," she shot back. "Mrs. Tyler would be the one to invite you in, not me. I'm just the nanny. If you leave a phone number, I'll make sure to have her call you when she returns. I promise."

Just then, the guitar player walked down the winding oak staircase. He looked to be about twelve years old. That would make him Josh, the youngest and sibling No. 5. The guitar he had strapped around his shoulders was a vintage Fender Stratocaster, something I could spot a mile away. Sledge had a 1961 cherry sunburst in the back office, but it wasn't nearly as cool. This one was white with dark rosewood fingerboard and an old black strap. It was connected to the amp by remote, which allowed Josh to walk anywhere he wanted in the house and continue playing. When he saw me, he stopped strumming and paused, almost as if he thought he knew me for a second. He turned to the nanny, "Who the hell is he?"

She thought carefully and said, "He's a friend of your father's. Nic, I'd like you to meet Josh."

We looked at each other, eye to eye. For me, it was a big moment. This was my actual half-brother. I did not see much resemblance between us—or Ben, for that matter—but he was a lean, good-looking kid with a dark complexion and obviously took after his Mexican mother.

"Nice guitar," I said, thinking I couldn't go wrong with that.

"You bet it is, pal," he smirked. "It used to belong to Jimi Hendrix. You probably never heard of him."

I tried to think of a comeback, but I was distracted by the guitar—right handed altered for left handed playing (strings backwards and a Hendrix trademark), even though Josh was playing right handed. He started up again, strumming choppy chords, and kicked open the kitchen door. For a brief moment, I saw a teenage girl preparing something on the stove. She looked to be a couple of years older than Josh and I instantly pegged her as Jessica Tyler, sibling number four in the half sibling chain. I only got a glimpse, but her most ostensible feature was long black hair that flowed down to her ass.

"Is Joseph here?" I said, turning back to the nanny and trying to refocus.

"No. He's in England for the summer studying genetics."

"Genetics? Isn't he like fifteen or something?"

"Yes, he is."

Just then, a loud crash came echoing from the kitchen—like a large ceramic bowl smashing against stone—accompanied by a seething feline shriek: "Get the fuck out of here, you little wart, pervert, scumshit, fuckface."

Without flinching, the nanny again suggested I talk first with Mrs. Tyler. "It's best that way," she said and then quickly retrieved paper and pen. I wrote down the phone number and room number for my hotel. She assured me Isabella Tyler would leave a message with the front desk if I wasn't there. I thanked her and left the house without trying to say good-bye to little Jimi Hendrix, or hello and good-bye to the screaming gourmet, both of whom were continuing to battle it out in the kitchen.

I then proceeded to walk almost three hours in the dark back to the hotel. I immediately checked with the night clerk and was told that no one had called for me. It was almost midnight, so I returned to Sunset in search of a late-night restaurant to accommodate my roaring appetite. I found a Middle-Eastern joint about six blocks away, devoured a hearty lamb and pita sandwich covered with raw vegetables, and washed it all down with three glasses of fresh carrot juice. Food never tasted so good after a full day of not eating and climbing mountains. I returned to the hotel and crawled under the covers, looking forward to the next day when I would talk with Isabella Tyler.

When I awoke the next morning, my hotel phone was already blinking. I immediately dialed the front desk and was informed that Isabella Tyler had called ten minutes earlier. She left a message stating that, regrettably, none of her children wanted to talk to me, and there was nothing she could do about it. She would tell her husband about my visit when he called, although she did not know when that would be. She was sorry she could not do more and wished me luck.

"That's it?!" I screamed into the receiver.

"Afraid so," said the clerk.

"What about a number? A phone number?"

"She didn't leave one."

"What do you mean she didn't leave one?" I persisted.

"We always ask for a number—she said it wasn't necessary. Sorry, man, I tried."

This was horrible news. A blanket refusal from my siblings, and no phone number to follow up. I got out of bed and walked onto the patio to think it over. This trip was turning into a miserable failure, and it deeply hurt, despite whatever nonsense I told myself in Detroit about how it would be a good experience no matter what happened. The goal, the reason for the cross-country journey, was to bond with the estranged bio-clan—my long-lost brothers and sisters—but the only person I bonded with thus far was Molly Sivad. And although I admired her in an unorthodox way (not something I would really choose to talk about), and perhaps learned a few things as well, she was a wine-guzzling sex maniac whose laissez-faire attitude of child-bearing and child-mating would be of no help to me. The cold hard fact was that these Tylers were not capable of accepting me. It was like wanting a vacuum cleaner to hug you. I had to seriously consider if I should risk further humiliation. I had been rejected by every sibling I had been in contact with, either by letter or proxy. The only one left was Stan Tyler, sibling No. 2 and Molly's second born. And what could he possibly be like? If he somehow was the exception, it was not his own mother's seasoned opinion. Besides, he was up in Alaska with his bleeding sister.

Bewildered and irritated, I jumped on the Sunset Boulevard bus again and rode it as far west as it would go—to the ocean. I then walked down a steep set of stairs dug into the coastal bank. Once I hit ground again, I crossed the coastal highway, settled onto the sandy beach, and stared at the mighty Pacific for about an hour. It was a new experience. Being a Midwestern boy, I had never heard ocean waves before, and it had a calming effect on me. The salty air tasted good, too. I inhaled deeply over and over again. All around me were bathers of different races and ethnicities, basking in the hazy sunshine. They seemed relaxed and satisfied, and I was glad to be near them. When I grew hot enough, I flipped off my shirt and walked into the ocean. The water was cold and seemed lighter than lake water. This water also had a slight greasy substance to it, like a light film of dish detergent. It was subtle, but the longer I remained in the ocean, the more I detected it. Later, I found out from one of the surfer dudes that the filmy texture is called pollution.

"Dude, like where have you been? It's a sewer. Especially after it rains."

I noticed the surfer dudes wore rubber wet suits which protected them, but I guess the rest of us were on our own. Still, I enjoyed myself, and I was glad to finally experience the sea. The next time, though, I should find one that's not so greasy.

On the way back to the hotel, I stopped in Westwood Village and visited UCLA. It was a pretty campus with plenty of restaurants, clothing shops, and movie theaters, and I'm sure I would have enjoyed spending the next four years of my life there, but probably not as much as I would have enjoyed Boston, San Francisco, or New York. I left UCLA with no regrets.

When I returned to the hotel that evening, there were no messages, as I suspected, and I made a final decision then and there to go home. Before I had a chance to change my mind, I quickly collected my belongings, said good-bye to the friendly hotel people, and jumped on the same Sunset bus heading east back into downtown Los Angeles. When I arrived at Union Station, I stayed put for most of the four hours it took for the next *Zephyr* to depart. My California visit was over.

A few days later, Stu picked me up from the train station and I was actually glad to be back in struggling, sweltering Detroit, my home, sweet home. I spent the rest of the summer working at Eclectic and preparing to go to Michigan. Sledge gave me as many hours as I wanted. A most generous offering, too, because he had other employees to consider, many of whom had been with him a long time. In the six months following the revelation of bio-Dad, Sledge and I had grown fond of each other. He also told me I had turned into one of the best assistants he had ever hired. That was a compliment I truly cherished, and it probably played a part in some of my future choices, including what courses to take in college.

Two days before I was set to leave for Ann Arbor, I received a letter in the mail. And once again, I thought, just as you finally accept things, things change. The letter was postmarked from London, England, and the return address was a hotel, *The Dorchester* on Park Lane. My name and address were hand-written on the front of the envelope in thin black ink. I opened it, unfolded the crisp, bonded hotel stationery, and read the following:

Dear Nic,

> *This is Ben Tyler writing to you. I've been in Nepal and Mongolia for many months and just got the news about your visit. I also was forwarded your letters and read both of them for the first time today. I'm sorry I wasn't there to welcome you to Los Angeles, but I guess that should come as no surprise to you since I've never been there for you, including when you were born. I also learned from my wife that my kids were not the most gracious, and I apologize for them too.*
>
> *I realize you want to get to know me after recently finding out that I am your biological father, but I must tell you you're probably better off not. I don't say that lightly because it hurts me to admit it to myself. My life is no picnic and I don't think I would be a good influence. I don't want to embarrass myself either. Just keep doing what you're doing. Continue to live a good life, something that you can be proud of later on when you get older. I can't tell my kids this because they're already too screwed up and they would only laugh at me anyway. And they have a right to laugh. I've been a terrible father and mentor. I'll probably never change. I hope you understand what I'm trying to say here. You haven't missed much, and it's to your benefit that we leave things the way they are. Please give your mom my best, although she may not be interested in hearing that. And thanks again for coming to California*

and dropping by and thinking of me and those kids. It was a very cool thing to do. Take care, son, if you allow me to refer to you as that. I'm rooting for you all the way, which is why I'm telling you this.

Love, Ben Tyler

P.S. If you should really need something, or you're in a jam, let my wife know. She'll know how to get in touch with me.

7
REPRIEVE

Bio-Dad's eleventh-hour Euro-letter masterpiece was a gift from the heavens. That was how I interpreted it. I was profoundly touched by his candor and remorse and did not need anything more from him. The letter was enough. (I even felt a little bad about my previous "your music sucks" postscript, but I guess we were both going to have to let bygones be bygones.) I chose to follow his good advice—a course I was already on—and concentrate on my own path. My Tyler days were behind me for good or bad, or so I thought, and off to Ann Arbor I went, a free young man.

*

College turned out to be a busy affair. I stuck to my plan to double major in music appreciation and world history and did rather well because I was genuinely interested. My extracurricular activities included writing music critiques for *Res Gestae*, spinning vinyl at WCBN, and hanging out on an almost daily basis with my roommate and best friend, the brilliant and wry Jonathan Castlelake.

Jonathan was (and still is, I think) a plump, erudite, didactic Southern boy from Charleston, South Carolina. His great, great-grandparents on his mother's side were slaveholders, and he grew up in the same master house that his ascendants inhabited when they were taking care of business around the old tobacco plantation. Not entirely proud of his Southern nobility heritage, Jonathan nonetheless held on to some of its more endearing characteristics, such as supreme confidence and entitlement. He was also the biggest slob I'd ever set eyes on before or since. But as I was quickly learning over and over during this time, nobody's perfect; and I chose to pay more attention to his intellect, humor and hubris, and not to the disgusting peanut butter and jelly stains on our couch.

Jonathan and I shared what we believed to be a metaphorical geographical nexus, because we both grew up in cities that played big in race relations throughout our nation's history. Charleston was the heart of the South and the slave trade leading up to the Civil War, and Detroit became one of the most segregated and antagonistic cities in the North during the twentieth century and one of the big riot hot spots of the 1960s. Granted it was a strange bond, and of our own invention, but a bond nonetheless, and Jonathan and I would spend countless hours milling over the historiography of racial conquest, whether it be on a grand scale, such as European colonialism over the centuries, or on a smaller but equally disturbing scale seen in, say, North America or South Africa in the previous century.

Since Jonathan and I hit it off so well, it was not long before I clued him in on bio-Dad and my evolving life history, beginning with my mother's early and brief groupie experience in musical Detroit, and ending with my elucidating *California Zephyr* trip (i.e., rejection by the siblings, being seduced by the mature poet Molly Sivad—with whose work Jonathan was familiar—and the out-of-nowhere, tenth-inning Euro-letter masterpiece from the legendary bio-Dad himself).

Jonathan wisely surmised that this tale of generational excess and sibling woe, coupled with its worldwide social significance, as reflected in both popular culture (international rock star) and urban phenomenon (everybody who listened), was nothing less than the stuff of modern folklore. To Jonathan, I was the forgotten seed of a petite cultural icon that only this vulgar, narcissistic, late-twentieth century Western culture could produce. My foul, bloodstained (and in bio-Dad's case, guilt-ridden) bio-letters were primary source material in the annals of American history, similar to the discovered diary of a Civil War soldier who was bludgeoned to death at Gettysburg. He also shared my opinion of bio-Dad, which had evolved from a belief that he was a lucky hedonist with limited talent to a belief that he was a lucky and somewhat honorable hedonist with limited talent who also possessed a bit of a conscience but was way too corrupted for that to matter.

I was always pleased when Jonathan and I agreed because it meant to me that I was of the same mind of a genius. But with genius comes arrogance and even though I asked Jonathan to be discreet with my bio-history, he did not, and soon everybody on campus knew me as the "cock bastard," a pretty feeble take on "rock bastard." At first I was upset by the betrayal, but I soon realized it was for the best because it took the novelty out of it—and probably Jonathon's true intention, knowing full well how hung up I was about it. True, Ben Tyler impregnated my mother on a hotel roof in Detroit. So what? Now, if he had pushed her over the edge, that would have been different. But he didn't. I was born. End of story. That became my attitude. Ironically, or maybe not so ironically, the net effect of this tawdry but accurate rumor that I was Ben Tyler's forgotten sperm cell made me somewhat popular and turned my cock into a wad of chewing tobacco for a couple of years. In fact, by my senior year, I was turning a majority of them down, which I kind of regret now as I sit alone in this mountainous jungle.

*

Despite my growing apathy and emotional distance, I did stay afloat of some Ben Tyler news, or rather the gossip surrounding his affairs during the college years. Essentially this was done by default and not by choice, like when I'd see a headline on a tabloid or a magazine cover as I waited in line at the supermarket. Most of it I filed away as rubbish, but there was one Tyler incident in my senior year that had a lasting impact. Young Josh Tyler, in a fit of retaliatory rage against his father, burned down Isabella's and Ben's Hollywood Hills home. The house was empty at the time, and Josh was never convicted for it, but it was understood by all knowledgeable parties that he was the guilty party. That house was the same one I had visited during my virgin California trip almost four years prior, and the electric guitar I saw Josh playing was the cause, or one of the causes, for his burning down the house.

As reported by both the legitimate press and the gossip rags—

along with a few bits and pieces I acquired on my own later down the line—the story unfolded as follows: Josh had a gambling problem and was rumored to be 250,000 dollars in the red from wagering on college and professional sporting events. That was a significant sum for anyone, but for a sixteen-year-old kid, it was astounding. But whether you're sixteen years old or sixty, people expect to get paid, or else, and Josh found himself in a serious mess. Fearing for his life, probably one limb at a time, he sought out his father's above-mentioned dark rosewood necked Strat and gave it to the bookie to cover the quarter-million-dollar debt. (The guitar may have been worth more, depending on who you talk to, but in my opinion it was a fair exchange.) At some later point Ben found out about his ex-guitar and punished Josh in an undisclosed manner. Josh then burned down Ben's house as revenge for said punishment. That, as far as I could gather, was the sequence.

Now the big question on everyone's mind who kept up with such things was: What punishment did Ben render to young Josh to provoke such an outburst of hate and vengeance as burning down a multimillion dollar home? Before conjecturing on such a thought, it should be remembered that Ben was from a generation that worshipped Jimi Hendrix. Hendrix was the real thing. He was a great innovator, a great musician, a great artist, and he would have been that in any era. Hendrix, you might say, legitimized the excess of that period and gave people like Ben a deeper sense of purpose. The guitar symbolized that purpose. It was an irreplaceable, timeless relic. So what did Ben actually do? Nobody knew. Not back then, anyway. Josh never talked about it, nor did any of the other family members. It was, I suppose, a well-kept family secret. Years later, I was to learn more, but I will wait until we reach that point in the bio-drama to disclose such information.

About three months following the torching, Ben and Isabella quietly bought another house farther east along Mulholland. They also purchased a condo for Josh in Venice, close to the beach, and that was where Josh was ordered to live. He was no longer allowed in the new house, or near it, for obvious reasons, until much later and then only for special occasions.

But other than the torching, there was no Tyler bio-news worth mentioning during my college stint that I knew of. No divorces, suicides, marriages, or anything else of that caliber. I, of course, being an outsider at the time and preferring it that way, knew only what was presented to me through popular media. In fact, my college years solidified my divorce from the Tylers and their affairs. I remained fond of bio-Dad because of his Euro-letter, but that was about as far as it went. Besides, there were so many other things to think about, such as what direction to take after graduation.

Originally, the choices were to go to law school or to go to law school. That is, until one morning when the phone rang, exactly five weeks before I was to graduate. It was Sledge. He called to inform me that he was returning to federal prison and would I be interested in taking over Eclectic Emporium. It was one of those matter-of-fact, no-big-deal, just-taking-care-of-business calls that I used to get when I was working for him. I still did work for him over the summers and holidays, but had no plans to return after college. This, however, was different. He didn't want me as an employee; he wanted me to take over the shop. To own it. He needed somebody who would do justice to what he had created, and in his opinion, I was that person.

"How long will you be away?" I asked, dumbfounded.

"It could be awhile. This is my second rap."

"What does that mean?"

"I'm going to have to do the mandatory. And the federal system doesn't offer parole. I hear they're thinking about changing it, though."

"Sledge, I'm graduating in a few weeks and all set to go to law school."

"How are your grades?" he asked, unfazed.

"Why?"

"Curious."

"3.8."

"I know I'm making the right choice here."

"I don't know what to say, Sledge," I mumbled.

"You don't have to say anything right now, but I want you to think about it. Okay?"

"Okay."

I thought about it for a week straight, but I could not look beyond his bizarre actions. Sledge was successful. People from all over the world shopped at his place. They all paid good money. Why would he continue with the phony cash? Sure, he could profit by having more purchasing power, but becoming wealthy and having a lot of "things" was not what Sledge was about. And yet this unique, gifted man was now going to spend his twilight years in a prison yard. What a horrible waste. The more I thought about it, the less it made sense. After another sleepless night, I called him and told him that before I would seriously consider taking over his business, he would have to explain to me why he kept up with the counterfeiting.

"Temptation," he replied.

"What does that mean?"

"To see if I could get away with it. I mean, I did get away with it for a long time, except that one other time, but I wanted to see how long I could keep getting away with it, again."

"I don't believe it."

"You don't have to."

"There's got to be more. It's too stupid."

"Like what?"

"Something else."

"You probably think I wanted to get caught?"

"What?"

"Go on, admit it."

This of course never occurred to me, but it was an intriguing concept, especially since he was the one who offered it up.

"Well, did you?" I asked, taking his lead.

"Hell no, I didn't," he snapped back with conviction. This was the first time he strayed from his casual cool.

"Okay."

"That's right."

I was then convinced he wanted to get caught. I also knew he did not want to admit it, another imperceptible subject.

"So it was just the temptation?" I asked.

"You have to look at it artistically, Nic," he said, returning to calm, cool, and in control.

"Go on."

"Say you're a really talented art forger. Would you want your van Goghs and Corots rotting away in a dark damp basement or would you want them hanging in the great museums of the world for everyone to see and admire?"

"Hmm, I guess in the museums, Sledge."

"Of course you do, damn it. It's the same for me. I want everyone to be using my money."

"Spend it? Buy stuff with it?"

"Exactly. I want the little old ladies to buy medicine with my money. I want young mothers to buy milk for their babies with my money. I want congressmen and senators to be bribed with my Ben Franklins. And most of all, I want people to buy my music with my own money. And they do, too. All the time. You have no idea how much pleasure I get when someone walks into the shop and hands me one of my own twenty-dollar bills. I could almost weep. Especially if they come from the suburbs."

It is a fact that very successful people do unforgivably stupid things all the time. Here, in my opinion, was another example.

"Let me think about it more," I said.

"I got a month before I go in."

"How much would you want for it?"

"Money? You got to be kidding, man. Didn't you just hear me? I don't want your damn money. It's free to the right person. I got fined quite a bit by the court, but I had just enough to pay them with their money so they can't touch the business. The shop is still mine. It's the only thing I got left, and I need somebody who will do it justice."

"I'll get back to you."

"One thing more."

"Yeah?"

"If you take it, I want you to make it grow. That's my only request. I want it nurtured, man. I want it to shine like the North Star after I'm gone. If you can't do that, don't take it."

After he hung up I sought out Jonathan, the best mind I knew, and asked him what he thought.

"Take the record shop. You can always become a lawyer, even when you're fifty."

"But what about all the time I've spent preparing to go to law school, all the work involved? I got into Chicago. That's one of the top law schools in the country."

"And what are you planning to do once you get your paper-work stamped?"

"Entertainment law."

"Well, in terms of what matters, there's absolutely no choice here, and I thought that should be rather obvious and I'm surprised you're even bothering me with this. Do you really think spending the next seven or eight years of your life preparing to negotiate and accumulate great amounts of wealth for fugacious, innocuous, self-obsessed, drug-addicted, emotionally insecure thespians or the like who pretend to be creators is more worthy of your time than preserving and propagating a timeless, life-affirming symphony of collective genius for the benefit of mankind? Do you really think there's a fucking choice here?"

He slammed the door on the way out. What a numbskull, I thought. What did he know anyway? What choices did he really have to make? It was all laid out for him. He was going to grad school to earn a Ph.D. with his eyes closed because he was not equipped to do anything else but read, write, extrapolate, consume, and defecate. The idea of him working with other people at a law firm or on Wall Street or, God forbid, as a physician in a hospital, was frightening. What would he tell the terminal cancer patient? "Congratulations, you have a clean way out. Refuse treatment. See what's next. I'm excited for you. I have to go now, looking at you makes me hungry."

I needed another opinion, so I solicited Stu. He was a lawyer, but so what? When I called, he was in a verbose mood, and I could tell that my conflict—ostensibly pertaining to a comparatively interesting life decision opposed to whatever tedious nonsense he was doing over there—was pure escape for him and should have been enough information for me not to choose the law profession. I listened carefully and he, too, had a few interesting things to say:

"I don't advocate the Bar because it is a ridiculous organization with ridiculous people with questionable habits who engage in hypocritical trivialities, and yet it has its merits because it provides one with a base to negotiate one's way through life. Because of that, I would recommend that you do not take over Eclectic Emporium, even though it's a great shop and I go there all the time. It's wiser to go to Chicago—which I couldn't get into—on the waiting list so I had to settle for Michigan—but getting back to you—and this is extremely important and something you may not fully believe at this point, just getting out of college—but as you get older, it becomes tougher to get into the good schools, like Chicago and Michigan. As life presents itself in all its splendor, especially if you're doing interesting stuff like running Sledge's cutting-edge music shop, the desire to hit the books and study your ass off diminishes. And if you get married and have kids—something which I avoided, thank God—you might blow it off altogether and regret it—hold on."

He then took another call. Thirty seconds later his voice came back:

"Where was I, oh yeah, like I said, law school gives you the skills to negotiate through life and in that respect it is invaluable, even if you don't stick with it as a profession. So again, if you're asking my opinion, I would go to Chicago and let Sledge figure something else out with the shop. He's a smart guy, even though I question his choice to live the rest of his life in a cozy, minimal-security federal camp where he can just think and do nothing, as opposed to living here in Detroit and running his music and counterfeiting businesses, both of which were tip-top operations that served a lot of good, honest people. But I guess he's doing what is best for him, and I think you should do what is best for you. I'm conjecturing here, but the timing is interesting, don't you think? Just as you're graduating, he's going to prison. You needn't be an accomplice to his desires, Nic. Live your own life. And on a small note, I think your mother would prefer you go to law school, too. She'll never say it out loud, but that's my fifty-three cents. Now I hate to end on that below-the-belt remark about Marge, but I do have to take this call. It's a slumlord who wants to bribe me. I'm not taking it of course, but I'm curious to see what he's offering."

Stu was a smart man, and as far as I'm concerned, he should have been accepted at Chicago. Perhaps the year he was applying was a very competitive one. He managed to shed some light on Sledge, too, identifying the deep-rooted psychosis of a man who would choose prison over Detroit; although the more I thought about it, the more it became less outrageous. And he shrewdly admitted that he was hitting below the belt to invoke Marge, probably the one person to whom I would defer. His mentioning her had the same effect as introducing inadmissible evidence during a trial: no matter what the judge says about deleting said information from the brain cells, the jury is not going to forget. His admission was meant to have that same impact.

Still, Marge might be the person to talk to. More than anyone I knew, she was unpredictable with her opinions and had been throughout my life (and before my life, too), but I knew she had my best interests at heart.

So I called her the next day and hinted that I could use a good meal with finals coming up. She immediately suggested that I come home that weekend for a Sunday dinner. Like many mothers, Marge interpreted Sunday dinners as a binding, nurturing experience. Growing up, I always looked forward to them, as I did in college, even though I felt unworthy with my lifestyle having changed so radically. In truth, I was no better than Marge during her groupie years.

We began eating at dusk, always a meaningful and reflective time of day for me. The fading evening light cast a soft phantasmagoric glow across the long dining room table. Marge prepared one of my favorite meals—pot roast and noodles with gravy, fresh asparagus, a knish casserole, cucumber salad, and black cherry pie for dessert.

"So what do you want to talk about, dear?" she asked.

"How do you know I want to talk about something?"

"Because you've never invited yourself to dinner in the four years you've been up at school."

"I thought you invited me?"

"What is it dear, tell me."

So I told her.

"I don't have any answers for you," she said.

"You don't have a preference or an opinion?"

"No. I just want you to be happy."

"I thought you were happy I was going to law school?"

"I was, and I still am if that's what you decide. But if you decide to do something else, I'll be happy to see you do something else, as long as that's what you want to do and you're not hurting anyone."

She was turning out to be of no help, but then added:

"You should know I've always done what I wanted to do."

"You have?"

"Taking care of you and Barney was pure joy to me and exactly what I wanted. It allowed me time to do all these other wonderful things I've being doing over the years. I was fortunate, Nic. I still am. And I want the same for you."

Throughout my life, Marge volunteered at hospitals and clinics and was involved in community activities, such as voter registration and local political reform (hopeless causes as I viewed it). After Barney died, she began attending religious services at this old crusty Episcopalian church near Warren Avenue, close to where she worked. I was surprised by the change of routine but never queried her. Growing up, she and Barney never went to church and therefore I didn't.

"How's Sledge doing?" she asked.

"He sounded okay for a man going to prison."

"Poor man."

"He knew what he was doing," I said, trying to keep things real.

"You know, he doesn't charge me."

"What?"

"When I go in there to buy music, he refuses my money."

"When did that start?"

"About a year ago or so."

"You never told me?"

"I thought maybe you knew."

"No."

"You know what else he did?"

"What?"

"After a while, I stopped going in because I felt awkward about not paying, and he must have figured it out. So he began calling me and telling me the new Van Morrison or Joni Mitchell albums were in and waiting to be picked up, and if I didn't come into the store soon he was going to mail them to me so could I please save him the cost of the postage and come in and get them."

"Did you ask him why?"

"I just figured it was because you worked there. All he would keep saying is 'Your money is no good here, Mrs. Reilly.' It's kind of funny he would say that with all the no-good money he had."

"This started about a year ago?"

"Last summer."

After I loaded up the car with enough leftovers to feed Jonathan at least twice, I drove to Eclectic Emporium to talk to Sledge. As I was driving, the snow in my mind started to melt and things became extraordinarily clear. First of all, Stu was dead wrong about Marge. Down deep she wanted me to take over Eclectic Emporium. Sledge convinced her of that in his own inimitable way and then kept reminding her every time she came into the shop. He understood that she understood the cultural significance of a place like his and the importance of sustaining such an establishment for the good of all, especially in an economically challenged city such as Detroit. He also knew me well enough to realize that I would consider Marge in whatever I decided once he offered me the shop.

On the other hand, Stu was dead on about Sledge. Sledge wanted to go to prison. He wanted to spend most of the rest of his days in some monkey federal camp eating slop food and reading and thinking and never once more having to worry about anything ever again, including his music business. And I'm sure there were other obscure reasons that only Sledge was privy to. His decision to go to prison can be traced back at least one year when he stopped charging Marge for her music in a well-calculated attempt to have me take care of his business.

And why not? I was his student. He groomed me himself. I understood what he created. He knew I was capable of maintaining and even improving upon what he started. And it worked like a charm because Sledge was going to prison next month, and next month I was to graduate from college and take over his prize enterprise. Law school can wait. Who cares if in the years to come I am not in love with the law or that I cannot get into Chicago? There were other law schools, but there was no record shop in the world like Sledge's, and if I did not take it over, it could dissolve or be defaulted to an incompetent or a mogul. Jonathan was right again. I would be an absolute fool not to take over his shop. Who knows more about it than me? I had been spinning vinyl for the past four years and was tutored by the master himself. Besides, I was a second generation music stud all the way, bio-Dad being the pioneer. It was in my blood.

When I arrived at Eclectic, I parked in front and looked in. The old shop had the aura of a prestigious institute, like the Library of Congress or Carnegie Hall, with its carefully quartered sections and myriad themes. Sledge was all alone, doing inventory, finishing up for the night. I felt privileged to be the one he chose to take this institution to a higher level.

I stepped out of the car and entered the shop. Sledge looked up at me, smiled knowingly, and said, "I've been waiting for you, young man."

8
THE ECLECTIC RECORD BUSINESS

The last thing Sledge said to me before he surrendered to the federal marshals was, "Don't ever give up on the vinyl." It was an unusual statement because, for those of us who understood where things were going, digital was the future—immediate or otherwise. Records and tapes were soon to be a thing of the past. But there was much fear, confusion and resistance about how exactly that was going to happen; although, initially, for many in the music industry, it was interpreted as a celestial windfall as people began to purchase music they already owned in the new CD format. And how can you lose when you're selling the same thing again at a higher price for a fraction of the cost? Right? Wrong. But nobody fully understood that part yet. Nobody realized that the giant, benevolent gift from God—CDs and digital technology—would soon become the monster demon from hell in the more advanced digital forms of the Internet and file sharing. But it took a while, some fifteen years or so, and it was midway during that stretch when I became the proprietor of Eclectic Emporium.

Since it is not my purpose to rehash the music industry twists and turns in the dawn of the digital era, I'm just going to say that I started out by riding the CD bump and profiting greatly from it, but I also began making adjustments and preparing myself for the bigger changes ahead. With reference to the latter, Eclectic Emporium also had three distinct advantages over comparable retail competition during this critical period.

The first was that we were a specialty shop that catered to the connoisseurs and the hard-to-please. Actually, we catered to everybody else, too, but that specialty niche was what set us apart. Thus, our clients, in general, because of who they were, were not overzealous to profit from the downloading frenzy once they figured out how to do it. A good many of them believed, as I did, that it was wrong not to pay for something you were going to possess and use over and over again. They further believed, as I did, the artist should be paid for his or her labor—if not the profiteering record companies who, without doubt, took full advantage of the situation, and were partially responsible for their own downfall.

In addition, we were buffered by a large in-place mail-order business, accounting for some 32 percent of our revenue. This type of you-don't-have-to-be-there-in-person exchange lent itself to the burgeoning Internet. The only difference being that, as the Internet grew, people could go online and order through our cutting-edge website instead of calling or mailing in the order. We would still mail them the merchandise, and they still did not have to come into the store to find and purchase rare music.

And thanks to Sledge's parting words of wisdom, we held on to our precious vinyl, a commodity that became more precious as time went on because it was not downloadable. If you wanted the real thing and not the digitalized hybrid, you had to purchase the analog record. This helped insulate us from the ensuing piracy.

Our second advantage was a most peculiar one and completely unforeseen—at least that was my initial interpretation. It was also indirectly related to the industry problem as a whole, a phenomenon that was completely misinterpreted, mishandled, and contrary to everything anyone knew about the evolution of the twentieth century music business. I'm referring of course to kids. Traditionally, kids are the solution, not the problem, when it comes to buying and selling music. That began to dramatically change with a new generation growing up on Internet sites such as Napster, Kazaa, and iMesh. These kids did not or could not see or appreciate the separation between music and the Internet. To them, the two were one and the same, like milk in cereal, and it was foolish to believe they were going to change or "grow up" and start buying CDs from a retail store. In fact the exact opposite happened and grown-ups began to follow their lead and stopped buying and began downloading.

The major record companies never fully understood this organic process. For them, file sharing was nothing short of blanket heresy—the digital Antichrist. The question they kept asking (and it was legitimate): "What would happen if this started going on everywhere, in every area of commerce?" Take the housing market, for instance. What if people no longer paid rent or bought homes, and they just took them over? What if no one bothered to go to the checkout line in the grocery store and just grabbed what they needed from the shelves and left? It was a new madness. The ancient laws that had hitherto protected investment and private property were no longer viable. And it was legal, too, in the sense that it could not be stopped, and it empowered a new generation from the impoverished adolescent class, some of whom would master the technology and use their initiative to become mega-millionaires and billionaires.

So what did they actually do—the large record store chains? The music label companies? The music publishing companies? The entertainment conglomerates? The big corporations? Not a whole lot because they couldn't buy or "own" the World Wide Web, nor could they shut it off like a faucet, nor would the legal process (which they do partially own) provide a speedy and adequate solution. Thus, many of them just began to bleed and defaulted to the more traditional strategy of gobbling up dwindling market shares and eliminating the competition, beginning with the small guy, a category yours truly fell into. Eclectic Emporium thus became vulnerable to the larger music retail chains and to one in particular called, strangely enough, Prostitute Records. Prostitute was a big, independent label with a massive retail operation, but it was not a major or a conglomerate, and therefore could not absorb revenue loss by shifting gears into other entertainment fields or other sources of non-entertainment income. With all their eggs in the same musical basket, so to speak, the rulers of Prostitute Records became monstrously paranoid by the growing piracy and file sharing and immediately began implementing strategy to preserve their future. They also happened to be championed by a maverick named Hank Tyler, who happened to be the brother of a musician named Ben Tyler, who happened to be my distant and estranged bio-Dad. As I saw it, at the time, this bio-connection—this blood link—was to my advantage, even though I did not welcome any of it and was ultimately driven to the point of no-return.

The third advantage I had (over other retailers) was in the form of personnel. Following Sledge's penal exodus, I inherited two of his key employees, Delco and Byron. Both stayed on with me for exactly one year from the date I took over. Both were, I believe, given bonuses or bribed by Sledge to do exactly that. And both were consumed by jealousy and resentment for not having been chosen as Sledge's successors. This last bit was exacerbated by the fact that both were closer to Sledge's age, both had been with Sledge much longer, and both happened to wear the same skin color as Sledge.

The purpose of their tenure was to provide our in-store customers familiarity and stability while I got up to speed: same music, same atmosphere, same service, and the same people except for the guy in the back office. It worked beautifully, too. We made the post-Sledge transition in a profitable and orderly fashion, but the big downside was my subjugation to a slew of unfair backstabbing and private bitching. So it should come as no surprise that I was not sad to see the tag team of Delco and Byron go their own way once the bribery clock ran out.

To replace them I decided to hire a full-time assistant manager and continue with part-time employees. My long-term plan was to expand Eclectic into other cities, and I needed a collaborator and confidant, someone who would be responsible for running things while I was not in town and who would be the future general manager of our many stores. It was a big choice and I had to be thorough. I even entertained the idea of going back to Ann Arbor to interview grad students and MBAs. I was willing to pay a good salary. We were doing well riding the CD bump, and I could afford it. It made sense to invest in the right personnel.

So, naturally, when it came down to the very critical selection process, I disregarded all my criteria and chose someone who knew absolutely nothing about the music or the record industry and had no business skills to speak of but who was undoubtedly one of the most beautiful persons on the planet. Her name was Karolina Torgustive. Karolina, or Karo, was born in Uganda, of all places, the product of a Ugandan diplomat and a Ukrainian housewife who met when the diplomat was studying in the old Soviet Union; back in the days when the United States and the Soviet Union competed for African influence and natural resources. Regrettably, the Soviet Union, who won the battle of influence in Uganda, could not do much about the Ugandan dictator Adi Amin, who had the tendency to kill anything and everything that moved, including Karolina's father, forcing Karo's mother to return to Kiev when Karo was three years old. In the Ukraine, Karolina—who took slightly more after her tall, black, muscular father than her chalk-white, beauty-queen mother—was raised by her mother and grandmother in a provincial setting where everyone was smallish, ashen, and wore a mustache if a member of the masculine gender. Karo, as could be expected, grew up feeling different and isolated in these quaint surroundings, and when she was old enough ran away to Western Europe where she became an underwear model and dabbled in the black market using some of her old Russian contacts.

This underwear/black market combination lasted for some time before she transplanted to the United States to study clothing design at the Detroit Fashion Institute, where she was awarded a partial scholarship. (If not for the scholarship, she would have chosen another city.) Becoming quickly disillusioned in the highly competitive, international fashion world, she decided to switch to the music business, where she felt her personality could play more of a factor and spotted my ad in the *Detroit Free Press*. I interviewed her about three weeks later, and I hired her a few seconds after that, telling myself she could speak Russian and that should be helpful somewhere down the line since the Soviet Union had since collapsed and the Russian market was wide open even though, at that time, I had only one customer on that part of the globe through the mail-order business, a Billie Holiday fan who would listen only to old 78 records, and he was actually a transplanted New Yorker living in Singapore (but at least he was barely on the same continent if you include Europe and Asia as one and the same).

The truth was, from the moment I met her, I had no defense against Karolina's beauty: her light cocoa complexion, her thick budding lips, her sad teasing eyes, her flowing blonde-streaked Jamaican hair that seemed to engulf her entire body, and her soft rubicund smile that hinted at innocence but was really a full on seduction. Below the shoulders was even more intoxicating, including long, artistic fingers that in due time would dig into my back and draw blood.

Karolina and I worked together for almost seven years, which is a hell of a long time when you consider our current ages: thirty and thirty-two, she being the elder. I can't give you the full history of the early years if I am to get on with the more important, larger bio-drama, but suffice to say that for much of this time we were periodic lovers but never "in love" because that takes two and there was only one of us who felt that strongly. That person was me. She, alas, did not share my excitement, passion or devotion, nor did she choose to exercise her option to marry me and become my equity partner, an avenue that was not really spoken about but was more than available to her if she wanted it. All she had to do was whisper. She did, however, become my business partner and collaborator, and was eventually positioned to benefit almost as much as I from our growth as a company.

At first, Karolina's duties consisted of picking up where the Delco-Byron tag team left off, but when I saw how fast she was learning and how much everyone liked her, I officially crowned her "manager" after six weeks and allowed her to hire part-time employees, which numbered as many as sixteen in the following years. As manager, she oversaw the advertising, promotions, in-store visuals (art, seasonal decorations, themes), and scheduling. Part of her success—our success—had to do with her being an artist in her own right, with a flair for color and design. She used her skills to transform the look of our shop to a more creative and inviting atmosphere, yet she was careful to preserve the essence of Sledge's creation in terms of his filing systems and thematic divisions of the music.

Another positive factor of having her as manager—I don't want to place too much significance on this, but to ignore it is to ignore reality—was her unusual Afro-Russian heritage. Many of our clients were black, and it did not hurt to have beautiful, dark Karolina on the floor running things after the departures of Sledge, Delco, and Byron. And for those, such as myself, for whom race is not an issue, she was first and foremost an exotic woman with a vibrant personality to whom customers gravitate whether they realize it or not. I calculated her presence alone increased the in-store revenue 18 to 20 percent from the time she took over the floor to the time right before we built the digital listening lounge. After the lounge opened up, our revenues went up another 7 to 9 percent.

Thus, the multi-talented, African queen was my third advantage to help offset the digital madness that was to consume us. Her capacity as my sometimes lover also served to fortify me as the industry conflict grew uglier.

*

As mentioned, one of my goals was to expand Eclectic Emporium into other cities, especially Chicago. Twice I came close to signing leases but each time I postponed at the last second. The first postponement was a result of simply being cautious. Due to our inventory, specialty status, and catering to exotic tastes, I learned it was going to cost me a bloody fortune to duplicate ourselves. We were that good. Sledge had been pounding away at his craft for a long time, and it showed in terms of dollars and cents. I was also bent on purchasing and installing the latest in digital sound technology and other acoustic amenities for customer convenience. I wanted everything to be state-of-the art for the future. So, like other business owners in my position, I applied for a loan and while waiting for it to come through Karolina suggested that we first enlarge the existing Detroit store because it made better business sense to maximize our profits locally, where everything was inexpensive, before venturing out to Chicago where everything cost nearly twice as much.

I thought it was an excellent idea and took the bank loan and built an eight-hundred-square-foot digital listening lounge in the Detroit store so customers could relax and listen to music before buying it. We also used the lounge as a platform for artists to perform and started a regular live gig. Karolina became the chief architect for most of this effort. She designed the lounge, chose the furniture and art, and organized most of the live activities. It was a tremendous success.

About fourteen months after the opening of our new Eclectic

Lounge, I was once again ready to sign the lease for a new Chicago store in the Bucktown area of Chicago. My construction plans had become more ambitious since the last time and I was going to pay for it by refinancing the existing loan. The bank was more than happy to accommodate me since I was generating sound income and never missed a payment. But again, I balked at the eleventh hour. The reason this time was twofold and much more complicated. To begin with, the Internet was beginning to grow by leaps and bounds since I opened the lounge, and it became clear to me that the new downloading problem was never going to disappear, despite whatever mixed nonsense I was hearing from confused insiders. Second, Prostitute Records purchased an old warehouse for pennies on a burned-out stretch of Gratiot Avenue and began converting it into a cutting-edge, industrial-style, retail music shop and lounge. This was within two miles of my store. The best part: they were going to call it "Prostitute Eclectic." Once I received confirmation from several sources that this was indeed true, I postponed the second Chicago lease signing. Sadly, I never opened a Chicago store.

*

Before I describe the details of this corporate marauding, let me first convey some interesting background on Hank Tyler, brother of my bio-Dad and president of Prostitute LLC. Before Hank became a record mogul, he was a used-car salesman off Route 22 in the state of New Jersey. And before that, he was a nightclub manager in Lower Manhattan. The reason he left the nightclub was because he got caught stealing 47,000 dollars from his bosses, thus destroying his reputation in the New York City club scene. He then crossed the Hudson River and entered the used-car title trade, where he purchased wrecked automobiles from junk yards and resold them to the general public without making the proper mechanical repairs. He covered this illicit activity by changing VIN numbers, an extremely dangerous and illegal procedure because it erases the accident history of the vehicle in question in the event of a title check. Many times, these Hank Tyler cars would be involved in new accidents within a couple of days or weeks of leaving the sales lot due to faulty axles, brake lines, steering columns, crankshafts, and other fundamental mechanical failures. Based on my research, there were fatalities in a few of these accidents. That, in my eyes, made Hank Tyler a murderer.

What brought Hank to his knees in this second arena was directly related to a familiar Tyler weakness: sexual obsession. Apparently, he was screwing the wife of one of his employees, and the employee found out and tipped off the State's DMV authorities using hard evidence he stole from Hank's office. The authorities followed up, and Hank was indicted for a couple of felonies, and would have been tossed into the slammer for a good twenty years if not for the remarkable success of his younger brother who had just hit it big with the aforementioned album *Elevator to Hell*. With more money than he knew what to do with, Ben hired a well-connected mobster lawyer who respectfully paid off everybody in New Jersey who needed to be paid off, including the judge and Hank's renegade employee. Hank was then quietly acquitted on a technicality and moved to California, where he lived off his kid brother's good will by managing some of his business affairs until he came up with the idea of starting the record label. Giving credit where credit is due, most if not all of Prostitute's success as a record label, recording studio, distribution network, and retail outlet was due to Hank's hard work and aggressive tactics. At the time of the opening of the Detroit Prostitute Eclectic copycat store, the *Wall Street Journal* reported Prostitute LLC to be worth about 800 million dollars.

*

The strategy that Hank employed to combat the Internet file-sharing frenzy was a rather crude and fundamental slash-and-burn campaign. Sensing doom—but not quite understanding it—he instructed his marketing research team to single out the smaller retail competition that were doing relatively well and steal their customer base by duplicating and underselling. And they were ordered to hurry up about it since they were not going to out-muscle the majors, who were also beginning to panic. This was meant to generate new business and help compensate for the loss of piracy income until this Internet mess got straightened out in the federal courts or Congress, or until the majors figured out a way to regain control of those markets in the new ubiquitous digital-information age.

It should come as no surprise that my beloved Eclectic Emporium jumped right to the top of that list for the Detroit market. We had an excellent reputation with a large, loyal customer base, made up of people who actually bought music and could afford to do so. We also had one of the top five inventories in the country in terms of variety and arcane recordings.

In fact, I'm positive they learned a few things by studying our operation, because the existing Prostitute retail stores were not special in any way and merely on par with other big record chains, providing popular music in trendy settings for the common denominator. So, just as it was going to take me some doing to duplicate Eclectic Emporium in Chicago, the same held true for Hank and Prostitute Eclectic in Detroit with one major exception: access to money. They had tons of it. And they were not shy about using as much as they needed to accomplish their goal—which was to put me, and people like me, out of business for good.

My rebuttal for all this was of course my unique bloodline in the guise of good ole' bio-Dad, Hank's brother. I would simply contact bio-Dad and work something out. But after doing my fact-finding, I was fairly certain bio-Dad was not aware of my status as owner of Eclectic Emporium or what his (or rather his brother's) company was doing. Technically bio-Dad had an office in the Prostitute corporate headquarters, but he was not involved with any of the details of Prostitute LLC, nor did he want to be. Instead he was off globetrotting with "his friends." So I decided the best course to reach him was to take his Euro-letter suggestion of years past and go through his wife, Isabella. But, again, since I did not have her private phone number, I mailed her a certified letter in which I asked her to forward another enclosed letter to bio-Dad. I also sent a certified letter to Hank Tyler at the Prostitute corporate offices explaining who I was and my relationship to his brother (and to him) and how flattered I was that his company singled out my business to duplicate and destroy, but perhaps there was another less punitive way to go about it. After all, I was not the real enemy, the renegade Internet was. And "by attacking me, you are attacking yourself," hoping this Biblical metaphor was not beyond his mental grasp, given our unexpected blood link and his maggot reputation.

Meanwhile, Karolina and I initiated a small local offensive of our own by increasing our existing in-store promotions (especially the hip-hop artists who were doing extremely well at the time) and by increasing the number of live gigs at the lounge. In addition—and I consider this a major boost for Eclectic Emporium—Karolina began sleeping with me again after a sabbatical of over eight months. She chose to do this because it was her way of showing support. She did not love me, but she had faith in me and wanted me to be a strong, courageous warrior and stand up to the corporate, copycat, bio-scum invaders in these new troubling times. Sensing my fear—even though I tried not to show it, just as I tried not to show my hurt after the withdrawal of her full love or commitment—she proceeded to smother me with passion unlike she had ever done before.

On most days, it started right after work and lasted through the harsh winter nights with one of us arousing the other over and over again. Indeed, our renewed bonding was becoming an almost mystical arrangement, its own fey reality, a dream within a dream, and growing more intense as the outside threat loomed larger and larger, pushing me deeper and deeper into those warm, dark motherly breasts. Many times, I would have to remind myself after waking with my head resting on her belly or between her legs that I mustn't get emotionally conquered or lose my soul. In my mind, a capitulation of that nature was just as dangerous as surrendering my business to the big, fat whore down the street—another incestuous paradigm. It would have been different if Karolina loved me. If she loved me, I would have "let go" and hoped for the best, but she did not love me. How could she with all those other lovers; none of whom I knew personally. She kept them private, off to the side, which was for the best. I suppose I sequestered some small, personal comfort from the willful assumption that she was not in love with any of them either, and I was on top of the list, for the time being, anyway.

*

Despite the amorous distractions and counterinsurgency efforts, I literally drove myself crazy waiting and heard nothing from either one of the Tyler brothers after a grueling month. Apparently, the Biblical touch had no impact on the thick-skinned Hank, and I was assuming my other letter had not yet reached my eternally elusive bio-Dad. It brought back bad memories of waiting for Tylers during my lonely senior year of high school after I lost Barney. Time was critical, though, in terms of strategy. I did not want to negotiate a truce *after* the completion of the new Eclectic Detroit store, after Hank had made his investment. It was better to talk while they were in the formative stages with the hope we could still unite as father, son, and musical brothers. And why not? Did not we have the same blood pumping through our veins? Were they not trying to emulate me and duplicate my business? And who knew better than me what I was doing? This was negotiable. And negotiation was my only recourse because they would outspend me ten to one. But, just like with love, it takes two to negotiate.

In my anguish, I reached out to my good friend Jonathan for guidance. Jonathan was now lecturing at Harvard and finishing up his postdoctoral degree in European history. His advice and commentary were typically unorthodox.

"You have to understand, Nic, he's (meaning Hank Tyler) second-generation Euro-bulk with Napoleonic low self-esteem who has experienced American dream success. That makes him dangerous."

"How?"

"His confidence level is rising as his life is fading. He equates this confidence with almighty power. He believes he can destroy anyone below him and he has the *right* to do so. That is his position toward you, or people like you, sacred blood or no sacred blood. If you're serious about saving your business—if you don't want an honorable institution plagiarized and falsified by scoundrels and pirates—you must be bold."

"How?"

"That's for you to decide. But it probably wouldn't hurt to blow up his parked car—something along those lines."

"What?!"

"Scare him. He'll respect that course of action given his background—that gutter-mentality retaliation—especially if he knows you were behind it and can't prove it. That should bring his ass to the table. Your alternative is to wait for wayward bio-Dad to return to Western civilization, and by then it could be too late, if he returns at all, given his wealth and existential dilemma."

"Existential dilemma?"

"Some other time with that. What exactly did you say to Uncle Hank when you called him?"

"I never called him."

"What did you do?"

"I wrote him a letter."

"You're kidding?"

"No."

"What is this, be nice to your fucking executioner week?"

"I had to write bio-Dad because I didn't have his wife's phone number, so I figured—"

"—You figured wrong. Call the scoundrel up. Use brother against brother. King against king. Threaten. This is fucking war. Use your cannons."

"Okay."

"By the way, have you heard the latest?"

"No."

"There's new DNA evidence that Jesus' crucifixion was a hoax."

"Really? "

"Yeah. Paul got it all wrong, bad secondhand information, despite the Damascus road LSD blast. Someone else was crucified in Jesus' stead. The Resurrection was a brilliant rationalization, and the rumors Jesus was spotted sneaking out of Jerusalem on his way to the Orient to transcend on his own were in fact true."

This, to me, was utterly fascinating and entirely plausible. Unfortunately, Jonathan had to go to class and couldn't discuss it at length. It reminded me how much I missed my college days chatting with him on a daily basis.

In terms of Hank Tyler, though, I decided to take only half his advice. I would not contract to destroy Hank's vehicle, but I would call Hank at his office and threaten him with the wrath of bio-Dad if we didn't come to terms. (I still fully believed bio-Dad would rectify the situation if and when he got my letter.) But again, it was a fruitless effort. I called thirteen times and never once got past the second secretary, a woman named Victoria, nor did I ever receive a call back. A couple of weeks after my thirteenth call, five weeks after I talked to Jonathan, and over three months after my initial discovery of the Detroit invasion, Prostitute LLC announced it would be opening its breakthrough Motor City retail lounge and specialty store, Prostitute Eclectic. This information was propagated through the traditional media outlets.

Apparently, there was a party, too. One not advertised to the general public and scheduled to occur the night before the Saturday opening. This was an RSVP affair and only the coolest people in the Detroit area were invited, in addition to other hip people from undisclosed hip places outside Detroit, such as maybe the Bat Cave or a castle in the South of France. These people would most likely fly in on private aircraft or helicopters or hang glide if the weather was right. Strangely enough, a Reilly from Detroit actually made the guest list. Not me (I'm sure they grew tired of my phone calls and letters), but Marge Reilly, my good mother. She called me on the day of the party and told me she had received her invitation that morning.

"Maybe they got me mixed up with someone else?" she wondered.

At first I thought she was right, but then I began calling clients just to say hi and talk music, and sure enough, everyone I contacted had just received an invitation that morning to the star-studded Prostitute gala, which promised "champagne, celebrities, live music, free CDs, and the best food in the Detroit area." Obviously, Prostitute obtained our client list and carefully timed the delivery of its local invitations so we would be unable to respond.

So, I thought, as I got off the phone with yet another client who was going to "check out" the party, not only did bio-Uncle Hank ignore my pleas, but he was now abusing me like I was a sissy bitch. Maybe Jonathan was right after all. Maybe I should quit playing "roll the ball through the puddle" and hire a local gangbanger to fly to Los

Angeles and toss a fucking bomb through that used-car salesman's gauche mansion. In the meantime, I instructed Karolina to borrow Marge's invite, put on one of her naughty, homemade Tunisian dresses, and go over to that oil-stained, burned-out warehouse on Gratiot (except now it was a fully stocked, state-of-the-art, music-purchasing paradise) and find out as much as she could.

*

As it was related to me, through Karolina and other sources, it took no more than seven minutes in a crowd of three hundred for someone to point her out to the store manager. From there, it took less than ninety seconds for the store manager to hit on her. His name was Jam (like Sting), and Jam, among other things, was a sickly-looking but self-assured man in his late thirties with an accentuated, malnourished jawbone that jettisoned from his throat like a duck's beak. This unappealing oddity had to be a queer physical manifestation of a lifelong struggle with self-obsessive, addictive behavior and intense pharmaceutical and tobacco abuse.

Not wasting a beat, Jam muscled his way through the crowd and over to Karo and unabashedly introduced himself as the boss. He then went on to give a lengthy account of his tenure at Prostitute and how he was hand-picked by Hank Tyler himself to take over in the Motor City because he, more than anyone else, understood the "Detroit contribution" to the international music scene.

But Karolina, having by that time taken serious notice of the obscene similarities between our store and theirs, had no choice but to interrupt and ask Jam—since he was the boss—if he was responsible for the store's name, design, themes, and inventory, because it reminded her of another Eclectic record shop not too far away that had already been "in Detroit for quite a long time." The main difference, she continued, was that this new Eclectic shop was bigger and had more stuff, such as space, inventory, equipment, furniture, staff, money, and heat. In fact, the only notable mark of originality she could ascertain was the garish artwork. But other than that, one could easily think the two stores were part of an "Eclectic chain," as she referred to it.

Matthew Benjamin

Jam, not expecting this, and confused by the resistance, was promptly informed by one of his leather-clad, spidery female assistants that Karolina was indeed the manager of that other Eclectic store. Jam then burst into a fit of riotous, billowing laughter that echoed throughout the noisy warehouse and screamed out for all to hear that he must be turning goofy to not have detected Karolina for who she was and how interesting and humorous (can't you tell) it all was. This admission was meant to be salubrious and should not be confused with embarrassment or foolishness for being such a stupid old ham, because none of that existed in the Prostitute world. And to prove it—after the sebaceous laughter subsided—Jam lowered his voice and, like a true pro, invited Karo to be his executive assistant or assistant manager, whichever title she preferred. He was willing to almost double her salary and allow her input on all creative decisions that concerned Prostitute Eclectic. It was an impressive response that reeked with unchecked confidence and was most certainly a trademark of bio-Uncle Hank's leadership style. But Jam under-estimated Karolina, who began to laugh out loud herself.

"Why should I work for you when all you did was copy me?" she screamed back into the crowd. "But I might consider working for Hank and Ben Tyler if they make me your boss."

For this, poor Jam had no immediate comeback, and there was a new and embarrassing silence in his circle. Jam then coolly and quietly suggested that Karolina consider his generous offer anyway because she may never get it again. Karo told him she would take her chances and walked away.

On her way out, she bumped into one of our former part-time employees, a guy named Jake who, months earlier, quit in frustration after Karolina rejected him as a lover. That night, he happened to be wearing a little badge indicating he was now an employee of Prostitute Eclectic. That explained how they got our customer list.

When Karo returned, she was fiery with anger. She hated Jam and traitor Jake for stealing her ideas and our client lists, and we made love all night. Between sessions, we talked calmly about what we were up against, how determined we were to defeat them, and how disgusting and unoriginal and corporate-anal Prostitute was despite the trendy lambency and bullshit talk. Overall, we agreed we learned a lot from her attendance at the party. The only person we did not learn more about was bio-Uncle Hank, who did not attend. It was possible that he had more pressing business and did not have time to fly in from Los Angeles, but my gut told me his no-show was calculated and had more to do with the fear of my crashing their party and confronting him. Either way, I would soon have my day with musical Uncle Hank Tyler. His disrespect and haughty contempt only served to embolden me.

9
HANK TYLER

Exactly seven weeks after the opening of *Prostitute Eclectic* in Detroit, I received a certified letter from Hank Tyler, president of Prostitute LLC in Los Angeles. The envelope reminded me of something I might get from an attorney or an architect. The letter was printed on thick, bonded, off-white Prostitute stationery that somewhat deceived the earthy tone of the actual correspondence, which most certainly was the product of a dictation between a tycoon and his obedient assistant. It read as follows:

Dear Reilly:

> *I couldn't give a rat's ass whose bastard you are. But since you've been such a nuisance, I'm willing to buy you out before your Detroit operation goes south for good. Contact us for a fair price ASAP. This is my one and only offer.*

H. Tyler

My initial response was one of morbid fascination. How true, I reflected, that ego defines humanity. The egotists delineate the landscape, they form the alliances, they determine the power struggles. This letter was further proof.

The timing was interesting, too. Hank had waited seven weeks to send it, not because I was a "nuisance," but because that was how long it took before my store began to feel the full brunt of the new competition. In that relatively brief period, our sales began to dip significantly, with the biggest slip occurring from week six to week seven when I lost a startling 38 percent in sales revenue. Being a veteran to the slash-and-burn campaign, Hank had to have known that was going to happen. To boot, his sycophant protégé Jam continued the sleazy tactic of hiring my ex-employees and using them against me. Somewhere in week five he brought on Sledge's old tag team, Delco and Byron, as co-assistant managers. Their first official action as Prostitute henchmen was to call my customer base and tell them that they, Delco and Byron, were the true heirs to Eclectic Emporium. Sledge "sold" the business to me only because he was desperate with legal obligations and I offered him twice as much money. But now, finally, after all these years, they could respectfully "carry Sledge's torch" with the help of benevolent Prostitute Records.

This was a remarkable lie, and it proved one thing: Sledge knew what he was doing when he chose me and not those two blockheads to take over his creation. The damage they wrought was profound, though, because it gave our clients—all of them decent people—a moral pass to be seduced by Prostitute's give-aways and celebrity-tinged promotions. Many of them were especially intrigued by two well-known movie composers who made an appearance at the Detroit Prostitute Eclectic store one week after Delco and Byron joined the team. These talented men, celebrities in their own right, gave interesting lectures on the details of composing for the movie business, complete with an outpouring of anecdotal, name-dropping gems that impressed the fawning crowd. Later, I'm told, there was a buffet and wine bar for cozy, informal post-lecture conversation and Byron and Delco got to chit-chat with all their (my) old customers and introduce everyone to everyone, and soon everyone was sucking everyone's swollen, merged, community cock in an orgy of new digital Eclectic fellowship.

*

In just a couple of months, it had become abundantly clear to Karolina and me that our worst fear was coming true: we would not be able to compete despite our convictions. We were getting our asses kicked. And if kept up, it would not be long before we were panhandling on Mack Avenue. So I did the only thing I could think of doing in those critical moments (which did not include selling out to sleazebag Hank) and decided to go visit Sledge. Talk to the master. Bring him up to date. He was still the toughest and shrewdest man I had ever known, and this was his masterpiece that was being destroyed.

Over the years, I had never visited Sledge in federal prison because he did not want visitors. I believe his reluctance was tied to being reminded of the old world he purposely left behind. I did write him periodically to inform him about some of the major Eclectic developments, but his response letters were usually brief, supporting whatever decisions I had made, with no clues of how life was going for him on Terminal Island. I never got around to writing him about the Prostitute debacle because I kept fooling myself that the situation would get better. But things were now going south at a blazing pace—or so it seemed—and I decided to overrule his isolation plea (which I always thought was rather stupid) and fly to California.

Terminal Island, I discovered, was geographically situated between the port cities of Long Beach and San Pedro, California, and together the three coastal communities constitute one of the largest industrial port complexes in the world. And somewhere nestled in that hypnotic maze of post-industrial cargo exchange stood a sleepy federal prison where Sledge made his home.

After flying into the Long Beach Airport, I rented a car and drove no more than twenty minutes through the city of Long Beach before climbing a long blue bridge onto the tiny Terminal Island. I then zigzagged for about seven minutes around cargo bins, trucks, refineries, railroad tracks, cranes and a few other rusty objects until I reached the T.I. Federal Correctional Facility. This particular facility was nothing like the prison horrors portrayed in the movies or on cable television. I did not spot one rifle, dog, or electrified fence, and the one and only visible guard tower was empty. It was peppered with small dumpy buildings and barrack-type structures that were sectioned off and dispersed in what resembled an oversized football field. To me it looked more like an outdated, underfunded, decaying community college than a federal compound. Esthetically, though, it wasn't too challenging given its purpose. In fact, the prison grounds were less of an eyesore than the island itself—which, as far as I could tell, no longer sustained a residential community, the prison being the sole exception.

My first impression of Sledge after not having seen him for seven years was that he looked trim, fit, and healthy. His hair was longer (higher) and had changed from more black to more gray and white, but if anything that hinted at dignity rather than age. He also seemed happier and more relaxed. In fact, I would say overall he looked remarkably well. He wore the typical prison garb consisting of a khaki shirt, brown work pants, and black, rubber-soled shoes, but that did nothing to diminish his imbued magnanimity. Despite his intellect, artistry, and excellent phony money, Sledge was not a pretentious man and this carried over well into prison life.

"There's been a lot going on, Sledge," I said after the formalities were over.

"Since you're here, why don't you tell me all about it," he replied, with a slight grin on his face. "I got some time."

And I did. I told him everything; every detail, angle, impression, sequence, philosophy, and solution—or lack of one—in reference to the Prostitute invasion, including my emotional state and the antics of our former employees.

Sledge was familiar with Hank Tyler and his reputation, and he fully understood the corporate fear of the Internet fiasco. Before I worked for him, he was a pioneer in using the Internet to seek out obscure labels and rare music, although he, like most, never foresaw the extent of the digital piracy that was to follow. And that happened while he was incarcerated.

"It's a tough turn," he said thoughtfully.

After three hours of intensive conversation, in which I did most of the talking, it was time for me to leave. Sledge recommended I stay in Long Beach and return to the prison for the next visiting session, which would be in two days. He also suggested I visit L.A., too, because it's less than an hour away. "You know people out here, right?" he asked.

"You got to be kidding? My siblings?"

"Why don't you try visiting someone new?"

And with those words of wisdom, I left the federal grounds. I drove south to Long Beach and booked a room in the Renaissance Hotel on Pine Street. After resting, I walked to a seafood restaurant and ate heartily. I then hit a few area bars, purposefully got drunk, and stumbled back to my hotel and fell right out.

The next morning, I decided to take Sledge's advice and visit Los Angeles. After forty minutes of driving, I began to see the downtown Los Angeles buildings and connected to the Hollywood Freeway, later exiting on the Sunset Boulevard ramp. From there, I headed to the Sunset Strip. I parked in a lot near Crescent Heights—close to the very spot where I stepped off the bus during my teenage visit.

I began walking. It was a beautiful day, clear skies, the sun shining, a cool wind blowing in from the not-so-distant ocean. At some point, I thought, I would choose a restaurant. This time a real one and not some pizza or gyros joint. But it never happened because my legs stopped working after four blocks or so when I looked to my left and saw a white, elegant, fifteen-story office building with ten tall metal letters situated above the main entrance that composed the word "PROSTITUTE." Had I not been standing directly in front and facing that direction, I would have missed it. I immediately began to wonder if this was my real reason for coming to Terminal Island—to seek out Hank Tyler. Although, to the best of my knowledge, I had no intention or desire to see Hank before or after I left Detroit. Sledge was the one who suggested I drive to Los Angeles. Yet I did vaguely remember Hank's building had a Sunset Boulevard address.

Either way, conscious or subconscious, fate or folly, I was here, and the question became: Should I go in and talk to the buzzard face to face? Technically, he was still waiting for my reply about selling the business, which gave me a legitimate reason to enter. But my feet were frozen. I'm almost embarrassed to admit it, but I was petrified. But why? What was I afraid of? Certainly not Hank, the copycat, used-car salesman from New Jersey who was trying to ruin my life. Or was I? This was, after all, big-league Hollywood, and despite my fading confidence, I was still just a Midwestern boy who owned one record shop. Then again, that was not true either. My blood father was the major partner in this business and if not for him, none of this would exist—including me. This was the same man who wrote me if I ever really needed him, he would be there for me. If I did not have a right to walk in that building and speak my mind, nobody did.

Without further ado, I marched through the revolving door. The lobby was pierced with a giant marble feng shui fountain large enough to drown a classroom of small children. I briskly walked past the fountain, into the elevator, and pushed the button for the top-floor penthouse. The elevator seemed slow which gave me more time to regain my confidence. Finally the doors opened and I proceeded onward.

Upon entering the suite, there were a bunch of things that immediately caught my eye and not necessarily in this order: the impressive view of the surrounding Hollywood community, visible through the floor-to-ceiling windows; the numerous large, hanging, black-and-white photos of rock stars and other musical talent, such as Ray Charles and Ella Fitzgerald; the very cool, light-purple, sparsely-decorated Art Deco furniture; and, last but not least, the beautiful and smartly dressed young women situated throughout doing various office tasks.

I walked up to one of these women, an emaciated blonde with an Eastern-European accent who was positioned in the circular control center near the middle of the room. She greeted me with a smile, no words, and I asked her if she would please let Hank Tyler know that Nic Reilly from Detroit is here to talk to him about his offer. She frowned slightly, routinely checked her appointment screen, and simultaneously asked me, with a tinge of doubt and condescension, if I had an appointment with Mr. Tyler. I told her I did not because I had not planned to be in Los Angeles today but some urgent business brought me into the general area and I figured I would stop by before flying back to Detroit.

"Really?"

"No, Reilly. Nic Reilly," I replied.

"You've called here before, haven't you?" she asked, obviously remembering the name from all the messages I left.

"Quite a few times."

"I'm sorry, Mr. Reilly, but without an appointment there's nothing I can do for you."

"I'm the one responding to Mr. Tyler's offer, not the other way around," I persisted.

"I'm sure you are." This was barely audible.

"Could you at least find out if he's interested in seeing me before I leave town and fly away for good," I said, not quite ready to give up.

She looked back up me, stared, mumbled to herself something like, "I don't usually do this," picked up the phone and began whispering into it. As she was whispering, she pointed to the purple couches, meaning that was where I should go and wait, which I did.

Exactly twenty-two minutes later, another well-dressed, attractive, slightly emaciated woman with a different foreign accent, clearly Italian, approached me and introduced herself as "Vicky." I immediately remembered this voice my from my phone calls. She told me Mr. Tyler would see me now. I followed Vicky's legs down a narrow hallway past a couple of opened and closed doors to another closed door, which she opened. She smiled and gestured for me to enter the office. I smiled back and entered Hank Tyler's office, allowing her to shut the door behind me. She did not enter herself.

*

He was seated behind his desk, squawking on the phone and staring out the window, his back to the front of the room. All I could see of him was the back and top of his oval-shaped balding head. I was certain he knew I had entered. I decided not to sit down in one of the brown leather chairs in front of his desk without an invitation. "I'll wait," I thought, and looked around: more candid black-and-white photos of rock stars, including a great shot of a full-bearded bio-Dad taken when he was about my age. *How I wished he were here instead of this grease ball.* Finally, the phone clicked down, the chair swirled around, and Hank looked my way. There was a long pause as we both stared into each other's faces—faces that closely resembled one another. *So close* that neither one of us could utter a word. The stunned silence was finally broken by a gruff, scratchy baritone.

"Sit down," he said.

I sat down. He lit up a Marlboro, thinking how best to proceed. "So I understand you were in the area?" he asked.

"Yeah, I'm visiting Sledge Parker. He's the guy who created Eclectic Emporium."

"What's he doing out here?"

"He's in prison. Terminal Island."

"Yeah? Well, he could be doing a lot worse than that joint."

He would know, I thought, after escaping the claws of a New Jersey state penitentiary by the skin of his ass. He paused again, staring blankly. His hesitancy suggested his befuddlement by these unexpected, undeniable biological similarities. I knew from reputation that it was not in his character to be this confused. As Jonathan noted, he lived in a black-and-white world.

"So," he started up again," what have you decided?"

"I'm not ready to sell. I want to talk to Ben."

"Wouldn't we all? He's impossible to get a hold of."

"I can wait."

"Listen," he said thoughtfully, inhaling deeply, perhaps reconsidering, "maybe we can work something better out."

"What do you have in mind?"

"First of all, I'll give you a decent price for Eclectic Emporium. Something you can feel good about. Once you sell, I'll set you up at the new Detroit store as an executive consultant or something. I can't make you the boss right away because it would complicate things, but you hang in there, learn the ropes of how we do things, and then we'll see about what's next. And if you want, we'll get rid of those two assholes who used to work at your store."

"That's it?"

"It's a start, isn't it?"

"It's not enough," I said, and meant it.

He smiled slightly. He was becoming more comfortable. The confrontation was sobering. "Nic, right?" he asked.

"Yeah."

"Nic, I know you're not stupid. And despite what you might think, I'm not stupid, either. Look around you. Does this look stupid? If you think so, you should get the fuck out of here right now, Ben

Tyler or no Ben Tyler."

I offered nothing, remaining silent. He continued: "If you need time to think, go think. Take all the time you need and call when you're done thinking, okay?"

"I'll call you."

"Good."

"When's Ben going to be back?"

"Who knows? He just appears like Houdini. But when he does, I'll tell him we talked, fill him in on what's going on."

"Fair enough."

I stood up to leave. "Where you staying?" he asked.

"Long Beach."

"Close to that prison?"

"Yeah."

"Next time, we'll put you up around here."

"Okay."

He stood up, walked around the desk and extended his hand. It took a second, but I shook it.

"I'll be waiting," he said.

We looked at each other one last time, eye to eye, both of us around the same height, weight and bone structure, and both of us still in an emotional cul-de-sac about the physical parity.

On the way out, I understood why the office women, especially the receptionist whose name I later found out was Sonia, didn't toss me out earlier. I looked like her boss. This time, she smiled brightly at me, "Good-bye Mr. Reilly."

Minutes later, I was back on Sunset walking west with my thinking cap on. Hank's new offer was interesting: a significant wad of cash and a future in the family empire in exchange for my business and possibly my integrity. But a compromise such as that seemed to be the norm in the adult world. Only the heroes, or the ones who have deep faith, go their own way and survive; I had not the stamina or characteristics of either. I wondered, too, Hank being Hank, if he would have offered the same deal had I not looked like him. Probably not, I thought. But that's how it goes. Life is a series of inches and all the rest is saloon talk. For Hank to have shunned me in this casting, he would have been shunning himself.

Yet there was more to his proposal than met the eye—or rather less. The offer to buy me out was not new, just the amount (and still no choice in the matter except sell or be destroyed). And I wasn't thrilled at the prospect of working in his Detroit store under the leadership of Jam until I "learned the ropes." Jam was another cunning narcissist with poor taste. He was also political. He would resist; sabotage. I would hate every second of it. It had all the markings of disaster.

But the last part—the promise of the future—was a legitimately good offer. As I interpreted it, I would first pay my filial dues in Detroit, and then I'd be invited to join Hank and bio-Dad in the upper chambers of Prostitute LLC in Los Angeles. It could serve to be the perfect and much-belated vehicle to establishing my status as the oldest Tyler child (Hank had no children) and thus my birthright to inherit what could be perceived by some as rightfully mine if not for the adoption. I was still Ben's oldest kid, no matter what any court said.

Adding it all up was a confusing process. As I drove back to Long Beach, I thought long and hard about it. I knew I'd be seeing Sledge the next day and was curious how he would respond to these latest developments, or if I should even tell him. It was important for me to remember that Sledge had made his prison camp decision, and I still had my whole life ahead of me. Thus far, my commitment to him and Eclectic Emporium and the ideal he started had never wavered, but at the end of the day, there was only so much I could do. Much of this I could not battle, such as the Internet piracy and the Prostitute war chest. I should not let my emotional preference blind me to these facts. My commitment had limitations, especially since, as mentioned, there was an exceedingly good possibility that we were going down anyway, probably within six months if I continued to lose business at the rate I was losing it.

That night, I did not sleep much. The next morning, feeling tired and lousy, I checked out of the Renaissance Hotel and again crossed the long Desmond Bridge onto bleak Terminal Island. As I drove, there was a dense, eerie fog smothering the industrial port landscape, and it gave me the helpless sensation I was entering some kind of apocalyptic *Bladerunner* nightmare from which there was no return. Towering Jurassic cranes—monster shadows in the fog—were waiting to crush me. Filthy, asthmatic refineries would soon erupt like devil birth. And all of it being fed and kept alive by the haunting, distant pirate ships fleeting in from evil Asia.

Sledge seemed to be in an upbeat mood, though, probably because living in this pit rendered the weather irrelevant, and gloomy days had long lost their meaning. "What did you do yesterday?" he asked cheerfully.

"I went to Los Angeles."

"Did you go see the Lakers?"

"It's summer. Basketball season is over."

"That's right. So what did you do?"

I was still undecided about how to approach him with Hank's offer. But, as usual, Sledge was two steps ahead: "Did you go see Hank Tyler at the Prostitute Records building on Sunset?" he asked, without waiting for an answer to the first question.

"Yes," I said.

"And what did Hank Tyler have to say?"

"He seems to have altered his stance a little."

"His offer to buy you out?"

"Yes. There's a little more to it now."

"You mean like a future?"

"That's what he was hinting at."

"If it's real, and the terms are reasonable, it might be a good deal for you."

"You think?"

"Yeah."

"You want to know the details?"

"Nah."

"We might go down anyway, Sledge."

"I agree. Got to think ahead."

"If I take his offer, I at least have a chance to include Eclectic Emporium in the stew. Once I secure myself."

"That's one way to go about it," he said. "And a smart way."

I looked at him carefully, not knowing if he was mouthing these things for my sake and hiding his true thoughts. He then, strangely, lowered his voice, his eyes still as a stagnant duck pond, and said:

"I forgot to tell you, but I kept some stuff in the basement near the sump pump. I can't remember what it is now, but it's all yours if you ever want to check it out."

"In the basement?"

"Yeah"

"Okay, thanks."

"Sure."

"So you think it's worth considering? What he's offering?" I said, getting back on subject.

"If he sticks to it. He may not. That's the one thing you need to be careful about."

"Okay."

"Another thing."

"Yeah?"

"If things work out, don't be too hard on Delco and Byron."

10
BIG CHANGES

It would take me months to fully understand what Sledge was talking about, but as I was learning, life has a way of unfolding secrets in its own time.

After leaving Terminal Island, I flew back to Detroit. Karolina was waiting for me at the airport, and we made love in a remote section of the airport parking garage. A faulty fluorescent light kept blinking above, adding a touch of staccato decadence to the carnal pleasure. She had new Prostitute info, too, which I heard while thrusting between those golden-brown legs, the tops of which were crammed upward, crisscrossed, and knocking ceaselessly against the roof of her old Dodge.

It was weird but good news. It turned out that Jam was as twisted as any of us had imagined and maybe even a little more so. One of his favorite hobbies was turd worshipping. For those who aren't savvy, turd worshipping is exactly what the phrase implies: the worship or idolatry of human feces—the size, girth, shape, and composition. Each piece (of shit) is examined, critiqued, admired, and ultimately ossified and displayed, if worth saving. The most important qualifying aspect is that it be in one solid unit in its natural form. So, in other words, a salty sailor after a drunken night in port would not be the prime candidate to produce a great work of art. The most prized pieces come from young, spruce, athletic teenagers whose metabolisms are in good working condition and who, because of their wholesome lifestyles and healthy appetites, are capable of producing prodigious and mighty specimens for connoisseurs such as Jam—who approach it like a piece of sculpture. I believe the phallic shape contributes to the admiration process, although I don't know if that is openly acknowledged.

Unfortunately, this good news interrupted my sexual performance and complicated what had already become a physical challenge due to the restrictive circumstances of the cramped automobile. Afterward, though, in the store, in my office, when I had time to reflect, I concluded there were more odious fetishes in today's skewed world than turd idolatry. But if exposed, it would certainly be frowned upon.

Karolina found out about Jam's passion from Jake, who quit working for Prostitute Records after he clashed with Delco and Byron, his new superiors. Jake imagined he was more up-to-date in the music scene than the two old guys, and apparently they did not help the situation by shamelessly abusing what little authority they had. Hearing about this, and knowing how Hank felt about Delco and Byron, reminded me of an old Chinese saying: *If you stand by the river long enough, you'll watch your enemies float by.*

I updated Karolina on the various developments from my new California adventure, including the surprise visit to Hank Tyler, our resemblance, his revised offer, and Sledge's flexible reaction to all of it. She was skeptical. She was also probably worried about what would happen to her if I chose to go in that direction. She did not bring that up—which I admired—but it was unspoken. I, however, had no intention of leaving Karolina behind no matter what transpired. Any deal I signed would include her.

For me, it all boiled down to what Sledge warned me about: Could Hank be trusted? And not just then, but in the future. What would happen if he and I butted heads down the line and he decided to cut me loose before I assumed my rightful place as an heir to the Tyler musical fiefdom? Despite our recent "reconciliation," I had no doubt he would toss me out on my ears in a heartbeat if the spirit moved him. I believed he was of that temperament, that psychology. He was also the boss, and based on how he acted in our meeting, I suspected that if I did not suck up 99 percent of the time, I could easily be demoted to a non-Tyler employee scum entity and treated accordingly. This needed to be considered even though it was probably the worst scenario and failed to take into account the quintessential blockbuster bio-Dad, who, sooner or later, would make his grand entrance onto the scene.

According to my data, bio-Dad was still the largest member-owner in the LLC. He and Hank, as a team, controlled the company with 51 percent. So on at least two important levels (as guardian and as owner), bio-Dad could prevent any serious harm to me if I accepted Hank's offer and later had a falling out. Nothing was guaranteed, of course, but that was a fair assumption.

The only possible complication regarding bio-Dad would be his caveat about my not becoming involved with him or his affairs, fearing I would turn into a pseudo-deviant twisted sponge like some of his other kids. That might extend to his jaded brother's enterprise as well. But in my defense, the circumstances surrounding my entrance into his affairs were not of my doing. Prior to the invasion, I stood on my own two feet, minding my own damn business, and running a small but first-rate operation in my home city. Things changed only after his brother's henchman marched into Detroit and tried to destroy me. I would be sure to point that out.

As usual, I checked with others before making a decision of this magnitude, and the results were surprising. Stu, who I thought would be gung ho, was hesitant because of his dislike for corporate monopolies and monolithic retail chains. Being primarily a labor lawyer, he never accepted the banality of the obscene proliferation of the same mediocre products and considered the cancerous growth to be one of the major contributing factors to the ensuing end of civilization (he had written off the United States years ago; his concern now was for the rest of the world). But, like Karolina and me, he saw no alternative in the long run. He was also keenly aware of my sensitivity to Tyler filial issues and quickly understood my new long-term goals of empire. I did not start this. But now that it had started, my ambitions began to grow. Ultimately, his advice was more conservative: "Get as much money now as you can, and don't rule out law school."

Jonathan, paradoxically, was all for the sale of Eclectic Emporium to Prostitute LLC, but for reasons that were consistent with his earlier appeal—to defeat the rogue tyrant, second-generation immigrant Hank Tyler, at any cost. I could hear crunching cereal as he explained his modified position to me over the phone:

"This is a unique opportunity, and probably superior to the gutter tactics I originally proposed. By taking this new route, you can penetrate the inner sanctum of his purulent mind and befriend the hooligan as a tributary and then, when he least expects it, crush him like a bug. It has its risks, certainly, but it's more suited to a thinking man. Follow me?"

"Go on," I said, wanting more.

"You see, Nic, a festering mind such as Hank Tyler's is also a guarded mind—guarded with barbed wire and hungry wolves. But if the wolves go to sleep—say they're drugged by a resemblance pill—the mercurial personality could enter into unfamiliar territory, perhaps an alien state sometimes known as vulnerability, and that is when you must attack with full force, straight for the jugular, no mercy. Got it?"

"Take his offer?"

"Yes, and then when you get close to him, destroy him. Right away. That's important."

"There won't be much time?"

"No. Because, eventually, the viscous mind will constrict again—the wolves will wake up—and the mercurial personality will become more rigid, more paranoid, more threatening, more dangerous, and more evil than ever before. You need to strike when you can."

"I see."

"Only the sociopaths and knuckle brains endure in his environment. For instance, that turd guy."

My last confidant, Marge, was the only one against it, and her reasons more instinctive than the others: "It just doesn't feel right, honey."

"What do you mean?"

"Isn't there another way than selling?"

"It doesn't seem so," I replied, filling her in on details about the changing industry and why both Sledge and Stu thought it was the thing to do at this point. It didn't faze her at all:

"Sledge is in jail, and Stu, well, he's a lawyer. I just want you to be happy, dear."

"I know you do, Mom."

"Eclectic Emporium is a fine store. It will always have a following."

That was probably true but Marge's thoughts had no lasting impact on me, and I decided to go along with the majority. I would sell Eclectic Emporium to Prostitute LLC for cash, work for Hank Tyler as a consultant at Prostitute Eclectic in Detroit (under Jam), and take my bloody chances.

The following Monday, I called Prostitute LLC in Los Angeles to negotiate the sale of Eclectic Emporium and discuss my new role in the organization. Vicky answered my phone call and promptly transferred me to Hank's office. Once again, I had to wait a few minutes and then no salutations, just, "So what's it going to be?"

"Let's do it," I said.

"You'll need to come out here again. When can you make it?"

"How about Friday?"

"Okay, Friday. I'll send you back to Vicky, and she'll set you up at a hotel around here."

"I'm going to bring my lawyer with me, if that's okay."

He chuckled, more smoke: "Sure, bring your lawyer. Bring whoever the hell you want. See you on Friday."

Later that day, I drove to Stu's office to talk things over. We decided $450,000 cash was a reasonable sum for Eclectic Emporium's inventory, client base, and name—even if they were going to stick with "Prostitute Eclectic" instead of "Eclectic Emporium." It was theft nonetheless, and everyone knew it. Stu also suggested we try to nail down a finite time schedule for my tenure at Prostitute Eclectic under the leadership of fecal Jam before I assumed control over the Detroit store or moved to California to become involved in the corporate business.

*

The rest of the week flew by in preparation and did not allow me the leisure time to brood over the shocking reality of saying good-bye forever to yet another great Detroit establishment. I kept telling myself that retail music was morphing into something else, and I was simply taking the next logical step to protect myself. Although in my heart, I knew I was selling out.

On Friday morning, Karolina and I woke at 4:30, dressed, and stepped outside into the pitch black, Detroit weather. We then hopped into her car and picked up Stu at his house near Tiger Stadium and drove to the airport. Despite the early hour and darkness, we were in a good mood, a mood of acceptance, for we had made up our minds and there was nothing left to do but go for it. We discussed how we would approach the subject of Karolina's role, and it was agreed that she would work closely with me in whatever responsibilities I assumed. She would also be given a title. Hank was getting what he wanted—our acquiescence, inventory, and client list—and Stu had no worries that Karolina's inclusion would be a deal breaker.

At the airport, I was sad to part with Karo, but she would serve our cause better by staying in Detroit and keeping an eye on the shop. She gave us both big hugs, wished us luck, and drove off.

Stu and I entered the airport. There was the typical post 9/11 line at our airline counter. As we began to hurry up and wait, I had the urge to read a newspaper. I told Stu I'd be right back, walked over to the newsstand, and purchased a copy of the *Detroit Free Press*. I looked at the front page. The headlines spelled out the latest local political scandal and mayhem. It was depressing. Why, I wondered, did the city of Detroit produce the most inept and foolhardy politicians on the planet? Couldn't they just be respectfully corrupt like everywhere else?

I was tempted to give it back, but I turned to page two instead. And that's where I saw it, on top: "Rock Star Ben Tyler Found Dead in Thailand." I blinked a few times to make sure my vision was sound. It was. Apparently, bio-Dad had expired. I began reading the story and then remembered, thinking calmly, that I should probably get back to the flight line before Stu reached the counter because this was going to change things. In retrospect, I consider my lack of emotion rather disturbing, especially upon discovering that my biological father was found dead in the streets—or an alley for that matter—of a foreign city. My next thought, however, wasn't that much more compassionate: *once again bio-Dad was not going to be there for me.*

I returned to the check-in line and showed Stu the newspaper. Upon reading, Stu went into his bomb squad deep-freeze, as he had the tendency to do now and then. I wondered about the complexity of his thoughts at that moment. For him, there were a myriad of new complications to consider, including the big one facing us at that precise moment: Should we even get on the airplane? It was doubtful we would be discussing Prostitute business.

I looked at my watch: 6:40 am (EST). It was still the middle of the night in Los Angeles. We were not able to call, nor would we be for many hours. Our plane was scheduled to depart at 7:15 am. Stu asked me if I still wanted to go. I thought about it calmly, just as I did minutes before when I first read the newspaper. "Of course I want to go," I replied. "He's my father. Right?"

Stu didn't respond immediately, the situation being too laden with irony and contradiction. But then he bent over, picked up his suitcase, and said, "Okay, let's go."

On the flight to Los Angeles, Stu and I speculated over what could have happened to bio-Dad. Both of us went to bed early the night before and missed whatever late-night TV and radio coverage there was, if any. The situation had not improved any now that we were 37,000 feet above the sea, hurling through space in a metal tube with no outside communication. Hence, the newspaper would have to suffice as our only source.

According to the *Detroit Free Press* article taken from AP wire sources, Ben's body was discovered in an alley in central Bangkok near Chidlom Road around 5 am Thursday, local time. The Thai medical examiner estimated the time of death to be approximately three hours prior to the discovery of the body—around 2 am—and the probable cause of death, a massive coronary. An official autopsy was scheduled to be performed within the next couple of days, after Ben's family was consulted.

Interestingly, the Thai police did not disclose to the public this or any information related to Ben's death until 7 pm that evening—a good 12 hours after the discovery. In addition, there were peculiarities, both stated and implied, that were not expatiated on in the article. For instance, when Ben was discovered dead, it was noted that his *pants were on backwards*. That is, the zipper was facing his ass—zipped up. The police offered no hypothesis except to say there was no physical evidence that he was assaulted, either physically or sexually, although most of this would have to be corroborated by autopsy. Nor, they reported, was he robbed. His wallet was in his back pocket (front in this case) with $3,020 American in it. The police acknowledged the facts were incongruous, but offered no real explanation of what happened after a full day of thinking about it. They confirmed bio-Dad had been staying in a small, obscure hotel in Southern Bangkok for the past eighteen weeks and the last time he was seen in public was two days prior to his death on Koh Mook Beach, sunbathing with three young Thai girls in string bikinis.

Stu and I agreed the Thai reticence may have had to do with the embarrassing implications, the least awkward being that bio-Dad was tipsy and mistakenly put his pants on backward (and zippered them?), walked into the alley to relieve himself, and had a heart attack before he could figure out how to whip it out. A more likely scenario was that bio-Dad died elsewhere—naked and probably in the act of fornication—and his hastily clothed body was transferred to the alley and left for discovery. That, at least, might account for the 3,000 dollars in his wallet. No respectable whore would walk away from that kind of cash unless, of course, she or he was fraught with guilt and in hysterics. Stu thought the latter scenario might explain why the police took so long to announce his death. They were looking for Ben's associates.

Over four hours later we arrived in Los Angeles. Unlike the second-page coverage bio-Dad's demise received in the *Detroit Free Press*, the Los Angeles media were all over it. Los Angeles was the heart of the music and entertainment industry, and Ben was one of its own. He also had quite a reputation as a sexual predator. The first headline I saw once I got off the plane was: "BEN TYLER DIES WITH HIS PANTS ON—BACKWARDS." Thus, I feared, bio-Dad's whole life would now be reduced to that one sordid little detail. That's what they're going to remember. And it could have easily been avoided had his sexual companions kept their cool and properly put his pants on before dumping him in the alley—if that is what happened.

*

As Ben's invisible oldest son, my sense of the surreal was heightened as I traversed the sugar-coated streets of Hollywood in the midst of this media firestorm. At one intersection on Melrose near Fairfax, I saw two middle-aged men dressed in thousand-dollar business suits buckle over with laughter as they read aloud the particulars of bio-Dad's postmortem wardrobe in the *Los Angeles Times*. It distressed me to see this, yet I felt beyond visceral reaction, as though I were a peripheral character in someone else's dream, shielded by the translucent vehicle. It was too strange, too surreal—as were my circumstances and timing. Bio-Dad was right to steer me away from this raw, public exposure. This heartless fucking cannibalism. That was the gist of his message in the Euro-letter masterpiece of years gone by; a message I fully heeded until the Prostitute invasion changed everything.

Once we settled into our hotel, I drank a pot of coffee to get focused and shake off the jet lag. I had been awake for about eight hours, but it felt like a week straight.

At ten minutes before 11 PDT, it was time to leave for our scheduled meeting at the Prostitute offices. No one called us to cancel, but I called anyway to confirm. Nobody answered. Not even an answering service. Who could blame them based on what we had seen so far? But I had a feeling they were over there just the same. I was hoping, too, that Hank would honor my relationship with his deceased brother and provide special information. My presence should not be strictly about business during this sorrowful period.

We left the hotel and walked fewer than two blocks. As we approached the Prostitute building, we saw a slew of media vans parked in front screwing up traffic, with 40 to 50 people loitering on the sidewalk bullshitting, smoking cigarettes, and ostensibly enjoying themselves. I would even go as far as to say the mood was festive. Had I not known the circumstances of the gathering, I would have guessed it was a celebrity appearance or a movie premiere.

There was also a salient private security presence blocking the front entrance, preventing anyone from entering the building. Stu and I pushed our way through the crowd to the entrance and explained our circumstances to the security men. As I waited for them to get confirmation, I noticed a few of the nearby reporters staring at me. Their curiosity, I thought, may have been inspired by my Tyler features. One of the reporters began to inch his way over to me. Surely, his intent was to question me. He would probably ask me who I was and what I was doing there. I shrewdly considered: Wouldn't this be the perfect moment to publicly announce my Tyler bastardship to the world at large? I couldn't ask for a wider or more receptive audience. But before he got to me, Stu and I were briskly escorted into the building, leaving behind the curious reporters who became even more curious after our admittance.

The lobby was silent and empty. The giant waterfall was turned off. It felt eerie. We took the elevator to the Prostitute penthouse suites where we found Vicky waiting for us in the lobby. She appeared frayed, edgy, unlike the poised professional I remembered, and apologetically informed us that Hank Tyler could not be here to meet with us for obvious reasons. We were free to stay the weekend at their expense, but she could not guarantee when they would be able to reschedule. I asked her if it was possible for me to contact Hank directly. "I have some personal issues I'd like to discuss with him." After I said this, I watched her big, dark Italian eyes grow soft and sad. I knew then, for sure, that she was aware of the emotional complexity of my current situation. "I'm sorry, Mr. Reilly," she replied, "but I don't have authority to give out Mr. Tyler's private numbers."

"Oh."

"But I guarantee you I will do everything I can to have him call you as soon as I talk to him again."

"Thank you."

"This is a tough time for all of us," she said.

And with that, Stu and I returned to the elevator. Our West Coast meeting was over. We descended to the lobby, allowed the security guards to smuggle us out to the street, and pushed through the crowd without talking to any of the nosy reporters, to whom I now felt a sudden and profound aversion. After we broke free, we walked up Sunset and found ourselves a little lounge. From there, we proceeded to get shitfaced. It wasn't a hard thing to do. The change of scenery, geography, circumstances, lives, plans, and expectations had altered our senses. We compensated with ice-cold Russian vodka and washed it down with warm Guinness from the barrel. This oasis allowed me new and uninterrupted moments to consider bio-Dad's demise on a purely emotional level, independent of the business of Prostitute Records or his mogul brother. Bio-Dad was no longer simply an aloof, distant, shadowy figure who spent most of his time in foreign lands chasing pussy; he was now a recorded statistic, a victim of his own obsessions and addictions. If I were to ever bond with this man who engineered my birth, it would have to be done elsewhere, in some other dimension. That was sad. I was also saddened by the persisting belief that he once again abandoned me when I needed him most—this time by dying. I knew it was a selfish thought, but it wouldn't leave me alone. I kept drinking.

Later that evening, I awoke in a dark hotel room painfully hung over and depressed. As Ben Tyler's oldest son, but with no family ties, I felt awkward, helpless and terminally unique—a feeling exacerbated by my being in Ben's hometown during this hellish period.

I did not hear from Hank or Vicky in the following days. My solution was to attempt to contact the poet Molly Sivad, the only person I had had any kind of relationship with in Los Angeles. She might be able to shed some light and share my grief. Her phone number was unlisted (she never gave it to me all those years ago), but I remembered where she lived in Topanga.

When I told Stu of my plan, I could tell he was relieved to hear that he would be on his own. Stu was a bachelor and used to his privacy, and I had always suspected him of smoking the magic peace pipe behind closed doors. Either way, it was irrelevant except for the curiosity of his keeping it a secret, if in fact it was true. He cheerfully told me it had been years since he was in Southern California, and he had much to keep him occupied. We went our separate ways.

After renting a car, I drove west on Sunset to the Pacific Ocean and turned north up the coast. The distinguishing characteristic of this relatively short stretch of PCH—from Santa Monica to Malibu—was creature-comfort excess. Here, I thought, was an insatiable, growing, irreverent population powered and sustained by the internal combustion engine. I constantly had to be on my guard about nonstop intersections, hidden traffic lights, cars jumping in and out of parking lots and gas stations, choppy highway, drainage canals, and most of all, split-second shoulder parking and accelerating. I had no problem understanding why people in this area had a reputation of anesthetizing themselves. I would too if I had to navigate this madness on a daily basis.

Fortunately, I survived and reached Topanga Canyon Road without incident and gratefully turned up the mountain. Once I reached the village, I was forced to stop at the post office and reacquaint myself with the area. After doing so, I easily located Molly's street and drove up the winding dirt road until I spotted the crooked mailbox. I parked and walked along the faint trail through the woods until I reached the infamous teepee outhouse. It was still, twelve years later, standing upright in all its lurid splendor. Beyond the outhouse, however, there was a noticeable change: the lighthouse had fallen over.

The three-story, cylindrical structure was now horizontal, opposed to vertical, except in a few places where a couple of stubborn, unyielding trees fractured the integrity of the tube and prevented sections from touching the ground. It immediately reminded me of photos I'd seen of a commercial jet fuselage after a crash in the wilderness. I walked closer and discovered the cause. The foundation beneath the structure had cracked like a jigsaw puzzle. From the looks of it, most of the rupture, or separation, probably occurred after the building had fallen. Thus, from this cursory examination, it appeared an outside force triggered the incident. What that force was, I had no clue. Bizarrely, the rest of the building still appeared intact, with much of the brick and stone in place, and one could even argue Molly's house looked better in its current wrecked fuselage state than when it was standing upright. I estimated, based on the decay and growth where the building met the earth, the fall had taken place within the past year. I'm sure I could have learned more by entering via one of the broken windows but decided against it for what I might find. These were not ordinary people, and I was not interested in the macabre possibilities.

But I was deeply curious about one thing, and I maneuvered to the "top" of the building. As I moved through the random growth, I tripped over a rusty beach chair organically cemented into the soil from neglect. I fell hard to the ground, bracing myself with my forearms. When I stood up, my arms and palms were scraped and bleeding. Feeling stupid but still determined, I kept going until I reached the end of the building. There, "above" the third floor, I searched diligently and found what I was looking for: the white flag with the black lettering. It was still physically attached to the roof with most of the pole and all of the flag seeped into the earth. Using my bloody hands, I grabbed hold of the midpoint of the pole and pulled upward with all my strength. It held firm, but I kept pulling and finally the pole popped up like a broken tree root. I examined the flag, or what remained of it. It was rotted, molded, decomposed, yet I could still read most of the angry black letters stretching across the sagging nylon: SURRENDER GOD—YOU PUSSY—FOR WE ARE MORE POWERFUL.

I walked to the front of the house carrying the pole. I dropped to my knees, dug a new hole, and stuck the pole in, twisting and pushing until it clung firmly to the earth. The filthy, matted flag now stood proudly in front of the torpedoed and misplaced lighthouse, and for the first time it seemed to make a little sense. I then thought about Molly. I still wanted to talk to her and hoped her fate was not the same as that of her sunken abode.

*

Later that night, back at the hotel, Stu had interesting news about Prostitute LLC. Through an old law school friend, who was partnered in a Century City entertainment law firm, he learned "the two brothers had a prenuptial" with regard to the business. Translated, that meant bio-Dad and Hank Tyler had an agreement that if one of them died or wanted out, the other had first rights to buy the deceased or disinterested member's equity in the company before it could be sold to an outside party. Together, the two brothers owned 51 percent and were the managing entity of the LLC, which meant Hank controlled everything because bio-Dad was off doing his own thing and did not want to be bothered. Technically, Prostitute was broken into six or seven LLCs for its various enterprises, such as the record label, the retail chain, publishing, etc., with Prostitute LLC owning 51 percent in each LLC, and with each one having its own set of investors and partners. It was smart business because it diffused the investors and allowed Hank to maintain rigid hegemony over his kingdom.

There was, however, one fascinating factor in this structure: of that 51 percent majority, Hank owned 25 percent and bio-Dad owned 26 percent, a slight but significant discrepancy. As some business people like to say, that's a big 1 percent. When the two brothers started the business, it was all bio-Dad's money and prestige and rock-star friends that provided the basis for Hank to build a successful enterprise, and the percentage split could easily have been more lopsided in bio-Dad's favor if not for his good heart and desire to provide a career for his nearly jailbird, East Coast refugee brother. Still, that tiny advantage meant that whoever was set to inherit bio-Dad's interest in the company would actually have the most control over Prostitute Records. They could sell it to Hank or not sell it to him, if they chose to sell (if Hank was not already designated as recipient). But it all got back to what bio-Dad's will looked like, or how his estate was set up through trusts, or both. There were additional factors, too, such as California being a community property state and other legal technicalities Stu understood. But one thing I did understand well: Hank did not get along with bio-Dad's side of the family, and they, or some part or combination of them, would be the PROBABLE recipients of that 26 percent, unless bio-Dad awarded it to me, the bastard. But if that were true, I had a feeling I would have heard from Hank already. I hadn't. Nor was I going to for a long time. But I heard from somebody else who proved to be much more important than Hank Tyler.

11
ISABELLA

I spent my remaining day in the Los Angeles area with Stu, sunbathing in Malibu on one of the state beaches. The shore was peppered with naturally sculpted rock formations the size of automobiles, and it was quite beautiful as the sun set to the northwest and threw long, shapely shadows across the sand. At this point my mental state was one of resignation to the bio-paradox of being Ben's oldest and not being included in any family mourning ritual. That paradox was heightened by my business with Prostitute Records and the timing of my visit to Los Angeles. But that's how it goes, I reasoned, and there was nothing more I could do. My further attempts to contact Molly Sivad had failed, and with all the fanfare and media obsession surrounding bio-Dad, I was not going to attempt to summon Isabella Tyler, Ben's wife, until things calmed down.

When I returned to Detroit the following day, I called Marge and we talked openly about Ben Tyler. She expressed little sympathy, but did manage to avoid mentioning the rumors surrounding his death, all of which were unflattering. I remember a couple of strange silent moments during that conversation when both of us seemed to be lost in the contradictions of our lifelines. In reference to the more practical matter of inheritance, she told me not to hold my breath "given his past performance," and unnecessarily reminded me that I was not entitled to anything by law since I was adopted.

"How did it go with the record business?" she asked.

"Everything is on hold."

"Maybe God is watching out for you," she said.

"Maybe God's watching out for somebody else," I replied.

"Whoever it is, it's not Ben Tyler, that's for sure."

And who could argue with that? Poor bio-Dad. The next day,

the media reported the official Thai autopsy confirmed the cause of death as ventricular fibrillation, or sudden heart failure, most likely triggered by "adrenaline released during intense physical or athletic activity." In addition (and I knew something like this was coming), there was dead spermatozoa on and around his genitalia. The good news was that it came from him and no one else.

In terms of the ongoing investigation, the Thai police still had no "solid proof" bio-Dad was with anyone when sudden cardiac death occurred (right), although they did not rule it out, nor did they rule out the possibility that he had died elsewhere and his body dumped in the alley. Still, they reported, he had a window of no more than a minute or two to successfully receive CPR treatment after the attack, and even then, there were no guarantees he would have survived. In other words, as I read it, bio-Dad basically dropped dead right after he shot his mighty load and nobody would be going to jail for mistakenly putting his pants on backward, celebrity or no celebrity.

Interestingly—but in retrospect, predictably, the family requested the investigation be ended. They were satisfied. That meant Isabella or Hank was not interested in finding out who Ben was screwing, especially if that person(s) was underage. The newspaper went on to say fans and mourners could pay their respects by sending donations to a private foundation labeled "S-A-D" at a provided address. The family would offer no further public statements ever again regarding this matter. The body was being flown back to Los Angeles where a private service would be held, after which he would be cremated, "as he requested." The "as he requested" part suggested to me that he did have a will.

Meanwhile, in Detroit, Jam and his cronies were maxing out on bio-Dad's untimely demise. A big picture of him was draped in front of the Prostitute Eclectic warehouse, like Stalin or Che', and they staged what could loosely be called a memorial in their copycat lounge. Visitors were invited for refreshments and given free Ben Tyler CDs and information regarding other promotions at Prostitute. Everyone was asked to sign the guest list and include as many personal details as possible.

The most bitter irony of all, though (and the ironies continued to mount), was my not being a part of any of it, anywhere. Not in

Los Angeles and not even in Detroit, my own turf. I have to admit, I was becoming debased by the experience and began to worry if there would be permanent psychological damage.

About a week later, I received a call from Stu, who obtained a copy of Ben's will through his Los Angeles contacts.

"Are you ready?" he asked.

"As ready as I'll ever be."

"It's not what I expected, but it makes sense."

"Tell me, for God's sake!"

"He turned everything over to his wife."

"What does that mean?"

"It means exactly what it suggests. Isabella Tyler now controls the entire Tyler estate."

"What about the kids?"

"That's up to Isabella."

"You mean, like everything stays the same?"

"Yeah. Unless she decides to carve it up with trusts and foundations and giveaways."

"No trusts?"

"Nope. I think he had a real problem with those kids. In his will, the only thing he requested besides being cremated was that Josh Tyler be disinherited. That's the kid who burned down their house?"

"Yes."

"I'm not sure how that would work since Isabella has a right to do as she pleases once the estate becomes all hers."

"And she inherits Ben's portion of Prostitute?"

"You bet she does. You should try to get in touch with her."

"You think?"

"I would. She distrusts Hank Tyler. According to my sources, she would periodically have Prostitute audited to keep track of what Hank was doing since Ben didn't care. Ben allowed Hank to run the show, but that's going to change now that Isabella controls Ben's share. I'm told she's a smart woman. She gets advice from her Marijuana rancher father, who is a shrewd if not an entirely honest businessman. Talk to her. Let her know what you been up to all these years. She should be easier to deal with than Hank and probably more straightforward. Did he ever contact you?"

"Not yet."

"All in all, this is not a bad scenario. Ben didn't give you anything, but he didn't give any of the kids anything. And more importantly, he didn't give his brother his share of the business. The estate is still intact. You're still in the game."

"Okay. Thanks."

"Get in touch with Isabella Tyler."

"Right."

Easier said than done, I thought, after he hung up. I was not sure what became of the last letter I sent her. Probably nothing since I never heard from Ben. The idea of sending her yet another one to the same address seemed fruitless, especially with all the recent publicity. So I decided on another strategy. I called Vicky at Prostitute LLC and asked for Hank and, as expected, was told Hank was still not available. I then told her to tell Hank it was absolutely crucial for me to send something to Ben's wife in reference to Ben's death and he would understand. She called back fifteen minutes later and gave me a private L.A. post office box through which, she assured me, Ben's wife would personally receive anything I sent. I thanked her and told her to have Hank call when he was ready.

From this, I gathered two things: (1) Hank was full of shit about calling me back, and (2) he probably changed his mind about our deal. Writing to Isabella thus became, in part, an indirect attack on Hank, and it felt satisfying that he was helping me do it.

In this new postmortem bio-letter to the widow Isabella, I gave her a brief history of the Eclectic Emporium/Prostitute Records conflict, the irony of the blood connection, and the difficulty I was having with Hank. I did not get into Hank's subsequent offer because I was not sure it was still on the table. Although, by not doing so, I was acutely aware of the omission and attempting to generate as much leverage as possible. I also reminded her that I had sent a letter to Ben in her care, and in that letter was a request to Ben to contact me in reference to this specific matter. I ended by expressing my genuine confusion and sadness about bio-Dad's demise, and the fact that he and I had never gotten together—I being his oldest offspring. It was an honest letter even though my intentions were pure self-interest.

Four days later, Karolina received a call at the store from Isabella. I was not there, but this time Isabella left her phone number (it only took 12 years). Upon hearing the news, I immediately called and Isabella answered the phone. Her voice contained the tiniest trace of a Latin accent, but her diction was exact, her vocabulary astute and appropriate, and it wasn't too long into the phone conversation before I surmised this was a woman whose current resume may have read "mother and widow of rock star" but should have read "director and owner of a significant fortune, including a substantial stake in a privately owned $800 million music entertainment business."

Her first course of business was to apologize for not getting in touch with me sooner and not inviting me to Ben's funeral, but with so much happening she did not remember my circumstance. She told me that she had read my letter carefully and thought it might be a good idea if I came out to Los Angeles to meet with her and talk about things of mutual interest. She would pick me up at the airport and I could stay at her house.

"When did you have in mind?" I asked coolly.

"As soon as you can make it," she said, "I'll work around your schedule."

What schedule? The schedule of insult, bankruptcy, and failure? "How about this Friday?" I shot back.

"Friday's perfect."

I considered mentioning that I had been out there during the time of Ben's death with the intent of talking business with Hank Tyler. But, again, I decided against it. Hank's reticence irritated me, and this relationship had the potential to blow his deal out of the water. I owed nothing to Hank Tyler—not as long as he did not call me back.

Karolina was ecstatic at the news and her energy level atomic. I could tell she was also a tad jealous that I would be leaving again. We talked it out and I stressed the value of her being patient. I understood well how she was becoming restless with so much at stake. The same was true for me.

Once again, I flew to LAX on a Friday morning and Isabella was waiting for me at the baggage claim area. She immediately spotted me out of hundreds of passengers, and I was beginning to grow accustomed to being recognized as a Tyler by people who knew them.

"Nic Reilly?" she called out from a distance, separated by dozens of airport pedestrians.

I walked over, put down my carry-on, and shook hands with her. She was about five-foot-five with a firm, shapely body and wore black, stylish sunglasses and a red silk scarf that covered her ears and compressed a full head of thick, black hair. Her facial features were a perfect mixture of chiseled, Aztec bone structure and soft, feminine beauty. I was immediately attracted to her despite her approximate fifty years. And the only reason I knew her age was because I could do the math. In actual appearance (despite the partial cover-up of glasses and scarf), she looked to be in her thirties, late thirties maybe, and whatever maturity she possessed in her rich olive skin was a welcome and defining characteristic of a timeless sensuality—similar to the qualities Georgia O'Keefe displayed when photographed in the last twenty years of her life.

She directed me through the parking structure, and I could tell this procedure of picking up visitors from the airport and driving them to her home was second nature. After we settled into her small Lexus, she began to open up.

"I apologize again for not inviting you to his funeral," she said with an intonation suggesting how unfair it was. "A couple of his other children weren't at the funeral either, but they were invited. My youngest son, Josh, missed it. So did Ben's daughter from his first marriage."

"That would be Megan," I said.

"Right. She may have had an excuse. She's in a rehab in Minnesota or someplace. But Josh refused to come."

Josh may have had an excuse, too, like being disinherited, but I did not dare reveal too much about what I knew.

"At least the others made it," she continued. "My other two children flew in from Europe, Joseph from England and Jessica from Spain. And Stan—that's Ben's oldest boy from his first marriage—he was there, too."

She stopped and thought a second. "Except for you, that is.

You're the oldest. Sorry."

"By about six months," I said. "Megan's six months younger. What are Joseph and Jessica doing in Europe?" I asked.

"Joseph just finished his doctoral program at Newcastle University—he's a geneticist—and Jessica is a chef in San Sebastian."

"Are they still here in Los Angeles?"

"No. Both of them flew back after the funeral and after taking care of whatever business they had in town."

The last part of her sentence trailed off a bit, hinting at a possible conflict of interest. Undoubtedly, Joseph and Jessica were disappointed to some degree that nothing had changed for them in terms of the Tyler estate.

"I know you never met Ben, but I want you to know something about him," she continued.

"Yes?"

"He was a good man. A trustworthy man—in his own way, despite what you may have read or heard."

"Thank you for telling me," I said.

"When we get home, we'll have lunch and relax and then I'd like to discuss why I asked you to come out. Okay?"

"Sounds good to me," I smiled back.

"You know," she said carefully, "you remind me of him. Of Ben. Much more than the other kids."

"Do I really?"

"Yes. But you look a lot like his brother, Hank." She turned and looked squarely at me. "Did you know that?"

Her question made me suspect that perhaps she and Hank may have had a chat about me already. I knew, at the very least, they were in contact of some sort due to their mutual business caused by bio-Dad's death. From her phone call the day before, it did not sound as though they had talked specifically about me, but that was early yesterday, and today was today, and any monkey can pick up a phone and press a few buttons. Even Hank. As I sat staring into her big, black sunglasses, I thought I should do my best to be most careful here. This exotic and interesting woman, who married my biological father and who now controlled everything he owned, was not to be taken lightly. So I answered in the following manner, thinking carefully about every word:

"Yes, I did. I met him in his office a few weeks ago when I was out here visiting the former owner of Eclectic Emporium, who is now in a federal prison on Terminal Island. I was scheduled to meet Hank again on the day Ben died. We were going to discuss a buyout offer for my store, plus my participation in the new Prostitute Eclectic store in Detroit—which is basically a rip-off of my store. I flew out here with my attorney, but we never had the meeting because of the tragedy. I haven't heard from Hank since. But I did manage to get your post office box from his assistant because I wasn't sure if you were receiving my letters."

I stopped there and waited. She waited, too, and then asked me, rather casually, "So you were going to take Hank's offer? The buyout?"

And it was here, at this moment, when I knew I had screwed up. Isabella and Hank were enemies, and she was looking for allies. I was attempting to cut a deal with the enemy.

"Yes, I was going to take it," I mumbled. "I felt I had no choice. Especially since I hadn't heard from Ben."

She didn't respond. I kept waiting as we drove deeper and higher into the opulent hills. When we reached the very top, she turned right, and I could see both the Valley and the Los Angeles basin by turning my head in one direction or the other. We continued to drive on Mulholland in silence for about three more miles, and then turned south onto a side street overflowing with cypress and maple trees. About halfway down that street, she pulled into the driveway of a medium-sized English Tudor house. This was the house she moved into after Josh burned down the one I had visited years earlier. Beyond the manicured landscape, I could see tennis courts and a swimming pool. I became intrigued by the possibility of exploring bio-Dad's habitat (part-time habitat), but I began wondering if I was going to enjoy it now that Isabella had grown mute and probably had a change of heart. Neither one of us said a word in nearly fifteen minutes.

She stopped the car at the end of the driveway, removed the keys from the ignition, put them into her smart leather purse, looked over at me again, and removed her sunglasses. Her eyes, which I finally got to see, were dark brown, penetrating, and as beautiful as I had imagined them. Unfortunately, the moment of discovery was wasted in my fear of what was to come or, more accurately, not to come. Finally, her full, painted lips separated and words flowed out.

"But you didn't take it?"

"Hank's offer?"

"Yes."

"No. I didn't."

"Ben died, and the meeting was canceled?"

"Yes."

"I forwarded Ben your first letter, you know," she said.

"You did?"

"Yes. Come on, let's get something to eat. We'll talk more later."

We both stepped out of the automobile, and I followed this enigmatic woman into the Tyler household.

12
ENTITLEMENT

On the back patio, overlooking the Valley, Isabella and I lunched on a guacamole salad, chipotle shrimp, and green chicken tamales. As an added surprise, we were served by an old acquaintance: the milky-white, Irish nanny whom I met years earlier in the previous Tyler residence. Her name was Claire. Claire had aged a bit since our last brief encounter, but still looked like a refugee from County Mayo and treated me as though I was just awarded the Nobel Peace Prize. I interpreted this reverence as having very little to do with me and everything to do with her lifelong disappointment with the other Tyler children.

As the meal progressed, they both were interested in knowing more about my background in Detroit, but there was no talk about the business at hand. Toward the end, Isabella asked me if I would like to go flying.

"Do you mean in one of those little planes?" I asked.

"Yes," she smiled, "little planes."

"I've never done so before."

"Would you like to give it a try?"

"Sure."

"Good. We'll go early tomorrow morning."

She then stood up. "Why don't you take the rest of the day off?" she said as she checked a text message on her cell phone. "Take a nap, go swimming, relax. If you need a car, there's one in the garage. Claire will give you the keys. There will be plenty of time for us to talk more. I have a couple of important errands, but I'll be back soon. Okay?"

"Okay."

"You don't mind?"

"Of course not."

She smiled and off she went. Claire showed me to my room, a guest bedroom on the second floor of the three-story Tudor, and I fell out as soon as my head hit the pillow. I awoke almost three hours later feeling groggy from a deep, midday nap, but was comforted in knowing I had been sleeping under bio-Dad's roof, in one of his bedrooms, with the renewed desire to explore his habitat. I wanted to see the evidence of his life, the artifacts, the patterns of his existence. He had been a world traveler, but this was still technically his primary residence, and he wasn't dead but a few weeks. I figured there should be plenty to discover.

I walked into the hallway from the bedroom. Most of the doors were closed. The exceptions were a bathroom near the staircase and, next to the bathroom, a den or a library. I entered the latter thinking it was a common room but soon realized otherwise.

The walls were lined with books and art. Many of the books were vintage and collector's editions with cloth covers, and the art work just as rare and included three original paintings by Frida Kahlo, Rufino Tamayo, and Roberto Montenegro. Against the back wall stood a lovely Windsor couch. It was fan-shaped with big, soft cushions covered in Navajo weaves and blankets, and it looked so inviting that I had to stop myself from nesting and returning to sleep land. I also noticed a personal journal on the edge of the couch. It was opened and I could see the handsome feminine penmanship. Needless to say, I was tempted to sit down on the lovely couch and read every word but restrained myself. In retrospect, that restraint became more important as time went on.

I moved away from the couch and walked over to a small desk near the windows. On the desk were framed photographs, five all together, standing upright, and not quite of equal proportion. They were the only visible photographs in the room. These I examined carefully. One was of a young, smiling bio-Dad in a wooded area holding a baby, I'm guessing Joseph, their oldest. A second was of all three children when they were toddlers, taken at the beach playing in the sand near the ocean blue. In another photo, this one an old black-and-white, a proud, austere Chicano man sits on a horse in a wide-open pasture, wearing a big, white rancher's hat, reminiscent of those Emiliano Zapata photographs you see in history books. I immediately tagged him as Isabella's father, Macro Vasquelez—the marijuana rancher, illegal labor transporter or, from Stu's perspective, "the shrewd business-man." Here, he looks invincible, and I imagined the pasture in which he poses belonged to him as well. This photograph could have easily been taken forty or fifty years earlier, perhaps around the time Isabella was born.

The remaining two pictures were of two women in their mid to late thirties, both Anglos—a blonde and a redhead—and I had no clue who they were or why they were chosen for this select group. Both photos were candid, un-staged medium shots, and captured the introspection of the moment, suggesting, perhaps, venturesome personalities.

After snooping around far longer than I should have, I began to feel guilty. This, after all, was not the public library on Woodward. This was Isabella's sanctuary. This is where she obviously came to think, journal and to be by herself, and I was intruding—or more accurately, I was acting like an adolescent peeping Tom. I might as well have been sniffing her underwear from her dresser drawer. I had to force myself to do the old and trusty 180 and shuffle out of the room. In truth, I was becoming infatuated with this woman, my bio-Dad's second wife.

As I walked down the staircase, I realized that what applied to Isabella's library should apply to the house in general because Isabella and Claire were probably the only ones who had ever lived here. Bio-Dad was a remote visitor at best, and the kids, according to my Tyler history book, were already gone by the time Isabella moved into the house, with Joseph and Jessica studying abroad, and Josh not being invited in after having burned down the first one. I told myself my bio-Dad treasure hunt was over. I was at the wrong address.

Once I hit the polished, hardwood ground floors, I kept walking through the living room, dining room, kitchen, out the back door, across the patio where I had eaten lunch, and into a yard that featured majestic Montezuma cypresses and a swimming pool at the rear of the property, partially hidden by the trees. Without hesitation. I stripped naked and jumped into the water to cool off my sizzling loins.

I stayed by the pool for the rest of the day, wrapped in a towel, lounging, listening to the birds and the wind blowing through the Montezumas, falling in and out of consciousness until it turned dark and nippy. I was then approached by a very respectful, ghost-like Claire, who first apologized for the intrusion because she could tell I was enjoying my privacy (something to which she was sensitive), and then politely informed me there was hot food inside when I was ready. And in the event I was getting chilled by the night air, she had plenty of sweaters stored in the pool house. I thanked her and told her I would be in shortly to eat. As I watched her disappear beyond the spruces, I wondered if this is what it would have been like growing up in this household, to be left alone to think aloud and to be waited upon and to have automobiles and warm sweaters at my disposal without ever having to worry. And if so—if given this privilege, this freedom, this adolescent playground—would I have stood up to the test of time and fared any better trudging through those impressionable early years than my half siblings had. Probably not.

Later that night, Claire and I ate dinner. She made poached salmon and offered to serve me in the dining room, but I preferred the intimacy of the kitchen. I was informed that Isabella had called while I was by the pool and, apologetically, would not be back for dinner, but wanted to assure me the two of us would go flying early tomorrow morning. I was privately disappointed and assumed she had a lover and was being tactful with bio-Dad still warm in his grave. And if true, there was, in my mind, no need for any stealth. Bio-Dad's self-imposed exile while he was alive, coupled with his raucous infidelity (in truth, infidelity no longer applied, they were way beyond that) most likely transformed their relationship decades before.

Claire was a lot of fun, though, and I enjoyed her company. She remembered when I came knocking twelve years earlier and "given Mr. Tyler's lifestyle" was surprised there weren't "dozens more like me roaming the countryside."

The next morning, Isabella knocked on my door at 7:00. We ate a light breakfast that she had prepared (Claire was still sleeping) and drove to the Santa Monica Airport to sail around in one of her flying machines. Apparently, she had a few of them, but not all were pressurized. Some were single engine World War I, II types, and some were miniature versions of today's commercial aircraft. The one we used that day was a small Falcon jet. It fit up to six people and was only five feet wide and twelve feet long, yet it flew over five hundred miles per hour and could climb up to forty thousand feet.

After taking off, we circled away from the ocean and flew in a southeasterly direction. It took a few minutes for my stomach to adjust, but once I stabilized I sat back and enjoyed. We flew over the California desert to the Grand Canyon, and I was awed by the rugged, cascading brilliance of that gargantuan hole, the first time I had ever seen it from any perspective. We then angled north and followed the Colorado River into Northern Arizona and Southern Utah. For most of the flight, we stayed up around twenty thousand feet, but once we hit the Painted Desert and Monument Valley, Isabella descended to the point where we could almost touch the naturally sculpted monuments. Such rare beauty, I thought, deepening my appreciation and fascination of the desert, until I would periodically glance over at my pilot, who in my eyes was just as alluring and exotic as the landscape below.

She was an excellent navigator, too. She told me she was trained by Navy Seal pilots and was capable of performing stunts such as twirls and spins and swan dives—the stuff you see in air shows— but would spare me on this maiden voyage. I almost wished she did not spare me because it would have helped me fight off the incessant amative thoughts, especially the ones that told me she fell into the Molly Sivad category of non-blood-relations and was therefore suitable for intense and prolonged lovemaking. The tight, black slacks covering her round sculptured ass didn't help either. With plenty of time to think, the obvious question kept presenting itself: What the hell was wrong with me? Why did I want to have sex with my blood father's wives? Was this an attempt to bring me closer to postmortem bio-Dad, my real subconscious quest? Or maybe I was just an idle perv and there wasn't any more to it. Take your pick because I sure as hell don't know the answer.

After we circled back and landed, we drove to a Persian restaurant on Westwood Boulevard for lunch. We ordered a hearty meal and got down to business, and there was much to feast on:

Now that bio-Dad was dead and cremated, Isabella had assumed his solid, 26 percent stake in Prostitute LLC, and was seeking the right person to represent her interests since she had neither the experience nor the time to keep up with the day-to-day details, or to adequately deal with Hank Tyler, a man whom she had never liked or trusted. Hank, as Stu pointed out, obtained first rights to buy her out because of the way the LLC bylaws were written, but Isabella resented Hank for the way he treated her over the years and refused to sell. Thus, when she received my letter from her post office box (which Hank helped to deliver), she considered it more or less divine intervention. I was the person she was seeking. But just to be on the safe side, she checked up on me through a private investigative firm and discovered I had not misrepresented myself in my writings and that I shared her concerns about Hank's business practices and probity. The fact that Hank was emulating me (Eclectic Emporium) was more than enough proof that I had the potential to be successful. True, I was not up to speed with all aspects of the music business, such as label and publishing, but Hank did not know everything there was to know when he started out, either.

For compensation, she offered me a significant interest in the company, a lucrative salary, and a still to be determined title. Because of her one percent advantage over Hank, she would force Hank to accept her terms. Once I was in as Hank's approximate equal, I, Nic Reilly, together with Isabella, would be able to impose our ideas on the stubborn and recalcitrant tyrant, who would most definitely fight this tooth and nail. But so what? The tides had turned, and Isabella was no longer putting up with his nonsense. Besides, this was something Ben would have wanted had he stayed alive to see it through. Finally, if I did choose to accept her offer, I would be welcome to stay with her until I got my own place in Los Angeles. Or I could just stay there for as long as I liked because I was, after all, part of Ben's family.

My only dilemma upon hearing all this was how to restrain my indescribable enthusiasm. All my dreams were suddenly coming true. Not only would this skyrocket me into a coveted position as a player in the music industry, but it would solidify my rightful place as a legitimate heir to the Tyler musical fiefdom—a position that I rightfully deserved for being the oldest of the clan and for putting up with Hank Tyler.

I was still deeply curious about one thing. And perhaps a wiser and more disciplined person would not have ventured. "Did you and Hank Tyler ever discuss me?" I asked.

"Yes, we did," she replied. "He told me you came to his office to compel him to buy your record store so you could squeeze money out of him. He said you couldn't be trusted and he wasn't sure if you were who you said you were."

"Did you believe him?"

"All I knew was what Ben and Claire had said about you, but that was a long time ago. You have to understand, Nic, when you're as well-known as Ben, people do all kinds of strange things. So I hired a private investigative service—the same one I use to keep tabs on Hank—and they told me Hank was the one who initiated the contact by trying to run you out of business in Detroit. They were concerned about your partner doing prison time for counterfeiting, but they doubted you were involved. Oh yeah, they validated your status as Ben's oldest child, too."

"I accept your offer."

"Are you sure you don't want to think it over?"

"I'm sure. I'll need about a month to work things out in Detroit before returning here."

"A month is fine. It will give me time to prepare Hank."

"I won't disappoint you, Isabella; that I promise you."

"I know you won't," she said softly, seeming to feel good about what was happening here.

"Do I really remind you of Ben?"

"You remind me of him when I was madly in love with him. How old are you?"

"Thirty."

"Thirty, yeah, that's about right."

13
KISS OF DEATH

I was worried I was falling in love with Isabella. That was how I felt, and of course this kind of thing is impossible to measure or stay objective about when you're in the thick of it. Again, I had to remind myself any indiscretion on my part could complicate and endanger my new position as heir, or one of the heirs, to the Tyler musical fiefdom. Hence, in the remaining hours that I was within close proximity to golden Isabella, I wisely switched my thoughts from her ageless beauty to another obsessive category: evil Hank Tyler.

Hank was a worthy and formidable opponent, but I was just as ambitious if not as ruthless, and I would be ready for him. I was still smarting over what he told Isabella about me—and this, remarkably, after the two of us were set to meet and work out a deal. If he was playing me the whole time, that would make him almost inhuman. I made up my mind to do two things: One, I would not take his phone call because I'm sure once Isabella told him about the new way of life, he would find the time to call me; and, two, I would send him a fax from Detroit after I didn't take his phone call informing him I would be driving to the Prostitute Eclectic store to fire that diseased, turd-worshipper and replace him with Karolina. That would be my first official act. And too damn bad if he didn't like it.

The next morning, I said good-bye to Claire, promising to return within the month. She and I had become fast friends, and I looked forward to the time when I would see her again. While Isabella drove me to LAX, she told me she had already contacted her lawyers about our Prostitute strategy, and we would be hearing more soon. She was planning to consult her father, too, and get his perspective.

"His instincts are good," she said, "although I haven't always agreed with him on everything."

"I would like to meet him someday," I said, knowing that Isabella, like many women, had a special place in her heart for her padre, regardless of his resume.

"Maybe when you get back we'll fly down together to see him," she responded.

"I'd love to."

When we arrived at the airport, I became nervous about saying good-bye. I warned myself that I should be on my best behavior in these sensitive parting moments. In my mind, my relationship with her had changed drastically from the time she had picked me up just three days earlier at this same spot. At that time, she was just a nebulous figure connected to the bio-Dad/Prostitute world. Now, she was my business partner with whom I was secretly in love, despite how goofy that sounded.

She advised we stay in touch as much as necessary until I returned. We hugged and stayed hugging for a while, and I sensed (or deluded myself into sensing) that this was a tad more than just an ordinary hug. That feeling was confirmed when I looked down into her sad, strained Amerind eyes and knew for sure something was going on with her. Perhaps she was confused by my Ben-like ambiance and was trying to work through it? With Ben having just died, my unforeseen visit may have evoked memories she did not anticipate and this intensified embrace was a matter of transference. In contrast, I had no ambivalence whatsoever about my feelings toward her. I was madly in love with her and always would be. I thought I was doing a decent job of not showing it, but maybe not. Much of this, I believe, is telepathic anyway, and people know what is going on in these circumstances without the spoken word (whether they realize it or not).

I remembered, too, she probably had a lover, and I respected that, as I respected her, her lifestyle, her choices, and her position as my boss (and savior). So, basically, all I was required to do here, at this particular moment in time, was keep hugging her as long as she wanted to hug me and release when she was done. That was all. But, of course, I did not. Instead, I did the unthinkable—the absolute fucking unthinkable—and leaned down and kissed her on the lips, deeply. It was probably the boldest thing I had ever done in my life and perhaps the stupidest, too. I don't remember how it happened, either, you know, how that split second transpired when I physically lowered my head and executed the kiss. But it most definitely occurred.

Afterward, she released me and looked haunted. I knew I had erred, radically strayed. I said to her, "I lost myself for a second, I'm sorry. Please forgive me, Isabella."

She kept staring at me, trying to get at the truth of what had just happened, and then whispered: "That's okay, Nic, I felt like doing the same. So we're both guilty. We just can't let it happen again. Okay?"

"Okay," I responded gratefully and said nothing more.

I thought about her during the entire flight back to Detroit—the way she looked at me, the taste of her lips, the curious, frightened look in her eyes, the dignified way she handled it, and, of course, this only made me want her more. In a sense, the situation was hopeless—an insurmountable burden I must endure, like that big rock Sisyphus had to push around. Still, maybe it was best we got it out of the way and I could commit to the role of dutiful son and business associate. I did, however, allow myself to obsess about her choice words, "we're both guilty." How exotic they were. How utterly mesmerizing.

The idea of the two of us as a couple was pure fantasy, and apparently completely unrealistic, and that may have been one of her many concerns. A union such as ours would appear ghoulish to even the most unorthodox, which would include Ben's twisted, narcissistic, and usually indifferent offspring. Their distress would center on their pending fortunes, and they would undoubtedly label this genuine bond as incestuous witchcraft and use it to attack Isabella's character and coveted position as executrix and sole beneficiary of Ben's estate. Most likely, it would segue into a media-sponsored bloodbath as Ben's children and their attorneys lined up to gnaw away at the Tyler estate. And as far as the rest of the world goes, we would fall into one of the multiple freak categories. It was barely okay for a wife to default to her spouse's brother in the event of her spouse's death, but son for father was still unthinkable, even if the blood was pure. Personally, I didn't give a damn, but I was only half the equation, the minor half. For Isabella's sake, that kiss could not happen again. But what a beautiful everlasting kiss it was, and I shall remember it until the day I die.

*

When I returned to Detroit, I threw a massive party and invited everybody I knew, including former Eclectic Emporium employees who now or once worked at Prostitute Eclectic. I wanted to make sure my enthusiasm was acknowledged at Prostitute Records, both in Detroit and Los Angeles. I spared no expense (the bank account was starting to hemorrhage, but there would be new money coming in shortly) and promoted it as Eclectic Emporium's anniversary party, which was technically the following month. The real reason was to celebrate my knockout victory over Hank Tyler; a victory that would have to remain a semisecret until Isabella and her lawyers ironed things out with Hank and his lawyers.

But that didn't stop Karo, Stu, me, and even Marge from getting slaphappy drunk and acting like teenagers on laughing gas. The highlight of the night was Karolina's striptease on one of our stage amps. Fortunately, she stopped at her naughty black bikini underwear because I was in no condition to protect her in the event of a stampede—a very likely possibility every time she bent over, tucked her head between her legs, and stuck out her tongue. She was so good I began to wonder if she did this kind of thing in Europe and the underwear modeling story was nonsense.

The next few days were spent recovering from that one night and beginning to map out the transition plan. I called Isabella nearly every day so she could keep me up to date on the negotiation developments, and as expected, Hank was resisting vehemently. She said there was a possibility of legal action if he didn't conciliate. She also hinted if Hank wanted to play the lawsuit game, he was going to lose. Now that she owned all of bio-Dad's assets, including his 26 percent of Prostitute, she could crush Hank in the long run. At first, that information frightened me because I did not want to delay getting started, but then I reasoned if a lawsuit would drain Hank financially and then force him to yield anyway, why not be patient? The more vulnerable he became, the better it was for me. The weaker he became, the stronger I got. Yeah, let's have some lawsuits and watch the fucker bleed. I'd probably get some good publicity out of it, too.

But by the end of the week, it was beginning to look as though Hank was on the verge of conceding much of what Isabella demanded. I believe, from reading between the lines, Hank was cautious about aligning the other investors to counter Isabella for fear he'd be opening up a whole new can of worms. By Thursday, Isabella told me my transition to Los Angeles might go ahead as scheduled and I should prepare. Knowing I was going to be very busy for a very long time, I decided to take a weekend camping trip in the Upper Peninsula. I invited Karolina, but she declined, stating she had too much to do in preparation for all the changes that were about to take place. She had already begun plans to consolidate the two Detroit Eclectic stores. So I went alone. It was further evidence of her ambitions and that I was not an integral part of her life on a personal level.

That Friday I drove to the Upper Peninsula. It was late September and the colors were beginning to change. The camping spot I chose was surrounded by tributary streams of Lake Superior and Lake Michigan. I settled quietly in the dense foliage, pitched my tent, and built a fire to cook the trout I had caught in one of the streams. After eating, I layered on some old sweaters and drank beer, watching the stars and wondering how our dust-like planet—spinning and rotating on its flimsy axis and held in space by a hypothetical gravitational field in the midst of billions and billions of galaxies—could ever have a chance at life. I mean, what were the Vegas odds? I once read a biography on Albert Einstein in which it was documented that Albert kept saying over and over again—especially as he got older and older when more people were listening less and less—that God doesn't play dice with the universe regardless of whatever overwhelming evidence there was to the contrary. That persistence may have been grounded in the belief that we, or at least Albert, had just not quite figured it all out yet, even though he was working his gentle fingers to the bone on his Unified Field Theory by wandering around the quiet streets of Princeton, New Jersey, for literally decades with his head in a thunderstorm.

Otherwise, it's all chaotic nonsense, right Albert? And that, of course, is the alternative argument, the quantum one—everything is random bullshit—which, paradoxically, Albert help to create with his brilliant quanta particles discovery when he 27 years old, three years younger than my present age. So I suppose Albert, if anyone, had quite a bit to think about. But the way I have come to view it is: Who cares what the latest theory is? Relativity, quantum matter, dark matter, dark energy. In a hundred, two hundred years—that is, if the planet doesn't melt into a fetid cesspool first—there will be a whole new set of discoveries and insights and theories, and it will just be more of the same thing. The more we know, the more we don't, ad infinitum. That seems to be the only fact that we know for sure. So why even bother? It's like trying to figure out relationships. You just have to wait until you're dead.

The next day, I fasted and hiked and swam naked in the warm, September lake water—warm because it took all summer for it to heat up, and I was catching it at its peak temperature before it began turning back to freezing, even though the air temperature had already dropped considerably. Much later that night, I swam again and the deepening contrast between air and water heightened my sense of being all alone in the wilderness and brought upon me an ethereal quality of being; like I was more spirit than flesh, more the same than different. It was a beautiful feeling and lasted for quite a long time.

Afterward, I drip dried under the stars, my skin steaming, dressed warmly, built another fire, snuggled in my sleeping bag in my opened tent, and slept like a rock for about ten hours. The following day, Sunday, I continued my fast and remained still most of the day, no hiking. Right before sunset, I was feeling as high as I have ever felt and I knew it was time to go. Going home would be painless and beautiful and I would know peace. I would drive in silence the whole way.

I packed in the dark—and had no problem doing so, in sync with my surroundings by that time—and walked out of the woods renewed, poised, and proud of myself for taking time to nurture my body and soul. I located my car and drove to the country store where I had purchased my fishing pole to buy coffee for the long ride home. I knew coffee would be harsh to my system, but I couldn't afford to fall asleep in my tranquility, not on the dark, winding highway. In this particular nondescript rural store, the coffee was thin and stale and tasted good-bad. I bought two cups just in case the first didn't work.

On the way out, I caught sight of the Sunday newspapers. After spending almost three days in the woods, fasting, the newspapers appeared fat, cumbersome, and a tragic waste of good trees. But it reminded me of baseball with the playoffs coming up. I wanted to know about the Tigers. So I stopped, put down my two coffee cups, and began to strum through the newspaper pages to locate the sports section. In doing so, I was reminded of the time I spotted bio-Dad's obituary headline in the airport. I don't know why that thought resurfaced, but it did. This was followed by a brief lapse of memory. A "What were we just talking about?" type of mental hiccup. Only there was more than one of them in a row, and they were accumulating. I didn't know why it was happening, either. Maybe it had something to do with the fast? I equated it to a childhood puzzle, or the experience of seeing someone who reminds you of something else but you aren't quite sure what that something else is but you know it's there—the feeling of knowing there's a connection somewhere.

So I stood motionless in the empty store until the puzzle started to take shape, and then the idea formed in my mind to buy the newspaper, even though it was such a horrendous waste of paper and I no longer had an interest in the baseball world. I put a dollar on the counter, tucked the newspaper under my arm, picked up both coffee cups, left the store, and after more juggling, got in my car and drove off.

It was sometime in the middle of the night when I pulled off the road to take a break and read the newspaper. I felt the time had come to do that. There was a story that caught my eye, although I couldn't remember exactly why I wanted to read it or what it was about. I knew it wasn't a sports-related story because I never took the time to glance at the sports section. I turned on the interior light and picked up the newspaper, turning to Page 3. I read the story beneath the small headline: "Rock Star's Wife Dies in Plane Crash." The gist was as follows: Isabella Tyler, the former wife of Ben Tyler, crashed her private jet in the Mexican state of Sinaloa near the ciudad of San Alto at around 8:45 pm local time Saturday night. She was flying alone en route to Presa del Rosano in Michoacán, Mexico, to visit her father when she encountered a sudden storm out of the tropical south. According to the Jalisco aviation authorities, she attempted to negotiate an emergency landing with their help at a small San Alto airport when she lost control of the aircraft. She died on impact. Her death occurred exactly thirty-seven days after her famous husband was found dead in an alley in Bangkok, Thailand, with his pants on backward. Isabella, born and raised in Michoacán, Mexico, attended college in San Diego, California, and was a performance artist before she married Ben Tyler of Iron Horse fame. She was survived by her three grown children and her father. She was forty-nine years old.

I read most of the article before I became vertiginous. I waited patiently for my equilibrium to return. It did not, so I continued to wait in the car in the middle of the night in the middle of nowhere. It was the strangest series of extended moments in my life, and I thought there was a chance I was going to expire. Maybe it was similar to what Barney experienced after his accident. About fifteen minutes later, I felt the energy return. The life energy. The stuff that Einstein alluded to. I finished reading the article. Then, using all my available concentration, I slowly and methodically switched off the inside light, fastened my safety belt, shifted gears, put my foot on the gas pedal, and drove back to Detroit, leaving the asshole universe behind.

14
PROBATE BARBECUE

I've always been a fan of the written word, so I don't know why I was being tortured by these bloody newspapers. It seemed particularly cruel that they followed me wherever I went, even to the upper regions of an isolated and vast natural preserve. And it angered me that their authors and editors showed distance and objectivity when describing the most horrible of personal tragedies. Had I been the one describing Isabella's death, my article would have been dripping with sorrow. It would have excluded the meaningless meteorological data and paltry aviation details and presented the only true account of what had happened in that stormy Mexican sky: The gods had become jealous and therefore decided they wanted Isabella all to themselves.

Once I surfaced from the initial shock (the word is you don't *know* you're in shock *while* you're in shock), I cried for the rest of the ride back to Detroit. I cried gut-wrenching tears. I cried because I loved her. I cried because I was looking forward to being close to her on a daily basis and now that would not happen. I cried because she was such a giving and loving and caring person. And then it all sort of blended together, and I began to wail uncontrollably, something I've seen only broken-hearted teenage girls do. A couple of times, I had to cease driving, pull over to the side of the road and calm myself. At the core of it, I knew it was all about me—my loss, my sorrow, my broken heart, and my inability to fathom what was going to happen next.

After three days in bed, I talked to Stu. He had news about what was to become of the Tyler estate and Prostitute LLC now that Isabella was incomprehensibly out of the picture. I assumed everything would depend on the specifics of Isabella's will, similar to the bio-Dad postmortem saga. I further assumed, either way, will or no will, it would not bode well for me for the following reasons: One, if she had a will, I would not be a part of it because she would not have had time to include me. Two, if for some reason she did not have a will, we were back to the traditional story of me being the adopted bastard, legally severed, and excluded from everything Tyler.

My only chance, I thought, given this post-Isabella scenario, was if I had signed documents establishing my new position as a principal in Prostitute LLC. But I had not, even though Isabella's lawyers did contact Stu for preliminary discussions. So there you have it. I was back to square one. Even Hank's earlier offers, bogus or not, had suddenly become ancient history, for he would sooner cut off his own fingers than reach out to me after what Isabella and I were trying to force down his throat.

Yet, as always, as it turned out, I was dead wrong, or mostly wrong. What Stu had to tell me was quite different from what I had assumed and much more complicated, but just as bad if not worse in terms of my fate.

To begin with, Stu explained, Isabella never officially satisfied the requirements established by the state of California to be a beneficiary and executrix of a decedent's estate. According to California probate law, a beneficiary must survive the decedent (in this case, bio-Dad) by 120 days for the transfer of assets to be legal and binding, and Isabella didn't even tick off 40 days before she crashed into the Mexican soil. Because she did not survive the probate incubation, all of Ben's assets would go to the "alternate beneficiary" on his will, which turned out to be Stan Tyler, Molly and Ben's second oldest, and Ben's oldest legit son. Stan was also designated the alternate executor of the estate, effectively filling the role Isabella played following Ben's death and prior to her own.

Therefore, one would naturally think—and this was becoming a problem, the natural thinking thing—Stan, Ben's alternate beneficiary and executor, would now be in complete control of the Tyler estate as Isabella was before she died. But that was not true either, because California is a community property state, which means almost half of Ben's estate was already owned by Isabella prior to her death. In community property states, married couples share everything they acquire while together, regardless of whom the breadwinner is. So when Ben transferred all his worldly possessions to Isabella and avoided taxation, she already owned almost half anyway (43 percent to be exact, the discrepancy being tied to what Ben owned prior to marrying Isabella, which was not common property, but some of which became common after so many years of marriage...). Hence, Isabella did not live long enough to acquire Ben's half, but she still, posthumously, controlled her own almost-half, which would now go to whomever Isabella designated in her will or trust, if she had one or both. And if she did not have either, it would be divided equally among her three surviving children, including Josh since this was not Ben's portion of the Tyler estate, and his disinheritance clause would not apply. Josh could be completely excluded from all Tyler assets only if Isabella specifically disinherited him in her will as well. So, in effect, with Isabella's death, the Tyler estate was divided, with Stan Tyler controlling 57 percent, and the remaining 43 percent distributed to either Isabella's designated beneficiary(ies) or, by default, to her three kids.

Another and probably simpler way to gauge all this was to look at the winners and losers. The big winner by a bloody knockout in the first round was Stan Tyler. He now controlled 57 percent of bio-Dad's and Isabella's estate. Stan was probably chosen because he was the least offensive or the oldest coherent offspring, with older sister Megan being diagnosed as dangerously volatile due to her substance addiction. Stu ventured, correctly I was to find out, that bio-Dad had no intention for Stan to benefit, but was forced to include an alternate name on his will as required by law. His intention was always to turn everything over to Isabella.

Other winners, but to a much lesser degree, were all of Isabella's kids because they likely would be entitled to something through her death unless she decided otherwise in her will, if she had one. And if that were true, Josh would come out on top because Ben wanted him disinherited and now he would not only not be disinherited, but he would get most of what he ever would have gotten rather quickly. This would be even more to his advantage because it would not allow him the time to royally screw up again and piss off his mother to such a degree she would disinherit him, too—that is, if she hadn't already and if she in fact had a will or trust.

As for the losers, that was easy. The two big losers by a landslide were Megan Tyler—Ben's oldest legit offspring, who would now become dependent on the good graces of her little brother Stan—and yours truly, Nic Reilly, the bastard who was on the cusp of scoring the victory of a lifetime in true underdog fashion and reclaiming his natural birthright as heir to the Tyler musical fiefdom, but was now suddenly and tragically sentenced to be transported back in time to freezing his poor ass off in the rugged Detroit winter while watching Eclectic Emporium go under for good. This was a particularly harsh fate after being so beautifully and poetically positioned to usurp the fiefdom via the tactful, willful and wise Isabella. One of the many ironies of all this was that Ben's two oldest offspring were the ones to benefit least.

Naturally, I became horrifyingly depressed by these new circumstances, in addition to being horrifyingly depressed anyway, and I'm sure Karolina would have been more concerned about my condition had she not become so horrifyingly depressed herself. Right before Isabella died, Karolina was nonstop busy, working out the details to consolidate the Prostitute-Emporium retail operations without any cooperation from Prostitute. A fine pair we made at 9:55 in the morning, sitting in my office too despondent to even open the front doors for business. We were proof positive that it is worse when you're given hope only to see that hope vanish, than to never have been given any hope to begin with. At least that was how I felt.

This pain was interrupted, or complicated somewhat, by a phone call from Claire inviting me to Isabella's funeral. The invitation took me by surprise because I was so used to being excluded from Tyler affairs. Claire's phone voice was docile and wounded, devoid of the Gaelic exuberance I had grown accustomed to. Selfishly, I gained comfort from talking to someone who was close to Isabella, even though I understood how much pain she was experiencing. Isabella and Claire had shared much history—such as the raising of difficult children and the burning down of their home. And all this coming on the heels of Ben's death, another person who had periodically shared the same street address with Claire.

With no alternative, I booked yet another expensive round-trip flight without advance notice using a credit card I knew I would soon be defaulting on. This would be my fourth trip to California in a seven-week period, beginning with my prison journey to Terminal Island to visit Sledge. Karolina hinted that she would like to come with me this time. I had to refuse her with the fear of bankruptcy and failure quickly seeping back into my consciousness. I don't think she took it well.

*

When I arrived again at LAX, I taxied to Isabella's house. I was greeted at the front door by my half-sister Jessica Tyler, Isabella's second oldest, who had just returned again from San Sebastian, Spain, where she was working as a chef. This was the same individual I saw for a flash in the previous Tyler house when I was a teenager. She was now tall, lean, shapely and all grown up. "Dick, right?" she barely asked, her cynical blue eyes hopelessly defiant.

"Nic," I corrected her, sensing a final farewell to my sibling novelty.

"Whatever," she murmured back.

Immediately declaring the situation hopeless, and fatigued, I brushed past her and began climbing the stairs to the guest room I had vacated not three weeks earlier. It was rude but less rude than telling her to go fuck herself and then climbing the stairs. Inside the room I plopped down on the bed wondering how I was going to survive this ordeal. My solution was to close my eyes and fall asleep.

Sometime later, I was awakened by a knocking sound. I collected my thoughts, wrapped a blanket around my body, and opened the bedroom door. It was Jessica, who once again looked me over like a piece of lamb before speaking. There was now a slight familiarity between us, however unfriendly or thin.

"Do you want to eat?" she asked, this time with a little less judgment.

"Sure."

"We're outside on the patio. Dinner is almost ready."

"I'll be down in a few minutes," I said, thankful for the molecule of civility.

I quickly dressed and thought about what Stu told me a long time ago: having siblings is overrated. He was dead on. Minutes later I walked outside and saw Claire seated at the table, jotting down information in a calendar book. When she heard me, she looked up and tried to smile. I bent down and hugged her. I could feel her bones tense up in my embrace and then melt again as I released her.

"God is full of surprises," she whispered.

That evening, younger half-sister Jessica presented us with food I had never tasted before: a foie gras dish with mango and caramel, grilled anchovies, roasted pasta, and slim baby eels. She uncorked a bottle of Basque wine, and the three of us settled into the cool evening, eating quietly. As time passed, there was no real exchange, and I detected the lack of dialogue had more to do with awkward tension than culinary narcosis. Jessica and Claire were at some kind of deep odds. Of the two, Claire, judging by her body language, was the more timid—seemingly careful not to cross any invisible boundaries—while Jessica appeared unhappily at ease and confident. As for me, I simply chose to accept my plebian ranking and stayed quiet and allowed Jessica to set the tone and serve the meal. I reminded myself that it was Jessica's mother, and not mine, who had just died, and not much more than a month after her father. She was experiencing incredible loss (whether she realized it or not), and this loss was entangled with the radioactive issue of voluminous inheritance. A sequence such as this could contaminate anyone's mind, even the soundest. So, just as she was being patient with me, I needed to be patient with her.

After dinner, Claire quietly and dutifully cleared the table and returned to the kitchen. She purposely left the wine bottle, knowing Jessica would want her to do so. Jessica filled her glass again and, with Claire absent, finally asked me about my business with her mother. It became clear to me she wanted details. I was more than happy not to disappoint her and informed her about Isabella's intentions as they concerned me, Hank, and Prostitute LLC after the death of Ben. She was a good listener and as I was watching her listen I have to admit I became a bit distracted by the way she kept crossing and uncrossing her legs, itching her shoulders, fidgeting, smoking, sipping wine, things of that nature. I thought, My God, what a sexy, edgy little bitch she is. In my defense, it should be duly noted that this was my first real encounter with Jessica in my thirty-year-old life, and she physically took after her mother, not her father, and we all know how fond I was of Isabella. There is no sin in acknowledging what is organically transpiring in one's mind although I shut it off like a faucet.

"So what are you going to do now?" she asked in a slightly authoritarian but curious tone.

"I don't know," I replied.

"Bullshit you don't," she sneered back, her intensity growing. "Didn't you talk to Claire?"

"About what?"

"She's in control—that's what!" she shot back. "My little nanny is in control—for the time being anyway."

She then stood up tall, "You don't fool me, ghetto boy," she said mockingly, her sobriety fading by the second. "I hear you're haggling with Uncle Hank."

"He started it."

"It's gotta start somewhere," she replied, as she side-armed her wine glass into the charcoal pit, the glass shattering. "I need sleep. I didn't nap after my twelve-hour plane trip like you did. Big day tomorrow. Mom's funeral. Poor Mom."

After Jessica retired, I stayed put on the patio, thinking about Claire, the person "in control," who just happened to be inside washing our dishes. "In control" could mean a lot of things, including executrix alternate for Isabella's portion of the Tyler estate. If so—and taking into account Claire's subliminal performance at dinner—I wondered if Claire's offer to have me stay at Isabella's house for the funeral had more to do with her protection than anything else. These were extraordinary times, after all, and Isabella and bio-Dad were no longer around to fight fire with fire. Claire could use as many weapons as possible. More importantly, according to my new impromptu calculations, Isabella's beneficiaries still owned about 11 percent of Prostitute LLC. (Stan, as bio-Dad's beneficiary, owned the rest at around 15 percent.) That 11 percent was a significant figure that could put me back in the Tyler music game if Claire was in a legal position to assign some of that ownership.

I walked into the house and found her in the pantry humbly stacking dishes. "Hi, Claire," I said softly, not wanting to startle her.

She turned and looked behind me. "Is Jessica upstairs?" she asked, almost whispering.

"She's gone to bed."

"She's had a long day," she said, unable to hide her relief.

"She cooked a good meal."

"I taught her some of that, you know."

"I'm sure you did."

"Everybody has a short memory," she said, more or less talking out loud.

"Would you like me to make you a cup of tea?" I asked.

"Tea?"

"Yes, I'm going to have one," I said, knowing full well it had probably been ages since anyone asked her.

"I'd love a cup of tea, Nic. Thank you."

I grabbed the kettle, made tea and we began talking, and what followed was an informative and remarkable exchange that lasted over two hours and served to strengthen the bond that had already existed between us; a bond that would serve me more than it would serve Claire as time went on.

Before I go into details, though, I want to pause here and consider my motives. In truth, I cared a great deal about Claire. She was a good woman, like my mother was a good woman and like Isabella was a good woman (it appeared, for the most part, that people of their generation were easier to get along with). And I, being a decent fellow myself, wanted to comfort her during this most unfortunate time, and so I offered to make her a cup a tea. I told her I was going to have tea myself but if she hadn't been there I probably would have grabbed a beer instead. I knew this tiny gesture would mean the world to her. She was alone, scared, widowed in a sense, and the bearer of a lot of new and unwanted responsibility. The question then becomes: Was this, in fact, a dishonest act? I mean, did I really offer her tea as a genuinely friendly gesture or was I thinking more about what Jessica told me before retiring for the evening? If the latter were true—which it was—then perhaps I was even more diabolical than my half siblings. They, for the most part, were up front about their greed and self-centeredness, whereas I was not. Hence, in retrospect, sitting in this dank jungle, I firmly believe this tiny tea episode was a crucial moment in my life history. A major turning point. It marked the beginning of my lust for wealth and power. Claire trusted me even though she barely knew me. I was well aware of that fact and took full advantage. But, still, does that mean I'm a rotten person for pouring a cup of tea for a tired, emotionally wounded woman who was scared to death? Would not someone else in my position have done the same? Was not that the decent and proper thing to do? Some may think this foolishness on my part to walk down this path; but I don't. I knew in my heart where my intentions lay. Prior to this, all of my actions were essentially defensive and retaliatory against mean-spirited rogues. This was something different. A baby step, perhaps, but a step nonetheless.

As it turned out Isabella did indeed have a will. In fact, she had two of them, but the second one—the one she began to draw up following bio-Dad's death—was a holographic will and never properly dated and signed. Claire believed Isabella was planning to turn it over to her attorneys for their review and to convert it into a more formalized document. But it was still a handwritten will and testament which does not need a witness in the state of California. In the holographic will, her plans were to set up conditional trusts for her children and Molly's children (Ben's dependents), and to create two nonprofit organizations for causes that were dear to her heart. One was a charitable foundation for Dependents of the Sexually Addicted (SAD)—the entity that Isabella set up following the discovery of bio-Dad's corpse in a Bangkok alley. The other was a Washington-based think tank to help solve the illegal Mexican immigration problem. According to Claire, Isabella believed jingoism on both sides of the border disguised the real problems of greed and poverty. It should be remembered that Isabella's father, Marco, who was now retired, had reaped huge profits by exploiting this labor market, and Isabella may have wanted to compensate for having indirectly benefited herself.

The holographic also included bequeathments to, among many, a few key people: Claire (the house and cars), Isabella's "good friend" C.J. Taylor (jewelry, art, the airplanes, and other personal possessions), and, yes, the beggar bastard from Motown, Nic Reilly. It was her intent to will me her remaining interest in Prostitute LLC. As usual this was not as simple as it sounds because Isabella obviously did not intend to include the portion she was already giving me prior to her death. So, I assumed (I know, not a good thing to do), her intention to will me her stake in Prostitute would now mean her entire stake as it then stood immediately before, and immediately after, she crashed her plane. But that remained to be seen and much would depend on the actions of the principal actors as the probate pudding thickened. It was a given that all would contest the incomplete and restrictive holographic or the court would deem it invalid and the first will would take precedence which was simply—are you ready?—the female version of bio-Dad's will and meant to facilitate an indisputable tax-free transfer of all assets from wife to husband. But with Ben having died first anyway, everything would defer to Isabella's alternate executrix and beneficiaries who—as in Ben's will—took the guise of one default human being. That person, as you may have guessed, was Isabella's longtime household companion Claire, or as Jessica called her, "the little nanny." Again, Isabella and Ben never thought it would ever come to this. But it did. Thus, much depended on what Claire was going to do, at least ostensibly. Overall, though, it was turning into a probate nightmare.

"They're going to fight tooth and nail," Claire said, referring to Isabella's kids.

"That makes you even more of a target," I confirmed, thinking that the holographic won't stand up and Stan and Claire would become the beneficiaries and administrators.

"They feel cheated."

"They want Isabella's share split up right away?"

"Oh, you bet they do."

"What about you?" I asked.

"I don't know," she said reflectively. "I think I should follow through with Isabella's plans. I should follow through with her written will. It seems like the right thing to do, if not the popular thing."

She paused and then looked squarely at me and asked, "What do you think, Nic?"

"Me?" I replied in a surprised voice.

"Yes, I value your judgment."

I thought about it perhaps five seconds more than I needed to, took a sip of ice cold tea, and said calmly, "I think you're on the right track. Follow through with Isabella's plans. That's what I would do."

15
BAPTISM

I sat quietly as we inched our way down the mountain into the Valley and over to a church called St. Charles Borromeo, near Lankershim Boulevard. Inside the limo, Jessica and Claire sat opposite facing me, both draped in black, and both preparing themselves for their second funeral in seven weeks. When we arrived, we were greeted by stiff Secret Service-like ushers wearing dark suits and dark sunglasses. They escorted us out of the limo and through the spacious vestibule into the cathedral, where hundreds of mourners sat waiting. Claire told me this was the same church in which bio-Dad had his service, and so I morbidly surmised that many of these same people were present for the first Tyler service and may have been positioned in the same pews. And if not the same pew, almost the same pew, or they would have remembered where they sat the last time opposed to this time. Why this ridiculous thought would come to me and dominate my thinking I have no idea, but I am quite certain that it was true.

As the three of us walked along the nave, I noticed heads turning like a Broadway musical. Much of this, I believe, had to do with me and my distinct Ben and Hank Tyler features. "Who is this Tyler?" I heard them thinking. I was not one of Ben's and Hank and Gertrude didn't have kids. And if I was related somehow, then why wasn't I around when it was Ben's turn to be eulogized?

We were seated in the very first pew, center-left, in front of Isabella, who lay in closed coffin on the foot of the altar—closed because her splintered body parts could not be sufficiently gathered, stitched, and powdered to suit the minimal aesthetic standards of an open-casket ceremony.

Anchored above her hung a beautifully crafted wood baldacchino and beyond her a magnificent reredos, the combination of which had a calming effect on me and I hoped on the elderly Chicano man in the next pew over whom I immediately recognized from the photographs in Isabella's study as Marco Vasquelez. Unless I was mistaken, Marco was by himself, reminding me that Isabella was an only child and her madre long deceased. This made Marco appear all the more destitute and lost. Here was not the proud bandido landowner I saw in that majestic photograph. Here was a grieving skeleton of a man with pagan eyes who probably blamed himself, as people often will. He was the one she was flying out to see when her plane took that fatal dive.

Other than Mr. Vasquelez, there were no others I recognized in the family pews, which was disconcerting because I thought Joseph and Josh, at the very least, would be present for their own mother's funeral. I was tempted to query Jessica, but I figured it was none of my business. I also didn't see scoundrel Hank Tyler, which was not too surprising given his caustic relationship with Isabella.

It wasn't too much later when the giant pipe organ began to swell and a chubby, balding Anglo priest appeared on the altar and began circling Isabella's casket, sprinkling it with holy water. He was trailed by a string of lesser-ranked clergy and altar boys who supplied burning incense, a series of crosses depicting Jesus in his worst moments, and one of those gold covered, super large-print versions of the Bible. Not having been to too many Catholic services, I was intrigued by the visuals, the pomp, the tradition, the church itself, but as time dragged on, I soon became disappointed with the substance, especially the sermon. For all of us, Isabella's death was untimely and premature and the best this ecclesiastic could manage was the old and tattered, "the Lord works in mysterious ways," coupled with "she is now at peace with God through Jesus Christ our Savior." Don't get me wrong, I respect the idea of "ever and ever," but I was discouraged by the lack of genuine insight and contemporary empathy and it started me thinking how these Roman ordained clergy were getting more and more incongruous in the modern day, both in public and private, and the medieval rituals they observed and theological dogma they espoused were antediluvian at best. So when an intoxicated Josh Tyler stumbled in halfway through the service wearing dirty jeans, sneakers, and a black T-shirt with a pregnant belly dancer ironed on it, I took it as a sign from the good Lord Himself we were not being forgotten in this modern Byzantine capsule. God was there with us after all, even if the messenger was an arsonist who was late to his own mother's funeral.

*

As it turned out, my first full Tyler gathering signified a major bio-shift, possibly even a revolution of sorts in terms of communication, access, acceptance and parity. My siblings could continue to despise me—and they did for the most part—but they could no longer dismiss me. Things had changed, despite my current vulnerability. My relationships with Isabella, Uncle Hank (whom they loathed but respected because of his wickedness and power), and Claire, the new executrix of Isabella's portion of their father's kingdom, were a daunting reality. And to add insult to injury, I looked more like a Tyler than any of them—a Ben and Hank Tyler. This was reinforced throughout Isabella's funeral and post-funeral gatherings as people gravitated toward me, curious and open to who I was, where I came from, and what I was doing. When I told them, they welcomed me with open arms and showed no surprise to hear that Ben had unaccounted-for offspring. As Isabella and Claire did before them, they saw me as a truer picture of a younger Ben, a Ben they loved, a Ben they missed, a Ben they remembered before he drifted away from Isabella into his sexual abyss. This attention and relevancy made my presence a distinct psychological reality. I had become a family player and dispelled forever the convenient illusion that I did not have Ben's blood pumping through my veins. Yes, there were legal distinctions, but there were also legal distinctions between Isabella's kids and Molly's kids, which they were now all grappling with since both Ben and Isabella left behind identical reciprocal wills.

This new bio-positioning was reflected in the conversations I had with half-brother Joseph, Isabella's oldest, whom I finally got to meet at her house following the ceremonies. I was wrong about Joseph not being present for the funeral. He was physically there but chose to sit upstairs in the rear choir balcony with the church organist, out of view. At first, I assumed his decision was spiritually motivated, but after being with him for just a short period, I discarded that benevolent theory and attributed it instead to old-fashioned Tyler peculiarity. This was the same person, I remembered, who wrote me that creepy letter all those years ago.

Like his younger sister Jessica, Joseph took more after his mother than his father. He was a tall, lean, good-looking man with olive skin and dark curly hair. His only physical drawback was an unusual downward slope on the left side of his face where his two lips met. This salient and seemingly permanent facial "smirk" defied, as far as I could tell, any observable characteristics of his mother or father or siblings or anyone else except maybe Popeye the Sailor Man and was exacerbated by an ugly half-ass British accent from being in England too long. His discolored teeth—another sign of good English living—and horribly bad breath didn't help either.

"I heard you file CDs for a living," he said with contempt after we were introduced by Claire, who was making it a point to introduce me to as many people as she could.

"I'm a musicologist," I said.

He paused, thinking about it, and then mockingly frowned: "How convenient and original. My father had something to do with music I think."

"What's that supposed to mean?"

"It means whatever the bloody hell it's supposed to mean."

"So what do you do?"

"Me? I'm an embryologist!" And with that, he began to laugh heartily, proud of himself for the witty response. When he was done, he became more specific and told me he worked at a privately-funded embryonic research firm in Newcastle, England, where he and a few of his colleagues were engaged in cloning human embryos for therapeutic purposes. Technically, that's not the same as cloning for "reproductive purposes," but it still involves removing the genetic material of a cell and replacing it with DNA from an embryonic stem cell in an attempt to create tissue or organs for the clonal donor.

It was controversial because of how easily the research and

procedures can be altered to create a human clone, an illegal practice in England as it was everywhere else in the world.

"It's really quite exciting," he said with a little too much assurance.

"I think I'd rather file CDs," I said.

"I bet you would!" he scowled.

As a geneticist, Joseph did not dispute my Tyler DNA, because if he did, I most certainly would have heard about it. He did, however, manage to ridicule me for being an emotional plebeian for believing in romantic love.

I'm not sure how we got on the topic, but he brought it up and was indirectly connected to his meticulous research and professional interests. Midway through, we were sounding like this:

"It's a story, a fiction man invented to justify his primal responsibility to propagate the species," he said. "The 'attraction' is really a biological mechanism for selecting a mate—it's like pissing. Nothing more."

"What about Shakespeare? He believed in romantic love," I countered, knowing in England, his adopted country, everybody accepts Shakespeare's divinity, including, I assumed, transplanted geneticists such as himself. He wasn't deterred.

"Shakespeare proves the point," he said mockingly.

"How?"

"All his characters who 'fall in love' act stupid and get themselves killed or turn into asses. You have to understand, man, it's all chemicals."

"Brain chemicals?"

"The serotonin levels plummet, the dopamine kicks in like a heroin fix, and that's what you call love."

"So you currently aren't in love and don't plan to marry soon?"

This struck a chord. "Marriage?" he asked.

"Yeah, marriage."

"I'll be married like my father was married," he shrugged.

He downed his drink, threw his cigarette butt on his mother's beautiful hardwood floor, and set the record straight: "Listen, you bloody knave. I'm not sure what your immediate strategy is, but I know your motive, and if it interferes with that which is legitimately mine, you had better watch out. And I mean it."

And off he went, pushing his way through the crowd.

He was rude, foul and smelled, but I fully understood his concerns, and they were reasonable: He was getting royally screwed out of his father's share of the estate by an unexpected and bizarre legal twist, and now this forgotten mutation (that's me) comes crawling into town befriending his mother and peasant, Claire, another major unexpected pain-in-the-ass obstacle that he finds implausible, and he's at the end of his already short rope.

He didn't trust my legitimate music association, and even though I may have had contact with evil Uncle Hank—another rogue who weaseled his way into Ben Tyler's fortune—I was still, at best, a beggar from Detroit with no real claim, despite my genetic link, which in this case conveniently didn't carry any significance.

After he was gone, I was free again to mingle with the other guests. Of the many, I liked the aging rock-and-rollers best, some of whom I recognized from old album covers we had in stock at Eclectic Emporium. In many respects, they were survivors, and I made it a point to do my best to support them in the uncertain digital age, if I survived this inheritance debacle and somehow came out on top at Prostitute.

I then met a very interesting woman named Cynthia. Once again, Claire introduced us, and when I saw Cynthia's face, I immediately recognized her as one of the chosen few who were photographically represented upstairs in Isabella's study.

She was probably in her late forties, although the age thing with women was beginning to confuse me because of the surgery epidemic. In Detroit, this was less prevalent because people couldn't afford it, but in Southern California, cosmetic modification was as common as going to the dentist for a teeth cleaning.

Surgery or not, she was an attractive woman with thoughtful blue eyes, flowing blonde hair, and a sleek physique. She talked softly, carefully and listened intently. She also gave clues—which I didn't catch at first—that she was still in shock over Isabella's sudden death. She revealed this altered state of mind by pausing periodically and staying paused for extended periods of time.

At first, when she took these breaks, I thought she was thinking about what she was in the middle of saying or about to say, or about what I had just said, or any variation of that verbal composite, but after it happened more than a few times, I realized she was pausing to regain her emotional balance before moving on with the conversation—similar to a mountain climber who almost slips off the mountain and then takes a few moments to recoup before continuing the journey.

Her lack of equilibrium gave me the impression that she and Isabella were more than friends (together with the upstairs photograph), and that Cynthia may also go by the name of CJ—one of Isabella's intended beneficiaries according to Claire. And this led me to further suspect that Cynthia was Isabella's destination that first night I came to visit.

For years, Cynthia made a living as an actress and was married to a very successful movie and TV producer, but was now no longer acting or married, both seeming to have dissolved around the same time. This opened up a new career of promoting and supporting various important artistic, humanitarian, and environmental causes throughout the world. Translated, this equated to that she was comfortably divorced with no kids, or the kids were grown-up, thus allowing her the time and means to do exactly what she wanted.

After talking with her for a good thirty minutes—pregnant pauses included—a decent spell considering her fragile condition, she abruptly told me it was time for her to "leave this house."

She handed me her wine glass and walked directly out the front door without saying another word to anyone. Clearly, she was haunted and needed to escape Isabella's nimbus, and etiquette was not a serious consideration or possibility. I privately wished her well. I had known Isabella for only a brief time and was infatuated; I couldn't imagine what it would be like to have fallen deeply in love with her for a long time.

After Cynthia, I noticed the crowd thinning, but at the same time quite a few people were digging in for the long haul. One of those persons was my old pal Molly Sivad. I was pleased to see with my own eyes that she had escaped her torpedoed lighthouse unscathed. She looked remarkably well, too, almost identical to the time when, over twelve years earlier, she knelt down and studied my cock, her litmus test for measuring my Tyler authenticity.

"I can't believe they both died and I'm still here, " she said, referring to Isabella and Ben. "It's a goddamn irony if there ever was one."

Speaking of death, her new collection was selling well for a poetry book, and not just to bookish teenagers going through a suicidal stage, although they continued to make up the majority of her sales. "I'm pegged by the publishers just like *Harry Potter*. I write teen books. That's how they look at it."

What about Stan? What was he doing now that he was set to inherit 57 percent of his father's joint estate?

"He wants to be the youngest principal owner of a professional sports team, or whatever they're called. You know, like the New York Yankees. I know he's going to lose his ass. He's not the smartest kid in the world."

"Where is he?"

"Wyoming. He has a ranch out there next to the Cheneys."

"The Cheneys?"

"You know, Dick Cheney, the warmonger."

"Wow."

"They're friends."

"How's Megan?"

"She's the same, I think. She refuses to talk to me while she's in rehab. But she's always in rehab, so I never talk to her. But I keep hoping for her."

I was curious and tempted to ask more but I didn't want to risk her slipping into one of her lubricated philosophical discourses, so I switched the conversation to her Topanga Canyon lighthouse.

"Oh, that. You noticed?"

"A little. What happened?"

"It kinda fell."

"How?"

"I blew it up. Or rather, I hired some local kids who needed the work to do it. They did it on the Fourth of July so it wouldn't draw attention. I told everybody it got struck by lightning because of the legal implications."

"Why did you blow it up?"

"I needed a change."

"Couldn't you have just moved?"

"I needed a push."

"A push?"

"Sometimes it takes a push to get me going. I'm a creature of habit."

"But isn't that excessive?"

"You don't understand, dear, I still lived in it for about two weeks after it turned sideways. The mailman didn't even stop delivering the mail. Familiarity breeds contempt, and I'm living proof."

"So what forced you to move?"

"I couldn't get anyone else to come inside anymore. Then I moved. Which was the original idea. So it all worked out."

She then offered me some friendly advice: "Be careful with the kids. They have a lot on their minds. I always can tell."

She was referring to Isabella's kids because hers didn't show up. But for Molly to volunteer that information meant something. Of all the Tylers, she was the most unaffected and seasoned. As an ex-spouse, she was floating in the same murky waters as I—unentitled, with nothing to gain unless singled out. Unlike me, though, I don't think she was seeking anything she didn't already have.

"Thanks," I said.

She gave me her card with her new address and phone number. "Come visit me in Marin. It's only about a forty-minute plane ride from here."

"How far from Detroit?"

"Detroit? Who are you kidding?" she snickered as she shuffled off.

There it was again, I thought. My presence was being interpreted as ambition and little more.

After Molly, I searched out Isabella's father, Marco Vasquelez, wanting very much to speak with him. I found him sitting on the living room floor by himself with his back to Isabella's purple stone fireplace. His legs were folded upward and pressed against his chest with his arms wrapped around his knees, just above his polished cowboy boots. Occasionally, he would bend his head slightly and rest it on his kneecaps. Within reach was a half-empty bottle of tequila with his name on it.

I sat on the floor next to him, not wanting to tower over him, and introduced myself. He was slow to respond because of the drink, but he eventually looked up and I could detect the tiniest bit of change in his heavily creased, sun-baked face; a face that was overwhelmed by a pair of dull, bloodshot eyes. When he spoke, his voice was gruff, tired, and thickly accented.

"Yes, I remember now," he barely said as he picked up his bottle and took another mouthful. "She mentioned you."

"I'm sorry."

"Yes. I'm sorry, too," he mumbled.

He was an old man, and I should have been worried about him in this condition, but his reputation preceded him and suggested he was also a man who knew himself, and the alcohol, though potent, was self-prescribed medicine for this intense period of emotional illness.

I couldn't think of anything more to say that wouldn't be somehow unnecessary, so I decided to let him be, as everyone else was, when he surprised me.

"She loved to fly," he said. "Me? I like to walk," he added.

And with that, I saw a small crack of a smile spread across his old face. What a generous man, I thought. He was doing this for me. He had no inclination for company.

"Me? I like to sleep," I responded, trying to reciprocate the kindness.

He technically laughed, which came out as one lazy, heavy grunt, his eyes still dead as a doornail.

"Nic?" he asked.

"Yes."

"Sometime we talk, but not now. Okay, my friend?"

"Okay."

"Don't forget."

"No, we'll talk soon."

I stood up and walked into the kitchen, leaving the old man and looking forward to the time when we would talk.

*

The kitchen and adjoining outside patio were cluttered with catering staff and hungry guests. I joined one of the inside lines and just as I was about to be dished what looked to be a chicken-mushroom casserole, I heard Joseph Tyler's warped British accent erupt like a terrorist bomb across the room, "THERE HE IS NOW, THE BASTARD, STUFFING HIS FACE."

My first and only thought upon hearing this was what a truly ugly voice he had. Everything else was secondary because it was so saliently disgusting, worse than, say, an Australian convict ready to be tossed into a shark-infested sea two hundred years before. And I could literally smell his breath from ten feet away. Thank God he stayed up in that balcony at church otherwise his vapor would have disintegrated the corpse.

I had no choice but to look over and confront his gawky frame leaning against the refrigerator, holding a glass of booze. Next to him, and staring me down like a small gorilla, was his younger brother, Josh, an even more unwelcome sight given his obvious level of intoxication—which at that point must have been about seven hours old since he was drunk at the funeral that morning. Josh wasn't quite as long as his brother but was equally angular and dark with strong facial features. At that particular moment his face appeared to be glowing like one of those exposed 200 watt colored light bulbs you see at Halloween parties.

Next to the wattage and holding him tightly around the waist (maybe to keep him vertical) was what had to be Josh's girlfriend, but the connection didn't automatically register because Josh was about twenty-four years old and she was, easily, in her mid-fifties, and this was not taking into account surgery, which would have made the calculation too complex to figure out in the shocking moment. Her face was a thickly powdered clown white and her head wasn't quite shaved but almost, which, in this case, made her look more like an escaped patient from a poorly run Eastern European sanitarium. On the bright side, she did have a hard, shapely body, which she did her best to exhibit by wearing a pink miniskirt (another anachronism, although it complimented her boyfriend's facial hue), no stockings, and a tight, black, embroidered blouse showing off her big, braless and probably fake tits.

This woman was not at the funeral because I would have remembered her, so Josh must have picked her up at the corner on his way over or purchased her in the concession area of a David Lynch museum.

I didn't have too much time to marvel over this lovely couple because, within seconds, Josh threw a beer bottle at my head. It missed its target and smashed against the kitchen wall, scaring the wait staff and bringing silence to the noisy room.

"Infidel," he threatened; a strange word to use I thought.

"He's not even an infidel, he's a bloody tramp," his older brother corrected him.

Mind you, I was not afraid of either one, and I would have loved to beat the shit out of both of them, but I didn't want to make the situation worse, especially for Claire. Fortunately Jessica came to my rescue. She was either already in the kitchen and I didn't see her, or she came in right after Josh threw the bottle.

"Stop it," she said in a slightly annoyed parental voice.

"Oh, fuck you, you fucking bitch," Josh replied.

"Shut up!" she wailed, using those good chords that I remembered from all those years ago. She then resumed the parental attitude. "Time to go boys—and don't forget to take that senior-citizen whore with you."

"Fuck you," Josh shrieked back, giving more evidence of his lurid unpredictability. He then pushed his girlfriend away because she was pulling at him to ease up. "Leave me alone!" he cried.

"Claire has the security here. I'll get them if I have to," Jessica warned, continuing to talk directly to Josh.

"Oh, isn't this sweet," Joseph jumped in. "Protecting this sycophant. What did he do to you to earn that?"

"Fuck you too Frankenstein," Jessica smirked back.

"I know you're up to something," he said, spraying half the room with his dribble.

"Up to something?" she asked in mocking disbelief.

"Yes. Up to something!"

"Like what?"

"I don't know. Something."

"Joseph, how come you're so stupid?" she asked as if dumbfounded. She then began to chuckle. "You got all those degrees and you're so fucking stupid. How can you remain that stupid?"

"Oh, fuck you."

"No, no, I want to know," she demanded as her laughter and jeering grew louder, more pointed. "I really do. Please tell me: How come you're so fucking stupid? Did they give you a "P-H-I" too for being a world class IDIOT? That's the one you should frame over the fireplace..." This kept up, her mocking him, and strangely the tension began to diffuse. Her laughter became infectious. Soon others joined in with muffled snickering—not necessarily to be mean, but because she was genuinely funny.

I, however, was in agreement with her one-hundred percent, although I did my best not to howl out loud at my stupid half-brother with the stupid accent and the stupid degrees—who, by the way, had now backed down and become seethingly quiet in his defeat as he stood in the patio doorway—when I felt a hard, pole-like object crush into the side of my head, instantly numbing my senses and forcing my body to free fall onto the stone kitchen floor.

Still awake, with my head flush to the ground, my cheek on the cold stone, I saw Joseph quickly run up to me and kick me squarely in the head, bursting my face into red pieces. That was the last thing I saw for some time, but I continued to hear random screaming from the crowd and laughing from Josh. His was a wild and frenetic laughter that began to fade as he raced off somewhere.

Soon after, I opened my eyes and I saw above me a group of fuzzy people touching, wiping, mending my face. Jessica was there, too. I heard Claire in the distance instructing the security people to keep Joseph and Josh from reentering the grounds. The doctors—plastic surgeon guests from the gathering—concluded that I may have suffered a concussion and decided to carry me upstairs to my bedroom where they could better patch me up and do further tests to decide if a hospital trip would be necessary.

16
LIES

It was a broomstick. While I was laughing at Joseph, Josh crept up from behind and whacked me over the head with a broomstick. Jessica told me this as the in-house physicians performed basic neurological tests and kept asking me questions, such as: Did I remember falling to the floor? (I didn't but I clearly remembered lying on the floor and watching Joseph golf-swing his foot into my face.) Did I know what city I was from? (Yes.) Did I feel like vomiting? The vomiting, I could tell, was an important issue. I did not feel like vomiting and repeatedly told them so. Eventually, there was unanimous agreement among the skin men that it would not be necessary to taxi me to Cedar Sinai Medical Center for brain scans and further testing. The nasty goose egg on top of my head would need to be iced. My nose (their specialty and not broken) and forehead would require cleaning and bandaging. And I would need plenty of rest in the next couple of days.

"You were lucky," one of them kept saying to me as he cleaned my scalp. "It could have been much worse."

They ordered Claire and Jessica to take turns watching and icing me for the next few hours in the event I became nauseated or forgetful. They also flipped me a vile of some major-league prescription dope—which someone had handy—for the pain and offered to hang around downstairs for a couple of more drinks just in case.

After they were gone, I told Claire she should not feel responsible for what happened. But she did, of course, and kept telling me so. She also told me she was now determined to follow through with Isabella's plans as detailed in the holographic will—if the court granted her that power.

"You sure you don't need more time to think about it?" I asked.

"No. I've made up my mind," she said.

As I drifted off, I figured Claire's decision meant a lot of things for a lot of people. For me, specifically, it meant I was earmarked to receive Isabella's revised 43 percent of Ben's 26 percent interest in Prostitute LLC. That figure would not restore me to my brief and coveted super-position as Isabella's partner, but it would certainly get me back in the game.

Hence, if this new arrangement held up—with Ben's interest now divided between Stan and me—Hank Tyler would become the largest single member with his standing 25 percent ownership, followed by Stan, who would inherit about 15 percent, followed by me at about 11 percent. And as the good surgeon said about my pummeled face, things could be much worse.

My one concern, however, was how brittle and ephemeral everything seemed in this strange Tyler world. It felt as though I were a traveling international businessman, and my major client a small hung-over third-world equatorial country where the officials are corrupt, the wealth hoarded, and the coup d'états as common as newborn babies. But I wasn't complaining, nor was I in pain anymore, for the magic medicine had begun to saunter through my bloodstream and provide a dense cerebral cushion. Soon I felt deeply, deeply at peace, and alone, with both Claire and Jessica downstairs somewhere, but as I drifted deeper and deeper into peace land I discovered that I wasn't alone after all and that someone else was there, present, close by, and then I realized it was Isabella, of course. Who else? She was nearby, possibly down the hall in her beloved study where she spent much of her time reading and thinking and I could tell she was friendly but curious, patient but curious—curiosity was the sensation I felt most—and she wanted to talk with me but she wanted me to start talking first and not wanting to disappoint her I began talking like she wanted and told her I was grateful for her hospitality and for her believing in me and for embracing me when no one else would and she was gracious to acknowledge my gratitude but I could tell she wanted me to talk about something else and then I knew what that was and I told her she should not worry because I had accepted the capricious nature of her children and I would do my best to act responsibly when the time came to deal with them over and over again because I knew better and they did not, I being the oldest after all with a more balanced upbringing and a better sense of right and wrong and then I realized she wanted me to include Molly's kids too not just her own and that was very important to her and so I told her this would apply to all of my siblings, all of Ben's kids, and with that she said, "Thank you, Nic, I have to go now," and she left, this time for good.

When she was gone, a couple of thoughts came to me. The first one had to do with how patient she was to have waited for the right time to talk to me. The second was that I was reminded about how ridiculously easy it would have been to really, really fall in love with her like Cynthia had and how Cynthia must be suffering horribly with such catastrophic loss with no warning, and I kept thinking about poor staccato Cynthia after all the other thoughts drifted away, and for some reason Cynthia's suffering became very powerful and all-consuming, and after I couldn't think about Cynthia anymore because my mind was exhausted and would not allow it, I became terribly, terribly despondent because I knew I had lied.

*

During the next two days, as I healed, I had time to evaluate the behavior of my siblings. I was surprised by the recklessness of Joseph and Josh because they were adults, or rather of adult age, and thus, by law, responsible for their acts of violence against another human being, openly displayed in a crowded room.

It was possible they understood what they were doing, and shrewdly calculated that I would not retaliate because I had other fiduciary interests in mind; or perhaps they perceived the loyalty I felt toward Claire and the publicity-weary Tyler family. And if so—and they were not in some sort of twisted blackout—then it was a wild, fantastic, barroom gamble few people would have chanced, because they could have easily been arrested and incarcerated. Attempted murder could have been one of the charges, too.

Joseph's shameful conduct was particularly screwball, considering his scientific career. What if his Nazi-like foot blow killed me? It was baffling. He was baffling. Wasn't it enough his disturbed pyromaniac brother knocked me to the ground, motionless? With a stick? That should have been enough for anybody, even the most heartless, and it suggested to me a dangerously dark side to Joseph, even more sinister then half-baked Josh. Paradoxically, though, I was morbidly fascinated by their actions on a purely intellectual level, for they were truly out of the ordinary.

Likewise, I was encouraged by Jessica and her performance both before and after the incident. She had become my one sibling ally, at least on the surface. Strategically, she did not factor much in terms of probate because she was not entitled to any of bio-Dad's portion of the estate until Stan declared his intentions (and unless Stan was magically transformed through exorcism, it was a given Isabella's kids were getting slammed). Her concerns, and those of her lawyers, were more about securing an equitable share of her mother's assets via Claire (my getting clobbered may have helped her there), and possibly contesting the wills and challenging Stan for a reasonable cut of bio-Dad's share of the pie. Fighting me for a sliver interest in evil, pain-in-the-ass Uncle Hank's Prostitute Records could not have been on top of her list. So, really, I had little to gain from her, and she had little to lose from me. Regardless, I needed and wanted a sibling ally in the event the probate situation spiraled out of control; an entirely possible scenario if recent history was any clue of what was to come.

My desire for Jessica's friendship did not overlook the fact that she was probably on excellent behavior during my visit and that I had not seen the "real" Jessica. There had to be good reasons why Claire was afraid of her and why Ben and Isabella refused to single her out as different from the others.

When I returned to Detroit, I immediately connected with the legal-minded Stu and talked about the latest developments and options. Stu was intrigued by my pummeled face and strongly recommended I sue Joseph and Josh. I told him I was more interested in directing all my energy into solidifying my latest position at Prostitute via Claire. (I also felt by not suing I would continue to gain sympathy in Tyler circles, but I didn't want to get into that with Stu.) Stu was not in full agreement with the strategy, and suggested that I should nonetheless continue the process of petitioning whomever in defiance of Hank, because Hank would be on the warpath again after my aborted plans to upstage him with Isabella as my partner. That meant I should approach Stan Tyler.

Stan lived in Jackson, Wyoming, a place I knew nothing about, but soon learned was a trendy and wealthy recreational ranching community and home to a wide variety of celebrity types, including talented artists and not so talented politicians such as Dick Cheney. Stan reportedly loved the wide-open region and took advantage of its topology, spending a good deal of his waking hours skiing, hunting, climbing, fishing, riding horses, and ballooning. He owned a fifty-acre ranch which he unimaginatively named the "KO Corral" (the opposite spelling of you know what), and he lived there with his fiancée, Ponderosa Crawford, a former professional cheerleader and current real-estate enthusiast.

Stan was unique among the Tyler siblings in that he did not drink or consume drugs, and that was a major distinction. The downside was that he was still a Tyler with a wayward Tyler disposition, and his rigid sobriety offered no release valve to vent that mysterious, swirling, kinetic-genetic Tyler energy, rendering him a bursting-at-the-seams paranoid zealot with a virulent temper who scared even the poor horses he kept on the ranch.

I obtained most of this info from his mother, Molly ("How's your face, sweetie? Does it still hurt?"), a fairly reliable source whom I telephoned in Mill Valley for help once I decided to act on Stu's advice. Molly was forthcoming and said she would do what she could but warned me not to expect much if anything at all. "He can be a problem," she kept saying. She proved to be dead right about that.

Another problem, a big problem, that came into being during this time period following Isabella's funeral clobbering was Karolina. When I returned from California bandaged up but with fair news of my new positioning via Claire's stated intention, Karolina's reaction was one of disbelief. Not ecstatic disbelief or happy disbelief but more like "uh hum" disbelief or "Are you sure?" disbelief.

I understood her caution because if I had learned anything up to that point it was that nothing Tyler was certain, but her lack of enthusiasm was disappointing, and I wondered if she had finally grown weary of the whole Eclectic-Prostitute saga and was thinking about moving on to something more stable. God knows I would not blame her one iota, because in many ways it was pure madness with no foreseeable ending and everything could change tomorrow anyway.

I recognized, too, it was a mistake not to take her along to the funeral. She wanted to go and needed a break from all her hard work and bitter disappointment and yet I ignored her needs because of the costs involved. She was wounded by my niggardly insensitivity, and my gut told me she probably picked up another lover or went back to an old one, or both, for spite if nothing else. More significantly, though, I sensed the Eclectic Emporium bond between us was damaged, a bond that I considered sacred.

From that point on, I made a solemn oath to myself to never again let money deter me from doing the right thing. It was only money, after all, and what's the big deal about having less of something you don't have to begin with? Had I done the right thing and taken Karo along, I'd still be penniless and living on broken plastic, watching the business tank as the bills piled up, but at least I would still have beautiful, creative Karolina supporting me 100 percent.

*

Theoretically my positioning had changed again in light of Claire's intentions, but in reality things were going to initially stay the same and then get much worse until I joined Prostitute LLC as an equity member and warped to the next level of becoming "one of them." Apparently there would be nothing in between and not a second before. On a local level, capital-intensive Prostitute-Detroit continued to steal my clients through bribery and coercion; and on the national corporate level, Hank continued to conjure against me, personally and professionally. His original and long-term strategy (dating back to before he knew who I was) of making me bleed to death was a damn good one, and he would now double his efforts. He wanted me small, obscure, helpless, and not to be taken seriously so he could trifle me into nonexistence before my time had come.

My recourse, of course, was to do the exact opposite and stay visible, vocal, and ballsy so nobody would dare to forget me.

But with no funds left in the treasury, no property to mortgage, and being confined to an industry that was getting its ass royally kicked day by day as the digital piracy blossomed, I was up against the proverbial wall. So I did what any respectable business person would do in my position and dusted off my one dark blue suit and moseyed over to the bank to see about a loan. This was not a new concept for me. I deferred to the bank when I expanded the Eclectic Emporium store and again when I was set to expand into the Chicago market. Both times, they were more than happy to give me as much money as I wanted, and I was still paying off the original expansion loan.

Staying consistent, I returned to the same bank, in the same suit, and sat down at the same banker's desk and requested the same type of loan—or if he preferred a simple bridge loan, or a refinance, or whatever suited him, since I wasn't too picky. This time, however, I was told the record industry had gone sour and the bank was no longer extending credit to enterprises such as mine, even though I had a good track record, I never missed a payment, my credit was still good (on paper), and the banker, himself, frequented Eclectic Emporium (although he admitted going to Prostitute Eclectic and liking that store as well). He was quite adamant about his negative position and encouraged me to try some other banks but was reasonably certain I would be confronted with the same concerns.

Naturally I took the rejection personally. Where's the loyalty? Where's the fucking compassion? After all, when push comes to shove, aren't we all flesh and blood? I marched out of there with vengeance and proceeded to prove the banker right and was turned down at every financial institution I made the mistake of entering. In my heart, though, I knew they were within their protocol. The year was 2004 and retail music was getting hammered, and I wasn't fooling anybody by walking in those tall brick buildings with last year's receipts. Hence, an extension of credit was now tragically out of the question. And just like everything else in my life at that time, it happened fast.

I was left with the dreadful alternative of borrowing directly from individuals, such as friends and family. This I most assuredly did not want to do for obvious reasons but also because of the inherent limitations. Stu told me if everything went well with probate—meaning quickly and in my favor—the Tyler estate should be settled in nine months. But the likelihood of that happening was almost nil, given the complicated legal arrangement following the deaths of bio-Dad and Isabella and the skewed and volatile personalities of those left behind. What I wanted to avoid at all costs was continually borrowing until my ship came in, like a drunken riverboat gambler. With a commercial bank, this was not a problem because I could ask for plenty up front and weather out the storm. But with individuals, there were limits to what they could afford and what my conscience would allow me to solicit. Furthermore, I could offer no collateral or guarantees because I was entirely dependent upon a legal process over which I had absolutely no control.

My centering point in all this was Hank Tyler. I was not going to let him win, to crush me, to humiliate me. And since he proved over and over again that he did not yield, or compromise, he had to be the one who was crushed, humiliated, broken. There was no middle ground with him. Jonathan was right when he stated that Hank never really wanted to help me; and if he did it was a momentary lapse in judgment that would correct itself by his hibernating, fermenting, reactionary wrath. He fluidly exhibited this behavior following bio-Dad's death when he canceled our appointment and left me hanging indefinitely, probably never planning to call me or take my phone calls again. Not a very nice thing to do to someone whose father had just died. And it made me wonder if bio-Dad was the real reason for Hank's change of heart. That is, I was beginning to suspect that Hank was actually in touch with bio-Dad when he was whoring in Thailand and bio-Dad was the one who insisted Hank work with me. When bio-Dad died, Hank no longer had to worry about me. My money was on the latter scenario, although I would never find out for sure.

Hence, Hank Tyler was rotten to the core. I had no choice but to destroy him before he destroyed me. To do that, I required credit to stay visible and defiant, to keep swinging away, to keep the Nic Tyler-Eclectic Emporium flag waving strong, and to let people know

I was not going anywhere except to the board room of Prostitute LLC. But my strategy to borrow money was not working. The banks turned me down and sponging from individuals (e.g., having Marge mortgage her home or tapping Stu, who was already fronting the legal bill) would not work, and actually played into Hank's plans by making me feel pressured as the clock kept ticking down, forcing me to compromise and possibly give up. I needed another source. I needed another lifeline. I needed money. And I needed it now.

17
HIDDEN TREASURES

It's funny how when you ask for things, you very often get them—but never in the way you thought.

This was especially true for me in the months following Isabella's funeral as I valiantly attempted to appear fiscally sound, while simultaneously dodging impatient and sometimes rude creditors, who began calling me at all hours and making a nuisance of themselves.

Not coincidentally, just as I was dodging one of those feisty leeches by putting him on hold to answer another call, Hank Tyler's voice resounded out of the dark oblivion. Actually, Vicky made the connection first and offered a prelude of pleasantries, as if I was her favorite eighteenth century French cousin, before Hank's course syllables began to grunt through the phone lines. It turned out to be another astonishing exchange in the analog of bio-conversations that were beginning to quickly accumulate.

"Nic," he said, "sorry to take so long to get back to you, I've just been so busy with Ben dying and all."

He was referring, mind you, to our aborted meeting months before when bio-Dad tragically died, and implying that nothing else had transpired since, such as Isabella's revolt, my big role in that revolt, her subsequent death and funeral, and now Claire's stated promise to follow through with Isabella's plans, allowing me to assume ownership of her reduced share of Prostitute LLC. That figure amounted to 11 percent of his company and not an insignificant sum.

"Oh, that's okay," I replied like I was the dimwitted cousin from Appalachia.

"A couple things have changed, Nic."

"Oh?"

"We're scaling down here, and I can't offer you a position anymore. But I'd like to still purchase Eclectic Emporium for five hundred thousand dollars."

"Really?" I said, trying to filter the myriad of thoughts and emotions streaking through my mind.

"Yeah, really, Nic," he said, disdainfully, as though he was now going through the motions and maybe he should have had someone else place this phone call.

"Well, that's not going to work for me, *Hank*," I said, making sure to stress his name. I truly hated this man.

"A half-million is more than generous, and twice what it's worth, and you know it."

"It doesn't take into account everything."

There was a smoky pause. "What do you have in mind then?"

"One million."

"A million?"

"Yeah. One million for Eclectic Emporium."

"Okay. A million. I must be crazy. But that's it."

Not bad, I thought. *Especially when you're penniless.*

"Okay," I heard myself saying. "We can settle it when I get back to Los Angeles. I have business with Isabella's lawyers concerning Ben and Isabella's estate."

There was another pregnant pause. "Nic," he said carefully, "one million is for everything. That would satisfy any claims you think you might have to Eclectic Emporium and Prostitute Records. You follow me? You'll have to sign some papers. Okay?"

"As it relates to Isabella's estate?"

"Everything. One million for everything."

"Hank?"

"What?"

"Go fuck yourself!"

And I hung up.

So there you have it. I needed money badly, and I was suddenly offered plenty of it, more than I ever dreamed of, but it didn't come quite the way I thought it would, and to refuse it felt unreal. I wondered if I had done the right thing or if I was letting my hatred of Hank Tyler blur my vision.

Following that conversation, Hank went full steam in the opposite direction, instructing his corporate lawyers to petition the probate court to make sure the Prostitute bylaws were being upheld as they figured into the Tyler estate transfer.

According to Isabella's estate lawyers (and now Claire's, and now mine, indirectly), with whom I was in almost daily contact because I never stopped calling, I was not buying bio-Dad's interest, I was inheriting Isabella's portion of it. I was assuming it as a family member or beneficiary, just as Stan was inheriting the remaining 57 percent of bio-Dad's membership in Prostitute. Thus, Hank had no case. His first right to purchase did not apply.

Hank knew that, but his strategy was to *Exxon-Valdez* the probate process knowing I was dead broke, and then take a wait-and-see attitude. It made perfect sense, too, with Jessica, Josh, and Joseph challenging Claire as Isabella's designated executrix and beneficiary; and Josh, Joseph, Jessica, and Megan challenging Stan as bio-Dad's executor and sole beneficiary.

California law allowed a one-year timetable to end probate with an extension of six months if the estate was complicated or problematic—the two defining characteristics of the Tyler estate. That meant, possibly, eighteen long, brutal months in financial purgatory, or worse.

My rejection of Hank Tyler's one million bitch buyout seemed all the more courageous. Yet I knew I could do ten times better and take my rightful place if only I could endure. The critical issue remained: How to do that? How to endure? Not only endure, but to have the means to take care of business and strike back if necessary, or at least appear to.

As mentioned, I flirted with the idea of asking Marge to mortgage her house and lend me the money. I knew she would do it in a heartbeat. Why? Because I asked her. She would require nothing more. And I believe the guilt associated with that cowardly act of desperation opened up the inspirational flood gates and brought me to the presence of God, and along with God comes cleanliness and orderliness. So I decided the time had finally come to clean, organize, and dispose of all the junk in the store. I would go from the bottom up, starting with the cellar.

Once the idea came, I followed through almost immediately. I drove to the shop early next morning and gathered cleaning materials and workman's tools in preparation. Karolina was late coming to work, and I decided to wait because I didn't want to be going back and forth, up and down, until she got there. When she did arrive, finally, I ignored her tardiness and told her I'd be downstairs cleaning and she was not to disturb me unless it was really important, such as a call from Claire's lawyers or something of that magnitude. She did not object or question me, even though it was an odd request (her new aloofness would not allow it, I suppose, or she just didn't care). After that, I descended into the dark, damp, concrete-pillared basement and began the arduous chore of cleaning. Nothing of musical value was kept in the basement because of the moisture. It was utilized for storage of miscellaneous bulk that had not been thrown out for one reason or another and then forgotten. Some of this stuff had been lying around for over forty years, dating back to when Sledge first began renting the store. For example: furniture stereos the size of washing machines; old jukeboxes with the 45s still inside but knocked out of place; dozens of "new" parts for vehicles long extinct; frail, oil-saturated workbenches covered with rusted tools; stacks of moldy *LIFE* magazines a couple of yards high; and other inanimate growth I could not accurately identify because I was not born when those items were in use or they were too transmogrified to label.

It was so repellent that I flipped my strategy. Initially, I was going to collect and dispose of all the junk and then hose down the place as though it were a recently vacated Latin American political prison or the L.A. County jail. Instead, I would hose everything down first and then remove the junk. This way, I reasoned, I might avert toxic poisoning, skin irritation, and strangulation from blanket-thick spider webs.

So I uncoiled the rubber and began hosing. Almost immediately a couple of inches of water accumulated on the floor. The liquid was foul and reminded me of overflow from a malfunctioning chemical plant. I turned on the old sump pump Sledge had installed for flooding. The pump did not engage. I would have to fix it. I knew how to fix things like this from growing up with Barney. I learned a lot from Barney.

I rolled up my sleeve and sunk my hand and arm into the putrid water and began disassembling the sump pump. I discovered that below the pump, the drain had been sealed with lead. That was unusual. Why would that be? And then, beside the drain, I felt ANOTHER lid of some kind. This one was rectangular, metallic-like but not lead, and seemingly part of the flooring. I could not actually see it through the colored water, and I probably would not have noticed anyway because it was beneath where the pump stood erect.

I pulled on the edges of this second cover and yanked it up. I was surprised by how light it was—titanium-bicycle-frame light—and large, perhaps 3x5 feet, but easily manageable because of its composition. When I lifted, the water flushed into the compartment.

I put down the cover and reached below inside the compartment and felt thick plastic. What came to mind was the rain tarp they cover baseball diamonds with. I grabbed hold of the plastic and tried to pull it out. It was too heavy. I repositioned myself—this time squatting over the compartment like a weight lifter with my knees underwater—and pulled using both hands. I slowly lifted out a bulky package that could have been mistaken for a packet of wet cement left out in the rain overnight. But it wasn't cement at all. It was a treasure; a treasure from the dark, deep underground. A treasure designed to solve most of my immediate, short-term problems and keep me on track to take my place in the sun as a rightful heir to the Tyler musical fiefdom.

It was money. Sledge's phony money. And there was quite a bit of it.

18
NATURAL RESOURCES
AND UNNATURAL THOUGHTS

No one trusted Stan Tyler to act fairly. Not even his mother. That would not negate his fiduciary qualifications since he was Ben's oldest legit son, and in the eyes of the court the perfect person to manage and distribute bio-Dad's portion of the estate. He was also a young businessman with a track record. I would now travel to Wyoming and talk to him, as Stu had suggested.

My goal was to reason with him on how the two of us could join forces against our nemesis Hank Tyler and gain a superior equity position at Prostitute LLC. I knew Prostitute was low on Stan's pecking order. His primary capital interests involved buying a professional sports team and expanding his energy and mining interests with the help of his political friends such as Dick Cheney and people of that caliber. I thought this would be to my advantage and he would think me a small fry, harmlessly working for his interests. That was how I would have played it had I been in his shoes with his ambitions. Let someone else do the dirty work for you.

So I flew to Wyoming and, as always, hoped for the best. And had I not felt an urgency to pursue my small stake in the pending Tyler inheritance turmoil, and only that, I probably would have taken time to detour down the cottonwood-pregnant Snake River, and from there maybe soar up to the slopes of the Grand Teton Mountains or over to the Red Desert or Yellowstone or the Continental Divide or any of the other ecological wonders of this region where Stan maintained his fifty-acre KO Corral ranch. But I was fiercely compelled to stick to the business at hand, which also means filling you in on a few pertinent facts in the counterfeit age of the post-Isabella period.

In order to successfully utilize counterfeit money on a regular basis, one has to let go a little bit—sort of like jumping out of an airplane with a parachute. Chances are, the parachute will open as planned and you'll survive, but if it doesn't open, you're in trouble, and that's always in the back of your mind before and after you jump.

Equally important, one is not allowed to be lazy or stupid or careless or arrogant about how or where to circulate phony money, just as you can't be cavalier about organizing your parachute gear and monitoring the weather conditions before ascending and jumping.

In addition, utilizing counterfeit money also involves—in my case anyway—a change of routine. For instance, I began paying all my bills with money orders instead of checks, because I was not willing to risk depositing fake cash in the bank. This took me to low-end liquor stores, rip-off check-cashing dives and budget department stores, where I would wait in line with dozens of poor people. It was humbling at first, but soon I adjusted and found myself bonding with my fellow money-order purchasers, especially the young mothers who had kids yanking on their arms and were schlepping shopping bags filled with discount clothes and bulk food items, and who would soon be returning to liability partners or none at all.

Occasionally, and with caution, I would slip these women two, three-hundred bucks on the sly, under the sworn condition that they tell not a soul. It had to be our little secret. "I can't have everyone coming up to me," I'd whisper as I palmed over a roll of twenties.

I don't recommend taking unnecessary risks like this, but it was more than worth it to see the joy and relief shoot across their weary faces. In fact, some of these women would start crying on the spot, tears rolling down their cheeks. That's when I would turn away, because I was fearful of making a scene. The one thing I did not want to do was draw attention.

Another awkward exchange in a counterfeit existence is the purchase of costly goods and services with cash instead of the usual plastic—for instance, my airplane ticket to Jackson, Wyoming, which I paid for at the airline counter by handing over 19 twenty-dollar bills to a young airline employee. Eventually, the conversations that ensued over the months with regard to this specific issue became routine, but the key, I learned, was to find empathy with the "wage-earning employee." That was crucial. A typical exchange:

"Cash, we don't see that too much," they'd say as they counted the stack of bills.

"Yeah, I'm through being a slave to credit cards," I'd reply. Or "It's six months since I've used them, and I'm almost out of debt."

"Good for you," they'd marvel, understanding well, and then, more than occasionally, would share their own nightmare credit card stories and often give me preferential treatment, sometimes upgrading me to first class if I was flying.

Don't get me wrong, I'm not bragging about my success in this endeavor. I never wanted it or enjoyed it (with the possible exception of playing Robin Hood, now and then), and every morning I awoke with the sickly thought of being apprehended by FBI agents. But sometimes, one has to take risks and choose the lesser of the evils for the greater good, and if spending 250,000 fake dollars to achieve my goals demonstrated more integrity and backbone than sponging off my mother and stealing her only source of security, or borrowing from a family friend who was already donating his precious time as my personal attorney, or soliciting from, say, Jonathan, the refugee of an impoverished aristocracy who had already shared with me a lifetime of priceless wisdom, then so be it. When doubt crept in, and it often did, I would repeat to myself the old jazz tune *God Bless the Child Whose Got His Own*. That's what this was all about.

My only legitimate pause with this counterfeit usage was purely metaphysical. I had become concerned I was choosing the same lonely path Sledge had taken. You know, the REAL road-less-traveled path which equated to: learning-the-lessons-of-a-meaningful-life-via-physical-incarceration. That path. It worried me for conventional reasons, but also because I felt I did not have a conscious choice in the matter—that my larger self was making the calls, and I was a helpless puppet on strings.

Putting all that aside, though, I didn't waste a moment making use of my new treasure. Molly arranged the visit with Stan so the two of us could discuss Prostitute Records, "but he's not too thrilled about it, honey."

It turned out to be an appropriate warning because Stan Tyler did not pick me up at the airport as his mother said he would, nor did he provide any communication that he would not be there or supply an alternative means of transportation. He just simply blew me off.

This allowed me the opportunity to wander around Jackson, Wyoming, for a spell and soak up some of the local sights before I took my $140 taxi ride through the elevated Wyoming topography to Stan's KO Corral nestled in the Rockies. A car rental was probably the correct way to go, but the rental companies wanted a credit card and I was in my new cash mode and did not want to incur any real expenses, thinking I had to be prudent with so much probate road ahead of me and so few legitimate cash-register receipts.

When I arrived at the KO, I was worried nobody would be there to answer the door, just as no one was there to greet me at the airport. So I asked the obnoxious, garrulous cabbie to wait, just in case, thinking I might be forced to go back to Jackson and book a hotel room. I made up my mind I wasn't leaving Wyoming before I talked to Stan Tyler.

I left the cab and walked to the large, two-story log cabin (the ranch was done in "log cabin") and rang the doorbell. As I waited, I looked around and saw about a half-dozen smaller, single-story log cabins scattered about, giving the ranch a tedious, summer-camp feel. I also noticed there were no auto-mobiles anywhere—another bad sign, although, I reasoned, there had to be garages somewhere, and I didn't see those either.

I rang again. I looked back at the cabbie, who appeared curious, and who, I'm sure, was betting he was going to make another quick 140 fake bucks driving me back to Jackson and have some new Tyler fodder to share with his pals. From my earlier walking tour, I was certain the Jackson community was small and thin and the gossip large and thick.

I rang a third time and just as I was about to spin the old 180 dance step and make this idiot cabbie's day, the front door magically opened. And even more magical was the appearance of a young, tall, blonde woman wrapped in a soft navy blue towel, fresh out of the shower. The towel was insufficient, too. As a gentleman, I did my absolute best to keep my eyes straight ahead.

"Can I help you?" she said in non-regional, non-identifiable, college-educated American.

"I'm here to see Stan Tyler."

She appeared baffled. "He's not here. Was he expecting you?"

"He was supposed to pick me up from the airport. I'm Nic Reilly. His half-brother."

There was a long, searching pause and then: "Ohhh, I think I remember him saying something about this."

This was spoken in a manner that suggested the few words Stan did say were not repeatable, maybe an explosive burst of rapid-fire obscenities on his way out the door.

"My name is Ponderosa," she said. "Why don't you come in?"

"Thank you," I said, not bothering to look back at the cabbie.

I patiently waited inside the spacious ranch living room while Ponderosa dressed upstairs. She was also talking on the phone, and as the conversation progressed so did the slamming of the dresser drawers.

About a minute after the last slam, she came down dressed in tight jeans, a loose-knit sweater, and dark blue Converse sneakers. Her long blonde hair was still drying, thickening, and when she spoke there was an air of confidence and thoughtfulness suggesting a much more complex personality than her wholesome, Teutonic looks suggested. "He'll be back tonight," she said. "He got caught up with some business in Denver. Sorry."

"It happens," I said, trying to defuse the awkwardness.

"I didn't even know he was in Denver. I thought he was ballooning. So you two have never met?"

"No."

"You look older."

"I'm Ben's first."

"Before Megan?"

"By about six months."

"I'm going to make some coffee. Would you like a cup?" she asked as she walked into the open kitchen and began grinding coffee beans. Her demeanor was poised and reminded me of a government bureaucrat in an old bureaucratic country where things never change despite the pleas of its citizens.

"Yes, thank you."

"I should warn you," she said, "Stan is not really open to discussing his intentions now that Ben and Isabella have died."

"I'm not interested in the Tyler estate," I replied. "I'm here to talk about Prostitute Records."

This information confused her, and so I quickly filled her in on the basic Prostitute bio-news since Ben's death, including the recent horror at Isabella's house when I got clobbered. She was not at all surprised by my tale, except for my brief but glorious rise to the top of Prostitute LLC.

"Isabella must have really thought much of you," she said.

"It was mutual."

"If she didn't die, you might be running Prostitute Records now."

"Along with Hank Tyler," I corrected her. "But there's still a chance I can do that with Stan's help."

This was followed by a long silence as she located the coffee cups and poured the boiling water into a glass coffee press. But I could tell what she was really doing was thinking about what Stan told her about me. She then asked, "Ben Tyler and your mother never married?"

"No. In fact, I think they met only once or twice."

This candor evoked not an ounce of surprise on her part. I was now positive that Stan trashed me and this endeavor was going to be problematic.

"Considering, you've done pretty well so far," she said, as a way of preparing me.

"Thanks," I responded, unaffected. I then asked her the obvious. The clue was balancing on her third finger like a cube sculpture. "Getting married?"

"In November."

"Congratulations."

"Thank you."

This was followed by more silence as I wondered if a prenup was in the works and at what point they decided to marry, before or after bio-Dad died. I was also curious if she was advising Stan in business matters, and if so, did he listen.

Later that day, as we continued to wait for Stan, we became hungry and she made an early dinner and served pasta salad, homemade bread that she baked the night before, and good red wine. After eating, she escorted me to a guest cabin, the one closest to the main house. At this high altitude, the temperature dropped into the twenties by nightfall, and I was glad the cabins were more rustic in style than in substance. This one was fortified with thickly insulated walls and burning electric heat.

She told me she'd call when Stan arrived. I thanked her for her hospitality, and I believe—although this may not be the objective truth—that we looked into each other's eyes for a beat too long.

In that extraordinary moment, I realized many things: First, I was not ever going to taste those bratwurst lips (I know, it's terrible but the way men often think). Second, she most assuredly had her own agenda. Third, that agenda did not include people like me—or *especially* people like me. And fourth, I shouldn't expect too much from Stan if he ever came home. If this was true—and not just a product of my budding psychosis—it was thoughtful of her to clue me in without appearing to do so.

*

Nobody called me that night, and I would have slept all the way into the early morning sunrise if not for the verbal brawl that erupted in the main house around 4:15 am. It penetrated the insulated walls of my cozy cabin. I kept hearing phrases like "fuck no" and "fuck him" and "I'll kill the bastard." It was a male voice, so I assumed it was Stan's.

I couldn't get the full gist of his onslaught because in between his booming phrases, he would subside into unintelligible rants, leaving me uncomfortably uninformed. But I'm pretty sure I had something to do with all the fuss.

About ten minutes into this raging monologue, I heard Ponderosa's soprano voice soar above her male counterpart's with a shrill, "Will you please shut the fuck up." This promulgated a cease-fire for about ninety seconds or so until Stan's baritone started up and down again. Eventually, they did quiet down, and I drifted back to sleep, wondering if what I had just heard was a common occurrence.

The next morning, the phone rang and it was Ponderosa inviting me to breakfast in the main house. When I entered some fifteen minutes later, Stan was still upstairs and "should be down soon." I noticed only two place settings on the kitchen table and I assumed "soon" was a relative term. I should mention, these delays and hostile acts did not faze me, nor did they make me feel unwelcome, because being welcomed or fazed was not a variable in this equation. I was way beyond that. I was on a life-and-death mission. My personal feelings as a brother, or a guest, were not important. The real problem here, as I saw it, was that Stan did not fully grasp whom he was dealing with. This lapse or misjudgment was understandable but, in my thinking, did not serve him.

To Stan, I was a nonentity, not worthy of even a phone call to let me know no one would be waiting for me at a remote airport, despite whatever plans were made. My paltry stake in Prostitute Records coupled with my bastardized Tyler status invited his disdain. Like a child, he was wishing I would wondrously disappear instead of making me disappear as a man would do. Without meeting him, I already knew he was not going to be a formidable opponent like his Uncle Hank.

Stan never made it down for breakfast. After breakfast, Ponderosa took me for a walk around the ranch because there wasn't much left to do. I was intrigued that she was not going to tell me to leave. Her blatant independence of Stan strengthened my belief that Ponderosa was on her own quest. She needed to maintain her boundaries, her control. Neither I nor the specifics of my circumstances had much to do with it, either. There were larger psychological issues at stake. It was about the long run for her. Although, I was mindful that one could never be too certain about such matters without knowing all the details or being personally involved.

During the ranch tour I learned that Ponderosa loved horses and owned about a half-a-dozen of them. They were of good stock and were allowed to graze freely outside the corral and stables but also could be saddled and taken for a ride at will. Ponderosa said she looked after them herself, grooming and feeding them, and I remembered that statement. It proved to come in handy down the line.

Adjacent to the stables, and, for me, the most interesting sight on the ranch, was a launching site for Stan's hot air balloon. The pad was circular and slightly elevated, like a gazebo without the roof. It was painted red, white and blue. On it sat a purple gondola. Spread out across the field was the extensive fabric of the balloon, or envelope. This, too, was red, white, and blue and ready to be rigged and inflated by a giant fan sitting next to the pad. Inside the gondola were two vertically-propped silver propane fuel tanks and a large burner centered above the railing. The simplicity was endearing: burn propane fuel, create hot air, the hot air fills the envelope, and because hot air is lighter than normal air, up, up, and away you go.

Ponderosa said she never sailed in these balloons because there was so little control over the craft while in flight. The wind—and not the navigator—was the major determining factor of how fast you drifted and in which direction. I understood her fear, but to me, these balloons seemed like great fun and relatively safe, and I really wanted to give it a try. Ponderosa said Stan usually went up every morning to start off his day, but not this particular morning. Seeing how the craft was set to launch, I thought he may do so later on.

On the way back to the house, we stopped at some of the other cabins, all of which looked similar from the outside but inside served a special purpose. There was a movie theater cabin, a gymnasium cabin, and a hunting cabin. The hunting cabin was stocked with rifles, fishing gear, traps, knives, and likewise objects. This was where Stan and his business and political pals could relax and watch the ball game and have drinks before and after their hunting expeditions. Overall, the cabins were pleasant but only confirmed my impression that I was in a commercial lodge or summer camp.

When we returned to the house, Stan was waiting for us, sitting at the kitchen table eating cornflakes. He was dressed in jeans, cowboy boots, and a tight black T-shirt that showed off a finely-tuned upper body. His frame, by contrast, was smaller than I imagined, and overall he took on the physical characteristics of his mother, especially in the face. He had Molly's piercing eyes and sharp cheekbones—that same intensity. In fact, my other two cowardly male half siblings looked more like Tylers than Stan did, despite Isabella's strong Latin contribution. And I, of course, looked the most Tyler out of all of them, which pissed off every one of them and gave Stan pause after Ponderosa introduced us.

Like his uncle, half-brothers, and half-sister, he was startled by my appearance, enough to stop munching his cornflakes. I took the hesitation as a renewed sign of hope and, not wanting to allow the situation to deteriorate before it started (small talk proved never to be a good idea with the half siblings—they had no patience for it), I jumped into my pitch about Prostitute LLC and what I thought was possible if we joined forces, not forgetting to trash Uncle Hank, who was so far my only successful subject of unity in Tyler circles.

After I was through, Stan looked over at Ponderosa and their eyes locked. Silent information was exchanged. "Thanks, but I'm not interested," he said without looking at me.

"Are you sure you don't want to think about it?" I asked. "There's enormous potential, maybe not immediately, but in the years to come."

"I already thought about it. I'm selling my interest to Hank," he said. "I just got off the phone with him."

He resumed eating his cornflakes. I looked over at Ponderosa. She remained poised, noncommittal. I turned back to Stan. "You could have saved me a trip," I said.

For some reason, these few words irritated him. I guess I was not supposed to speak further or offer a rebuttal. He threw down his spoon. The spoon bounced off the table onto the floor, making a lot of noise. It was meant to be dramatic. He looked my way and stayed looking—possibly for the first time. "I have plans," he scowled, "and they don't include you or Prostitute Records. I'm taking the cash. Okay? Is there anything else you want to know before you leave here forever?"

"I guess not," I said, feeling unexpectedly wounded. I then added: "You sure you didn't sell yourself short?"

With this, he abruptly jumped up, the veins in his neck bulging and threatening to burst. He was hinting at a physical confrontation, but I wasn't sure how much of it was real.

"Who the fuck do you think you are?" he shouted. "Do you know where you are, man?"

I knew where I was. I was in kiddie summer camp sparring with another imbecilic Tyler on my way to claiming my rightful prize.

"I thought I was in a place of reason, but apparently not," I shouted back, curious to see what impact my rising voice would have.

"Reason? You want reason, man? I'll give you reason: The only 'reason' you think you can come here is because your mother is a fucking whore. How's that for a reason?"

Stunned silence followed. This, I had to think about. My mother is a whore. Perhaps there was truth to it, way back when. But it was ancient history. The real reason I was there was because *his* mother is a whore, not mine, but I chose not to get into that. The subject was too dark, and it almost made me sympathetic. He started up again:

"You may have fooled that Mexican freak (meaning Isabella, and for me another extremely sensitive subject), but you don't fool me. You're a loser. I'd rather deal with Hank than you any day. I hate him to the core, but at least he's a winner. I'm used to winners, man, all my friends are winners, all the people I do business with are winners, you should see the people who walk through that door. Why would I ever want to become partners with you?"

I looked over to Ponderosa. She wore one of those disappointing, blank expressions, eyes straight ahead like a grade-school teacher who walks into a classroom filled with screaming kids following a sugared lunch. She offered nothing. She had warned me. I turned back to Stan. It was time to leave.

"I don't appreciate your comment about my mother," I said. "And you still should have saved me the trip."

"You coming here made up my mind for me," he smirked. "He's going to crush you, man. It's already done."

He grabbed his cowboy hat and snakeskin jacket from the counter. Without looking at Ponderosa, he said, "When I come back here, he better be gone."

Ponderosa waited until the door slammed shut and then walked over to me and put her hand on my shoulder. "Are you alright?" she asked.

"Yeah. I'm going to call a taxi."

"I'll drive you."

"No, it's better this way. But thanks."

"You sure there is nothing I can do?"

"You can answer a question."

"Okay?"

"Do you find him unpredictable?" I asked.

"No," she said with her scientific, Aryan calm; her eyes as clear as mountain stream water flowing through these highlands. "Not at all."

"I'll wait in my cabin," I said.

"I'll call you when the cab comes."

I walked back to my cabin. I packed the few things I had with me and sat on the bed. As tempting as it was to stay and pick Ponderosa's mind, it was better that I be alone and think.

About 90 minutes later the taxi arrived. I walked out into the open air. Ponderosa was standing there with a lunch bag filled with sandwiches for my trip back. I accepted the food and thanked her for her hospitality and said, "Maybe we'll see each other again." This evoked a curious and doubtful "maybe" in response. As far as she was concerned, that would never happen. We both smiled politely. And then something extraordinary occurred. I looked up into the sky and saw Stan's hot air balloon in full flight, a little to the west. I almost couldn't believe my eyes. Just before, in the cabin, I was hoping for inspiration, and there it was floating above me in patriotic red, white, and blue, sailing through the heavenly clouds. I was deeply moved by this sight. It generated within unfiltered exhilaration—electric-current exhilaration, such as I had never felt before.

I kept looking up at the balloon, but I could not see Stan's figure in the gondola. He was too high up. I wasn't sure if he was peering through binoculars, looking down at us, but I had a strong feeling that he was. I smiled brightly up, as brightly as I could. I wanted him to see me smile. I wanted to thank him for such wonderful inspiration.

I then turned to Ponderosa and said: "Those balloons seem to work fine." She nodded slightly. "So far," she replied softly.

I could tell she had been staring at me and not the balloon.

19
TAKING ACTION

The ride back to the airport went quickly. The same irritating man who took me out to the ranch two days earlier was driving again. This time, I chose to be charitable by returning his conversation. I even offered him one of my sandwiches. He gratefully accepted the sandwich. This backfired on me when he began talking with his mouth full.

When we arrived at the airport, I tipped the cabbie 30 bucks—a ten-dollar bill he gave me as change for the cab fare, plus another one of my crisp twenties. (For the record, I usually held on to the bill change from my twenties to build up a Treasury Department reserve of tens and fives. In certain delicate situations, I would defer to this reserve.) The cabbie and I parted on friendly terms, which was my goal.

After a lengthy but relaxing wait at the airport, I flew into Detroit, taxied home, dropped off my belongings, jumped into my car and drove to the library on Woodward. In the library—where I always felt safe—I indulged in a little research the old-fashioned way, through books and technical magazines and not via the budding, digitally traceable Internet (a phenomenon that had now taken over the world, not to mention much of my long-term record business).

About three hours later, I returned home and amassed the following: insulated gloves, two flashlights, my toolbox, a variety of liquid and synthetic adhesives that dated back to the Barney days, camping gear, a road atlas, layers of warm clothing, a portable alarm clock, a thermos I would fill with hot coffee in the morning, a jar of natural peanut butter, and a loaf of rye bread. I put most of the items in the trunk of my car and went to bed early.

The next morning—it was a Tuesday—I made coffee, filled my

thermos, and drove to work. After about an hour or so, I told Karolina I was feeling lousy, probably coming down with something, and I was going back to bed. As I was leaving, she offered no sympathy and perhaps was glad to see me go. This hurt my feelings even though I wasn't really sick.

I walked back to my car and started my 1,700-mile drive due west—almost directly west as the crow flies—staying mostly on two Interstates, 94 and 80, and stopping only twice, not counting gas stations. My first stop was in Chicago to purchase two 40-gallon liquid-propane tanks at a large sporting-goods store. My second stop was in Denver to get some rest, choosing a run-down motel on the outskirts of town.

Denver was a little off the interstate, but I did not want to risk Cheyenne, Wyoming, where I might stick out or be remembered. I could afford this slight excursion because I was ahead of schedule. Detroit to Chicago took about five hours, plus a little downtime for shopping, and Chicago to Denver only about fourteen hours—driving straight through the night at 69 miles per hour.

I arrived at the Denver motel on Wednesday morning at about 7 am local time, or 9 am Detroit time. From the seedy motel, I called the shop and left a message for Karolina (who normally got in around 10 am), stating I was in need of further rest and I would check back with her the following day. I turned off my cell again, not wanting to talk to anyone for the duration of my trip.

In the motel room, I set my portable alarm clock to 6 pm MST, and, exhausted from driving all day and night, fell right out. I slept deeply and dreamt vividly about wild buffalo herds stampeding slaughter houses and the men who operated then and their wives and children, too—a lot of blood, horror, screaming—before awakening at the sound of the alarm bell, as planned. Sufficiently rested, strong, alert, focused, I ate two peanut butter sandwiches for protein, filled up the thermos with coffee at the nearby 7-Eleven, reviewed my plans, double-checked my gear, returned the motel key, and began driving again.

Almost eight hours later I was back at the KO Corral in western Wyoming. It was now Thursday and the time 3:17 am local time, an excellent hour. I parked the car in a hidden cove off the county road adjacent to the east side of the ranch. I suited up warmly, chose specific tools and adhesives from the tool box, and put them in my carrying sack. I then grabbed one of the cylinders of propane (leaving the other for reserve), strapped both the sack and cylinder to my back, and like an Eskimo on a hunting campaign, I began my trek across the sloping tundra beyond the fake log cabins.

I brought two flashlights but had no immediate use for either with the moon being almost full and the skies clear. The moon was a lucky break, I thought, although that could have been taken into account by checking the almanac. The temperature was in the teens, the ground frozen solid again after the sun had gone down; but no snow, no precipitation. The clear skies suggested that I could expect more of the same for the new day ahead.

As I walked, I could see in the distance, in silhouette, the two-story main ranch house where Stan and Ponderosa lived. No inside lights were visible, just as there were no lights visible anywhere else, and at 3:43 in the morning, it appeared that I was the only soul awake for hundreds of miles in any direction. It was a lonely but powerful feeling.

About twenty minutes into my journey, my chest started to burn from the freezing air, shortening my breath. I had in total about seventy pounds of weight strapped to my back, in addition to my heavy, layered clothing. The farther I walked, the heavier it got. But I kept my swift pace, crossed the ice-chunky stream, and reached the hot air balloon launching pad next to the stables in less than thirty-five minutes, as scheduled.

After resting and clearing my chest by spitting out mucus, and a little blood, which I covered with earth, I climbed into the gondola and got to work. I ignited both flashlights, positioning them at a low angle in the basket and pointing them on the propane tanks. I knew if anyone was looking in my general direction from afar—unlikely but still possible given the rising and vast terrain—they would probably notice a small light source emanating from the general area of the stables. This should not, I reasoned, be looked upon with any suspicion, but rather as an ordinary early-morning activity having to do with the stable or horses (which Ponderosa took care of—no helping hands that I knew of) or even the balloon itself.

The only danger would be if Stan or Ponderosa saw the light. I did not know which way their bedroom windows faced because I was not thinking in those terms when I was at the ranch. I also was aware they had the tendency to quarrel, sometimes late at night or early in the morning, but that was the one chance I had to take.

Inside the craft, I carefully examined the two vertically propped fuel tanks. One cylinder gauge read 85 percent full, the maximum capacity level for hot air balloon liquid-propane tanks. A tank that is 85 percent filled allows the remaining 15 percent of the tank to be consumed by propane vapor, the byproduct of the liquid and the actual substance that is burned after it is pressure-released from the tank.

The level of liquid propane in the second tank was at 62 percent, thus allowing 23 percent of the remaining 38 percent of space left in the tank to be topped off with liquid propane, which Stan was likely to do himself in the morning or the next time he was set to fly the balloon.

I should note a few important facts about propane before we move on: First, liquid propane expands substantially with heat (25 percent compared with water, which expands only 2.2 percent when heated). Second, all propane tanks have pressure-release valves if the propane pressure gets too high. Third, in order for these balloon crafts to work properly, a certain amount of vapor pressure is essential—90 to 160 PSI is recommended for performance and safety—which means when ballooning, one sets out to heat the tanks to increase vapor pressure, especially in cold climates.

The key to all this, as is the case with many things in life, is balance, proportion, measurement, restraint. The goal is to have the tanks pressurized enough to fly the craft but not enough to leak propane through the safety valves.

But, as we all know, sometimes goals are not met and, as it applies here, there are times when the equilibrium is off and propane is leaked into the atmosphere. And since propane vapor is heavier than air, the propane falls to the bottom of the gondola and collects and expands exponentially, seeking out an ignition source. If it finds one, this becomes the classic example of hot air balloon misfortunes. It does happen, rarely, although most times when propane is released into the craft, disaster is averted because there is time to vent and safely continue.

Without trying too hard, it is easy to understand how these release valves can be dangerous, by providing the means to release temperamental liquid petroleum vapor into the gondola. On the other hand, without the valves, one is left with the even more risky proposition of the tanks pressurizing to the point of explosion. Technically, tanks explode when the internal liquid expansion sucks up the vapor until there is nothing but liquid and then continues to expand beyond the capacity of the steel canisters.

Given these variables, this is what I was forced to do in the bitter cold on that mid-October morning: I had to re-calibrate the tank measurement gauges (something I learned from Barney) so they did not accurately display my increased liquid propane adjustments in the tanks—up to 97 percent instead of 85 percent. I had to apply a clear, synthetic, liquid-petroleum-based coating to the tank exteriors, which traps heat and accelerates the internal temperature increase of the tanks to pressurize them. Finally, I had to seal off the safety relief valves with liquid-steel adhesive.

It may sound simple, but it was just the opposite and I had to use a lot of brain power to get everything just right. For instance, I saw evidence of electrical heat tape on the tanks, and it was logical to assume Stan would use more of this insulating tape to increase vapor pressure in the cold Wyoming climate, and I had to recalculate how much this increase would be in relationship to the increase I would be generating with the liquid coating.

I also had to account for the outside air temperature rise from 20 degrees Fahrenheit at 4 am (on average, a 10 percent temperature rise will result in a 2 percent increase in propane volume expansion) to the mid-30s in the late morning with the sun shining. And I had to calculate that Stan would top off the less-filled tank to 85 percent, but what he'd actually be doing would be topping it off to 97 percent with my new calibration, once I contributed my additional portion from the liquid-propane tank strapped on my back, which in effect would allow only 3 percent tank space for vapor—just enough to get his balloon far enough into the air before the liquid-propane expansion kicked in from the combination of the heating tape, liquid canister coating, and air temperature increase.

This rising heat force would, after a brief period, surpass whatever pressure loss resulted from burning propane vapor to lift the balloon into the sky and destroy the structural integrity of the steel tank with the safety valves sealed, and culminate, I hoped, in a magnificent mid-air fire explosion that would almost certainly consume the gondola, the balloon, and Stan.

I repeatedly cautioned myself that one can never be too careful when experimenting on this level of danger, and there was absolutely no room for error. This was a one-shot deal. If my plan failed and the craft did not ignite into chemicals and flames and fall out of the sky like a comet, the consequences could be harsh given the abundance of irrefutable tampering evidence (sealed relief valves!) and kick off a new and unpredictable phase in the Tyler bio-inheritance saga involving the police and possibly the FBI.

It would also, probably, generate support and sympathy for Stan in probate court and other legal circles. I had no doubt, however, that there would be huge disappointment with the siblings if it was revealed that Stan escaped death.

But what tormented and plagued me with waves of sickly depression was something I was completely powerless over no matter how perfectly I carried out my plan: What if innocent people became victims due to unforeseen events or weird coincidence? What if Ponderosa, for starters, suddenly got the urge to go ballooning? What then? A scenario like that or some other freakish twist involving unsuspecting innocents was abominable. I had no way of controlling or planning against it.

Indeed, as I saw it, my cause, my bio-quest was important enough to plot against Stan (it had become personal for me), but it was still only for my own material benefit and ego gratification. I was not fighting fascism or trying to save loved ones from harm's way, yet a human being was to perish if all went well.

These thoughts tormented me, but I made a decision to take the chance and, once decided, never looked back. I planned and executed as best as humanly possible, and the results were now out of my hands.

Careful not to leave a trail and double-checking my work as I went along, I packed my belongings, and trekked back across the range as a trace of morning light was hinting at the big day ahead. When I reached my car, I dumped my materials into the trunk, shed my layers of winter clothing, secured myself behind the wheel, and drove straight back to Detroit. My only stops were gas stations to fill up on gasoline and relieve myself, and, at around 7:20 am Mountain Time, or 9:20 am Detroit time, to call the store and leave another message for Karolina stating I would not be in that day. To do this I pulled over to the shoulder of the road and used my cell phone.

During the entire return trip back I did not once turn on the radio. I had not the least desire to hear news of any kind until I was safely back home. I also listened to no music. Instead, I sunk into a deep meditative trance, buzzing from the adrenaline, and followed the unending white line. This adrenaline—or raw power—surging through my body was new to me and not a particularly healthy thing, either. Surely too much of this would distort one's perception of reality. But it was there, and to deny it was to deny who I had become. Even if my plans failed, and Stan survived, I had crossed a line with my intention, and it was both tragic and exhilarating at the same time.

20
DOUBT

Strategically, Stan made sense. He was subject to the same California statutes as Isabella, which meant he had to survive his benefactor by at least 120 days to secure or bequeath his inheritance. So if Stan vanished, so would his fortune. Equally relevant, Stan was the last listed beneficiary in Ben's will, and if he did not survive, the state of California would be forced to intervene and distribute Ben's fiefdom among what was left of his legit kids, with the possible exception of Josh, Ben's disinherited son. This would diffuse the grossly unfair and unintended estate cluster that Stan had lucked into and give me more time to negotiate with the others about Prostitute LLC. I was not absolutely certain but I was reasonably sure not all of my siblings would go along with Uncle Hank, despite whatever hatred they had for me and whatever compensation Hank might be offering.

I realize this may sound cold, my calculations, my lack of compassion, but I truly did not believe (at the time anyway—it has changed somewhat since) that my decision to eliminate Stan Tyler was strictly the deed of a ruthless opportunist. Serendipity and fear contributed just as much, if not more. Take, for instance, the sighting of Stan's balloon. Moments before, I was anchored in Stan's guest cabin meditating for guidance and direction and then I walk outside and there it was. Coincidence? I doubt it. To ignore that moment, that sign, that balloon, would have been to ignore my instincts, my being, my very essence. In other words, it was not some bozo psychotic delusion. It was inspiration, plain and simple.

In addition, on the long drive back to the airport (an important journey), I kept thinking how remote and inaccessible this territory was. So isolated, in fact, you could start a war and nobody would find out about it until you sent a postcard. This lent itself to a thoughtful examination of Stan's rugged personality. If he acted that brazenly and disrespectfully toward his own brother—however estranged—he most likely was doing the same with others. He was probably labeled "impulsive" and "off the handle" by his friends, enemies, and acquaintances. Upon hearing the news of his crash, many would immediately blame poor judgment. He was in a rush or being careless or not thinking. It was Stan, after all, and he was playing around in a balloon filled with nothing but hot air, and these things can and do happen.

And then, of course, underlying it all, was fear. Stan scared the hell out of me that morning. He told me he was selling Ben's portion of Prostitute to Hank. He said Hank, the "winner," had plans to "crush" me, the "loser." Those were his words. "It's already done." And I believed him and became frightened. To the core frightened. Thus, in my mind, it was fear, serendipity, and greed (desire for my rightful place in the sun) that spurred me to the point of no return. I wasn't simply sitting around plotting to kill a belligerently base but technically innocent person for malicious profit. That was how I viewed it.

*

Whatever excuses I entertained for my barbarism, it did not, of course, justify the deed, nor did it lessen the grizzly reality that I was spilling my own blood and, biblically speaking, committing the second-oldest crime: fratricide. Equally troubling was my callousness. I had not one ounce of sympathy for half-brother Stan Tyler before or after I took action against him, and that deeply bothered me—the fact that I could not *feel* anything for him. No guilt, remorse, ambiguity, sympathy. Nothing. Yet I was very much aware of the monstrosity of the deed or the idea of acting heinously against my own blood. It was truly awful and wrong, as wrong as anything can be. Yet killing Stan Tyler meant absolutely zilch. In fact, once I was inspired to do so, I could not wait to do so and— as you read—did not. This conundrum, this awareness of lack of conscience, was most confusing and plagued me on a regular basis. I really needed to talk to someone about it but of course could not. I even fantasized about discussing it with a good psychiatrist. A competent psychiatrist, not some quack. He could, I thought, this trained psychotherapist who possessed license to dispense the latest in pharmacological intervention, prescribe appropriate daily medication, and on a twice-a-week basis he and I could explore my behavior in a manner that would be civil, informational, and healing. And if necessary, he would increase or alter the daily medication as he saw fit after a reasonable period of time. And soon, say in a couple of years or so, I would get better, which would coincide with the long term chemical reworking of my brain.

He might also suggest that I—a victim no doubt on some important if not obscure level—should not single out fratricide as being more odious or deviant than good-old regular murder, and therefore I should not go to "super hell" with all those curious souls who do similar stuff, such as kill their wives and maybe their kids, too, and then lie about it to the authorities as though they are performing in a bad parochial-school play. This typically buys them about twenty minutes of skewed infamy on a sickly cable television station before they're proven guilty and sent packing to rot away in a forgotten, hazardous wing of a maximum-security state penitentiary.

This fantasy therapy, I felt, would be an important step toward the improvement of my mental condition, but it would not diminish the debilitating and nightmarish prospect of innocent people being inadvertently sacrificed by my willful sabotage. That horrid possibility began to eat away my internal organs until—I'm ashamed to admit—it was usurped, massively usurped, by a new and much more powerful and frightening "I don't want to get fucking caught" illness. Because as time dragged on, there was no word or news or rumor of any freak accidents coming out of lonely Wyoming. Not even a skiing accident. Not from the TV or the radio news stations, the newspapers, the Internet, or any person connected to the Tyler estate who knew me personally, such as Claire, her lawyers, Molly, or Jessica.

After the second consecutive twenty-four hour period of eerie silence, I became hopelessly paranoid. I tortured myself by reviewing every detail of the sabotage mission, especially the few places I stopped en route. But nothing stuck out. Every gas station I frequented was located on an interstate, where I would hardly be noticed. Every item purchased—from petroleum to helium to coffee—was acquired with cash, or fake cash. My one motel break in Denver was at best an invisible dive where I registered under a false name and false license plate number and never left the room or talked to anyone. There were no accidents, incidents, almost-incidents, imaginary incidents, flat tires, or anything else that would draw attention to me. I never drove faster than 70 miles per hour. A good portion of the driving was done at night. I don't remember seeing more than one or two state or highway patrol cars either way.

At the balloon site, I was careful not to leave any objects, tools, fragments or clues (outside the gondola). The only trail I left, that I could think of, at anytime, anywhere, was the phony money, but that was a chance I took every day of my life, and I made up my mind from the get-go not to worry about it. So if, perchance, Stan did discover that someone had tampered with his balloon and called the police—the least desired explanation for this delay out of many—I remained confident that I would not be suspected. And if by chance I was suspected anyway, I was equally confident my lies would hold water.

And—to take this to the worst scenario (this is how my mind was working)—if somehow I became a suspect anyway, I would simply turn it up a notch or two and act like a politician under indictment and go to the grave with my sins, like every other treasonable, perfidious scumbag who ever planted seeds in between sea to shiny sea: "There was no conspiracy involved in the assassination of President John F. Kennedy," just a lone assassin and a kooky, dancing bullet that wouldn't stop bouncing around a topless convertible which was remarkably void of shielding secret service agents (for those low grassy knoll angles) and motorcycled police. If they can do it, I can do it, too, if it ever came down to that. But it shouldn't come down to that, I reasoned, although the longer I waited without hearing, the more my mind went straight to hell. And having moody, distant Karolina around did not help matters either. I was beginning to feel as though I was interacting with a complete stranger—a stranger who did not like me and who would spend most of her time talking on the phone and refer to me only when it was convenient or self-serving. Gone were the delightful conversations about music, business, the store, evil Prostitute Records and its unsavory cast of characters, or the precious, obtainable, golden future. This transformation began after I returned from Isabella's funeral but had become much worse and seemingly permanent since then.

Curiously, her only subject of any interest outside of herself was Stan Tyler. When I briefly returned from my first Wyoming visit (Wyoming 1), I told her about Stan's stated intention to turn over Ben's Prostitute ownership to Hank. At that time, Karo did not appear interested or even reply, which made sense given her new aloofness and cynicism. But since my return from the second Wyoming visit (Wyoming 2), she started up with questions about Stan, questions such as: "Do you think he'll change his mind?" and "How stable do you think he is?" and "What's his girlfriend like?"

All legitimate queries, to be sure, and all answered with restraint (I was, after all, hoping he was going to fall out of the sky at any moment and burn to death), but if she had already emotionally abandoned Eclectic Emporium, why the sudden interest? And why just Stan and no one else, such as Claire, Hank, and all the other pieces to the Tyler bio-inheritance puzzle?

Out of respect for our history together, I remained tolerant of her erratic behavior, including enduring her nonstop yapping on the phone at the expense of our customers—something she had never done before. It irked me that she could be so disrespectful after all the time we worked together, and it drove home the reality that I was soon going to be losing an incredibly creative person whose unique signature was all over Eclectic Emporium. In fact, after the opening of the lounge, more people aligned Karolina with Eclectic Emporium than me, or even Sledge, and it was nothing less than tragic that it might end in such an uncomfortable and unfriendly manner.

On the other hand (if there was a bright side, this was unfortunately it), I was now actively engaged in unforgivable criminal activity that could land me in prison for the rest of my natural life. I'm not referring to some cozy, minimal-security federal junior college like Sledge secured, either, but a brutal, hard-core, state penitentiary where I'd be coexisting with the dredge of society on a good, sunny day. And it was entirely possible, if things went astray, Karolina could be implicated by association. We were viewed by most as being creative partners and lovers, and I had no right to endanger her, especially without her knowledge or consent. So perhaps, I reasoned, it was best she took this turn on her own. Yes, maybe it was for the best after all.

21
THE MILES DAVIS TEA PARTY

On the TWELFTH nerve-racking day back without news from Wyoming, I interrupted one of Karolina's phone conversations to inform her that if she needed to leave the store for a few hours, or even days, at a time, she should feel free to do so, and I would take over the floor. After we went broke, I laid-off all the part-time help and Karo was required to be in the store. But no more. She was now free to go about as she used to when we had plenty of help. Her absences would not affect her paycheck (partially funded with counterfeit currency), and if there was anything else I could do for her, she should not hesitate to let me know. I offered this thinking it would assist her in whatever plans she was making and precipitate her final departure. I wanted her gone.

Not surprisingly, she acted surprised by this generous overture and gladly accepted, thanking me, and then returned to her phone call. The next morning, she told me she had some personal business to take care of and would return around 1:00 that afternoon. I said "fine" and took over the floor as I said I would. The following day, she did the same, only she left in the early afternoon and returned around 4:30 pm.

This kept up for the next week or so, her leaving for a spell and returning later, and I was encouraged my plan was working and that she would soon be breaking the news to me that she would be leaving for good. But that did not happen. Instead, on my nineteenth nerve-racking day back after Wyoming 2—early November—and nearly three weeks without word of an accident or a police investigation or whatever was or was not happening out there in the Wyoming hinterland, Karolina took the entire day off and reappeared moments before the store was about to close, and asked me, "Why are you trying to get rid of me?" Mystified by her timing, I replied stoically that she appeared unhappy and I thought she could use the free time to figure out what would make her happy again.

"You mean, like find another job?"

"If that's what you want."

"That's not what I want," she moaned. "Why don't we have dinner tonight?"

Suspect of this attempted reconciliation, if that is what it was, I took her to this new Ethiopian place down the street on Woodward because it was close and we could walk to it. Her extended period of restrained aggression did not impress me as ephemeral, and I was on my guard.

During dinner, she sounded like her old self and talked about some new bands she liked and how she was struggling with depression and what new medication she was taking, things of that nature. Then, toward the end, the name Stan Tyler came up again: Had I heard anything more from his camp? Had the situation changed? What were my thoughts? Feeling pressured and uncomfortable, I told her the truth: nothing had changed.

And nothing *had* changed. I tried to kill him, but as far as I knew, I had failed and the end result was the same. "I don't expect much more from him," I said.

"But they can be unpredictable. Don't you think?" she persisted— "they" meaning my half siblings.

I didn't agree at all. The siblings were a lot of things, but unpredictable was certainly not one of them. In fact, they were militaristically consistent in their debauchery, selfishness, and uninhibited cruelty and not prone to sway too far from those unholy paths, with Jessica possibly the sole exception.

But what I said was this: "Unpredictable? What do you mean, Karo?"

"I don't know. They're so crazy," she replied.

That was a red flag. Calling the Tylers crazy was like calling water wet. She was obviously reaching. It reinforced my belief that she had absolutely no faith in me anymore.

"You think I'm going to fold, don't you?" I asked her directly.

"Well, are you?" she asked back.

I have to admit I was considerably hurt and my pride begged me to shout back, "Over my dead, rotting flesh will I ever fold to Hank Tyler." But instead, I somehow said, halfheartedly, "I don't know. Maybe."

Then I watched her eyes. I watched them like I was studying cancer cells through a microscope. They did not move. They were ice. Frozen. Frozen with contempt, disdain, and fucking venom. This long time partner and lover of mine had most assuredly written my sorry ass off as a big time loser and she hated me for it. I saw it as clear as day. I purposely showed a little weakness, and it revealed her true feelings. No matter what came out of her Cleopatra mouth, I was the village idiot about to get his head chopped off. And maybe she was right on.

Following this revelation, I did not even bother listening. *So why this meal?* I wondered. And what was all this nonsense about her not wanting to leave? Maybe she enjoyed seeing me suffer. In reality, the suffering I was experiencing she knew nothing about and hopefully never would, but she was right to sense I was suffering unbearably.

On the way out of the restaurant, I told her I was tired and going home to sleep. She laughed.

"What?" I asked, responding, even though I didn't care.

"I know you have a girlfriend," she said.

I wondered why she would think that, but I let it go. I paid the check with phony cash. We walked back to the lot, into our cars, and went our separate ways.

The next morning at work, I told her the arrangement was still on for her to come and go as she pleased.

"Still trying to get rid of me?" she asked half-jokingly.

"That's not fair."

"Actually, there are a few things I must do later."

When later arrived, I came onto the floor to take over and she left without mentioning where she was going. I looked around. The store was empty of customers. That was happening more as time dragged on. It made me ill along with everything else that was going on. I decided to step outside and get a breath of fresh air.

Once outside, I observed Karolina across the street walking to her car. Watching her drive off, I once again felt as though she were a stranger, only this time I was one of those poor suckers in *Invasion of the Body Snatchers* witnessing his wife leave the house in the middle of the night to collect his duplicate pod.

It was then I had the urge to leave the store. I quickly locked the front doors. I hustled around the corner to my car, jumped in, and waited until I saw Karo's car pass through the intersection. I kept waiting while another half-dozen cars went through and then swung into traffic and followed her at a safe distance.

I understood this vehicular perversion was senseless but minor compared to some of my other actions of late, so I didn't worry too much; although on paper it looked terrible. Jealous lovers stalk all the time and make idiots of themselves, but I was not Karolina's lover and I didn't give a damn who she was fucking. I was her employer. And what could I possibly discover about her that would be revealing? My goal was for her to drift away to different coordinates. So why was I engaging in this petty, reality-TV behavior?

Perhaps, I thought as I followed her down Woodward, I was becoming addicted to subterfuge. I was finding comfort in surreptitious, petty criminality. Or perhaps the stress and uncertainty of all my recent actions was taking its toll, and I was, as feared, losing my fucking mind. Only now, people were going to start noticing.

Her first stop was at a Starbucks near downtown. She entered the store and, five minutes later, came out sipping a frozen Frappuccino and carrying a little Starbucks bag with something inside, probably muffins. Once again, the idiot bell went off in my head and I thought about bagging it. What could possibly be next? A boutique? A salon? A movie theater? How about a steamy bedroom with soiled sheets and a stiff cock to kill the lazy hours of the afternoon since I was stupid enough to encourage it and pay her for it? What a damn fool I was, and yet I kept trailing anyway.

I followed her onto Gratiot heading north past the Renaissance Center and guesstimated her destination to be one of the less burned-out neighborhoods along the river and she would soon be cutting over to Jefferson. But she slowed down near Mack Avenue, parked her car on the street, stepped out, and began crossing Gratiot. This confused me because there was not much going on in this wannabe, renovated warehouse section except odious Prostitute Records. I then remembered hearing about a few sewing shops operating in the old warehouses and thought, perhaps, she may have started her design work again. If so, this gave me hope she was moving on with her life.

But hope is a funny thing and can vanish in a heartbeat (proof of unrequited love, for instance), which is exactly what happened when she did not turn down a side street as expected and kept walking until she reached the front entrance of elegant, trendy Prostitute Records.

As far as I knew, there was nothing special going on there that day, such as a promotional event or party, but I no longer kept up with the details of the local Prostitute operation, focusing instead on the bigger picture in Los Angeles and Wyoming. Karolina still did, though, or she had until recently, and maybe there was something happening.

I started driving again, slowly, and looked through the new glass portion of the warehouse. I saw no gathering, no special event, nothing exceptional except Karolina interacting with Jam at his pretentious stone desk. From the looks of it he was telling a long-winded story and gesturing wildly with his hands and arms for emphasis and she was responding by laughing her tits off.

This forced me to stop the car in the middle of the street. In my mind I was witnessing an obscenity. A perversion. What was Karolina doing hanging out with the turd worshipper—and on my time, too? This was not a "keeping an eye on the enemy" exchange, like Coke and Pepsi; it was friendship, camaraderie and collusion. And it kept getting worse, the gesturing, the flirtatious laugher. Finally, like a sexual climax, Jam delivered the long-awaited punch line, and they both exploded into glorious, carefree hilarity. And then—if that were not enough—he reached into the Starbuck's bag on his desk and took out a Frappuccino and began sucking through the straw. They sucked together. The Starbucks bag was for him! She left my store to have a coffee break with this fetid, shit-loving amphibian! What a disloyal, treacherous bitch! What deceitful, blasphemous duplicity was this Idi Amin, Russian roulette, black market wench up to anyway?

I had seen enough. If they started kissing I was afraid I might accelerate through the store window and road kill both of them. Instead, I drove directly back to the store, reopened, and tried to calm myself so I could think. This was not a simple matter. Their relationship was undoubtedly tied to the larger Hank Tyler-Prostitute LLC onslaught. Karolina was now working for the other guys, the bad guys. There was no other logical explanation. They got to her and convinced her I was a lost cause and promised her something for her efforts. Or she went to them. Either way, knowing Karo, the pay-off was major, like taking over Prostitute Detroit or a corporate position with Hank back in L.A. If he was offering me a million, Karolina was well within his budget, even if he didn't really want her.

Hank understood well the Tyler inheritance battle was about his autonomy, his empire, his dominion, and therefore Karolina may have become a necessity. Her recent and scripted statement that she was temporarily distraught and not interested in leaving Eclectic Emporium was proof positive that she was sticking around to spy. This vile corruption was most likely perpetrated after I rejected Hank's million-dollar offer and flew to Wyoming to lure Stan to my corner. They knew I was up in those mountains and Karolina was by herself in the store. I would not be surprised if Hank himself approached her to make a play while I was scheming against him in Wyoming and failing miserably.

Karolina's satanic conversion put a new spin on things and what Stan Tyler was really up to. There had to be more to it. If Karo was working for Hank, why was she pestering me about what I knew about Stan? It could only mean that Stan was playing Hank, too. Stan may have told me he was selling out to Hank, "the winner," but now I would have bet my last fake dollar he told Hank he was thinking about backing me, "the loser," and milking it to death, too, probably to raise Hank's price (and punish him), which I had no doubt Stan would succeed at unless something tragic and unexpected happened to him, a scenario that was fading like a pair of old jeans.

Unfortunately, because of my radical lawlessness, I could share none of this with anyone. I had no one to turn to. It was all mine to whimper about. As I waited for Karolina to return, I don't think I ever felt more alone or isolated. Her defection coupled with the deafening Wyoming silence, once again put me behind the eight ball.

Mercifully, a group of high-school kids walked into the store and started asking questions about Miles Davis. They were taking a jazz history class and were directed by their teacher to my store to find out more, which made me feel proud since we had everything there was to have on Miles and the other jazz greats. They also reminded me of me when I was their age and would come in here after school to talk with Sledge, the master. I was not at Sledge's level, of course, and if the truth were known, they probably were disappointed I was not Karolina, but I took advantage of the distraction and brought them into the lounge. I started spinning vintage Miles, talking about his influences and choice of musicians and how he was breaking ground musically, paving the way.

As we settled into it—Miles' trumpet, the orchestration by Gil—I could feel the torturous anguish festering in every cell of my body begin to melt away with each riff, each musical space. There was so much of it, too; so much wickedness, vengefulness, hatred, evil, poison, tension. I could almost see the toxicity drip out of my decomposing body like dirty oil from an accident-wrecked automobile.

So much sheer willpower and blanket perfidy to fulfill the elusive bio-quest. Was it really worth it? Maybe the universe was designed so people such as Hank Tyler would win. That was their role, their destiny, their contribution to the drama of life, so it would not get boring, and to teach the rest of us how *not* to behave. And the price they paid was to be eternally miserable.

I looked at these kids, bopping their heads, high-fiving one another when awed or inspired, being fused and uplifted by the ostinato genius, and I remembered why I chose to take over this old shop in the first place, way before it spiraled into moral degradation and self-loathing. Maybe, I thought, *I should abdicate if given the chance, if Stan beats the death sentence*. I could walk away unscathed, still able to hold my head in the air morally intact. If Stan discovered the sabotage and that was the cause for the delay, then I should take it as another blessing, another gift, a cue to stop before it got any worse. End it now. Throw in the proverbial towel.

It was still doubtful the authorities would ever connect the dots to me, especially with Stan's notorious, lunatic siblings openly calling for his demise after he miraculously inherited the bulk of bio-Dad's estate. They would be the obvious first choice, especially Josh and Joseph (dozens of people witnessed them almost kill me). In the meantime, I could negotiate with Hank and take the million, maybe more, if Stan was playing Hank, like I now thought he was doing. A million bucks was still quite a wad for a young man my age.

I could burn the counterfeit bills and start anew. Maybe New York City or Berlin. Somewhere away from California and Detroit, away from all the bio-madness. Or maybe I would go to law school after all and contradict Stu. There were so many choices for someone with the right attitude. But most of all, I could go back to living peacefully without constant conflict and guilt and have my spirit renewed and swear never to go down that dark, lonely path of murder again.

Yes, that's what I will do, I thought. I had made up my mind. I looked at these young, innocent teenage faces, and I knew for sure that was the new direction. And, as if being mystically sanctioned, just as my decision was made Karolina returned from the Prostitute brothel and joined us in the lounge. This inspired big smiles from all the boys, and guess who else: Me. I had a big, fat smile that said, "Look who's here."

Karolina was no longer the deceitful, traitorous, disloyal enemy slut bitch, but just another struggling soul along the path to enlightenment, coping with earthly challenges.

Karolina made tea for me and the boys, and I became quite happy, uplifted. It felt like the old days when it was all fun and music. We drank peppermint tea, and Karolina and I learned all about what was going on in high school these days and how these guys were forming a band and what instruments they played and the other types of music they liked and what they sought in a girlfriend and how they all thought Karolina was the most beautiful girl they'd ever seen. When I contradicted them to start a little playful controversy with Karo the phone rang and she answered. It was Stu.

We were having so much fun, I didn't want to take it, but I felt obligated and excused myself and went to my office. Stu's voice was loud and clear over the phone. "Guess what," he said.

"What?"

"Stan Tyler is dead."

This *actually* caught me by surprise. "You're kidding?" I asked.

"Would I kid about something like that?"

The darkness started to descend again like a thick coat of London fog. I was right back in the muck, the bottom of the coal mine covered with black soot. Yet I managed to ask the obvious because it was the appropriate question, and I wanted to stay appropriate.

"What happened?"

"It looks like an accident."

I kept it up: "What kind of an accident?"

"In a balloon—one of those hot air balloons. He was flying one, and it caught on fire."

"That's incredible."

"Yeah. According to the police, he was fried before he hit the earth. It's going to be all over the news soon. Just giving you a heads-up. Claire's lawyers called me about it."

"Just him?" I asked.

"What do you mean?"

"Was anybody with him in the balloon?"

"Oh, no, just him."

A deep, deep sense of relief filled my body. My worst fear did not come true. I felt my strength resurging.

"This changes things again," he continued.

"How?" I asked, as if I didn't know.

"Stan was the last name on Ben's will, and he did not survive, so the state of California will most likely step in and distribute Ben's portion of the estate. Probably to his kids."

I was taking a little bit of a chance here, but I needed to double-check: "Does that mean Josh, too?"

"No. I don't think so. Ben's only request was that Josh be disinherited. Josh should get something from his mother's half, so

I'm sure the judge will uphold that. Josh is probably out."

That's what I thought, too. He then added, "The Tyler estate is starting to look like a curse."

"Curse?"

"Both of Ben's beneficiaries have died in aviation accidents."

"I never thought of that," I said, which was partially true in terms of aviation being a common factor.

"This could be to your benefit, though."

"Yeah?"

"Stan was being obstinate. You might do better with the others."

"I can't do any worse, I guess."

"If I hear more, I'll call you."

"Thanks, Stu."

I clicked off the phone and walked over to the big peacock-shaped mirror on the office wall. It belonged to Marge's grandmother, and Marge gave it to me as a gift when I first took over the shop. I looked into the mirror, into my own eyes. They looked exactly the same. I kept looking, searching, but saw no evidence of change. I took that as a good sign.

I then walked back into the lounge. Karolina turned her attention my way, curious. She was still the double agent, I remembered, having almost just forgotten—but not really. *God, how things change so quickly, in my mind and in my heart, and always when least expected.*

"Everything okay?" she asked.

"That depends," I said.

The boys looked up, too, sensing the importance.

"What do you mean?" she asked.

"There's been an accident."

"What kind of an accident?"

"Stan Tyler. He's dead," I said.

Shock registered in her face like an electronic bulletin board changing slowly to the next advertisement.

"What?" she uttered in disbelief.

I'll tell you what: You backed the wrong horse, you bitch. That's what.

"Stan Tyler is dead," I said again, only with more volume. "His hot air balloon caught on fire a little while ago, while we were here listening to Miles. It killed him."

There was a long moment of silence. We looked at each other intensely. It was a complicated stare, both of us harboring dark secrets. I was waiting for her to say something, but apparently she could not. The nostalgic Miles Davis high-school tea party had come to an abrupt end.

22
A WALK IN THE PARK

The delay, as painful as it was, was worth it. I could not have dreamed of a better alibi: playing records to a bunch of high-school kids at the same time Stan was burning out of control some 1,700 miles away. It was invincible. Or so it seemed.

Much depended on the ensuing investigation, a mandated procedure for any aviation mishap. The chances of the Federal Traffic Safety Board or the Federal Aviation Administration collecting incriminating evidence with the propane tanks, gondola, and envelope all consumed by flames were not high. Those agencies knew that, too. This was not a major commercial aircraft carrying, say, three hundred people. It was a balloon, probably the simplest of all aviation vessels, with only one person involved. There was no reason to suspect foul play.

Most likely, they would conclude after a delay of about six months or so one of the following: the propane tanks pressurized and exploded from an accelerated increase of temperature, or the safety valves released propane first and the vapor ignited, exploding the tanks. Either way, human error or oversight should be the cause.

Human error or weather conditions (such as what happened with Isabella) are typically the causes for these types of small aviation crashes and not some sinister and diabolical plot in which sabotage and murder are factors. Stan Tyler accidentally screwed up and perished by his own actions. It should be that simple.

Confident in my planning and cover-up, I was troubled by my embarrassing emotional flip-flop and this needs to be addressed before I can rightfully move on with my story. I am referring of course to that brief interval of surrender in the lounge when I suddenly became willing to settle with Hank Tyler and abandon the mighty bio-quest.

I attribute this gyration to a few things and in the following order: One, the severe mental stress I was experiencing with the debut of desperate extremism (I hate that word "murder") into my up-to-that-point rather tame arsenal. Two, the debilitating and torturous waiting period that followed. And, three, the heartbreaking discovery of Karolina's defection to the turd-worshipping enemy camp. The combination was simply too powerful and I surrendered or transgressed to the higher road.

Then, as if that were not enough, within an hour or so I reversed myself again at the precise moment Stu informed me of Stan's final departure, with not the slightest consideration for the new surrender position I had just adopted. This shows a lack of character on my part (am I still allowed to say that after Hindenburg 2?), as well as an irreverence for the important, sacred higher road.

I offer no further defense for this capriciousness except to say that I did not have any conscious choice in the matter. It was an organic process for which I have no adequate psychological explanation. It revealed how miserably inept and vulnerable I really was and still am.

Having acknowledged the treason (awareness is the first step to recovery), there was much to think about in the rejuvenated post-Hindenburg 2 era. First and foremost, what should I do about Karolina? She was the enemy. I suppose if I tried, really tried, I could forgive her, because what she did with Prostitute LLC was not so different from what I had just done regarding the bio-quest. I got scared, lost faith, and flipped my position. But even if this were possible, I still would never be able to trust her again. That was unequivocal. So in reality, forgiveness, as a practicality, was not a viable option with regard to Karolina. My real choices were limited to simply firing her with no good explanation or playing her as a double agent, as they do in those old, Cold War espionage movies I was so fond of.

If I chose the latter, it would go something like this: Karo would not know it, but she would be working for me even though she'd be thinking she was working for Prostitute and only pretending to work for me, and I in turn would be feeding her bogus and viral information to mislead them. The absolute best part of the whole double agent thing was she'd be earning her salary—the bitch—for being my spy without knowing it. I still did not know what her financial arrangements were with the enemy turd faction.

This latter choice sounded super sexy on paper (in my head), but I was not sure how pragmatic it would be in the new era since I was skeptical about leaving Karolina alone in the store. Why I should worry about this was complicated by the fact that she was synonymous with Eclectic Emporium and helped invent it in its present form.

On the other hand, if I fired her, what would everyone think? I did not want to let on that I knew about her duplicity, therefore I could not use that as a reason to cut her loose. It was one thing for her to quit, it was quite another thing to toss her out on the street. And if I tossed her, would Prostitute publicly take her on or cut her loose, too?

My real concern in all this was Eclectic Emporium. I was fearful it would transform into a giant prop or a highway billboard while I chased after the bigger Prostitute prize. It was essential that I hold on to those customers who remained loyal, many of whom were still on board because of Karolina. That took precedence over everything else. Ultimately, I decided not to do anything (which was something), nor reveal anything. There's an old adage: If you don't know what to do, don't do anything. I hoped the right answer would present itself in due time.

*

Karolina's departure, emotionally if not physically, probably had a lot to do with my new fascination with Ponderosa, a woman who possessed quite a few admirable qualities of her own, such as discipline, patience, and ambition. She also knew the Tylers well, or their insanity, and could provide some much-needed feminine camaraderie, which I so dearly missed.

And how sick was that? I erase her abundantly rich boyfriend right before she was going to cash in, effectively destroying her dreams, and then I contemplate seducing her and converting her to my side for my own selfish means. What kind of Shakespearean rogue was I turning into, anyway? This pang of self-loathing was the only thing that prevented me from calling her at the ranch and inviting myself to Stan's funeral just so I could see her again. Instead, I sent her a sympathy card that included three of my phone numbers and a pitifully-overstated offer to be of assistance should she need anything during these trying times.

Following the public acknowledgment of Hindenburg 2, my next move was to go back to the drawing board and see where my other qualified siblings stood regarding their newly acquired stake in Prostitute. From my experience, none of the ones I met would be shy about their good fortune and Stan's tragic reversal and might be willing to negotiate with me if they felt it was to their advantage. Again, they had just acquired an unexpected windfall, and unlike their claim to Isabella's portion of the Tyler estate (Megan not included), Ben's inheritance would be forthcoming following probate and not subject to conditional trusts. Their new cut of Prostitute would be about 5 percent each, a smaller percentage than Stan's hefty 15 percent, and that, I hoped, would make them more flexible.

With regards to the cowardly Joseph, I had a specific plan in mind about how I would approach him. With Jessica, I would rely on my friendship to cushion the solicitation. But Megan, the rehab queen, and the only Tyler whom I had not yet met, was going to be a problem. She would also be attending Stan's funeral, whereas I was reasonably certain that neither of the Euro-based half siblings would be doing so (unless, in Joseph's case, it was to urinate on the casket).

Hence I would wait on Megan but go forward with Jessica and Joseph, Jessica first. I called the Basque restaurant in Spain where Jessica worked and using my broken Spanish managed to get her on the line. She was not the least bit surprised to hear my voice, and I instantly became sensitive to the possibility that she knew me better than I knew myself. Back in the innocent pre-Hindenburg 2 days, when I was still under the impression I was an honest man seeking that which was legitimately mine, she suspected me of cunning avarice. Maybe she was right after all, and I had just not been tested at that point. In Wyoming, I was tested, and I responded as forcefully as one can respond—like an electric current.

"You don't waste much time, do you?" she said thoughtfully.

"Why should I?" I responded, trying to act casual.

"You're right. Let's not waste time," she dictated. "I understand I'll get a 5 percent stake in Prostitute? Is that why you're calling?"

"Yes. I'd like us to team up to oppose Hank, like your mother and I were going to do."

"That's fine."

"I'm going to contact Joseph, too. Do you have any objection to that?"

"No. Did you ever talk to Stan?"

"Yes. I went out there to see him."

"I didn't know that."

"About three weeks before he died."

"And what happened?"

"He blew me off."

There was a thoughtful pause, and then, "That sounds like him."

"Are you coming back to the States, soon?"

There was another much more thoughtful pause.

"Not unless I absolutely have to" she replied, and then left with me with a quick, "Got to get back."

I hung up the phone. I felt uneasy about that exchange but did my best to shake the feeling.

I called Stu and asked him if he could send a letter to Joseph's attorney stating my intention to sue Joseph for his physical attack on me at his mother's funeral reception. I'd be willing to try to settle privately first, but if that didn't work, I was going ahead with the lawsuit. I also asked him if a civil suit could affect probate and if it was possible to put a lien on Joseph's inheritance based on the outcome of a pending court case.

"I'm not sure how that would work," he said, "but I can find out."

"Thanks."

"Why did you change your mind?"

"Hank is starting to scare me," I replied. "I need to do everything

I can."

That was true, Hank did scare me, but the real reason was that I never imagined—at that earlier time—that Stan would be dead (I know, I killed him) and Joseph and the others would pick up the slack.

"We'll keep each other posted," he said and hung up.

The next few weeks were spent on the offensive. I had gained an advantage in this post-Hindenburg 2 era and I was going to capitalize as best I could. I sent a wonderful letter (brought tears to my eyes) to Hank in Los Angeles reminding him that I would be acquiring substantial ownership in Prostitute LLC and we should get together because I had some ideas that could help "us" in the downloading age. This little business rendezvous could happen the next time he was in Detroit, implying he could come to me and not vice versa. I was positive this correspondence would pop a few blood vessels in his thick head, and it was indirect payback for his corruption of Karolina, if in fact he did approach her personally and was in contact with her. I still did not know the details of that corruption.

On the local front, I threw another freebie party using freebie cash and went all out. I did not gain any business or win back any clients, but that was not the point. The point was to flex my muscles so Prostitute Detroit would take notice and report it to Hank. At the very least, I knew he would get a briefing from Karolina. In preparation, I took care of the details myself and included Karo as a conduit and not as a creator.

I kept saying: "Don't worry, I got it covered" and "You go do whatever you have to do," like I was trying to be a nice guy and was oblivious to our changed reality. "I guess I'll just keep going for it now," I remember saying a couple of times, as if Stan's recent death was nothing more than a lucky break. This kept her at a confused distance. She was, in my view, haunted by her flawed decision to switch sides, and could not break free. Nonetheless, this did not stop her from continuing to ask questions about the Tyler inheritance and Prostitute Records. I reciprocated with information that was common knowledge, such as the state of California would now step in and distribute Ben's half of the Tyler estate, and Stan's share of

Prostitute would be divided among Jessica, Joseph, and Megan, but probably not the disinherited Josh. Obvious stuff.

She specifically asked about Jessica, and I told her I was confident Jessica and I could work things out but provided no details. I wanted Hank to think that. I kept quiet about my plan to prompt Joseph to negotiate but revealed I was told he might be willing to listen. I didn't mention Megan because she never asked.

About two weeks after Stan's funeral, I was surprised and thrilled to receive a phone call from Ponderosa, although it quickly turned into a clumsy conversation. I sensed she was questioning her intentions—not so much out of loyalty to Stan but because (and I'm fishing here) her instincts were whispering caution. Eventually, she let me know that she was flying to Chicago to visit her parents for Thanksgiving. Her parents lived in Evanston, a suburb just north of the city. I took the bait and arranged for us to meet for lunch that Friday, the day after Thanksgiving, at *The Four Olives* in Lincoln Park, a restaurant I became familiar with when I was planning to open the Chicago Eclectic music store.

"Isn't that a little out of your way?" she asked.

"For me, Chicago is down the street."

"Okay, then. How about two o'clock?"

That Friday morning, I called Karolina at her home and informed her she should not plan to leave the store that day because I wouldn't be in. "When will you be back?" she asked, not wasting a beat. I told her, "later in the day," knowing well it probably wouldn't be until the following morning. I didn't want to think about the possibility of Jam slithering over to my sacred Emporium supplied with Frappuccinos for a cozy chat. She could go over there but I didn't want him at my place. I even toyed with the idea of installing hidden security cameras, but I didn't want to waste good fake money. I still had a long way to go before the real payday.

As planned, I took a commuter flight to Chicago and had lunch with Ponderosa. Despite all that had gone down since we last met, we had become slight friends in Wyoming and that was what I was trying to rekindle. I enjoyed our meals and walks around the ranch. We also shared an understanding concerning the difficulty of her former partner and my former half-brother—although that was all unspoken. "How are you holding up?" I asked, legitimately interested.

"Getting better," she said.

I noticed she no longer wore her engagement ring, a good sign. "Are you going to stay on the ranch?" I queried, curious about that arrangement.

"Yes. The ranch is mine. Stan willed it to me."

"That's good," I replied, privately guessing how much more he would have been worth had he lived another couple of months.

"It's still not fully paid off, but it's mine."

"It's beautiful out there," I said, now trying to veer away from property and finances.

"So how are you doing, Nic?" she asked with a tiny bit more energy.

"About the same, I guess."

"Now that Stan is dead, it should be easier to consolidate your position at Prostitute Records. Shouldn't it?"

This directness I did not expect. And so soon in our conversation. Once again, I was on the defensive. Jessica made me feel this way when I talked to her over the phone. I felt it even more now, with Ponderosa staring right into my eyes. The trick was not to back down. Exhibit no hesitation.

"Yes, it is," I answered confidently. "I talked to Jessica about it, and she's going to support me, and I'm planning to sue Joseph for attacking me at Isabella's house to force him to negotiate."

"That's smart."

"Josh, I don't think I have to worry about because he's been disinherited by his father. According to my lawyer, it's going to stick. I haven't yet approached Megan. I'm not looking forward to that. But I will."

I was expecting a response, but I didn't get one. She was thinking—really thinking. She reminded me of a laptop, how you have to sometimes wait until the information is processed before completing the task. Ponderosa, again, was processing...

"Is Ponderosa your real name?" I asked, interrupting.

"No."

"Do you mind telling me what it is?"

"Heather. I changed it in college."

"Why?"

"Because Heather is so common."

"And you've never felt common?"

"Most of the time, I don't feel common. No."

"Me neither."

She swallowed more wine, processed more. "You're more common than Stan was," she said. "At least I think you are. Are you?"

I truthfully did not know how to answer that question. How common is a murderer? And how do I compare that with irascible Stan Tyler?

"Well, are you?" she persisted.

"I hope so," I replied, not knowing what else to say.

After lunch, we took a walk in Lincoln Park. The lake was to the east, always to the east, and a brisk north wind blew directly in our faces. Swirling all around were tiny cyclones of foliage and soil. We walked mostly in silence. There was tension between us and it seemed to be getting worse with each step. I had no idea why I thought it would be so easy to be with her. I suppose I underestimated her, or I was not the closet sociopath I gave myself credit for being.

Our situation as it related to me and my lawlessness was becoming, as usual, complicated. The more resistance she presented, the more I liked and respected her. I killed Stan and was not bothered by it, but strangely, my sympathy for Ponderosa was genuine, empathetic, and growing. I felt bad for her. I felt bad for her great loss, both the financial and the physical. I understood what it was like to lose someone close who could have changed my life. I also believed we had much in common. This is not to imply that she was murderous like me—she was not—but she was capable of extremity, such as conquering Stan, an incongruous and impossible person. Yet, unlike my half siblings, she understood balance and poise.

"What are you going to do now?" I asked.

"I'll go back to real estate. I have an office here in Chicago."

"Ever think Detroit will bounce back?"

"I've never been to Detroit."

"A lot of people haven't."

"I guess not."

More silence, and then, from me, "So you'll hold on to the ranch for the time being?"

"Yes, I'll keep the ranch," she said almost impatiently. It was becoming more and more awkward.

"I'm sorry if I seem like I'm prying," I said. "I'm interested in you."

She ignored my excuse. She had something else on her mind, and I was now going to hear it. Again, I was caught off guard, and I think this was the reason she wanted to see me:

"I have to share something with you, Nic," she said in a slightly different tone of voice, softer, yet no less direct and slightly more intense.

"Yes?"

She stopped walking, as did I. "That morning when you left the ranch, you looked up into the sky and saw Stan in his balloon, and I don't think I've ever seen anyone's eyes change like yours did."

"Change? Like how?"

"Color."

"Color? Really?"

"Really. They changed color, from blue like they are now to a silvery gray. You were experiencing something extraordinary, and it was showing on your face. Watching you at that moment reminded me of those people you see on TV who have religious experiences with evangelical preachers. You were transfixed. I don't know how else to describe it."

"Really?" I said again.

"Yes, really, Nic, really. Maybe you don't remember the moment?"

"No, no, I remember it. How can I forget it? It was the first time I saw a balloon in flight, you know, for real. It was exciting. I told you I wanted to go up."

"Yes, I remember," she said firmly.

This was followed by another long silence as my internal siren began to scream. She was on to something here. This was not my imagination. I was not being paranoid.

"You know," she continued with the same soft intensity, the same pursuit, "that was the last time I saw Stan in his balloon, too. When you saw him. That time. The next morning, he went to Houston for business about his basketball team. He stayed almost three weeks to work out most of the details. When he came back, the first thing he did was go up in his balloon, and he died. I heard the explosion from the house. When I heard it, I knew it was him."

She paused, perhaps waiting for a reaction. She got none. We both stayed quiet, stationary, still staring at each other, the bitter Lake Michigan air blowing in our faces. I don't even remember blinking. From a distance we could have been mistaken for statues.

During these moments, I tried convincing myself there was a possibility that she was not implying anything malicious or incriminating and was simply recounting a sequence of events she had remembered leading up to Stan's death; a sequence that was peculiar to her and that began with my ocular transformation.

But I didn't convince myself. Ponderosa was a deceptively deep thinker, and she obviously had done some serious thinking about Stan's last balloon ride. My only recourse, again, was to be bold, super bold, for I knew of no other way, and I broke the poisoning silence.

"Did the police ever tell you what happened up there?" I asked. "Why the balloon exploded? I heard they think it was a faulty helium tank. That's what I read."

I purposely said "helium" instead of "propane."

"Propane," she replied.

"Oh, okay, propane tank."

"Yes, something happened with the tank," she said mundanely, that Teutonic constitution revealing itself again.

"Sometimes people make mistakes," I said, giving the impression I was either being insolent or trying to be helpful, but really coming off as irritating and painfully obvious, which is what I was striving for. When I receive obtuse advice and I'm deeply troubled by something, it drives me crazy, but I never doubt the sincerity of the giver.

"He never made one before," she snipped.

"I'm sorry it doesn't make sense to you, Ponderosa," I continued. "How anxious was he to get back in the balloon after being away for three weeks? Maybe he wasn't paying as much attention as he should have?"

She did not answer, but I could tell she had already considered that. He had to have been anxious. It was his favorite thing to do besides acting like a jerk.

"Do you want to get a cappuccino?" I asked.

"Cappuccino?"

"Yeah, cappuccino. It's getting a little windy."

She stood there, again thinking—about what, I didn't know anymore.

"We can get one at the museum," I said.

"The Art Institute?"

"Yes. We can walk. It would only take about twenty minutes or so."

"I know where it is. I grew up here."

"Sorry, Evanston, I forgot for a second."

She smiled, barely, which could have meant she was impressed by my performance or the museum was a wonderful idea or anything in between, but the bottom line was the mood had shifted, the clouds had parted, the poetic investigative searching had ceased, and we were on our way to Michigan Avenue.

At the Art Institute, we nursed cinnamon-flavored cappuccinos and marveled over the visiting Sumerian exhibit, a brilliant display, just as the Sumerians and their ziggurats were brilliant when they ushered in civilization.

We then checked out some of the regular sights from the permanent collection, such as Matisse's *Bathers by a River* (her favorite) and Munch's *The Girl by the Window* (my favorite) and quite a few others with which both of us were familiar having visited this museum all our lives.

After about three hours, we took a cab to Milwaukee Avenue and drank beer at a crusty old tavern discolored from a century or so of smoke, despite the many coats of cheap paint. And I would say from this point on whatever subliminal challenges existed between us that would momentarily pop up stayed below the surface where they belonged.

At the bar, her mood improved even more. Her demeanor was open and alive, her smile more revealing and beautiful than when I first saw her in Wyoming. She knew I wanted her, and of course

I did, but she was nice enough to clear that up by saying she had come to Chicago to spend time with her parents and they would be disappointed if she didn't do exactly that. They were worried about her, with her fiancée dying so suddenly and tragically (it was not clear they actually liked him, but likability has never been a Tyler strong point or a reason not to have a relationship with one of them).

When it was time to go, she expressed concern about my getting back to Detroit, just as she had done in Wyoming the last time I was with her and before I looked up in the sky and saw my future. I told her I still had time to catch an evening shuttle flight from Midway Airport to Detroit.

"Are you sure?" she asked. "I don't want you spending your night in some lonely hotel."

I interpreted that remark as pure flirtation and the first real episode of the whole day.

"I'll be fine tonight," I told her. "I just hope we can do more of this, soon."

"Why don't you come to Wyoming again—when you have time?"

"Okay."

"Call me."

"I will."

"Oh," she said, "I might have some ideas about Megan. How to approach her."

"That would be great. Thanks."

We hugged warmly and got into our separate cabs. She went up to Evanston, and I rode south to Midway. Once again, things had turned out well despite the steep, winding, and at times heart-pounding roller-coaster journey.

Overall, though, I experienced a reasonable amount of guilt throughout the day, which, as mentioned, meant to me that I was still human, still capable of knowing what I had done was reprehensible, even though I felt nothing toward Stan Tyler. According to Jesus and other great philosophers, guilt is not meant to serve as reflective self-punishment; rather, it is a strictly human mechanism to remind one to not sin again. "Go and sin no more," the great one said.

Unfortunately, in my case, this didn't really apply. Yes, I should not continue to kill people, siblings, whomever, but my circumstances were such that I was actively profiting from my sin and would continue to do so for some time, perhaps for the rest of my life. And if all went well, or rather my way, there would be no retribution, no acknowledgment of wrongdoing, no redemption—just a march forward into the glorious empire with fresh blood on my hands, and my own brother's blood at that.

In addition, the grotesque lying would continue, and not just about Stan Tyler, but about everything. I found out that once you start lying, it just keeps expanding exponentially, for it knows no boundaries. For example, there is no such thing as "I'll be honest about everything in my life except about Stan and his fucking balloon." That is pure fluff. The brutal reality turns out to be more like, "Why try to be honest about anything when you're fundamentally dishonest?" Which then segues into "What difference does it make, really?" And of course, the counterfeiting ritual didn't help either—that being another ongoing daily lie that further reinforced the cycle. This, alas, was my life in the post-Hindenburg 2 era, where every single response had become a calculated decision and not an honest reaction.

When I returned to Detroit, Karolina informed me that Stu had called to tell me Joseph Tyler was willing to talk to me about Prostitute.

"The lawsuit threat worked," she said.

At first, I became irritated that she knew about this, and I made a mental note to tell Stu not to discuss any more business with her. But then I realized there was no harm done here because now Hank Tyler knew about it, and this was something he should know.

The next step with Hank was to force him to negotiate with me as an equal and nothing less, something his ego would not permit him to do thus far. Soon that would change, though, just as everything else was beginning to change. Despite the moral and emotional setbacks, and my new and less honorable way of life, I was now empowered and emboldened as never before.

23
EUROPEAN TOUR

Joseph Tyler's terms to begin negotiating his pending stake in Prostitute LLC were that I fly to Newcastle, England, officially known as Newcastle upon Tyne, and talk with him face to face. It was a strange request because he despised every cell of me, and the last time I saw him he kicked me in the face. I thought any exchange between us should be through lawyers or proxy but agreed, nonetheless, providing a third party be present at the meeting and it take place in a public setting.

I also instructed Stu, my proxy, to tell Joseph's lawyer that I planned to alert the Newcastle police of my arrival and the nature of my visit should I somehow disappear or be found at the bottom of the River Tyne with a log shoved up my ass.

There was much irony in all this, too, because I was, in fact, a real killer—a calculated first-degree fratricidal murderer, to boot—and this potential meeting was a direct result of that execution. But perhaps Joseph hadn't truly been tested yet, like I hadn't been until Wyoming.

In truth, though, I was less concerned about my safety than I was about Joseph complicating matters by making a remarkably stupid move. His sister, Jessica, made it wonderfully clear that he was scientific but foolhardy—a man skilled in grasping facts and minutia but not too dependable when it comes to life, laws, and society. I agreed with her assessment.

Stu was less concerned about Joseph than he was about my finances and how I was going to manage another trip, this time to pricey Europe. He knew (as did Hank) about my dwindling sales figures and offered me a personal loan. I refused, of course, reminding him of how much he was already helping by acting as my attorney without pay. But just to be on the safe side, I lied and told him my bank credit had been extended.

I also used the opportunity to clue him in about Karolina and her unfortunate defection and requested that he not discuss any further business with her. He was stunned and almost as hurt as I was by this revelation. Karo had a way of growing on people, Stu was not immune to this. I also requested he continue to be amicable toward her because I did not want her to suspect I was on to her. So in effect, with Karolina, I was choosing the double-agent strategy— yet another thing to worry about along with counterfeiting and murder.

Before flying to Newcastle, I made arrangements with a local travel agency for my plane tickets and paid using a money order I purchased from an inner-city discount department store. I utilized the retail detour strategy because I did not want to draw attention by handing over forty or fifty $20 bills to a travel agency or airline. I did it for domestic flights but the inter-continental flights were much more expensive.

This "volume" issue (as I referred to it to myself, since I could share it with no one else) was a problem from the day I dug up Sledge's treasure gift in the basement. Fortunately, I discovered a way out once I was overseas, and any idiot could have done it sooner.

In England, and elsewhere in Europe, foreigners routinely and ubiquitously change currencies into pounds and euros. As I was doing the same, I realized I could convert it all back into authentic U.S. Treasury paper once I returned to the States. From there, I could deposit the good money in the bank and start writing fat checks again.

This important discovery of turning phony dollars into real dollars by crossing borders was, by itself, enough to make my Euro-visit worthwhile.

*

Joseph and I were scheduled to meet in a pub in the Pink Triangle section of Newcastle near the Centre for Life bio-technology village. This village was advertised as the U.K.'s first attempt at creating a science city. Joseph's privately funded research firm was associated with the Centre for Life, as were most of the other biotech companies in the area. The focus of their activities was stem-cell research, cell morphology, and cloning.

As an oblique layman (early in life, I developed an antipathy for stale-smelling laboratories, microscopic germs, and the mutilation and torture of little, defenseless animals), I cared little about any of this science. However, because of the deafening moral debate over stem cells, I did come to understand that there were differences between adult stem cells and embryonic stem cells, and the latter (at the time) had the most potential for scientists in their attempt to generate solutions for disease and extend human life.

Adding to the controversial embryonic dabbling was the corresponding controversial cloning part, which I interpreted as a necessary step in the painstaking sequence, because any tissue generated by these magical, chameleon super-cells must be organically compatible with the donor patient. Therefore, cloning, or duplication, would not foster bodily rejection by the immune system. And this is what a lot of these science village people were doing—that and going to pubs.

Once in Newcastle, I followed through with my public declaration and stopped at the local constable office to inform the two gentlemanly Bobbies of the purpose of my visit. I was careful to include the details of Joseph's past violent behavior and my potential lawsuit. They in turn went through the motions of recording my information, itinerary, phone numbers, and so forth for my sake and then suggested, in their thick Geordie accents, that I should visit Hadrian's Wall—Newcastle being an old Roman domain way before the Anglo-Saxons took it over and built a "new castle."

From the police station, I walked to the designated pub on Osborne Road and met with Joseph, who was there waiting with one of his co-workers, another young scientist named Sascha.

Sascha was stocky and horizontally proportioned but appeared to have the same unattractive hygiene issues that my lean, elongated half sibling had, as well as the same type of warped ingenuity and focus. As the conversation progressed, it was apparent Sascha was officially the third party I requested and the two of them had been in the pub for some time prior to my scheduled arrival.

"So what are you going to give me for my parcel of Prostitute Records?" Joseph demanded.

"Whatever it's worth. Market value."

"The placenta will double that out of his own pocket," he said. "His slaves keep calling me. "The placenta was a reference to Hank, the slaves, Hank's employees.

"I can't do that," I said.

"You can't?" he mused.

"No, and you would have to wait until after probate for payment."

"Well, mister fucking music man from Detroit, you're not offering me too much here, and I can use the money bloody well now. I won't need it so much after probate. Will I?"

"You know I can bloody well see the resemblance," Sascha interrupted, seemingly fascinated by my appearance.

"Shut up," Joseph commanded.

Sascha burst into laughter, his bad breath breaking over me like a blast of Canadian wind over a defenseless, naked plateau. It was so foul I almost gagged. But it must have jolted my mind, because I then proposed the following to Joseph:

"How about if you give me a notarized letter stating your intent to turn over to me your pending stake in Prostitute. I can bring it to the bank along with everything else I have and see if they'll give me a loan, and if so, I'll pay you right away. There's no guarantee, but I can try."

Joseph and Sascha exchanged glances. "That's not good enough," Joseph said.

I didn't believe him. Or rather, I believed this offer was not ideal for him, but he would take it. He obviously had his reasons for wanting to deal with me and not Hank, and given their personalities and lifelong association, I could not fathom the level of animosity they had for each other. And just in case I was wrong, I felt the time was now right to remind him of the lawsuit.

"I've been very open about where I stand with all this, Joseph," I said. "I don't want to sue you and slow everything down, but I will, and you know I will."

Another drinking pause, then, "You don't scare me, but okay. And you better be fast about it. That letter will be contingent on the loan."

"Fair enough," I replied. "I'll call my lawyer. As soon as he gets the letter, I'll have an answer and possibly payment for you within a month."

Sascha once again interjected, unable to control himself. "You know you do, you know?"

"Do what?" I asked.

"Look like your dad."

"Shut up, you idiot!" Joseph blared.

"Oh, bugger off. He's just as much as you are, and you know it, you heinous liar."

"Fuck you."

"Fuck you."

"Fuck you."

"Fuck you."

This went on, the fuck yous, accompanied by spraying, toxic mouth liquid and garbage-dump breath, and it was satisfying to see them going at one another, but I was curious. "What are you guys working on at your firm?" I asked, jumping into the condemned air space.

A big smile materialized on Sascha's face. "The future. What else?" he replied.

"And what is the future?" I asked.

There was a naughty pause between the two, and then Sascha screamed loud enough for the entire pub to hear: "I'm looking at it!"

And they both burst into laughter, riotous laughter, with Joseph almost falling off his chair. Finally, they calmed just in time to save me from asphyxiation.

Sascha addressed me again: "You're not such a bad chap after all, despite what this moron says."

"Thanks," I said, desperately wanting to know what they were up to. "Is that why you need money, for your work?"

This question brought on a little sobriety.

"We have certain expenses sometimes. Unexpected expenses," Sascha answered cautiously. Joseph became uncomfortable.

"Okay, we've had our meeting," he said. "You got a bloody month." And then, in what appeared to be a remarkably generous gesture on his part, he added: "Thanks for coming."

This also meant for me to leave, but it still showed a sign of civility, however small. I obediently stood up, said my good-byes, and left the pub. I knew Sascha, for one, was sad to see me go.

Later, after making five stops at various currency exchange venues around town, building up my pound reserve, I took a bus to see the Roman wall as the two nice constables suggested. I was impressed, especially by the enormous size of the bricks and the way they were piled directly on top of one another without the use of diesel engines, cranes and tractors.

I decided to walk along the weathered path adjacent to the wall, through the English countryside. The sky was heavy and thickly overcast. The air raw, fresh, and pouring in from the sea. Scotland was to the north, and that was what the wall was for, to keep the ancient Scots in their place. I thought of *Wuthering Heights*, the faded black-and-white Laurence Olivier movie that gave me my first visual impressions of ye olde England.

As I tracked deeper into the rolling pastures, I fantasized I was being cleansed by these fair meadows and the more I walked, the purer I became, almost as if I were going backward in time. Yet I knew in my heart it was all fancy, because I would always be stained, tattooed by the devil for committing fratricide (and still no genuine remorse for Stan). It was foolish to hope for absolution. I was cursed and these settings and these moments a tease and nothing more.

I still didn't understand why Stan had to be such an insanely difficult and mean creature. His death was gratuitous. Had he not been so cruel, I would not have been inspired to kill him, even if he denied me. I was sure of that. The inspiration would not have come, and I would have figured something else out.

And what was the other one up to, Joseph—he and his malodorous but lively co-worker? Surely they had to be in some kind of ugly, unspeakable quandary to summon me, the scourge;

although I was satisfied with the result. I knew beforehand he would not simply hand over his share of Prostitute just because I threatened him with a lawsuit. He wanted fair compensation, and that was reasonable. But they were so queer, both of them, and I just as queer and secretive, only more presentable to the outside world.

When I returned to the hotel, I called Jessica in Spain. I wanted to tell her about what had transpired in Newcastle and to see if I could obtain a letter from her stating her willingness to partner with me. Legally, I would not be assuming or purchasing her shares, but combining our pending equity. That would equate to collective control of 21 percent of Prostitute LLC, still a little behind Hank, but a significant portion nonetheless.

"Are you in Newcastle now?" she asked, the noise of the restaurant in the background drowning her out.

"Yes. I just had the meeting with Joseph."

"Any new head injuries?"

"No, not this time, fortunately."

"Why don't you cross the Channel and come to Spain and tell me all about it then?"

"Sure. I'll cross the Channel. How do I go about that?"

"Last I heard, you get on a boat. When you hit land again, take a train through France to Spain. Unless you want to fly. Call me when you're close." She gave me another phone number and got off.

Sadly, this was my first trip overseas, and I was not in a touristy state of mind. Being in England, I naturally wanted to visit London and maybe detour to the Irish island, and then from there maybe Greenland or Iceland. But I decided to save the North Atlantic sightseeing for another time when I was more at peace mentally, and instead caught the Newcastle ferry and crossed the bumpy North Sea to a Dutch seaport, where I hopped a commuter train to the old Central Railroad Station in Amsterdam. From there, I switched trains without leaving the station and journeyed directly to Paris. Once in Paris, I needed to rest and secured a hotel not too far from La Gare Montparnasse.

The reason I purposely chose to ignore Amsterdam was because all my life I heard about the hashish cafes and the whore boutiques. I did not want to be tempted, especially with a growing wad of real cash bulging out of my pants along with my swelling cock. I easily might never have gotten out of there. I figured it was safer to rest in Paris, and then take an overnight TVA train to San Sebastian. I must stay on track, I kept telling myself. I must take care of business first.

This plan failed miserably, because I made the mistake of stepping outdoors in Paris and became lightheaded from the sights. Before I knew it, one thing led to the other (as always), and I wound up hiking around the city for three straight days, literally mesmerized by the tapestry of architecture and neighborhoods, and all the time wondering how a ridiculously ill-tempered people such as the French could create such an urban masterpiece.

I started out on the iron footbridges of Canal St. Martin in the 10th arrondissement and, drawn by the lure of the nineteenth-century architecture, ventured aimlessly north to Montmartre and climbed all the way up to Sacre-Coeur, where I stayed put for four hours just staring out at the city. Satisfied, I climbed down again and kept walking the streets until I reached an old cemetery somewhere in the 20th arrondissement and picnicked by Oscar Wilde's grave and bonded with what seemed like hundreds of people without uttering a word.

It was a mystical experience, and I knew it would not be easy to leave this metropolis. That proved to be the case when two days later I was still wandering the Left Bank—and this was without once entering a building, with the exception of my three random and tiny hotel rooms (one in the Champs Elysees area, one near the Paris Opera, and last one in the Latin Quarter).

I can't remember when, or on what day, but at some point it became more than obvious to me that it would take years to leave this city if I started going inside the cathedrals and museums and all the rest; so for about eighty hours I stayed outside, walking, soaking it up, eating all my meals at sidewalk cafes, and getting little or no rest. When I finally returned to La Gare Montparnasse, I was fortunate to pass out on the correct train heading to the Basque region of Northern Spain and awoke in San Sebastian some time the next day.

*

San Sebastian was another visual feast, but at least I had a plan to distract me from the alluring natural beauty, and that was to meet with Jessica and formally consolidate our interest in Prostitute LLC, something I had not thought about once while sleepwalking around Paris. None of that mattered in Paris. Paris was a drug.

I called Jessica from the train station and shortly later met her at her bistro, Restaurante Sabino, located off Plaza de la Trinidad in the middle of Parte Vieja.

I was nervous about seeing her again. As mentioned, she was dark, unpredictable and understood well the poison in my blood—much better than I did. Overall, at this point, I'd say our relationship above and below the surface was complex and cautious, with me being the needier of the two. Yet, as the inheritance saga continued to play out, she began to see the value of having me as an ally, and that may have contributed to her open invitation to Spain.

When I entered, she was sitting at one of the back tables in the front barroom wearing her white chef's uniform, drinking espresso, and making changes to the menu. She appeared to be more Spanish than the Spaniards with her long, black, Mediterranean hair, the dark complexion she inherited from her mother, and her fluency in Spanish. She also spoke Euskara, the Basque dialect that has no known origin.

When I approached her and our eyes met, I was not sure if I should hug her or not. My instincts told me to do so—she was my sister, after all—and I wanted to, but I restrained myself, still not quite understanding our tentative relationship.

"Sit down," she said.

And that took care of that. She spoke English to me and Spanish and Euskara to everyone else. She ordered me an espresso and explained she was creating menus and she'd be busy most of the day and evening but later tonight we could talk. She also suggested a couple of hotels where I could stay.

"My place is small," she added.

"That's fine. The one by the beach sounds good."

"Careful, you might wind up never leaving."

"There are still a couple of things I have to take care of back in Detroit."

"Of course, Detroit," she uttered with disbelief. "How could I forget?"

Later that day, in the cool off-season weather, I fell asleep on La Concha beach, allowing my body to recuperate from my Paris marathon. Upon awaking, I returned to the hotel, bathed, and joined hordes of San Sebastians as they barhopped through the old section, wolfing down tapas or pinoxs and consuming large amounts of alcohol. Apparently, this was a daily ritual, and I fit right in and enjoyed meeting lots of pretty girls to whom American basketball was a popular subject. I also got drunk rather quickly.

At some much later point, I made a pit stop at Restaurante Sabino to check in with Jessica, who was almost finished and insisted I eat more, serving me her walnut soup and baked crab, which was excellent, although my taste buds were pretty much gone.

Afterward, the two of us walked to a bar near the Urumea River, a tiny place with blue-flecked walls and soft lighting, and I drank more. Jessica knew the bartender and all the men in the room, and they were very friendly toward her. She introduced me as Nic but not as her brother, which disappointed me. Yet, amazingly, this did not stop me from becoming slightly protective in a brotherly sense, which was nothing less than absurd for a myriad of reasons (the biggest one: I had the distinct feeling she had already slept with everyone in the room). I'm sure this sentiment, however anachronistic, had something to do with my not ever having that kind of an experience growing up in Detroit.

After the introductions, we were left alone and I finally tried to talk business. "Joseph is willing to sell me his shares, " I said. "He needs money right away."

"So buy it," she snapped back.

"I plan to, but I need to get a loan to do it."

"Then get one."

She then barked at Gustavo, the bartender, to serve us vodka. She was done with wine for the night, and I guess I was, too. No longer distracted by running a restaurant, the real Jessica was emerging—the one who briefly showed up on her mother's patio in California.

"Why do you think Joseph needs the money so bad?" I asked.

"Because he's an idiot. I thought that should be clear to you by now," she said, looking me over with disdain. "What does he need to do before you get that—shoot you through the neck with a fucking harpoon?"

"I was just curious," I said, feeling my anger rise from the insult and not being able to arrest it with so much alcohol inside of me. "Jessica, why are you so angry?" I asked.

"I'm not fucking angry."

"Yes you fucking are."

"Then that's who I am. At least it's something. Who the fuck are you?"

"I'm your fucking brother. Remember?"

She looked at me. I looked back at her. It was a peculiar, maudlin, drunken moment. I felt it profoundly.

"You're more like my father," she said quietly.

"Well then stop cursing at me. You didn't curse at him?"

"Who?"

"Ben, your father. Who are we talking about?"

"He was never around to curse at."

"Okay, then," I said, not knowing why, except that I was ready to say something more and then became confused and that was all that came out of my mouth.

"You're like the other one, too," she mumbled.

"Who?"

"Who? Uncle Hank, who else?"

"I look like him?"

"Yes, but that's not what I mean."

And then I heard the words, "Then what the fuck do you mean?" come screaming out of my mouth. Hank was the enemy. Hank was what was wrong with the planet. Hank was famine, disease, nuclear warfare, and politics as usual in the midst of polar meltdowns. Hank was why I was doing what I was doing. In my mind, Hank was also the reason Stan was dead. He had just as much to do with it as Stan did.

"Forget it. I could be wrong," she said weakly, as if she no longer cared one way or the other. "But I don't think so. Come on, let's take a walk, I spend too much time in this dump."

She swallowed her vodka, stood up, and walked out to the street. I reluctantly followed, not knowing what else to do and worried about my drunkenness; worried I would not have the necessary patience for this explosive and reckless young woman.

I caught up with her, and we walked away from the river to Calle de Aldamar and stopped at another bar, this one lively with music and dancing, a real Euro party scene: smoking, drinking, snorting, kissing...

"Where's your boyfriend?" I asked her as we settled into the bar.

"I don't have one."

"Why not?"

"Good God, shut-up. Come on, let's dance before I croak."

She pulled me through the flesh to get to the floor, and we started dancing to pounding 1980s techno, the Juan Atkins, Kevin Saunderson stuff that was born in Detroit when I was in grade school and which the ongoing eurotrash apparently couldn't get enough of. And of course Jessica could dance, her long black hair flailing over her moist, Latin skin, reminding me a lot of Karolina, although I tried not to think about that.

Instead, I tried focusing on my pitiful coordination and how I could not dance to save my ass. Eventually, I stumbled off the floor to find refuge and bullied my way to the bar for more booze. About 20 minutes later, she found me. For the first time that night, I saw a slight smile on her face.

"What happened to Fred Astaire?" she asked.

"He has two left feet."

I ordered more vodka for both of us. "I want to know something," I said.

"What?"

"What the hell is Joseph doing? Why does he need money?"

"He's cloning humans."

"No!"

"Ah, yes!"

"How do you know?"

"Because he's been blabbering about it for the last decade. He can't keep his fat mouth shut."

"His firm is doing it?"

"They do therapeutic cloning. But it's not a big jump from there. He's got his own operation."

"That takes money?"

"I guess. I heard him once say they have problems with the carriers."

"Surrogate mothers?"

"Yeah. They come out oversized. Like the sheep did. It's too weird."

I swallowed more vodka and ordered more. "Shouldn't somebody try to stop him?" I asked.

"Why? It's all going to be legal soon anyway."

"When?"

"When it's safe. Wake up, Detroit. Nobody gives a shit."

She was absolutely right. Who was going to prevent people from immortalizing themselves on this ego-driven, narcissist, capitalist planet? It was inevitable, even if it was dead wrong.

Still, I thought, perhaps I should kill him just the same. By killing Joseph, at least I would have the excuse that it was for the good of mankind, not just my ugly greed, although that would certainly play into it.

"He'll be set once probate is over," I said. "He can fertilize the whole English countryside—create his own fucking planet."

"What about you?"

"What about me?" I retorted, knowing she was going to be mean.

"Oh, come on Mr. Music Mogul."

"What do you care? Bitch."

She paused. My drunkenness was showing.

"Or do you?" I added.

Another big smile crept across her face. She stared me in the eyes. "I like you better when you're mad," she said.

"That's because you're sick. Like your brothers."

"Maybe." She paused, smiling. "It doesn't change it."

"I'm stronger than all of them, you know, Hank, too."

"We'll see about that," she said, and ordered more vodka.

"What are you going to do?"

"I'm opening some restaurants," she said.

"Where?"

"New York and Los Angeles."

"What about Paris? Now there's a fucking city."

"Paris can wait" she replied, still amused by how drunk I was.

More drinks arrived. I reached for mine and slipped off the bar, the glass breaking in my hand, and landed hard on the floor. My head was wounded, too, having scraped the bar top edge on the way down. Both my head and my hand were bleeding, but I felt no pain, just the sensation of warm blood on various parts of my body, dripping.

With the help of a patron, she lifted me up off the floor, positioned me upward against the bar again, like a mop in a kitchen corner, and dipped a napkin in the iced vodka to clean my head wound. I was so numb and obtuse that any stimulation was welcome, even if it should register as pain. Extreme drunkenness is a form of self-mutilation.

She then cleaned my hand and requested a towel from the bartender and bandaged it.

"It looks like it's time to go, strong man," she said.

She grabbed hold of my arm, swung it around her shoulders, and guided me through the maze of sound and smoke into the cool ocean air, which brought on more stimulation. She called over to a cabbie, and the two of them placed me in the back of the cab.

"Tonight, you stay with me," she said.

After arriving and paying the driver, we climbed her stairs and entered her third-floor apartment, the top apartment. I remember the door was unlocked.

Inside were a lot of windows, windows in every direction. I saw the bay through one window and the river through another. I sat on a thick white sofa and felt at home.

This was the first time I had felt at home since my Euro-tour began in the north of England. This was a new experience, too, a sibling taking care of me, looking after me, and that is what she was doing—that and drinking more vodka. She was used to this, I could tell, taking care of drunken people, having drunken people around her, incapacitated.

And then she ripped my heart out: "I've always wanted to fuck my father," she said. "You're the closest I'll ever get to it."

I looked over at her, and she was taking off her dress. Once again, I did not see it coming, and once again, I was out of my league. Only now, I was helpless.

She was gorgeous, too, with large breasts that expanded as they drooped lower; a flat, tight stomach; slender, angular legs that looped into her hips; and perhaps the most confusing feature of all, her resemblance to her good mother from the neck up, a woman with whom I had been infatuated.

Never was anything more tempting and wrong at the same time. But was it really wrong? Why did I always stop and pause at these flimsy roadblocks prior to jumping over and doing whatever evil I was going to do anyway? Who was I kidding? Certainly none of the Tylers, the ones still alive, anyway. And they were dead on about me. I was the only one of them who was a murderer. How much worse can an incestuous murderer be? Why did I keep pretending my life was still on the family farm milking the cows and feeding the chickens? I left the farm when I took that second trip to Wyoming.

But she hurt me; she deeply hurt me, because all I really wanted from her was a sister. That's all I ever wanted with any of them from the very beginning, to be their brother.

Naked, she walked over to me and sat on my lap. She planted her feet on the couch, raising her thighs upward and revealing her vagina in full, as she pressed down on my lap. I knew if I were sober this would not be happening. I could handle this if I possessed just the tinniest bit of sobriety. I could slip away, talk my way out of it, even be forceful if necessary. But I had not the strength for any of it.

"I can't fuck anyone right now, Jessica," I said.

Her body was moist and warm and glistening from the soft lights through the open bay windows. She lowered her mouth into mine and began kissing me. When she stopped, she said, "That's what they all say."

I noticed speckles of wet blood on her forehead from my head wound. She reinserted her tongue deeply while she shifted on my cock, moving ever so slightly, just enough to miraculously arouse me.

"Jessica, I don't want to do this. Please."

"Talk about Dad," she said.

"Jessica, no..."

"He wrote you a letter, right? What did it say? Tell me what the letter said. Tell me what he said to you."

And that was that.

I told her.

24
BACK TO THE RANCH

Once again, I found myself teetering on emotional and spiritual collapse. I had no comeback for this latest bio-obscenity. When I awoke the next morning in Jessica's apartment, I felt suicidal. Jessica had already gone to the restaurant and left me a note to call her. I interpreted her absence as divine reprieve. I flipped the note over and scribbled, "Gone back to America."

I returned to my hotel, collected my belongings, and took the first available airplane to New York City. From there I waited another three hours before securing a connecting flight to Detroit. After arriving at Metro I walked out of the plane into the terminal and stopped in my tracks. I could not, or would not, convince myself to go home or to the shop. I was too morbidly depressed. I did not want to see anyone, especially Karolina. Karo used to mean comfort and family, and now she was the fucking plague. But it wasn't just her, it was my entire world. It had become contaminated. Every aspect of it. So I paused and sat down in the gate area and waited until something better came to mind. It was the most homeless I've ever felt in my entire life.

I was also in need of rest. Institutional-type rest. I had not slept the entire trip back from Europe and got very little real sleep the night before after I passed out from booze, incestuous sex, and self-loathing. And now, after fifteen hours of hung-over flying and airports, to say that I was jet-lagged was to say O.J. Simpson needed counseling. I thought about a dark hotel room with the drapes pulled, but I did not have prescription sleeping pills (the over-the-counter kind never worked for me) and risked not being able to fall asleep. Sleep was the only thing that could stop the emotional hemorrhaging.

It was then that I thought of Ponderosa. Maybe I should call her?

When I met with her in Chicago, she invited me out to the ranch. I knew it was a risky move. Anything remotely Tyler-related was risky at this point. My having killed her fiancée only increased the odds of it resulting in some kind of disaster or potential disaster. Besides, if I had a shred of decency, I would leave the woman alone forever. But I called her anyway because I was weak and in a dark, lonely place.

"Where are you?" she asked softly.

I've always wondered how those you connect with always sense when you're not anchored. When I called, I gave no indication that I was not at home or in my shop or that I was sitting in an airport having just spent the previous week wandering around Europe. All I said was, "This is Nic."

"I'm in the Detroit Metro Airport," I replied.

"What are you doing there?"

"I just got off a plane from Spain."

"Plane from Spain? Is this a joke?"

"No. I was in Europe with Jessica Tyler, and before that Joseph Tyler."

"Are you alright?"

"I'm not sure."

There was no immediate response, then, "Do you want to come out here?"

"I was thinking it might be a good time."

"Why?"

"I don't want to go home."

"Then why did you fly back to Detroit?"

"I don't know."

There was more silence.

"Why don't you come out then," she said. "I'm leaving town on business soon, but you can stay as long as you want."

"Okay."

"Call me again when you know the details. I'll pick you up at the airport."

"Thank you."

I clicked off the phone and felt a sense of relief. I did not have to go home or get a hotel room.

I walked out to the main corridor and over to the proper airline counter to buy a ticket only to discover I had no Yankee cash on me. I had exchanged every phony bill while in Europe.

I detoured to the currency counter and converted all my Euro-dollars into healthy Ben Franklins, a little over $17,000 worth. I then purchased the ticket to Jackson.

I had to switch planes in Denver, but it was not a difficult journey in comparison to what I had been through for the last 24 hours. The only discernible awkward moment I had en route occurred after I had landed in Jackson and noticed that annoying cab driver loitering outside the terminal—the same one who drove me to and from the KO Ranch on my first Wyoming visit.

This obnoxious creature, from his expression, must have registered that he did not see me come in for Stan's funeral but I was now visiting solo Ponderosa not even a month after Stan was planted. I should not have cared, but I did. A little bit. He was a loose end of sorts, although I was not sure how. I remembered treating him with kindness the last time I was trapped inside his cab, but that was because I was under a spell triggered by the sight of Stan's balloon. This time I ignored him, pretending not to see him.

*

Ponderosa did not appear too uncomfortable with my mental state of mind and ragged appearance. I attributed that to her unique disposition and being used to guys like Stan Tyler. I had Tyler blood pumping through my veins, therefore I was given slack. "How are Jessica and Joseph doing?" she asked, as we drove through the snow-covered Wyoming wilderness.

"About the same," I replied, not having the energy or aptitude to honestly answer the question.

"That could mean anything."

"How well do you know them?"

"I met Joseph once at a party at Isabella's house when Ben was in town, and Jessica calls every once in a while. Or she used to."

"How often would Jessica call?"

"She would call for Stan but would wind up talking to me. Sort of like what happened to you. She hasn't called since Stan died. And she didn't come in for the funeral."

"Did you talk to Joseph?"

"No. He never acknowledged me. As I recall, he was too busy yelling at his father when I saw him."

"About money?"

"Yes."

"That hasn't changed. The money part."

"Who was more challenging for you?" she asked. "Joseph or Jessica?"

It was a strange question, I thought, but a good one. It proved that she understood well the Tyler blood. Joseph almost killed me at one point and she knew that, but there was no doubt about the answer. "Jessica," I replied.

Ponderosa looked over at me. I looked back at her. "You're tired," she said. "Why don't you take a nap when we get back?"

When we got "back" to the KO Corral, my third visit, I tried not to recall my historic second visit—under the moonlight with a propane tank strapped to my body in the freezing darkness— and told myself to ignore any of Stan's remaining artifacts. I was depressed enough.

I was also uneasy about where I was going to nap, and I decided I would preempt the confusion by requesting the cabin where I stayed on the first visit. I was not prepared to be with Ponderosa after Jessica. I may have been assuming much more than I should, but I could not take the chance. I was fragile and knew it, and if I did not get good solid sleep, I would chance a breakdown.

"Are you sure you don't want to stay in the house?" she asked.

"I remember sleeping soundly in the cabin," I replied awkwardly, almost as if it were someone other than me talking. Someone I didn't know.

"Okay," she said, curious probably about my motives but in no rush either.

She took my bag, and we walked into the cabin. She turned on the light and the electric heat. There were warm blankets at the foot of the bed. I began to settle in. The awkwardness continued. I felt I owed her an explanation.

"Ponderosa," I said nervously, "if this is weird, I'm sorry. I'll be okay once I rest."

"No worry," she said pleasantly, almost amused, almost as though it wasn't the first time she had heard something like that. "If you get up and it's not too late, come over and have something to eat. The door is unlocked."

"Thank you."

After she left, I undressed, showered, and fell asleep for the first time in over sixty hours. When I awoke in the middle of the night, Jessica was on my mind. I kept seeing blood. Blood on her face, body, dripping on her nipples—my blood, her blood, our blood.

We had sex for over two hours. The whole time, she was grunting about Ben, what he said, what he was like, what he bought for her, the movie stars and rock stars he fucked, the parties, the teenagers, the things she knew. It became abundantly clear why her mother and father did not single her out despite her level head and professional success. I understood why Claire was afraid of her. I understood why I was afraid of her.

I have never had sex like that in my life. Despite my pitiful and immobilizing inebriation, I had multiple orgasms and literally fucked myself into sobriety. I was almost cold stone sober by the time I passed out covered with our fluids.

I dug into my soiled suitcase and put on dirty, wrinkled clothes and walked over to the house. It was the usual dark and freezing in the familiar wee hours of the Wyoming morning. Ponderosa was upstairs sleeping. I entered. I felt my equilibrium returning. I walked into the kitchen and opened the refrigerator. There was a six-pack of Moosehead beer in the back, probably Stan's or left over from his funeral-related festivities. I pulled the six-pack. My throat was dry.

As I stood drinking, I wondered if I could do this—drink Stan's beer in his house—if I had killed him point-blank, say, shot him in the head at close range, instead of sabotaging him from afar. The end result was the same. I was just as guilty. He was just as dead. And yet, it did make a difference that there were no idiosyncratic physical details or extended memory close-ups to second-guess myself and magnify the guilt.

I uncorked a second bottle. I thought about Ponderosa upstairs sleeping, how attractive and desirable she was. She allowed me to come here, and she invited me to sleep in the house. Perhaps she was mine if I wanted her.

I was curious, though, how in tune she was with her instincts regarding my probity. During that memorable walk in Lincoln Park, she was on to me and probably still was (how does one dismiss such intense feelings?). So she was either ignoring her instincts or giving me the benefit of the doubt. Or both. Or perhaps she was adopting a position of which I was not fully aware. I had to remind myself—however ostensibly incongruous—that this woman lived and dealt with Stan Tyler on a daily basis for a much higher purpose: her own. I was the one seeking her out, and she was *allowing* it. Maybe *she* was the one who could have me if she wanted rather than the other way around? Either way, neither way, I did not want the recent San Sebastian episode to transform me into a nihilistic casualty. Historically, what happened with Jessica was roughly consistent with the litany of bio-atrocities committed thus far (although for me, more reprehensible than Stan's murder). I needed to get back on track emotionally and physically. I needed to resume the bio-quest whether I liked it or not, for there was really nothing else left for me to do in my wretched, deprecatory life.

Later, I thought, I would call Stu and ask him to contact Joseph's and Jessica's attorneys and request the appropriate letters for the bank loan. I never found the right moment to ask Jessica for a letter, but I had no doubt that she would agree to it, especially now that our relationship had warped to another level that I could not yet adequately define or label.

After finishing a second bottle of beer, I felt tired and went to sleep again, this time on the living room couch. I awoke a few hours later to cooking sounds coming from the kitchen. As I sat up, a blanket was covering me. The blanket was new. I walked into the kitchen and said hello to Ponderosa, who was drinking coffee and scrambling eggs.

"Feeling better?" she asked.

"Much better."

"You're sure?"

"I'm not losing my mind," I said. "You don't have to worry."

"Just checking," she said with a smile, as she poured coffee and ordered me to sit down.

After breakfast, we spent the day skiing in the Rockies, and toward the end of the day, I noticed myself cartwheeling down the mountain at a great speed, my skis spinning like helicopter blades. Fully convinced I was going to break my neck and die, if I was lucky, and if not, be on a life-support machine for a couple of years and then die (an unconscious death), I had—in that furtive sequence of moments when time stands still—an epiphany of sorts, and that was that God, in His great irony and wit and wisdom, was going to make it easy for me. He was going to give me a way out of this moral garbage dump I dug myself into by permanently transposing me, and my bone-crunching, contorted demise in the presence of Ponderosa, in the state of Wyoming on my third visit, would be a most appropriate thematic farewell as well as a respectable contribution to the trail of mounting Tyler deaths which appeared to be progressing at a healthy pace. In the eyes of those who kept up with such things, such as Hank Tyler and the lawyers, I had become a Tyler, and like a true Tyler I was on the verge of acquiring something big but would now not get it because I suddenly expired. But alas, God fooled me again. I did not die. I did not even fracture a leg, because the skis broke free just at the right moment allowing me the flexibility to brace myself and slide and roll to safety before any structural damage could occur.

Minutes later, Ponderosa came to my aid and assisted me off the slope. Accidents such as this serve to bring people closer together, and we were no exception, especially when I said, "I bet this never happened to Stan," knowing full well Stan was a competent skier and most likely would have frowned upon my performance. Her riotous laughter was proof that I was correct.

Soon after we went to dinner and Ponderosa got talking about Megan. This is what she told me: About six weeks earlier, Megan checked into a new rehab in St. Petersburg, Florida, a very high-end, exclusive, all-women facility that her counselor recommended. Her mother thought it was a good idea too, but paying for these rehabs was starting to become an issue. Up to the point of Ben's demise,

Molly and Ben had an arrangement whereby they shared Megan's rehab expenses, but this was not formalized or written down. With Ben gone, Isabella inherited Ben's share of the expenses and was planning to willingly follow through for as long as necessary. But once Isabella died, Stan, the next in line, began quarreling with his mother about the bills. His position was one of "tough love" and believed Megan would never change unless forced to and that she should get a job like everyone else.

This, like pretty much everything else Tyler, was never fully resolved before Stan died (was killed), and now with him gone and California taking over, there was no longer any arrangement in place, verbal, written, or otherwise. Thus, Megan might be willing to negotiate her pending interest in Prostitute for some immediate compensation or to have her rehab expenses covered until the estate was settled. She, like Joseph, had a lot more coming, probably a third of Ben's share once probate played out.

It was a good idea, and we both thought Molly would be receptive if she was going to be Megan's sole provider until Megan cashed in. Neither one of us was sure if Molly would first need to get Megan's permission or petition for power-of-attorney due to Megan's instability. Regardless, Molly was the first person I should approach, but I knew that was not going to happen because of the guilt I harbored for killing her only son. I could not ignore the maternal bond, just as I could not ignore Marge's love for me. (True, I was surviving the Ponderosa ordeal okay, but I believed Ponderosa always had her own agenda.)

Without explaining myself to Ponderosa, I decided to bypass Molly and go directly to Florida and talk to Megan and hope for the best. I was not optimistic because of Megan's history and reputation but, as with others, I could still give it a shot.

Ponderosa also mentioned that Megan was uncharacteristically quiet during her brief stay at the ranch for Stan's funeral and stuck close to her mother with whom she apparently had stopped quarreling. She slept in one of the cabins—my cabin, to be exact—before returning to rehab the following morning after the funeral. This restraint on her part gave me more hope that there was a chance of my coming to terms with her.

When Ponderosa and I returned to the KO Corral that night, we were left with the option of a romantic evening. I was feeling almost "normal" again, but remained deeply confused about Jessica. I could still taste her every time I swallowed, and probably for the first time in my life I felt a need for continual abstinence. Time heals, I kept reminding myself.

I told Ponderosa after she opened a bottle of Merlot that my body was hurting from the ski plunge and that I should take a warm bath and get a good night's rest. "I don't want you to think you're running a clinic as I continue to make an ass of myself," I said in an attempt to be stupid-funny and hide my reasons.

"Do you want to go back to the cabin or the couch or... where do want to sleep, Nic?"

"In the cabin."

Again, she walked me to the cabin, only this time she helped me draw a bath and we hugged good-night. A long, strong hug but nothing more.

The next morning, we drove to the airport. She was flying to Denver for a real-estate closing, and I was off to Florida to talk to Megan. I would call her when I was leaving Florida so we could coordinate our schedules to meet up again, possibly even in Detroit, if she was willing. Sooner or later, I had to resume my old life, and to have Ponderosa visit would be a huge shot in the arm for my morale. It was not that my situation was not under control—it was, within reason and barring the unexpected—but I dreaded the people, the routine, and the unspoken deceit that was permeating every level. When I talked to Karolina, I was talking to Hank and Jam. When I looked around my shop, and saw all the wonderful things Karo had done, it now depressed me and reminded me of failure. It was what I imagined an ugly divorce to be with both parties still living under the same roof.

But now with Ponderosa, there was new hope.

25
REHABILITATION

Megan's Harmony House rehab facility was a lily-white castle set on a few acres of lush green landscape right on the banks of the blue Tampa Bay and surrounded by a grove of giant pines and weeping willows.

It had tennis courts, volleyball nets, croquet fields, cycad gardens, walking paths, and a marvelous, elevated shrine overlooking the bay, where I imagined yoga, meditation, tai chi, and other holistic activities took place.

As I stood outside, looking in through the glorious trees, I became jealous that I wasn't stationed here. I was now just as screwed up and spiritually bankrupt as any of the Tylers, and this little palace, with its carefully groomed gardens and playgrounds, was far superior to any urban county hospital. But it was not a place—I quickly discovered—where one could arrive unannounced and expect cooperation.

My reluctance (guilt) to call Molly, coupled with the historically successful bio-routine of simply showing up on the unsuspecting siblings before they could negatively react, blinded me to Megan's unique circumstances. Clearly, this institution had rules and regulations that protected its clients from undesirables and passersby, even if they happened to share blood.

I had no clue what Molly had told Megan about me, if anything, and my one and only communication with her dated back some almost thirteen years in the form of a letter-shaped sanitary napkin. This was hardly the intimate background that gave one the right to barge in without invitation. After traveling almost two thousand miles, I decided to change my strategy and call first. When I did, a strong, Southern female voice answered. I introduced myself as Megan's half-brother. I told her that I happened to be in St. Petersburg on business and wondered if it would be okay to drop by and say hello to Megan.

"Did you talk with Megan?" she asked sternly.

"No," I said, knowing that Megan would be consulted and lying was not a possibility.

"When was the last time you talked to her?" the strong female voice asked.

"Actually," I replied casually, "I've never seen or talked to her before in my life."

This was followed by a long, hollow silence, as it should have been. When that eternity ended, she requested a contact number and promised to get back to me one way or another. I clicked off the cell thinking my chances were poor, but I was already there so I would wait it out.

I returned to my hotel and was informed by my desk manager that the city of St. Petersburg, Florida, is home to one of the most important Salvador Dali museums in the world. This was excellent news, and I killed the rest of the day inside the museum and was glad to do so.

The next morning, with nothing to do, I called everybody I knew to let them know I was still breathing. I had not been in contact with anyone except Stu and Ponderosa since I left for England almost two weeks earlier. The last person I called was Karolina, who, remarkably, during our conversation, told me that she was "worried about sales," as though that were somehow news.

"We haven't been doing well for quite a while," I retorted, stating the ridiculously obvious.

"Yeah, I guess you're right," she said.

"Yeah, I guess so," I murmured back, thinking her remark might be connected to surreptitious plotting and it motivated me to tell her that I was now in Florida courting Megan. I wanted Hank to know this, but I also suspected it would evoke thoughts about how I was managing to pay for all the traveling and add bitterness to our riff, which dated back to my costly mistake of not taking her to Isabella's funeral.

I didn't enjoy the sparring, but it was a war. Her wicked defection was irreparable, and my hands were tied. It made my abhorrence of Hank Tyler all the more powerful because down deep I blamed him. I wanted him to fully understand my strategy of consolidating my assets by uniting the siblings against him. He risked being swallowed up by the people whom he despised most.

After murder, counterfeiting, and now bloody incest, conquering Hank was becoming almost second nature.

*

On day three of my St. Pete excursion I spent the afternoon on the beach, and it was there I received a phone call from the female rehab voice informing me I would be permitted to see Megan that evening during "family hours," beginning at 7 pm.

I was delighted for the good news. I then became a tiny bit nervous, knowing that I was going to actually meet her face to face. By trade, Megan was a musician and singer, but her addiction problem overshadowed everything in her life and left a long trail of destruction. Of all the Tylers, she had the worse reputation— not an easy accomplishment. I also harbored the knowledge that I had killed her one and only full sibling. This would be the most challenging meeting yet.

To stay upbeat, I told myself if nothing materialized I would still mutually control 21 percent of Prostitute LLC, providing that I could secure the loan for Joseph. That did not surpass Hank's 25 percent, but it still put me in a strong position to raise hell over there until I could figure out something else. Megan's support, of course, would mean the golden 26 percent.

That evening I drove back to Harmony House, and upon entering was greeted by a tall, well-dressed female administrator, Dr. Ferris. Dr. Ferris provided guidelines on how to interact with the inpatients and requested that I not carry drugs or medication of any kind inside, prescription or otherwise. I did not happen to have any on me, but I appreciated and respected the caution involved and thanked her. She told me Megan was waiting for me in the south wing.

I left Dr. Ferris and walked through the grand foyer into a

spacious sitting room speckled with fat sofa chairs and large potted palms beyond which was the entrance to the south wing. I kept walking past the chairs and felt the fear growing inside me with each and every step. Before entering the wing, I stopped altogether, looked down at my hands, and noticed they were trembling. It didn't make sense. Why should a Tyler-weary, incestuous murderer be nervous about yet one more Tyler? The only answer that came to mind was not an answer but a fact: She was the last one. She was the last Tyler. There would be no more after her. This gave me back some strength.

I took a big breath and entered. She was sitting alone at a folded card table with her back to the entrance, drinking from a paper coffee cup and smoking a thin, dark cigarette. She wore a tight, gray pullover that hugged her slight frame and edgy bones. Her hair was blonde, highlighted, and cut short, revealing an attractive, Modigliani profile, as she stared downward into the table. She looked as if she was thinking about something dense, important, and way beyond my paltry comprehension.

I walked up behind her and was careful not to startle her. "Megan?" I asked softly, looking down at her.

She turned slightly and looked up. "Yes, that's me," she answered, snapping out of it.

"May I sit down?"

She didn't respond. She was too busy staring a hole in my face. I waited for the recognition process to synthesize. I was now more than used to it with the Tylers.

"Sure," she finally said.

I sat down opposite her at the table and fell victim to the same spell. Staring directly at her, she resembled Ben. All the others took more after their mothers—except for me. And that meant if the old "$a = b$ and $b = c$, then $a = c$" logic held, she must look like me, although I could not recognize our resemblance at that moment. Perhaps I had become too jaded to conceptualize myself anymore.

"Is it Nic or Nicholas?" she asked.

"Either one is okay," I said, knowing almost no one called me Nicholas. Not even Marge when she was upset.

"Doesn't matter?"

"No."

"If it doesn't matter, how about Nicky then?"

"Nicky?"

"I like Nicky."

It sounded like someone else's name, but I was so disgusted by who I was and what I had become, I said, "Nicky's fine," and meant it. It felt good to be someone else. Maybe that was my solution: become someone else.

"So, Nicky," she said, "tell me the truth: Do you really have business here in St. Petersburg, Florida, former home of the Triple A?"

"Other than you, you mean?"

"Yes."

"No. Not really."

"That's what I thought."

She crushed out her cigarette. I watched her closely, not sure if she was annoyed or amused. It was also difficult to gauge how old she appeared. I knew how old she was—six months my junior—yet from my perspective, she looked both much younger and much older than me. Her body was thin, small, rubbery, and could have belonged to a twelve-year-old. But her big, broken eyes sunk deeply into her skull and suggested a much older person. Thick war paint filled in her sockets. And if separated from the rest of her, they could have belonged to an octogenarian. Alcohol and drugs have a way of both stunting and aging the addict at the same time. Here was proof.

"Sorry," I said. "I didn't know what else to tell them."

"They're used to being lied to," she said with an empathic grin.

"I fit right in, I guess."

She continued to stare at me. "My mother didn't exaggerate about you."

"How?"

"How much you remind her of Dad."

"I never met him, you know."

"That's too bad," she said disappointingly.

"Yeah."

She stared blankly ahead and thought carefully about what she was about to say: "Nicky, I gotta tell you right from the start, we can't catch up. It's too late. So let's not try. Okay?"

She didn't wait for my response. It was a dead topic for her. "Do you want some coffee or something?" she asked.

"No thanks."

"Cigarette?"

"I don't smoke."

"Good for you. I can stop for like a half a day, and that's it, then I lose it—go nuts. I go to yoga here. I try not to smoke for a few hours before I go to class. That helps a little."

"Not smoking sucks too."

"Yeah, I know. Life's a bitch."

"You're different than what I'd thought you'd be," I said with a slight hesitation. I fully meant it, but wasn't sure it was the proper thing to say.

"When you say 'different,' you mean like 'better' or 'not too crazy.' Right?"

"I wouldn't put it that way."

"How would you put it, Nicky?"

"Well, okay, maybe a little."

"Well, maybe let me tell you something, Nicky-boy. I change pretty fast. You should know that. It's been a problem for like almost everyone I've ever known in my life."

I didn't challenge the statement but I did change the subject. "This is a good place?" I asked.

"It's a place to go when the over and over is over. I think. I'm not sure yet. But I think."

"I don't understand."

"Well, I've been going to places like this over and over for a long time, and I think the over and over is over."

"How do you know?"

"I don't. I just said that."

"Sorry. Does it help with this place being all women?" I asked, trying not to sound too stupid, but wanting to better understand.

"Kind of," she said thoughtfully, "but it's more like women talking about God."

"That's good," I replied, not sure of the difference between women talking about God opposed to men talking about God, or both men and women together talking about God, although not being a woman, and with God mostly referred to in the masculine, there most definitely could be a difference.

"Yeah, it's good. But I'm finding out it's not so good, in a way."

"How?"

"I don't like what I'm starting to see."

"You mean about God?"

"No about me."

"Oh, okay."

"Yeah. I don't think I've ever been conscious enough to really hate myself. That seems to be changing."

"I'm experiencing similar feelings, recently," I said. "Sometimes I loathe myself."

"You keep reminding me of Dad," she said. "He didn't like himself either. It must run in the family."

I stopped dead. This was the first time one of the siblings ever included me as a family member—like I was an actual brother, like we were roughly the same. Yes, Hank and the business world were starting to recognize me as such because of my creeping stake in Prostitute, but an acknowledgment by a sibling, as a sibling, was a breakthrough for me, if not just a tad too late on the bio-calendar.

She paused reflectively, thinking about who she was looking at. "What's the main reason you're here, Nicky? What's your business?"

"The truth?"

"Why not—just for the hell of it?"

"I'm trying to take control of Prostitute Records, and you're going to inherit five percent of Ben's ownership. I wanted to talk to you about that."

She nodded slightly to confirm what she suspected, and then stayed right on topic by saying, "Things have really changed since Stan died. Haven't they?"

"Yeah, they have," I replied almost in whisper.

"Everybody did okay by him getting killed in that balloon. Didn't we?"

I thought it was profound that she said "we," meaning that I was included in that group who did okay. I said nothing in reply, but I felt our intimacy disintegrating.

"Don't be shy, Nicky. Look around, does this look like Disneyland? When Dad died nothing changed, and then when Isabella died, things changed but not necessarily for the best; but now with Stan gone, things have really changed. For me, too."

"Megan," I said, "you wanted the truth and I told you, but we can do this some other time. I'd prefer we did."

"I know we can. Do you want to help me, Nicky?"

"Yes."

"You sure?"

"Yes."

"Pay the bills."

"To this place?"

"Yeah. It's twenty-five thousand a month."

"Okay."

"You sure?"

"Yes, I'm sure."

"You're a sucker, Nicky. I warned you."

"Maybe. But I don't care."

"You may later, down the line. That's what usually happens."

"You can always pay me back if you want to."

"Or maybe we can work out something with Prostitute?" She smiled brightly.

"That's not the reason I agreed to pay," I said, realizing that she may be playing with me.

"Are you sure about that?" she asked.

I had to think. Was it or wasn't it? Was I just bullshitting myself again and all I wanted was what I wanted, similar to what happened with Claire? I honestly didn't know.

"I don't know," I said. "I mean, before I came here, that was one of the main things I was thinking."

"To pay my bills in exchange for my Prostitute interest?"

"Yes. I thought that could be a possibility. But —"

"But what?"

"All of a sudden, it's not important. The Prostitute thing. I mean, you don't have to do anything about Prostitute, and I'll still pay. And you don't have to pay me back if you don't want to. You don't have to do anything."

"Okay."

She looked at me carefully and waited to see how I'd react.

"Okay," I said. "Is there anything else I can do for you while in here, in the home of the former Triple A?"

"No, that's plenty. Just pay the bills," she said casually. "Where are you going after this?" she asked.

"Back to Detroit, I guess."

"Leave me a number."

I wrote down my numbers on a newspaper and handed the paper to her.

"Call me anytime," I said. "I don't care if you're taking advantage of me. I want to be taken advantage of."

Our eyes locked. Hers turned sad. They were now broken sad instead of broken old.

"What?" I asked.

"Nothing."

"You know," I said, "we're about the same age, but you seem older."

"That just happened."

"What do you mean?"

"Me being older, that just happened. It's not important."

"No?"

"Nope," she confirmed, not wanting to discuss it. "Thanks for coming."

"Thank you for letting me see you."

It was time to go. I stood up from the card table. I did not try to hug her, but I wanted to. "Good-bye," I said.

"Bye."

I turned around and began walking out of the south wing.

"Nicky?" she called out.

I turned and looked at her. "Yes?"

"I'm sorry."

"About what?"

I could see the war paint begin to smear down her cheeks.

"About that letter. A long time ago."

"Oh, that," I said.

"I'm truly sorry."

"I forgive you. Can I ask a favor?"

"What?"

"Can I hug you good-bye?"

"Okay."

I walked back to her, leaned down and hugged her strongly. She was paper thin, but her frame felt sturdy and resilient. She had fire in her.

"I'm sorry, too," I whispered. "About Ben. And Stan." The last reference was a confession.

I straightened up. She looked at me strangely, almost as if she knew. "That's the way it goes sometimes."

"Yeah."

"Good-bye, Nicky."

"Good-bye."

26
MISUNDERSTANDING

I was going to have to burn a lot of good phony money to pay for Megan's St. Pete Harmony House retreat, but I could not remember ever having felt so good about anything. After a lifetime of emotional scarring and artificial medication, Megan was attempting a genuine transformation. She was finally going to break through the addiction web. It was my responsibility to do what I could.

I might be getting suckered, but getting suckered, or being suckered, was not a significant factor in either of our current realities. In fact, money in general, I believe, at that particular point in Megan's life, was not important to her. It was just something that had to be dealt with. I—out of the blue—had become the new vehicle for her. I would provide for her until the next person or situation came along, which might or might not be the inheritance itself.

On the way out of the rehab, I checked with Dr. Ferris to see when Megan's next payment was due. She directed me to the accounts manager, another middle-aged, Southern woman (I did not see one man the whole time I was there) who told me the bill would go out in two weeks and she would be happy to send it to me. This expense would force me to make some adjustments, such as, for starters, leaving the country again (and again) to convert, and then reconvert, suitcases full of fake twenties into good currency. It would be a risky venture but paled in comparison to the benefits derived, such as the fulfilling of my original dream of bonding with a sibling—a dream I had abandoned countless times for the last thirteen years. And maybe, just maybe, I thought, God was giving me a shot at redemption. I may have killed her brother (my brother, our brother), but I now had a chance in assisting in her rebirth. If that was the case, then I was being handled with kid gloves.

The next day I was back in Detroit infused with a new spirit. I wasted no time in getting Karo/Hank up to speed on all the good transcontinental bio-news. I told them Euro-based Jessica and Joseph were game to join forces and, on this side of the Atlantic, Megan needed time but "probably won't be a problem." I then laid into Hank good, by telling Karolina that he would soon be "rotting to death in his own cigarette ash."

The reality of my position did not warrant this level of arrogance, but it was all about conveying confidence. They needed to know I would never go away. The goal, of course, was to get Hank back to the table way before probate was through. I did not want to wait forever. But I could and would if forced to, and it was important he understood that.

I also did my usual 30 to 40 percent lying and told her I obtained a personal loan from an unnamed source and now had sufficient credit to weather out the Tyler probate drama, despite the poor sales here. This was payback for her curious comment over the phone, which I subsequently interpreted as a reminder from Hank, through Karolina, that things were getting much worse for me.

Once I was finished with Karolina, I called Ponderosa and asked her if she wanted to go to Paris for a few days.

"How can I refuse Paris?" she said with naked enthusiasm.

"You can't, nobody can," I replied.

Yes, Paris was an extravagant way to convert money, but so what? The smart thing would be to drive into Toronto (I wouldn't chance Windsor, across the river, too small) and save myself 5,000 dollars, but Paris was embedded in my mind, and I thought it would be a great way to get to know Ponderosa better. It was also nearing Christmas, and I wanted to get out of the country so I could be spared the monotonous, ubiquitous "holiday music" that was starting to bleed my eardrums. As cool as we thought we were, we still had to play it in the store for business sales. I booked reservations for Ponderosa to fly into Detroit and then for the two of us to fly to Paris via Chicago that same evening. I would tell Karolina I was going to Wisconsin on a camping trip and leave it at that.

Later that week, I went out to dinner with a curious Marge and

Stu but was not forthcoming about the siblings. Memories of San Sebastian continued to haunt me. I also disliked thinking about Joseph cloning humans or about Josh and his broomstick. In truth, it was a bio-washout of sorts, and I basically revealed nothing about any of them except Megan. Megan had become dear to my heart. My life was no longer only about usurping the Tyler musical fiefdom and becoming wealthy—not that there was anything dishonorable in that quest—but also about the recovery of my sister. I was hoping that once Megan left the rehab she would spend time in Detroit with me. As a musician and a Tyler, no one was more suited to help run Ben Tyler's music label than she.

"Who's paying for the new rehab?" Stu asked, referring to Harmony House and knowing well the legal nightmare that was going down in probate court.

"I don't know," I lied, not wanting to discuss my intervention and where the money would be coming from.

Later, he told me he received correspondence and documentation from representatives of Claire, Joseph, and Jessica supporting my bid and set up a meeting with his law firm's primary bank. We were scheduled to go in together the following week as a client-lawyer team. "I think we're ready," he said with a big smile.

I reassured him that if I did get the loan, I would finally compensate him for his legal services. "I hope you've been keeping track."

"I'll get my money tenfold," he replied. "I'm no fool."

After dinner, I returned home and was confronted by yet another ghost of sorts. This one was sitting on my front steps, smoking a cigarette. She was wrapped in a scarlet scarf and a beat-up leather pilot's jacket that hugged her Greek torso. Her long bell-bottomed legs crossed in a lazy fashion as she leaned backward almost at a 90 degree angle, supported by folded elbows. She reminded me of an old Jimi Hendrix album cover. Her name was Karolina Torgustive. But as beautifully vintage as she appeared—iconic even—it did not have any impact because I was on a mission that did not include her. Back in the days before Isabella's funeral, this was a common and welcome sight. Now, like everything else about her, it was painful.

"I was just about to leave," she said, noticeably withdrawn as she flicked her cigarette butt into the street.

"I was out with Marge and Stu," I said.

"How's Marge?"

"Good."

"I thought maybe you were with your girlfriend."

Again with the girlfriend, I wondered. I did not have a local girlfriend, and Ponderosa was just starting. She, Karolina, was my last real girlfriend. I let it alone, not wanting to waste time, thinking her motives convoluted.

"Everything okay, Karo?" I asked.

"Not really."

I sat down next to her on the steps. I had no choice. I was not inviting her in.

"What is it?" I asked.

"I'm not happy, Nic."

"Not many people are," I replied, invoking the universal axiom and trying to diffuse the real issue: she was having doubts about her espionage career.

She could not admit that, of course, nor could she vent the disadvantages of whatever sicko politics was going down in the sleazy Prostitute world. She would, I thought, be better off if she came out of the closet. But maybe they weren't open to that.

"Are you thinking about leaving?" I asked, pretending to refer to Eclectic Emporium, but I could have been referring to Prostitute Records.

"I don't want to," she replied.

"What do you want? Do you know?"

"I want it to be the way it used to be with us."

That was not possible. Although I was intrigued by what I could learn from her if we were to put all our cards on the table. It was tempting but way too risky. She could easily flip again, and where would I be then? Besides, there was no guarantee she would put all her cards on the table anyway. Like me, she was a fucking liar. If she had come to me prior to Hindenburg 2 and following the second Wyoming visit, it might have been a different story.

"I didn't start this," I said firmly, but actually giving in slightly.

"I was mad at you."

"I told you I was sorry."

"I guess I didn't hear you."

Her eyes filled up with holy water. This was a crucial moment. I was vulnerable to the extent that she never loved me, and I loved her. And because I never had that love, I'd always want it. But she was coming to me now not out of love or true friendship, but because she sensed I was going to win or her dealings with Prostitute were going south.

The bottom line: If she still thought I was going to lose, would she be sitting on my steps weeping? Would she be begging forgiveness if Hank was about to crush me into shit dust? The answer was obvious. Too obvious. I had no choice.

"I'm tired, Karo," I said. "Can we talk about this tomorrow?"

Her expression turned to one of insolence. She wanted to scratch out my eyes.

"Fuck you, Nic," she whined as she quickly stood up. "Mister fucking perfect."

And with that she was gone, her boots clicking hard on the pavement until the sound faded away.

The next morning, she did not come into work. I called her a few times, but she never answered or returned my messages. I was now in a quandary about what to do because I was scheduled to leave town the following day. With no one to replace her on such short notice, I might be forced to close down for the duration of the brief Paris trip. I had no intentions of canceling.

Still, I reasoned, despite the inconvenience, this was a step forward. Maybe she would quit for good, which is what she should have done when she first became disillusioned instead of turning into a despicable mole.

Her comments the previous night revealed much about her true thinking: "Mister fucking perfect." What was that supposed to mean? That I should be more imperfect, like her twisted, hypocritical, turd-worshipping coffee pal or, even better, like soulless, corrupt scourge Hank Tyler? Those guys were okay? They had acceptable flaws? Was that just part of their humanity? Or maybe she was making reference to my perseverance, which was beginning to pay off? Either way, she was a sore-loser bitch. I would not be surprised one bit if Prostitute had turned on her. That was what Hank was all about. She should have known that by the way he treated me. Her downfall was her own fault.

When Ponderosa flew in the next afternoon from Wyoming, she taxied to my shop at my request. This would allow me more time to keep the store open before shutting it down for four days during the Christmas season. When she arrived, I gave her the ten-cent tour. She was reasonably impressed. "I can see why Hank would want to copy you," she said.

Afterward, we hung out in the lounge and ordered in a late lunch. She was curious about the latest developments with the pending inheritance (a touchy subject for us) and how things panned out in Florida with Megan. I told her quite a bit, but I noticed I was forced to lie on a fairly consistent basis.

Lying to people was as common as breathing at this stage in the bio-quest, and I wondered if this perennial covering-up would forever deprive me from having an authentically intimate relationship with another human being. It was a terribly lonely feeling. I had to be especially cautious with Ponderosa given her relationship to the deposed Stan Tyler.

At about 5 pm, one hour before I was set to close up shop early and leave for the airport, Karolina entered the store. She seemed buzzed—weed high—and not at all angry, and I suppose more or less resigned to her circumstances, whatever they were. She apologized for being unavailable for the last couple of days and said she would work that night and be around during my absence. I thanked her for coming in and let the matter drop, not wanting to get into anything before leaving town. But I made a mental note that at some point soon she would have to be fired if she would not leave of her own accord.

She was intrigued to meet Ponderosa and was relieved to finally meet the person whom she thought I had been seeing for some time now. The reality, of course, was that I was not seeing Ponderosa for some time now or anyone else, and that Ponderosa was a person with whom she was familiar as Stan's fiancée. She just didn't recognize it yet.

I was more than willing to leave her in the dark because it was none of her goddamn business anyway, but soon after, she did figure out the Stan connection ("Wyoming? Where in Wyoming?") and from there her curiosity became excessive and inappropriate. Yet I still did nothing to set the timetable record straight. As I viewed it, there was no major drama here. Yes, I was hanging out with the woman Stan was planning to marry, but he was no longer planning to marry her because he was dead. It may be a little soon after his death, but not that soon. (The invisible fact that I had everything to do with his death was irrelevant because nobody knew about it. Furthermore, I did not kill Stan for Ponderosa, but obviously Ponderosa's subsequent availability could not be avoided. I was not a magician, just a last-resort murderer.) And Karolina—more than anyone I knew, or have ever known—made a mockery of the concept of boundaries when she jumped ship to Prostitute and started eating her Jam in between foamy cappuccinos. So in my mind I didn't care what she thought, true or untrue, and slipped into my office to take care of some last-minute business while they continued to yap away. Shortly later, Karolina entered alone. She wanted to talk to me in private.

"Now I understand," she said.

"Understand what?"

"Oh, come on."

"What?" I responded with more irritation. I was beginning to loathe her.

"I just remember when you suddenly disappeared, that's all," she said.

I stopped being annoyed for a moment and thought about what was being suggested. "Disappeared? What are you talking about?"

"After you got back from their ranch."

"You mean when I got back from Wyoming?"

"Yeah, when you suddenly got 'sick.' Remember?"

"So?"

"I called you a couple of times from the store, but no one answered and the machine wasn't on. I tried your cell, and it was turned off.

"So. I was sick."

"Stu called looking for you, too. I became worried."

"You did?"

"Yeah. I went over after work to check on you."

"You did?"

"Yeah."

"You let yourself in?"

"With the spare. You weren't there."

I paused, thinking carefully about where she might be going with this. "I can barely remember," I said shrugging it off. "I probably went to the store or something."

"I went over a second time."

"Oh?"

"The night before you came back to work. I think it was around midnight. Everything was the same. The kitchen. Your bedroom. You still weren't there. So I figured maybe you went away somewhere. For a few days."

"I see."

"Well?"

"Well what?"

"Just well."

"And where do you think I went?"

That was a stupid remark because it implied I agreed with her and that I actually went somewhere. But it was too late. The words had already slipped through my lips.

"It seems rather obvious to me now," she said.

And then I understood: Karolina was suggesting, in her relaxed hashish state, that once I returned from Wyoming the first time, I called in sick to rendezvous with Ponderosa, on the slant, free from Stan's presence, who was still breathing at the time.

It was an interesting theory but completely untrue, otherwise known as a misunderstanding. I was actually off sabotaging Stan's balloon and not meeting up with Ponderosa. Ponderosa, at that time, would have nothing to do with me. I looked at the clock. Ponderosa and I were set to leave in fifteen minutes to catch our flight. What should I do? What should I say? It was a little messy. I suppose—if push came to shove—I could live with the accusation of running off with my half-brother's fiancée when I was actually off killing my half-brother. But I preferred not to.

I doubted Karolina would be tactless enough to bring this up to

Ponderosa. Not right away. That was why she came in to talk to me alone. But if she did, Ponderosa would rightfully deny it, and that would leave open the question of where, in fact, was I during that time. It would still not be significantly meaningful or consequential because there was nothing to be suspicious about. I mean, I could have been in some whorehouse in New Orleans. It was my business what I was doing. Stan did not die until almost three weeks later while I was playing Miles Davis tunes to a bunch of school kids. Yet the circumstances were vaguely incestuous and potentially awkward, and I had to be cautious. So this is what I said to her: "Karo, you're clever, but for obvious reasons, I'm not going to comment on it one way or another. Excuse me."

And with that, I stood up and left the office. As I was walking through the stacks, I kept searching for more negatives about Karolina's discovery and wrongful conclusion, and the only other thing I could muster up was that she might tell Hank and Jam. But, again, that was another big nothing. In Prostitute circles, behavior of that type (true or untrue) was to be applauded and serve as resume material for promotion.

When I reached Ponderosa in the lounge, she asked me if she should continue to keep Paris a secret, and I told her, "Yes, definitely."

"She seems nice," she said, referring to Karolina.

"She's working for Hank Tyler," I said.

"What?"

"It's a long story. I'll fill you in later on the plane."

27
MELTDOWN

As it turned out, it took a long time to fill in Ponderosa about Karolina because it became a temporary non-issue.

As we were gathering our belongings to leave for the airport, Karolina entered the lounge and declared, "Molly Sivad is on the phone."

At first, I interpreted this as a good thing because I assumed Megan had talked with her mother and let her know I was picking up the tab for the rehab and thus provide me the important opportunity to break my guilt-ridden silence with Molly for killing her only son. But that was not why she called. She called to tell me—and I still have problems thinking about this—that Megan had relapsed and died.

Initially, I had no reaction because it did not, could not, register. But when it finally did, it felt like long pins were pushing through my eardrums. It dulled my ability to react out loud, and in retrospect, I believe I was close to fainting. I didn't faint, however. And that was probably a mistake because after I hung up with Molly, it became more ghoulish, if that were possible. I looked over to Ponderosa and remembered Molly and Ponderosa were on the verge of becoming in-laws before I changed that. Ponderosa knew the phone call was important. She was waiting for me to say something but I could not find the right words. I turned to Karolina, who appeared equally curious. Both were waiting for what I had to say.

I sat down on the couch and pointed at Karolina's cigarettes on the table. I did not smoke, but I needed something, anything, and a cigarette would have to suffice. My mind was saturated, and I recognized that it was not easy to be a habitual liar during an emotional crisis. Details and people were starting to blur. I lacked the ability to remember what to say and what not to say to whom, about whatever, wherever, and whomever.

I looked again at Ponderosa, who remained curious but patient. I so admired that about her. That poise. Karolina, on the other hand, could no longer tolerate the suspense and, after lighting my cigarette, said irritably, "Well, Nic, you have your cigarette, are you going to say something?"

"Megan Tyler is dead," I replied. "She overdosed in rehab."

I looked at Ponderosa. She said nothing, but she had that same faraway stare she had when we took that historic walk in Lincoln Park. I interpreted that as a sign of deep confusion. We were both deeply confused, although I had a suspicion her confusion was a much different strain than mine. My confusion was mixed with profound melancholy and unknown fear. Her confusion might have had much to do with me. But it was there, I saw it in her sky blue eyes.

"That's terrible," Karolina said when she realized no one else was going to say anything. "That's another dead Tyler."

With that, Ponderosa broke her stone silence: "I don't think we should go to Paris, Nic," she said, forgetting about Karolina or not caring.

"Paris?" Karo wondered out loud, looking right at me.

"Would you mind leaving us alone for a few minutes?" I asked her.

Her face turned ugly. She did not want to go. She wanted to stay and listen. It was then I knew for certain that she would indeed go, for good. Forever. Her rebellion and indignation were out of control. Perhaps she was punch-drunk from bouncing back and forth between me and Prostitute. Yet in her mind, this was still very much her store, her domain, and I was just something she had to put up with. Now she had turned openly defiant. And in front of Ponderosa.

My circumspection was no longer appropriate, regardless of the consequences, which at this stage seemed rather tame, if not stupid. Who cared what anybody thought? Karolina's lack of judgment and recklessness would sooner or later cause a crisis anyway. I would most definitely fire the traitor at the first appropriate moment, probably right after Megan's funeral.

I sucked up the rest of my cigarette as I watched Karolina finally leave the lounge.

"I'll be in the front if you need me," she said, talking directly to Ponderosa.

I waited for the blood to start flowing again and turned back to Ponderosa. "Are you alright?" I asked her.

"No. I'm not. Maybe I should go back to Wyoming."

"Now?"

She did not respond, and again she gave me the impression she was under the spell of some powerful hallucinogenic.

"Ponderosa?"

"I don't feel right," she said.

"I don't feel right, either," I said. "But I feel right about you."

She remained pensive, haunted. Her continued silence was deepening my despair. It was as if my emotional immune system had collapsed. Any more uncertainty would bring on a meltdown.

"Maybe it's best we don't go to Paris," I said." But why don't you stay here in Detroit for the night and decide in the morning what to do next. How do you feel about that?"

About a minute later: "Okay, I'll stay."

"Good."

"It's strange how these Tylers keep dying," she said.

"What do you mean strange?" I asked, the fear intensifying again.

"Unusual," she said.

"You mean like 'curse' unusual?" I asked, trying to lodge that idea into her head if she had not already thought about it. The alternative, in my mind, could only be foul play.

"I don't know what I mean," she said.

"Why don't we go have a drink?"

"Okay."

On the way out, I was forced to interact with Karolina again. It was early for a Saturday night, but I wanted her off the premises, which made no sense because I wasn't ready to fire her. Not until after the next funeral. But making sense no longer made any sense.

"Karo, why don't you take the night off." It wasn't a question. "I wasn't planning on staying open tonight."

"That's okay, I'll stay." She then quickly addressed Ponderosa before I could appeal, "I hope we get to talk soon."

"I'm sure we will," Ponderosa said.

"Are you coming in tomorrow, too?" I asked, knowing I had no say in what she was doing with my store for the immediate future.

"Of course. How about you? Or are you still going to Paris?"

The last question was laced with venom.

"I'll call you in the morning," I said, and walked out with one arm wrapped around Ponderosa's shoulder.

*

Later that night, in the bar with drinks in hand, Ponderosa asked me if I thought Megan was suicidal. I told her I did not.

"What was your impression of her then?"

"I thought she was healing."

"You mean getting better?"

"Yes.

"Did you offer to pay the bills?"

"Yes. She asked me to, and I agreed."

"That was part of a Prostitute agreement?"

"There was no agreement."

"Why not?"

"We didn't really talk about it," I said.

"You didn't talk about Prostitute? I don't understand. Isn't that why you went all the way out there?"

"Yes. But she didn't want to talk about it."

"Did she want to talk about Stan?" she asked.

"No. Not really," I said halfheartedly.

"Nothing?"

"She mentioned how things had changed since he died. But that was about it."

"And you didn't talk about Prostitute at all?"

"I don't think she was too concerned about the inheritance—if that's what you mean."

"But you agreed to pay for her expenses at rehab?"

Maybe I should not have told her that, I thought. Maybe I should have lied. Lying seemed to be more effective, more predictable, more simple. This was true even if there was no reason to lie, which was technically the case here. But, again, it was too late.

"I wanted to help," I heard myself saying aloud.

"Nic? Come on," she said.

And I have to say, it hurt me that Ponderosa continued to doubt me, but who could blame her? I did not fully understand my intentions either. Megan was the one who had pointed that out to me.

"I'm an only child, Ponderosa," I said, not knowing what else to say.

"Only child? I don't follow."

"I was an only child until I was seventeen years old. That's when I found out Ben Tyler was my biological father. When I tried to contact all my new siblings, they rejected me. Of all of them, Megan was the meanest. If it hadn't been for Hank Tyler and Prostitute Eclectic trying to put me out of business twelve years later, I never would have contacted them again. And you know the rest. But I never lost the desire to have a sister or a brother. That never changed.

"So when Megan was kind to me this time at the rehab, and in a sense reached out, I forgot all about Prostitute. It didn't matter. Her friendship and health became much more important. I believed something was going on for her. She was experiencing some kind of powerful spiritual change, and she embraced me. I wanted to help if I could. So, yes, I agreed to pay her bills expecting nothing in return."

Ponderosa looked deeply into my eyes and then, as if to say "I believe you," she grabbed hold of my hand.

"I'm an only child, too," she said softly, earnestly." This must be really hard for you. Her death."

"It's shocking. Unbearable. There's way too much going on, Ponderosa. That's why I don't want to lose you, too. We were just starting to get to know each other. I like you. I like you a lot."

She then whispered the following beautiful words: "It's okay, Nic, I'll be your sister. I'll be more than your sister."

Ponderosa and I slept together for the first time that night. I hadn't slept with too many natural blondes in my life, and she was blonde all over. And patient, too, just like she was when vertical with her clothes attached. She helped ease the pain I was now allowing myself to feel about Megan with my "Nicky" days suddenly and forever over.

Megan's recovery, Megan's rebirth, Megan's brilliant triumph over the evil forces into which she was born, had become my adopted cause. And now it was gone, as she was gone. My sister was gone. It made me realize how difficult real change is. Megan was fighting the demons of her character, her biology, and her environment, with most of it ingrained in her psyche before she had a chance to learn how to think or choose. Like most of us flesh-and-bone types, she came up short. But she tried. In the end, Megan had proved her worthiness through painful self-examination, whereas all I had gained up to that point was learning how to murder and succeed in the Hank Tyler primal universe. I was now left with the chore of choosing another way to redeem myself, if that was possible.

*

In the morning I made coffee, and Ponderosa and I took a tour of Detroit—her idea. She grew up in the Chicago suburbs, not terribly far away, but never had cause or ambition to visit Detroit, like so many other Americans. It had been a long time since Detroit was a tourist attraction, and unless you were studying the phenomena of urban decay and the tragic demise of the American automobile industry, it was perfectly normal never to come here.

"It's not Paris, but I'll do my best," I said as we drove down Grand River.

This was more than a private joke, because I recently fell in love with Paris, and I knew from grade-school civics that Detroit was once known as the *Paris of the West*. Many people today would scoff at the comparison, but after roaming Paris, I could see what the historians were talking about.

A good reminder is the Gilded Age, stone-carved urbanization on Woodward, exemplified by the Traver Building and the Schwankovsky Temple of Music (which later turned into the Wright-

Kay Building). So are the neoclassical and neo-Renaissance designs by Albert Kahn and Daniel Burnham. They produced, among others, the Dime Building, the Whitney, the Ford, the Fyfe, Cadillac Place, and Savoyard Centre. There's also the Art Deco preponderance of the 1920s—my favorite style of all time—led by Wirt Rowland and others, who architected the Penobscot, the Guardian, the Stott, the Fisher, the Buhl, and others.

In addition, Detroit, like Paris, has a plethora of outdoor monuments, sculptures (Corrado Parducci's Indians being the most known), fountains, facades, Baroque roadway designs, and, of course, the wonderful neo-Gothic churches, some of which are so old and decrepit they blend seamlessly into the dismal blight of the decomposed neighborhoods. But they're there, or partially there. And if it all got cleaned up and renovated properly, and a new middle class was created out of stardust, Detroit would be one of the most beautiful cities in North America, if not the world. So there was a lot to show Ponderosa, but just to be on the safe side, I boomeranged up to Grosse Pointe for lunch to make her feel at home.

Following the tour, we drove back to Eclectic Emporium. Before entering, I gave Ponderosa a brief account of Karolina's traitorous activities with Prostitute Records. Ponderosa listened in disbelief, partly because of her initial impression of Karo, which was good, and partly because Karo was still working for me. I explained the logic of my double agent activity, but Ponderosa thought it foolish. "I don't know if that was a wise thing to do," she said.

As we entered, and before I could open my mouth, Karolina preempted us with colorful news—news she was dying to relay.

"Guess what," she said, "Jessica Tyler called from Spain. I told her I wasn't sure if you'd be in today because you had company from out of town and you might be flying to Paris."

This could only be interpreted as Karolina and Jessica had a little chitchat and Karolina graciously volunteered that Stan's former fiancée was with me and our union had nothing to do with business.

"Thanks, Karo," I said not looking at her. "I might need to talk to you when I get off the phone." I walked into my office, leaving

Ponderosa on her own to be interrogated.

I shut the office door, locked it, and called Jessica at her restaurant. This was a long-overdue phone call, and it would be my first time talking to her since I left her blood-soaked San Sebastian couch. I had no clue what to expect. The restaurant was buzzing. It took three to four minutes to get her on the line. She got right into it:

"Molly called yesterday," she dictated, "and after telling me Megan was dead, she said you were Megan's last visitor."

"I visited her about a week or so before she died. I didn't know I was her last visitor."

"She also said nobody knows how Megan got the drugs."

What was she really saying here? "I don't understand, Jessica," I responded. "Are you suggesting that I gave Megan drugs? Because if you are, it's absolutely untrue."

"What I'm suggesting is it's open season on the Tylers. And every time it happens, your name is on the visitors list."

Despite her dizzying accuracy on a certain level, with regard to one Stan Tyler, she was making a wildly irresponsible insinuation, and I wondered if this ruthless attack had more to do with my not calling her since I fled Spain.

"You're out of line, Jessica," I said.

"Everybody is out of line, Nic. Why should you be any different?"

Again, as with Karolina, I knew it was a mistake and even dangerous to engage, but I felt compelled to state the obvious. "It's paranoid nonsense," I said. "What about you and Joseph? I visited you two, and you're both still breathing?"

"We're doing what you want. That's why," she replied angrily. "By the way, what's Stan's fiancée doing in ugly fucking Detroit besides fucking you?"

I was stunned into silence. "Listen to me," she continued. "I'm going to Megan's funeral. You had better be there. We need to talk. Otherwise, I'm going to start calling everybody I know, and you can kiss good-bye to my now seven-and-one-half percent of Prostitute Records. It will be in Hank's pocket."

She slammed down the phone. I remained seated, in silence, not able to fully comprehend the magnitude of that brief tirade. This was yet another monstrous development. Would they ever cease? In addition, Jessica's rebellion opened up a slew of frightening possibilities that hinted at serious complications.

I decided to light up another cigarette. I didn't have an ashtray in the office, so I used a coffee mug for the ashes. The room was now perfectly quiet as I turned my head and looked through the soundproof glass window into the store. Karolina and Ponderosa were yapping away, completely absorbed with each other. I continued to sit in silence and think. I knew something important was to be revealed. I felt it coming in the pure white silence. And then it came. I looked through the glass again: What were those two dangerous women doing in the next room at this stage of the bio-quest? Especially in the post-Hindenburg 2 era? Was I trying to sabotage myself? Was I trying to hang myself?

I remembered once reading about former President William Clinton in a prominent psychology journal. After Clinton was overwhelmingly reelected to a second term as president, and had successfully revamped the country and the economy and the Democratic party, and had become, arguably, the most respected and powerful figure on the planet, he started to screw around with this chubby, dumpy, below-average, almost-teenager in the sacred Oval Office. He's got, like, Yasser Arafat on Line 3, Queen Elizabeth on Line 2, and Monica's fat lips wrapped around his cock at the same time. And this was despite a couple of sexual harassment raps awaiting him once he finished his tenure.

It was too easy, right? He *wanted* to get caught. He wanted the challenge of impeachment and the personal disgrace for all of history to gawk at. It was too easy. That was my conclusion.

But unlike Bill Clinton, I did not think my chore was too easy. Murder is not easy. Habitual lying is not easy. But the presence of both Karolina and Ponderosa hanging around in my shop at this crucial period had to be fingerprint evidence that I was doing my best to get impeached and go to trial and possibly be disgraced for the rest of my life. Or worse.

The phone rang. I was sick of the phone ringing, but I quickly picked up before Karolina could. When I did, I watched her watch me through the window. She was disappointed she didn't get to it first. I wanted to flip her the bird, but I held off. On the line was Stu with more news.

"I just got a call from Rex" (his lawyer friend from L.A. who was occasionally smoking his peace pipe). "There's a story about the Tylers in today's *L.A Times*."

"Oh yeah?"

"You can go online and read it."

"What's it about?" I asked, none too eager.

"The number of recent Tyler deaths and how that's affecting probate. I'm sure you'll find it interesting."

"Oh, okay."

"Not to belittle the tragic death of Megan Tyler, but this does make it easier for you. Joseph and Jessica Tyler now pick up Megan's share of Ben's inheritance. And both of them are with us."

"That occurred to me," I said, choosing not to clue him in on Jessica's conversation.

"I'm sure I'll be hearing from Joseph's lawyer soon. They're going to expect more money."

"I guess we have no choice."

"I'll do my best."

"How's the loan coming along?"

"As soon as I hear more, I'll let you know. Look at the article."

"Stu?"

"Yeah?"

"Does it mention me in the article?"

He hesitated, perhaps thinking my vanity was showing, but the question was completely fear-based. I was preparing myself for more outrageous news. Recently, the newspapers had been especially brutal to me in conveying information. I was petrified to read them.

"No," he said. "You're still off the radar."

"Thanks, Stu."

I hung up and went online to the *L.A Times* website and printed out the article. It was on Page 1 of the California regional section.

The headline read: "Death Toll Grows Among Recipients of Ben Tyler Estate." I read the article carefully. The story was chronological in its presentation and implied no foul play, just a lot of Tyler rotten luck, as it spelled out the progenitive break-down and the default role California was now playing in distributing bio-Dad's estate.

As Stu correctly noted, there was no acknowledgment of the aspiring bastard from Detroit, but pretty much everyone else in Dodge was singled out, including Claire as the only living willed beneficiary (alternate for Isabella), whose intention, the article went on, was to "follow through with Isabella Tyler's plans" to distribute what eventually became her posthumous share of the Tyler estate.

Some of the reporter's finest paragraphs were devoted to fiery Josh Tyler and his history of burning down houses and selling priceless guitars and Ben's subsequent insertion of a disinheritance clause in his will as retaliation. Josh was fighting both his father's will and the separate inheritance through Claire from his mother's side. Apparently, the conditional trust that Isabella's lawyers were setting up for him (as told to me by Claire; this development was not in the article) was not enough for him.

With regard to my heinous actions against my half sibling Stan Tyler, there were a few related items. According to the article, Stan's death was due to a "ballooning accident in Wyoming still under investigation with the FAA and the NTSB," but the length of the investigation was considered "routine by federal standards."

Also, since Jessica brought it up earlier, the St. Petersburg, Florida, police were investigating Megan's overdose and awaiting the autopsy and toxicity reports. Dr. Ferris, the director of Harmony House, was quoted as saying that she and her staff thought Megan was "doing remarkably well" and were "shocked" by her actions and had "no idea" where Megan got her drugs or "how long she had them in her possession before using them." Dr. Ferris did admit, however, that Megan was taking prescribed antidepressants and they could have contributed to her death when she combined them with other pharmaceuticals.

No one ventured to guess whether Megan planned her death or if it was accidental. Megan left no note behind. The toxicity reports, once they were in, would reveal more in terms of Megan's motivation.

Overall, the article showed me three things: One, public interest in the Ben Tyler family was on the rise again. Two, although the article was not sensational by any means, there was reference to the "curse" phenomenon when the reporter made a comparison between the Tyler family and the Kennedy family. (I only partially agreed. I understood how Isabella's stormy crash and Stan Tyler's balloon travesty—being murdered is, I suppose, just as much a curse as accidental death—could contribute to that edgy comparison, but the demise of both Ben and Megan Tyler were the result of well-established addictions and should not have seemed too surprising.) And, three, I remained unscathed.

Furthermore, none of the below-the-surface details of Prostitute's or Claire's intentions were publicly known or reported, which I preferred at that time. Anonymity was the desired state until I was safely positioned at the top, or near the top, at Prostitute.

So, I thought as I sat quietly, the L.A. newspaper account actually turned out to be slightly good news for a change. In the public and legal eye, I was a nonentity and free from suspicion. This, however, would not change Jessica's misgivings. European Jessica did not give a damn about what anyone thought, especially some stupid American newspaper. She was a Tyler. She knew the nature of the Tylers, she knew what they were capable of, and in her mind, I was running amuck in the genetic minefield with Josh, Joseph, and her now that Megan and Stan were gone. In her thinking, the stakes were getting that much higher. She would protect her interests at all costs.

I decided there and then I needed to be more proactive. Jessica was the wakeup call, and the newspaper article was a reminder of growing public scrutiny. If I could help it—that is, if I was conscious enough—I did not want to sabotage myself. As mentioned, I was not up for the challenge like Bill Clinton was.

To prove this to myself, I got off my ass and walked into the shop. The time had come to have that talk with Karolina. She was a fucking catastrophe in the waiting. Sooner or later, she would damage me if I let her, either through Machiavellian deceit or with a broken coke bottle dug into the back of my neck. The double agent experiment was over.

Trance-like, I walked directly over to the counter where she and Ponderosa were talking. I asked Ponderosa if I could have a word with Karolina, alone. Ponderosa showed concern in her expression, but she agreed to wait in the lounge until we were done.

I then turned to Karolina, who appeared curious but fearless. She was not afraid of me in the least. I interpreted that boldness as permission to be as direct as I needed.

"Karo?" I asked.

"What?" she replied.

"What are you doing hanging out with that fucking turd-worshipping Prostitute fuck-face Jam?"

"What are you talking about?" she replied, not expecting this.

I pretended I had just gotten the news and I was uncontrollably livid. Sadly, I could not even be legitimately pissed off without a spin.

"It's all over fucking town," I screamed. "Are you denying it?"

I watched the boldness in her face change to strategic contemplation, and I knew she would admit to something because she had no idea who I just talked to on the phone. And once she did admit—no matter how she lied about it, no matter how half-true or untrue it was—I would have her. I would swing the self-righteous ax. "Are you?" I said, raising my voice higher.

"I've had some meetings with him —"

"GET THE FUCK OUT OF HERE. NOW! TAKE YOUR SHIT, AND GET THE FUCK OUT OF HERE. YOU'RE FIRED. GO!"

In all the years I'd known Karolina, I had never once raised my voice to her. Yes, she had seen me angry and obnoxious, but that was always directed at other people, such as Hank Tyler. I was hoping this unruly behavior would come as a shock, and it did. She was confused and wounded by my volume, uncertain how to fight back. She was caught off guard.

"I'll put your check in the mail," I continued. "Now get out of here, and I mean it. And tell your good friend Jam I can't wait for the day when I get to fire his sorry ass, too. Now go!"

She stood still for another few seconds, the mind unable to command the body. But then she moved. She bent down slowly and picked up her bag from behind the counter. Her eyes showed sadness, not anger. The strategy was working. She would go peacefully. She would choose to fight this at some later time. For a few brief seconds, I felt sorry for her. She deserved so much better. She deserved to be the creative director for all Eclectic Prostitute stores in North America. She deserved to be rich and successful and have an army of lieutenants running circles for her. But that was not going to happen.

Right before she walked out the front door, she stared at Ponderosa, who was still waiting in the lounge. They both looked like schoolgirls who had been scolded for smoking in the bathroom. Clearly they were bonding before I interrupted the smelting process.

After Karolina left, I picked up the phone book and called a 24 hour locksmith, requesting emergency service to replace all the locks in my store and my rented house.

I then turned to Ponderosa. Unlike Karolina, I wanted to keep Ponderosa, despite the risk. Ponderosa had taken a liking to Karolina, not a terribly difficult thing to do. She had fallen under Karolina's seductive spell. But Karo was the enemy. Karo felt perfectly at ease befriending my friends while serving my executioners. Toleration and intrigue were no longer official Eclectic Emporium strategies for in-house operations, especially now that I had my hands full with Jessica, a potential nuclear missile gone astray. I needed clarity and loyalty, not ambiguity and treachery. And if it was not going to work out between Ponderosa and me, better I know sooner than later. It would be much more painful to lose something that good after getting used to it. It would be easier and wiser not to discover the nuances, the hidden treasures, the deep arcane desires that only repetition and daily exploration can unearth. If she was to go, now was the time. I was more than prepared to get rid of her.

"I didn't enjoy that, but I meant it," I said to her without hesitation.

"Are you apologizing?" she asked coolly.

"No," I said. "Not at all."

"She couldn't be trusted. You had no choice. You should have done it sooner."

Yes, Ponderosa was worth the risk.

28
SERMON ON THE MOUNT

Megan's ceremony was to be held in California as her father's before her, only further north in beautiful Marin County, where Molly now made her home. Molly had chosen a small non-denominational church house buried deep in the redwoods overlooking the Pacific.

Following the ceremony, Megan's ashes were to be poured into the sea from a spot on the cliffs that Molly and Ben frequented many years earlier when they were together briefly, before or around the time Megan was conceived. Molly told me this when I called her to see if I could assist with the memorial expenses.

During that conversation—which occurred a few hours after I fired Karolina, and about a week before the St. Petersburg county coroner's office released the pharmacology report—Molly asked me if I had given Megan any drugs while I visited her in Florida. This marked the second time that question had come my way, and once again, I was offended and hurt by the accusation. I realize many could write off my complaint as ludicrous, due to the morbid fact that I did kill Stan, and if I could manage that I could manage anything, but nobody knew I killed Stan except me; nor did anyone realize Megan's recovery had become my *raison d'etre*, an ambition I could not readily express for fear of being labeled insincere.

Later that night, seeking a little sympathy, I told Ponderosa about Jessica and Molly, and discovered Ponderosa had secretly wondered the same but had chosen to stay quiet about it. This never-ending slander was further perpetuated by the St. Petersburg police, who called me the next evening and reminded me I was Megan Tyler's last "registered visitor" and inquired if Megan had "requested" any prescribed or un-prescribed "mood-altering medication of any kind." And if so, did I oblige her. I understood this inquiry to be a police formality because the suggested exchange could be considered criminal activity, but it made me even more paranoid and depressed. Besides, the whole thing was perfectly ridiculous. Suspecting me of supplying Megan because I was her last guest flowed counter to everything I knew about addiction. Addicts find ways to feed their habits no matter what, and it was naïve, and even stupid, to think that Megan needed me. She could have been quarantined on Mars and still had a stash big enough to anesthetize the solar system. Regardless, the bottom line was that quite a few people suspected me of enabling Megan, and in one instance— with Jessica—the suspicion included malicious intent, however speculative, irresponsible, and unverifiably intuitive.

*

Ten days after Megan's death, I closed down the shop and Ponderosa and I flew to Marin to attend Megan's memorial. After landing at the San Francisco airport, we decided to rent separate cars to drive up to Marin. Neither one of us thought it was a good idea to allow Molly to see us arrive together, despite whatever unorthodox and permissive values she claimed to espouse.

I gave Ponderosa about an hour head start, and then I took to the road myself. I crossed the Golden Gate Bridge into Marin and followed the coastal highway for about forty minutes before turning onto the winding side roads. From there I needled up and down through the brilliant sequoias and redwoods until I reached my lonely destination.

The chapel was isolated and situated along a high creek, partially obscured from view by the patchy hinterland, and not too far from a rambling cliff that overlooked the sea. I say chapel because that was what Molly called it, but as I got closer, I saw no crosses, symbols, icons, statues, effigies, or anything else that would single it out as a house of worship in the traditional sense. It looked more to me like an old barn or a backwoods storage facility, or perhaps some kind of rural community building where people gather for recreational activities on weekends.

Adjacent to the chapel was a weeded parking lot filled with

expensive-looking vehicles. I parked next to Ponderosa's rental, stepped out, and walked along a narrow, shiny stone path that connected the clearing to the front of the chapel. The crushed stones beneath my feet were tiny, bright white, and cuneiform, and it looked to me like the path glowed in the midst of the density and richness of the gray, overcast Northern California afternoon.

When I reached the chapel, I saw a simple, rectangular wooden sign with gold-stenciled lettering above the entrance. This, as far as I could tell, was the only token provided to indicate that I was not entering, say, a bingo lodge. The sign read: "WE ARE A SPIRIT HAVING A PHYSICAL EXPERIENCE."

I pushed through the doors and entered into a room the size of a school gymnasium. And like a gymnasium on graduation night, or some such affair, it was filled with folding chairs. What made it different, however, was the beautiful, cream-colored marble podium that stood about five feet high in front. This podium appeared permanent and statuesque in the midst of the faded woodcraft and was clearly the focal point. All the folding chairs directly faced it and gave the room a swirling effect, similar but smaller in scale to the U.N. General Assembly room.

As I moved closer, I calculated no more than thirty-five or forty people in the room, most of them clustered up front. I recognized about half of them from Isabella's gatherings, but personally knew fewer than one-sixth: Molly, Jessica, Ponderosa, Claire and, shockingly, Hank Tyler.

Hank was sitting by himself off-center a half-dozen rows back and was the first person I passed en route to the front. When our eyes met, he showed just as much surprise as I felt. He also looked vulnerable and accessible. With no back office to hide in, and no emaciated corporate Prostitute soldiers to guard him, he was just like everyone else.

Before settling down, I paid my respects to Molly, who was sitting in the front row. She appeared aloof and distracted and said nothing in return to my whispers. Obviously, the loss of both her children was taking its toll. I left Molly and sat down next to half-sister Jessica, perched near the end of the third aisle. She appeared impenetrable with her dark sunglasses and long, black hair. She, too, made no effort to acknowledge me.

Over to my left and a couple of aisles in front sat Claire, looking Irish and sad; and not too far from her was platinum-blonde Ponderosa, standing out like the luminous Virgin Mary in all this Tyler gloom and darkness. I did not spot the bio-tag team of Joseph and Josh, but that was for the best. There was no need for further drama here. I already felt saturated.

Flanking Molly were two people I did not notice at first but who now stood out to me. On her right was a big, round man, about sixty, wearing a dark, old-fashioned cross-tie suit, the kind newspaper editors wear in old John Ford Westerns. He had long, stringy white hair and a frizzy beard, and had I lived in an earlier age I could have tagged him for a bloated Walt Whitman. His girth was substantial enough to physically connect him to Molly's slender frame despite their separate chairs. On occasion, he would lean over and whisper into Molly's ear, providing further evidence of their bond.

On Molly's other side sat a compact woman whose complexion was so keen and shiny and athletic that I thought I could ice skate on it and not leave a mark. She wore a knitted gray smock, a simple black skirt, and below the skirt, rugged, tan cowboy boots. Her rich, ultra-thick brown hair was graying naturally and beautifully and once I noticed her I couldn't see anyone else. Nor did I want to. Calamity Jane was what came to mind, but minus the "calamity" and double the confidence as she radiated beside Molly. She then stood up—all five feet of her—and, burning with poised contemplative energy, climbed onto the marble podium to begin her sermon. The time had come to redirect her stray, wounded flock. Her voice was strong and clear and filled the empty seats. This is what she had to say:

> *Friends, I welcome you all here today on this beautiful winter day. I know many of you have traveled from afar, and I thank you for your presence and for your love and for your support of Molly, who has been challenged lately by the transitions of first her son, Stan, and now her daughter, Megan. Molly thanks you, too.*

I want to begin by stating a fact. And the fact is, it makes little difference how one dies. You can die of disease—as many people choose in this toxic age—or warfare or through natural disasters, or perhaps a random traffic accident with impeccable timing and unique telepathic agreements. Like I said, it doesn't matter. What matters is that we've made that choice. To leave. To move on. And all of us do that. There are no exceptions. No matter how young or old you are.

Likewise, we also choose the circumstances into which we are born. For instance, some of us are born into specific economic and social conditions that are so severe, so extreme, so depraved, that by the age of three or four years, they are competing with the dogs and rats for their meals. A city like Mumbai comes to mind. And then, of course, some of us are born into abundant material wealth, such as certain neighborhoods in our California.

With regard to our beloved Megan—she chose a difficult path. She was born into that second category, yet she was perhaps challenged much more than many of those who were born into the first category. And if we are to look at this correctly, we know that only Megan can be the judge of her progress here on Earth. No one else. And I will tell you this, too, through much recent prayer and meditation, I have come to believe that Megan has achieved remarkable growth in her brief thirty years. Astonishing growth. And every one of us in this chapel today should be proud of her and hope to gain as much as she did from our time here, even if we live to be one hundred and fifty years. I say this not for Molly's sake. I say this because it is the truth.

Still, we're struck by our loss. Her youth. Beauty. The loss of precious life. The loss of an individual who is unlike any other individual who has lived or whoever will live. God has challenged us with a formidable paradox because all we really have here on Earth is life,

life itself. Everything else is disposable matter, quickly forgotten by future generations. But as we have learned over and over again, this same heartache that we experience by the loss of life plays an important role in the progress of our collective consciousness. Awareness is an elusive virtue that is sometimes ushered into view only by sorrow or apparent acts of cruelty. We know this. This helps explain wars and other demonstrations of barbarity. So we must be strong. We must have faith. We must make better use of our own time here on earth and honor each moment for all of eternity. We must be soldiers of God. And most of all, we must not judge.

Now I want to take a moment to talk about the Tyler family and the recent string of transitions, beginning with Ben Tyler, Megan's father, the former rock star. I know this is a subject that concerns many of us today. I know because I can see it in your eyes, from up here. And I want to stress that we must be careful not to place too much emphasis on family—blood—relations. Yet we cannot ignore it, either. We've all made choices before entering this sphere, and much drama plays out on our humble, earthly playing field. It's called free will. It is our God-given right.

Yet, I do perceive some complications with this Tyler lineage, complications that are really none of my business. But I'm going take this opportunity to remind everyone anyway that every choice we make is recorded in the Akashic Records. Resolutions can be temporal and responsibility eternal. You must understand that. And so I say unto every one of you here today, in confusing and vulnerable times, you must concentrate on the third chakra and use your physical experience to increase your integrity, your self-respect, your self-discipline, your self-esteem, and your ability to handle a crisis. It is truth that heals. It is truth that sets us free. These are not hollow platitudes, sisters and brothers. Honor the truth like you would honor God, for they are

*one and the same. Do the right thing, for there is still
time to make the correct choices for your true eternal
sake. Take the righteous path, for surely that will be
your salvation...*

It was right around this point when I put on the old Detroit
earmuffs. I could listen no more. In my mind, Preacher Jane was
talking directly to me, despite the forced generalities. Evidently, she
had been tipped off by her spirit friends that I had killed one of the
Tylers—one of my blood—and as a mediator and a conveyor of
truth, she decided that it was her job to let me know there was still
time to consider the big picture and not just Hank Tyler's miserable,
earthly pot of gold. Or something along those lines.

Granted, it was more than possible she was a misguided,
wildwood, Northern California flake, but my gut told me otherwise.
This was the same gut that told me Isabella's surprise visitation in
her house after her memorial was exactly that, a visitation, and not
some half-ass, narcotic hallucination. Isabella said few words that
night, but three of them were "Molly's kids, too." I disregarded that
request but I wasn't sure if I could ignore this latest ethereal plea
from Preacher Jane.

So after turning off the volume, I stood up from my chair and
walked out of the chapel (past Hank Tyler, who appeared to be wisely
sleeping) into the cool Pacific air. I was now carrying cigarettes with
me, and I guess you could say I had started smoking. I lit up and
looked to the west, watching the sky. It was growing darker. Below
me, the stones connecting the chapel to the lot appeared to glow
brighter. I felt my equilibrium slipping—just a bit. The preacher
had struck a chord. Yet despite her accuracy, her good intentions,
it was an old story for me: *victims having to choose* and something
I struggled with every day of my life. The fact still remained that
Hank Tyler started this ugly mess, not me. And Stan Tyler was a
cruel son-of-a-bitch. He had no right to treat me or anyone else
the way he did. He deserved what he got and it was a mini-miracle
someone didn't beat me to it. I inhaled deeply, crushed my cigarette,
and felt the strength returning. The God-given strength I suppose.
Where else could it possibly come from? No, I *will not* acquiesce on this

sacred ground, despite the sermon. I *will not* turn the other cheek. I *will not* do the right thing. The third chakra/integrity stuff would have to wait until I claimed my earthly treasures and defeated Hank Tyler. Hank Tyler would be held responsible for his odious behavior in the here and now—and not when he was good and safely (or unsafely) dead. I had traveled too deep into rugged, surreal Tylerville to turn back now. I would finish what I started. Preacher Jane could go to hell. And fuck eternity. I'll cross that bridge when I get to it.

When the service ended, I joined the congregation as they filed out of the chapel and trekked about a quarter of a mile through the darkening coppice to the edge of the cliff. Here we watched Molly pour Megan's ashes into the angry sea. Preacher Jane said a final prayer, her voice clashing violently with the pounding of the surf below, neither one willing to surrender. It was moving and made me think about my last image of Megan, the one with smeared war paint on her face. She had not forgotten who she really was despite all those years of addiction and abuse.

As I stood high on that cliff, looking down into the abyss, the cold wind blowing right through me, I knew my unwillingness to do the right thing, as outlined by Preacher Jane, was the major difference between Megan and me and the reason why Megan had transcended and why I was still stuck on this dirty little planet—and probably would be for some time to come.

29
CAPITULATION

After the cliff ceremony, our congregation marched back to the chapel, back to our respective vehicles, and followed the taillights to Molly's residence in Mill Valley.

To my great relief, the house did not resemble a giant penis or a spaceship from a destroyed galaxy. Instead, it was rather ordinary and attractive with a sloped rock garden out front, pretty bay windows, and a cozy sitting room in the rear that looked out onto the scaling backwoods. I mention the back room because I found myself escaping to it now and then as the evening progressed.

My first course of action upon entering was to engage Jessica and get that over with. A lot of my concern about San Sebastian was overshadowed by her latest remarks accusing me of purposefully, maliciously supplying Megan with drugs. Unfortunately, it took that type of malice to dull my sensitivity to what had happened between us.

"We need to establish boundaries," she said to me.

"Boundaries? You're kidding, right?" I shot back, thinking it was light years too late for that.

"I've decided I don't want to have any more contact with you—personally."

This, I had to think about. Her demand made sense if it was to be interpreted as a practical measure to prevent another San Sebastian blood fest. But I don't think that had anything to do with it. I looked deeply into her eyes and sensed her intensity softening, weakening; a phenomenon that I had never witnessed or recognized before. It was so unlike her. I mean, she was a fucking battleship off the coast of Guadalcanal. I even detected a tiny bit of old fashioned human fear. Yes, fear! And then I knew. She was scared. Jessica was scared that I MIGHT TRY TO KILL HER—like I killed Megan. SHE COULD BE NEXT, as extraordinary as that sounds. But how extraordinary was it? I did kill Stan, after all, although I was not sure she suspected me of that, too. But she might have, despite the concrete evidence of my geographical innocence. She, more than anyone I knew, was ruled by her instincts.

I also wondered how much my running away from her into the arms of Ponderosa played into this equation. Quickly, in my mind, it was becoming complex. I decided to stick to the immediate business before us. She could think as she pleased.

"Okay," I said. "Does this mean everything else stays the same or not?"

"Use the lawyers," she snapped, and then abruptly walked over to Molly, who remained glued to her paraclete, Pastor Jane.

I stood, smarting, and then detoured to the bar to pour myself a real drink. From there, I sought out Claire, my bedrock in this Tyler swamp. She, along with everyone else, was curious about my visit with Megan before she died.

"Was she in pain?" she asked me, her eyes wide and full of hope for good news.

"That's not what I saw."

"What did you see, Nic?"

"I saw more change than anything else. Even though I didn't know her, I saw change. That's the only way I can describe it."

"She had a tough life."

"I know."

"It will be easier for her now, God willing."

"How are you getting along without Isabella?"

"It's lonely. I think when everything is all settled, I'm going to sell the house and move."

"Where?"

"I don't know. Maybe Ireland. I still have family there. Maybe it's time to go back."

Her eyes then fixed on someone beyond me. I turned around. Hank Tyler was standing nearby talking to the Walt Whitman guy.

"He was her godfather," she said.

"Hank?" I asked.

"Yes. Of all the kids, she was the closest to him."

That I did not want to hear. Megan had a special place in my heart, and heartless Hank Tyler should have no link to my sanctum.

"Claire," I said, changing the subject, "I want to thank you again for all that you've done for me."

"It's what Isabella wanted."

"I won't disappoint her," I said, knowing full well I had already done so.

"This may sound unnatural to you, Nic, but you're probably the head of the family now, or what's left of it."

"I don't know about that," I replied, not sure if I felt flattered. "It's really a vacuum."

And it was. Ben and his two children from his first marriage were now gone, Isabella (the matriarch) gone, Josh sanctioned and partially disinherited, and Joseph and Jessica self-exiled in Europe. Besides, I was never a part of it to begin with. My belated blood role had more to do with Prostitute Records and Hank Tyler's wrath. Once Joseph sold his membership to me, Jessica would be the only sibling I would have any reason to interact with, and she just made it clear to me that it would only be through mediators. That is, if she did not change her mind again. Or if I did not kill her (her thinking, not mine).

Later, after retreating to the rear sitting room to avoid Ponderosa, who I was afraid to be seen with for fear of possibly igniting Jessica into a public outburst, I was confronted by Preacher Jane, another person I was purposely avoiding. She walked serenely into the sitting room, aware of my recluse status. I could tell she was anxious to talk even though she was doing her best to appear constrained.

"And you are Nic." she said, not asked.

"Yes, I am Nic."

"Are you feeling okay, Nic?"

"Not really," I replied, hoping she would interpret that as a sign to leave me be.

"Is that why you left the chapel early?"

"Yes, I was feeling faint," I said. "Sorry about the timing."

"It's not the first time someone's walked out on me," she smiled. "I'm surprised they all don't."

This was an attempt at humor but, again, I wasn't interested. I was on edge. "I doubt that," I said politely.

"It became very clear to me today you and Megan really connected. Is that true?" she asked.

"What do you mean?"

"When you were with Megan in Florida—the two of you connected?"

"Yes, we did."

"After all those years, too?"

"Yes. I don't know if everyone realizes it, though."

"I do."

"You seem to realize a lot" I replied, knowing the more this went on, the worse off I'd be.

"It's a gift. But I have to nurture it or it will go away. You understand?"

"Yes. I can understand that."

"That's my excuse for being nosey," she smiled. "Megan was a courageous woman," she continued, inching closer, her eyes beaming bright like the Crab Nebula.

"Yes. That's how I felt about her."

"You two were about the same age?"

"Six months difference."

"Same father. I don't think it was a coincidence you met when you did, Nic. Right before she died."

"What do you mean?" I asked, her face now 18 inches away from mine.

"You attracted one another. You must be sailing some stormy weather yourself. Like Megan was. Aren't you?"

Yes, I was sailing through a hurricane in a canoe, but I was not taking the bait. I was not going to discuss fratricide and incest with Pastor Jane, not in this lifetime anyway. It was time to be rude.

"I have to go, Pastor," I said, "but thank you for your interest." I then stood up and walked past her, down the hallway, and into the main room where I almost collided with Molly, who was still looking like she needed directions to the Eiffel Tower.

"Did I tell you?" she almost screamed.

"Tell me what?"

"I got the toxicity report from the coroner."

"No, you didn't tell me."

"It wasn't good."

"No?"

"She had phenobarbital, diazepam, alprazolam, oxycodone, and ketamine in her bloodstream."

Molly's condition was beginning to frighten me. Whatever guilt she harbored for a lifetime of artistic self-indulgence had finally surfaced, like an iceberg, after Megan's death. I was partly to blame, too, for having destroyed her other child.

"When I talked to her at rehab," I said with the utmost sincerity, "she didn't mention drugs. I swear. She was on a path of a remarkable transformation."

"I'll never write another poem."

This was becoming painful. Molly was in a dire state. I saw Preacher Jane approaching. I turned back to Molly.

"Do you want another drink?" I asked.

"Make it a strong one."

"I'll be right back."

I hurried into the kitchen, not planning to return. I grabbed the bottle on the table and poured more vodka over ice for myself. I guzzled the vodka. I knew I had to escape. There were too many people I could not talk to without consequence, immediate or otherwise. And hiding in the back room was no longer effective, after being smoked out by Preacher Jane.

I decided I would make a beeline exit without saying another word, a trick I learned from Cynthia at Isabella's gathering. Only I would go out the back door. But then I considered Ponderosa. We had already booked a hotel for that night in San Francisco, and I should at least tell her before I left. I still hadn't uttered one word to her since that morning at the car rental agency as we attempted this ludicrous estrangement amongst people who knew me and my affairs better than I did.

When I reentered the living room, I found her talking with Jessica. As I walked closer, they both stopped talking and stared right at me. They both had strange, unflattering, noncommittal expressions on their faces, and I couldn't even *imagine* the contents of their conversation except that I was a major part of it. I immediately changed my mind. It was too risky to talk to Ponderosa, and I aborted the notification plan. Ponderosa would have to figure things out for herself.

And just as I was about to pull the trusty 180 and disappear via the rear, I heard a deep, scratchy voice address me. It was a familiar voice, but one I hadn't heard in a while.

"We need to talk," the voice said.

I turned to my left, and there was Hank Tyler, saddled with cigarette and drink, looking wishy-washy from all the booze. I actually had forgotten all about him with all the occult intrigues going on. At that particular moment, he was the least of my worries.

"I don't want to talk now," I responded rather directly.

He winced slightly, not expecting the curtness. He readjusted. "How 'bout just a couple of minutes?" he said.

"Make it fast."

"I underestimated you," he said, gulping down another mouthful of scotch. "I'm sorry."

I didn't quite believe him, and his verbal gesture seemed more strategy than sincerity, but this was, by any standards, a magnanimous concession. Unfortunately, his timing was off. I was not in a generous mood.

"So does that mean you're sorry for your behavior or that you just miscalculated?" I asked.

"Jesus Christ, don't get fancy on me."

"I'm listening."

"We need to work something out."

"Maybe I'm not ready to work something out."

"It will be worth your while."

I gazed around the room, and I noticed quite a few people looking our way, in pairs. There was Ponderosa and Jessica, and Claire and the Walt Whitman guy, and Molly and Preacher Jane. In fact, as I recall, it seemed as though almost everybody in the room was paired off and giving us their attention in one way or another. I looked back at Hank and realized that he had no real friends here in this Tyler collective his brother started many years before—a brother who was now gone, leaving Hank to fend for himself. Hank was all alone.

Normally, of course, that would not have mattered to him because he was used to being alone and unliked, but then I came along and screwed everything up for his business. Prostitute Records was the only Tyler thing he cared about. I had to overrule myself and take a few moments. I had Hank exactly where I wanted him. This was a long time coming. This was the moment I had been waiting for. The filthy bitch was mine.

"This isn't the place," I said.

"When?"

"In Detroit. At Eclectic Emporium. I want you to come."

"When?"

"Tuesday morning, 11 am."

"Okay, I'll be there."

"Before you come, I want you to fire Jam."

"I already got rid of him."

"Oh?"

"Karolina took over the Detroit store."

"She did?"

"You fired her, right?"

"Right."

"What the hell."

"Yeah, what the hell."

30
PARANOIAC CHIEFDOM

Ponderosa and I spent the night in San Francisco. Before we fell asleep, I couldn't help but ask her what she and Jessica were talking about at Molly's house.

"Don't you trust me?" she asked. "Or is this just a game the two of us play with each other?"

It was an excellent point and a competent response, but I still wondered how she could *not* comment on my sexual encounter with my half-sister and Jessica's subsequent murderous accusations, assuming Jessica was still Jessica and acting like Jessica while in Marin.

"Before I was on your side, I was on Stan's side. Remember? Or have you forgotten?" she added.

I remembered all too well, but then, of course, there was a big pot of gold at the end of that dark tunnel. My situation did not parallel Stan's, but clearly I would soon start reaping Tyler benefits with Hank's long-awaited capitulation.

Ponderosa was different from anyone else dear to me because she knew the Tylers and their associates better than I did. She had history with Jessica and the others, and God only knows the pillow talk and creepy things Stan told her all those months they were together. I was also the one who happened to kill him, which, I fully believed, she suspected me of at least on an intuitive, walk-in-the-park level, but chose to suppress or ignore, consciously or unconsciously, using her finely tuned disposition. This led me to believe that she *should not* trust me—whether she did or not. It was convoluted, hazy, paranoid thinking for sure, but Megan's death threw me for a loop. On a strict Hank Tyler business level, her demise strengthened my immediate inheritance position. But it also brought forth enormous personal heartache and a lot of vague and not-so-vague reversals from people about whom I previously did not have to worry. Jessica, Molly, and Ponderosa all now unnerved me in one way or another and to varying degrees as a result of Megan dying.

In addition—and this was more than loosely connected—Karolina refused to go away. She proved to be ten times smarter than Jam (no prize there), and used him instead of the other way around. Once her double-agent charade was up, she obviously persuaded Hank to ax Jam so she could take over. But the problem remained that I still did not trust Karolina, just as I did not trust Hank, even though we all soon stood to be on the same team, as fantastical as that may sound.

Hence, my world had become a much more complicated arrangement, and it made me all the more willing to trust Ponderosa because I needed to trust her, *whether she trusted me or not.*

*

The next morning, Ponderosa and I went our separate ways. She flew to Wyoming and I back to Detroit. From the Metro Airport, I taxied directly to Stu's office and filled him in on Hank. He was pleased and assured me that once the bank received this information, they would give the green light for the loan. He would then be free to contact Joseph's lawyer to complete the purchase of Joseph's stake in Prostitute LLC.

The loan also meant I could finally ease up on the phony cash. I did some cursory bookkeeping and discovered I had already burned over 237,000 dollars in twenty-dollar bills. That was a decent wad in a relatively brief period of time. I was running out of them, too, and this timely influx of U.S. Treasury bills through a sanctioned and regulated financial institution would save me the delicate task of approaching Sledge and asking him where I might dig up some more of his currency.

Sledge and I never talked or corresponded about the basement stash, with the exception of his key but incidental reference to the sump pump during my visit to Terminal Island. In my opinion, the paper was intended exclusively for me in the event that I needed it.

It wasn't simply forgotten about. As it turned out, I needed it badly and it served to be the deciding factor that kept me afloat long enough to outlast weasel Hank Tyler. Therefore, I needed to do my part and follow through in every respect, devoid of sentimentality, and take care of one last bit of unfinished business before Hank arrived on Tuesday and fire Karolina again. Yes, I could let bygones be bygones, and if she stayed, she would be involved with retail in Detroit and do a wonderful job and my responsibilities would be elsewhere, but I knew her ambitions would not stay in Detroit, nor would her relationship with Hank. She was potentially hazardous. And she hated me.

I questioned my true motives and wondered if retaliatory testosterone coupled with bitterness over her never having loved me had more to do with this tough decision than her potential future danger to my fiefdom (which was unquestionably real), but I called Hank anyway and requested that he get rid of her before he came out. He was hesitant at first, which made me more than certain the two of them had an understanding and I was doing the right thing. But he wisely said, "No problem, see you on Tuesday."

I then considered buying a weapon to protect myself. Karo had a temper, and she would not be happy about losing another job.

*

At 10 am on a freezing, snowy Tuesday morning in the first week of the New Year, Hank Tyler arrived at my Eclectic Emporium store. He entered sporting a long, green fur, Peter-the-Great caveman suit, otherwise known as a winter coat.

He walked directly over to the unattended counter, not once looking around at the store. Apparently, he was not interested in the physical details of a long-standing institution that he tried to arbitrarily destroy. I was in my office, alone, and feeling rather ambivalent for not alerting the media of this historic moment. Surely, there should be at least a couple of journalists and photographers present to record it for posterity.

Leaving that thought behind, I stood up and walked out to the counter and shook his hand. It wasn't tremendously uncomfortable since I had just been with him in Marin, but it was still awkward with both of us sober and no one around to distract us. Before directing him into the lounge, I offered coffee. He declined but asked if he could smoke. I was tempted to say no because I knew he really wanted to and therefore it would be to my advantage if he didn't. But I allowed it because I was now smoking and dying for one myself. So we lit up, settled in, and got down to business.

What was at stake was simple: the future of Prostitute LLC. I would soon be in control, or partial control, of Ben's original 26 percent, once probate was over. That was over one-quarter of the company. He was there to offer me something that would reflect my new equity-position and attempt to preempt a potential confrontation somewhere down the line. He was quick to warn me that despite my gains, or potential gains, he would still have the upper hand if he so chose by uniting some of the other long-standing members in his corner. "You must have considered that already?" he asked, almost rhetorically.

"Yes, but for how long?" I answered.

"As long as I want to."

"We'll see."

"Let's cut the bullshit."

"Okay."

He offered me the title of company president with the verbal and written understanding that he would be the CEO and maintain his role as the ultimate decision-maker. As an LLC, Prostitute had no board meetings and could do whatever it pleased providing 51 percent of the membership supported it.

He used to be, along with the silent Ben, the 51 percent, and now, if I wanted, he and I would be the 51 percent. "This way, everything stays in the family."

Averaging two cigarettes to my every one, he went on to say that he could offer me no better and if I declined, then it would indeed turn into an ugly war, and no matter what I thought, he would have the advantage. In addition, it was important that I appreciate the fact that he created Prostitute, and, thus far, he had done a pretty darn good job increasing its value over the years. He was now diversifying outside the music industry and would continue to do so because it was the smart thing to do. "And that's not going to change, either," he barked, as punctuation.

My first rebuttal was to correct his revisionist history. It was actually he and Ben who had started Prostitute, not just him, and he should not forget it. (I refrained from going into the jailbird yarn, but he got the idea.) I then went on to tell him his family reference as it regarded me was offensive after the way he treated me and he should "show more respect."

To that, he bowed his head and stared a hole in the floor and kept that way until I began discussing the specifics of his offer: the new title was acceptable, but I wanted to effectively take over the music, both label and retail, in the new digital age. "You can be doing a much better job, and you're not," I said, almost condescendingly. I had no problem with his diversifying, but it "shouldn't be at the expense of the music." My taking over the music was for his own good and my own good and to save everything he and Ben built.

"That's all you want? To take over?" he asked.

"The music."

"You think you're ready?"

"Yes."

"I'm not so sure."

"Go back to Los Angeles and think about it. I'm in no rush."

He lit up another smoke and changed the subject: "You know," he said, "your Karolina turned out to be a real pain in the ass. I had to fly my general manager in with me to take care of it."

"You started it."

"Yeah, I guess I did."

"Yeah, you did."

"You remind me of Ben. He was ballsy, too."

This quieted me, quieted both of us. I had almost forgotten about good old bio-Dad with all the tragedy, death, and murder. Ben and I had never bonded face to face, and perhaps this partial conciliatory exchange between his only brother and his first son would be the closest I'd ever get to it. Still, Hank was a scorpion, and I had to stay tough or get bitten again. "Those are my terms," I heard myself saying aloud. "That's final."

"Alright, alright," he moaned, before pulverizing yet another cigarette into the glass ashtray. "I'll agree in principle. You run the music. Satisfied?"

"Yes."

"Good. Now that you're in charge, you can take care of that mess down the street. I just pumped two million into it."

"Don't worry. I'll take care of it. I have something in mind for the whole retail operation. I want to coordinate it with what you already have in place."

"Fine," he mumbled, "just make sure it doesn't cost too much."

*

Exactly four days later, I proudly pushed open the glass doors of Detroit Prostitute Eclectic and claimed my token prize. To my bittersweet surprise, the place was busy and I recognized many old faces that used to frequent Eclectic Emporium. No hard feelings, I told myself, they were now customers again. I also recognized Karolina's unique touch in the choice of furniture, colors, and artwork.

I marveled over how she could have accomplished so much in just a few weeks' time, and then I remembered her extended coffee breaks and figured a lot of what I was looking at could have been implemented through Jam while she was still working for me, or rather for both of us. That possibility erased any guilt on my part or business acumen I credited her with, and I was glad the duplicitous heretic was forever banished. Even if it took firing her twice.

Hank left me Kim, the Prostitute retail general manager who accompanied Hank to Detroit to fire Karolina. Kim was a handsome, compact, shaved head, 35-year-old Korean émigré who, to my great relief, did not bear any behavioral or self-inflicted esthetic resemblance to Jam. Instead, he was soft-spoken, pleasant to be around, and assumed an almost militaristic obedience to my requests. He was also up to speed with the bio-complicated Eclectic Emporium/Prostitute history and was therefore impressed if not awed by my startling rise to the top. And how could he not be, knowing Hank as he did?

I immediately liked Kim, and I needed him, but I had no illusions about his guile, for he could not have survived otherwise. I told him up front that he was now working for me first and Hank second, and he would need to remember that order if he wanted to hold onto his job. After Karolina, I was taking no chances. Kim assured me that he understood the new hierarchy.

My first task in my new role as the hands-on boss of Prostitute Records was to consolidate the two Detroit retail stores. The Detroit market could barely support one, and I was forced to make a tough decision and close one down. Unfortunately, the right thing to do was obvious. The Prostitute Eclectic warehouse, which we owned, was over twice the size of the Eclectic Emporium rental, with newer facilities, more sophisticated technology, a bigger lounge, three times the parking space (for the suburbanites), and a growing or stabilizing client base. Thus, I would swallow my pride and transfer my inventory and my remaining customers to Prostitute Eclectic. I reminded myself that I, and not Hank, had won the war, and this move should be viewed as an act of selfless professionalism. To compensate, however, I was going to change the name of the company to Prostitute-Eclectic Records. It would be my first order of business once I moved to Los Angeles.

My next major decision was to incorporate (and this may sound heartless, because it was) the changes Karolina had implemented at the Detroit Prostitute store to all our stores throughout the country and the European continent. I told Kim about it, and he thought it was an excellent idea, too. We were unsure of the costs involved, but neither one of us doubted Hank's approval because it was so much in the spirit of "business as usual" at Prostitute Records, a tradition that Hank heralded: steal, claw, undermine, do whatever it takes to increase business.

I put Kim in charge of following through with the new retail plan. He would operate out of our Detroit store alongside me while I continued to familiarize myself with my new job. I called Hank and requested that he send out Kim's equivalent for the music label end of the business to help educate me until I was ready to make the permanent move to Los Angeles. Hank offered no resistance, and I assumed the prolonged physical transition suited him.

Underneath the surface, however, things were moving at

full speed, as he well knew. My bank loan had come in, and Stu was simultaneously finalizing my purchase of Joseph's pending Prostitute stake while ironing out my new contract as president with the Prostitute lawyers. For the first time in my life, money—fake, real, or otherwise—was no longer an issue. And on paper, I was beginning to live the life I had only dreamed about. True, it did not come without sacrifice, loss, and mortgaging two-thirds of my soul, but it felt good, despite my sleepless, creeping paranoia.

The one thing left to do to complete the circle was to persuade Ponderosa to move to Los Angeles. I wanted her close to me. I would have asked her to marry me if I thought it would serve me better, but I knew it would not and would likewise incite the wrath and contempt of many people. Besides, I knew she would balk. But I wanted all of her. That I knew.

*

As I was busy familiarizing myself with the intricacies of Prostitute LLC and courting Ponderosa from afar, I received a surprise visit from a most unlikely guest. Josh Tyler. His visit marked the second time a Tyler had come to me in Detroit, Hank Tyler being the first. Josh was sober, well-mannered, cleanly dressed, and apologetic about hitting me in the head with a broomstick the last time we met. "I was a little stressed out with my mother dying and all," he told me.

"Forget it," I said, trying to let bygones be bygones.

"It won't happen again."

"Thanks."

"I hear you're kicking Uncle Hank's ass."

"We're working together."

"That's more than he did with anyone else."

"He's got no choice."

"You gambled, and you won," he said in full admiration.

"Sort of," I replied, trying to be humble. "A lot of it has to do with your mom. She gambled on me."

"That's why I'm here."

Humility, I've learned, is not always the correct choice. He then proceeded to tell me the following: He was distraught about being disinherited by his father and having to wait over five years or so to cash in on his mother's inheritance in the guise of a restricted trust. He wanted me to talk to Claire on his behalf and try to persuade her to alter the trust arrangement so he could collect more funds up front. He was having difficulties coping with some existing gambling debts, and Claire and the lawyers were no longer accepting his phone calls.

"It really sucks," he kept saying. "My lawyer told me yesterday once the estate is settled I'll still be disinherited by Dad, and I'm still going to have to wait five years for my mother's share. I can't wait five years."

"Why not?"

"Because I might not make it. For me not to have money is a bad thing."

"Have you talked to Jessica and Joseph? They're due to get quite a bit from your father's side."

"Jessica hates me, and even if she broke down she'd torture me to death over it. And Joseph has his own things going on that cost a lot of money. I want my own money. I need my own money. I can't be dependent on Joseph and Jessica. It's not fair. I deserve my own fucking money."

I understood his position. He needed a cushion given his history and burden. That was legitimate. Overall, though, none of this was surprising or persuasive, nor was there anything I could do for him.

"I can talk to Claire," I said, "but she's just following through with what your mom wanted as spelled out in her holographic will. If Claire starts changing things, she risks being challenged and possibly losing. To Hank, for instance. Technically, Claire's the beneficiary, but as it now stands, she's just the executrix and simply finishing up what your mom spelled out. I really don't think Claire could help you even if she wanted to."

"That's what my lawyers said, but I'm trying everything I can. And now it's going to get worse."

"Why?"

"Because my lawyers want to get paid even though they're not helping me."

"Are you working?"

There was a long pause.

"Working?" he asked, but it didn't sound like a question.

"Yeah."

"I guess you can say I'm working. I started writing music again."

"Do you have a day job?"

"You're missing my point, Einstein. I could work for the next ten years at a straight gig, and I'd still be in debt and destitute. I need a lot of money, and I'll always need a lot of money."

He was becoming morbid and I kept seeing his mother in his face. "You may want to consider working here at Prostitute-Eclectic Records," I said. "That's going to be the new name. I'm thinking about starting a new mini-label that deals exclusively with Internet garage bands. I haven't figured it all out yet because I'm still learning, but it's on the agenda. I can use some help."

He was not too thrilled by the prospect. "Work for you and Hank? Fuck. I got a better idea. How about you work for me?"

"Maybe that day will come. But for now, it will have to be the other way around. And don't worry about Hank. You'd be dealing with me."

"What if he doesn't go for it?"

"Let me worry about Hank," I said, as if Hank did not really matter, which was not true.

"I'll think about it," he said.

"Okay, think about it."

"I would have to be paid well."

"Of course."

"I'll think about it."

"Okay."

"This place looks different from the other stores."

"They're all going to look more like this one."

He then became quiet, sinking into his own thoughts. I let him be. We both sat in silence. Eventually, he spoke up again, "If Hank wasn't such a dickhead, I would have come around more. I had some good ideas, but Dad never forgave me and always backed Hank. Then he died."

"Maybe if you just sold the Strat and didn't burn down the house, he would haven't been so hard on you."

"I don't know about that. After I sold the Strat, he told me he was disinheriting me. That's why I burned down the house."

After he left, I was convinced that he was incapable of working for anyone except possibly me. And that was going to be a tremendous challenge for both of us if he decided to do so. But I knew in my heart that I had to do my part. I sympathized with the unresolved guilt he harbored about his deceased father. They never came to a resolution. I had similar issues, but at least Ben sent me his Euro-letter to confirm his love. If Ben were alive, I believe he would want me to help Josh if I could, despite his bitterness regarding the loss of his wife's house and his sacred Strat. And I know damn well Isabella would have insisted upon it if the circumstances were right. Again, I felt I had no choice in the matter. Broomstick or no broomstick.

*

As we were finishing the consolidation of the two Detroit stores, I received an ominous phone call from Ponderosa. Her stoic, monotone phone voice reminded me of the old walk-in-the-park days.

"I received two calls today," she said, barely.

"Okay."

"From the government."

"Government? What part of the government?" I asked.

"The FAA and he National Transportation Safety Board. They're completing their investigations into Stan's balloon crash."

"Good," I replied, the words coming out effortlessly as I switched into autopilot fabrication mode. I knew the findings would be public sooner or later. "So what did they say?" I asked.

"There were unusual circumstances."

"Unusual?" I said, minimizing. "It's all unusual, isn't it?"

"They found something wrong with his propane tanks."

I stopped. This I did not expect. I assumed the tanks had been blown to bits and what remained consumed and melted by flame.

"So that's what caused the crash, the tanks?" I asked, knowing that her two most irritating traits when she acted like this were calculated reticence and intuitive observation.

"Yes. There was something wrong with a release valve," she replied softly.

The time had come to dumb down again. "It didn't work?" I asked obtusely.

"Yes. The valve didn't work."

"Well, at least they know what happened. What do you do now, sue the manufacturer?"

Here she hesitated, and then replied, "No, I don't think so. I don't think I can."

"Why not?"

"Because they said it was sealed shut."

"What was?"

"The valve."

"I don't understand."

"The valve was supposed to open up if the pressure in the propane tank became too great. But it never opened, because it was sealed. That's what they think caused the explosion."

"Why was it sealed? That doesn't make sense."

"They don't know, but they think someone must have sealed it."

She waited. We both waited. "Why would Stan seal it?"

There was even more silence after that. And then, with slight resignation, she said: "I don't know, Nic, but it's going to be all over the news tomorrow. They're releasing a statement. I thought you should know."

That rendered me speechless, and not on purpose. The implications, the publicity, were more than I cared to think about at the moment.

"You know what else they told me?" she continued.

"What?"

"They were about to conclude the investigation and declare human error on the part of Stan as the probable cause, but when they heard Megan died of an overdose they decided to keep it open and take a closer look. They reexamined everything and discovered the valve was sealed with a petroleum compound and not melted shut from the fire."

"What did they ask you?" I said, no longer able to pretend to be surprised or stupid. This time, she responded immediately, almost as if she was waiting for the question to be asked.

"They wanted to know how Stan and I were getting along. They wanted to know if Stan had any enemies. And they really wanted to know who would benefit most from Stan's death."

"Well, did you tell them?"

"Tell them? Tell them what?"

"Jessica and Joseph Tyler. Who else? Before Stan died they may have gotten nothing, and now they're due to split most of the estate."

31
INQUISITION

The news of Stan Tyler's sabotaged hot air balloon hit the gossip-obsessed public like an alcoholic tidal wave. They absolutely could not get enough. The TV news and talk shows, the tabloids, the blogs, the AM radio weirdoes, foreign countries, communists, the Bible Belt, everybody was tuning in. The lure, of course, was good old-fashioned juicy gossip. Who killed Stan Tyler, the heir to the Tyler fortune? The theatrics of Stan's little hot air balloon blowing up in the big Wyoming sky only served to heighten the dark comic appeal. It was a little too cartoonish, a little too British, and not the grisly, face-to-face, gang-bang murder that we loathe. It also connected seamlessly with rock star Ben's farewell, another wayward Tyler who expired rather comically—with a hard-on. Hence, it was all sort of "fun." It opened up a floodgate of grand theories about the string of Tyler family deaths. Who could resist? The most popular one being that all four of the deceased—Ben, Isabella, Stan, Megan—were killed, not just Stan. Isabella's plane was tampered with, the Thai authorities covered up Ben's sexual murder, someone forced drugs down Megan's throat, and so on. It was not entirely unfounded either. Had not Megan tragically died, the NTSB might not have discovered the truth about the propane tanks. From that perspective, even I, who knew the truth, understood the public's skeptical enthusiasm.

Likewise, most of the main suspects were Tylers, too. Staying consistent, the media portrayed them as caricatures. There was the secretive expatriated geneticist; the bitter but struggling record mogul (Hank); the mysterious and exotic San Sebastian chef; and the disinherited house-burner, Josh, who was by far the hands-down favorite as the "guy who did it."

Not to be excluded from this elite list were a few people outside the bloodline, such as Ponderosa and Claire (neither one made any sense to me), Isabella's lawyers (they were surreptitiously expropriating, and they hired trained assassins), and a couple of young Southern California rocker druggy dudes who were allegedly in cahoots with Josh. But no matter who your choice might be for multiple Tyler murderer, everyone was in agreement about motive: the pending almost half-billion-dollar Tyler estate.

As for *moi*, the only genuine culprit, I was finally picked up on the public radar as the ambitious Detroit bastard who was challenging the bitter record tycoon. I was a long shot, though, because of my small chance of draining the entire estate. For me to score like Jessica or Joseph, every single Tyler would have to be dead first—including Hank, and probably Josh, too, especially if he kept fighting. My financial reach was limited to Prostitute Records, a battle initiated by Hank Tyler and not me, and acknowledged as such. This sidetracked most serious conspiracy pundits, and they foolishly disregarded me as a suspect.

But—and I can't emphasize this enough—within the Tyler camp, and soon other key groups, I was not the long shot candidate. I was a prime fucking suspect.

Jessica, for one, was absolutely certain that I had killed both Megan and Stan for reasons already stated and could not be convinced otherwise. She never talked to the press, but within her own network she never shut up about it.

I had an inkling that Joseph shared his younger sister's suspicions, but he apparently did not care because of his magical reversal. He was too clone-obsessed to concern himself with frivolous details of who killed whom. As long as it was not he who was being killed. He was also satisfied with my loan (bribe?) money to help him bridge the gap and keep his pathetic Newcastle operations going until his real payoff came in.

Josh, I believe, suspected me, too, but remained noncommittal. One thing he was certain about, though: *He* was not the guy who did it, despite the unwanted and overwhelmingly negative publicity he was receiving. I had a feeling that he suspected Joseph, too. He knew about Joseph's habits, his clinical expenses, and, most of all, his hatred of Stan.

Molly was a big question mark. The sabotage of Stan's balloon craft must have induced some thinking about my visit to him a couple of weeks before he went down. She arranged it, after all. I was also Megan's last registered visitor, a fact that Molly brought to Jessica's attention. On the other hand, as a true follower of Preacher Jane's, revenge was a waste of time and none of her business. So I don't know if she even bothered to concern herself, regardless of what she suspected. In fact, I was more worried about Molly's health than her suspicions. I'm sure she loathed the public fascination that her children's deaths were attracting. She reportedly began to drink heavily and reclusively, and, as we know, she was a heavy drinker to begin with.

Hank Tyler was another puzzle of sorts. He never once revealed his thoughts on the matter to me, even though we were in regular contact during this time. Perhaps it had something to do with his prison mentality and the fact that he was once involved in murder himself. I am quite certain, however, that he considered himself better off without Stan Tyler, even though that meant he was stuck with me. For him, Stan was a lucky idiot who, among other things, had used me to blackmail him. (In retrospect, Stan clearly overplayed his hand, but was fooled about who would be the one to retaliate.) Stan was also on the verge of pissing away his father's fortune on money-losing sports franchises and highly speculative investment packages. Perhaps, like Joseph, Hank didn't give a rat's ass about it either way.

Interestingly, Hank chose not to use this new criminal investigation as a stalling tactic. He had nothing to lose by doing so. But for whatever reasons, he did not delay and instructed his attorneys to finish up the details of the contract.

Claire, I do not think suspected me or would ever suspect me, nor did she ever make a public statement that I knew of. My gut told me that she went along with the bloodsucking public and leaned more toward Josh and Joseph. She watched them biologically evolve as creatures and knew better than anyone how erratic they could be, especially when in an inebriated rage. She also hadn't forgotten how mechanically sophisticated Joseph was growing up and may have connected that with the altered propane tanks. I was fairly certain she would remain loyal to me.

Ponderosa I could spend an eternity dwelling on. She was drenched in subtlety and intuitive reflection, yet this had no effect on her cerebral prowess and methodical reasoning. Her complexity unnerved me. If held at gunpoint and forced to give a decisive opinion, I would have to say her unspoken position regarding my innocence was the same as her friend Jessica's. Strangely, that might have been a separate issue of whose side she was on. Nonetheless, I fiercely held my ground with her, as I had been doing since the post-Hindenburg 2 era began, and the two of us remained friends, lovers, and confidants (with limits).

In fact, our attraction and sexual appetites increased in the midst of all the edgy ambiguity and led to us fucking like rabbits. We were definitely living dangerously and enjoying it. When the subject of Stan came up, my attitude was simple: Where's the proof? There was too much speculation, publicity, and hearsay to take anything seriously, or so I proclaimed. She never challenged it.

In private, though, and despite my official party line, I carefully monitored everything that had to do with who killed Stan Tyler and the ensuing federal criminal investigation that began following the NTSB findings. Given the post-September 11 political climate, the United States government frowned upon any hint of foul play related to aviation, including a single-manned balloon.

The NTSB, I discovered, is an independent agency set up by Congress to determine probable cause in aviation mishaps that involve loss of life. That is their sole purpose. They do not prosecute or regulate. Instead, they draw conclusions, publish them, and then let the regulatory and investigatory agencies take over from there. In the Stan Tyler balloon case, the FBI and the U.S. Department of Justice were the two agencies that would take over. And as a paranoid saboteur who engaged in one tiny personal—not political—attack against one wretched half sibling during an elongated panic attack, I can attest to their accuracy, thoroughness and truthfulness.

Initially, they determined that electrical heat tape (applied by Stan) and liquid coating (applied by me) were used to increase the pressure in the propane tanks, and the probable cause was the ignition of vapor and liquid overflow brought on by rapid increase in tank pressure. The tanks were blown to bits, and the tape and coating were easy to detect. Stan was flying in the Wyoming morning when it was freezing outside and he needed to heat up those tanks. He screwed up. Hence, another case of human error or miscalculation on the part of the pilot, just as it was 99 percent of the time for small-craft, single-manned flights. Case closed.

And not to brag here, but that was exactly what I thought they would conclude. But then Megan Tyler died—the fourth Tyler to do so in six months—and they decided to scrupulously double-check their findings before publishing and discovered ethylene methyl acrylate copolymer resin on the release valve of the blown tank. That was a problem. Why would anyone seal the valve unless, you know, they understood the tank could blow as a result and kill ballooner Stan Tyler, who, at the time, happened to be the newly designated beneficiary and executor of Ben's portion of the Tyler estate?

One final and interesting note. Josh's lawyers, in an attempt to diffuse the unfair negative attention surrounding their innocent client (who would not and did not benefit one iota from the deaths of Megan and Stan), suggested the possibility that Stan committed suicide. The logic was a little fuzzy because if Stan was trying to kill himself he went about it in an extremely unorthodox way. But their point was well taken, and until specific incriminating evidence was produced fingering someone other than Stan, or definite proof of intent was established, nobody could be sure of what really happened up there.

*

Given the above, I wasn't entirely surprised when Kim entered the office and told me that FBI special agents Valarie Hunter and James Agee were outside waiting to talk to me. I knew it was coming sooner or later.

I finished my phone conversation and walked into the lounge, where the two agents were seated and waiting. Their visit marked my transcendence from closet observer of the Tyler criminal investigation to firsthand participant.

Both agents were in their 30s, well-groomed, and looked like actors who portray FBI agents on TV. They were also courteous (without being polite), methodical, direct, took notes, took turns asking questions, exchanged glances (some longer than others), and were extremely knowledgeable about my specific affairs as they related to the Tyler musical fiefdom.

"We tried the other record store first, but it was closed," Agent Agee said as a way of introduction.

"Yes, it's closed," I replied, not venturing anything more.

"Does that mean you've dissolved your first record business?"

"Merged."

"Congratulations," the other one said, her fine brown hair cut squarely and not quite reaching her shoulders. "So you are now partners with Hank Tyler?"

"The details are still being worked on."

"But it's being settled before probate ends?"

I paused, impressed by how up-to-date they were. "Evidently," I mumbled. "Can I get either one of you something to drink?"

They both shook their heads, "Naw, we're fine," said Hunter. "I understand you visited your half-brother Stan Tyler approximately three weeks before he died?"

"Yes, that's correct."

"This was on his ranch in Wyoming?"

"Yes."

"Did you see him after that?"

"No," I said.

"Did you see him before that time?"

"Never. That visit was the first and only time we met."

"So you didn't really know him?"

"Not at all."

"How did it go between you two when you did see him?" Agee asked, jumping back in.

"Not good."

"Why not?"

"He blew me off."

"Blew you off? You mean in terms of your business at hand?"

"Yes."

"That's the reason why you went to see him?"

"Yes."

"And this had to do with Hank Tyler and Prostitute Records?"

"Yes."

"So when he blew you off, he in fact rejected you or your offer? Is that what you mean?"

"Sort of."

"Sort of?" Agee said, coming alive like Nazareth. "Do you mean he was unclear about what he said?"

"Not exactly."

"So he was clear?"

"Yes, he was clear."

"Didn't he say he was planning on backing Hank Tyler and not you?"

"Yes. And if you know that, why are you asking me?"

"Please, let us do our job, Mr. Reilly, Agee said rather directly. "You need to explain what 'sort of' means."

I quickly surmised that "sort of" was a mistake. It implied ambivalence. Ambivalence could only suggest guilt. I needed to repair the damage, so I said, "He was playing us. Hank Tyler and me. Against each other."

"So you went to Wyoming to see if Stan Tyler would support you in your effort to merge with Prostitute Records," Agee continued, "and he told you he was backing Hank Tyler, and you interpreted that as him playing you?"

I had to think about that one. So I stayed quiet, thinking.

"Is that correct, Mr. Reilly?" Hunter asked as reinforcement.

"Well... that's what I was thinking."

"Was he direct in how he told you what he was going to do?"

"Yes."

"There was no doubt about what he was telling you?"

"No."

"But you still felt he was playing you?"

"Sort of."

"We're back to 'sort of,' Mr. Reilly?"

"I knew how much he didn't like Hank."

"So ultimately," Agee marched on, "you're saying you thought Stan Tyler was going to back you because he didn't like Hank Tyler, even though he made it quite clear—unequivocally clear—that he was going to back Hank Tyler?"

"I'm saying it was a possibility."

"But Stan Tyler was clear about what he said?"

"I told you, very clear."

"At the time, Stan Tyler was in control of the Tyler estate?"

"Ben's portion, not Isabella's. The estate was split."

"Of course. But when Stan Tyler died, the terms of Ben Tyler's inheritance changed?"

"Yes. Jessica, Joseph, and Megan Tyler became the new beneficiaries as mandated by the state."

"But you profited, too. Didn't you, Mr. Reilly?"

"Not directly."

"Come on, Mr. Reilly," Hunter said, her voice filled with serious doubt. "Look where we are. This is now your store, isn't it? Along with all the other Prostitute stores throughout the world? I understand your new title is President of the company. Isn't that correct?"

They were too sure of themselves, too sure about the facts. They must have gotten this from Ponderosa. Hank would not have told them about the details of our agreement until it was final and they were still in the process of being hammered out.

"It could have happened anyway," I said, not backing down. "Stan was playing us. That's how I felt. Maybe you should talk with Hank Tyler. See what he thinks."

They ignored that suggestion.

"After you left Wyoming that day, when Stan Tyler told you he was backing Hank Tyler, did you ever talk with Stan Tyler again?"

"No."

"Never emailed him or had any kind of contact at all?"

"Nothing."

"How about with his fiancée?" Agee asked. "Have you been in touch with her?"

Again, this was to be expected. I did not kill Stan for Ponderosa, nor did we as a team plot against him, but it still looked bad and there was no getting around it. I was bothered that Ponderosa didn't call to tell me that she had talked with them because they clearly talked with her. She told me about the NTSB but not the FBI. Three days earlier, she flew to Colorado for real estate business. I hadn't heard from her since.

"Yes, I have," I said.

"At Stan Tyler's funeral?" Agee asked again.

"I didn't go to the funeral," I replied, as if they didn't know. Bizarrely, I felt myself becoming insulted. They should not have been this suspicious. My record and background were clean. Initially, Hank Tyler attacked me, not the other way around, which brought me into this quagmire. Maybe they thought I was motivated by Ponderosa? But that line of reasoning did not make great sense either because if I had killed Stan because I loved Ponderosa, I also killed her chance of cashing in on the Tyler estate by permanently abrogating their planned marriage. If Ponderosa and I were on the sly for real, it would have made more sense to let Stan inherit the estate first, marry Ponderosa, and then kill him.

I was starting to confuse myself by trying to figure out how they should be deciphering this. Perhaps there was better logic and I was not seeing it.

"So when did you talk to her?" Agee asked.

They both waited patiently for the answer.

"I talk to her quite often," I said. "She's my girlfriend." I would have been a fool to say anything else.

Neither one blinked an eye. "And did this start before her fiancée died rather suddenly?" Agee asked.

"After."

"Can you be more specific?"

"I met her in Chicago for a day when she was visiting her parents. Around Thanksgiving."

"That was the first time you met?"

"We spent time together in Wyoming."

"Time together? You mean with Stan Tyler, too?"

"He was not immediately available when I went out there. So she entertained me. We got to know each other a little. After Stan died, I called her to see how she was doing and we met up in Chicago."

This triggered a seemingly unending series of questions in

which I was asked to provide many details about my brief history with Ponderosa. I told them the truth because I didn't know what Ponderosa told them and because my relationship with Ponderosa was separate from my killing Stan. At that point in time I could make the separation in my mind with no problem.

After Pondersoa, then they wanted to know all about my trip to St. Petersburg, Florida, to visit my sister Megan Tyler. This is when I lit up a cigarette. I didn't care if the smoke bothered them. It was my place, as they so clearly pointed out. They were starting to really piss me off.

32
DARK VICTORY

Losing my criminal investigative virginity could have gone better. My main mistake was that I tried to defend myself when I did not have to. It was true that Stan was playing Hank and me against each other, but I did not know that at the time of my first Wyoming visit. The FBI agents seemed to be aware of that. I fell into their trap. If it was a trap. Technically, I did not incriminate myself, but it gave them reason to believe. I threw lumber into their fire and possibly became a legitimate suspect. I doubted that I was their prime suspect, if they had one, but being on that list was not a comfortable feeling because nobody else on the block counted except them. Not the media, the public, or the Tylers. Everybody else could go to hell and think what they wanted except for the law enforcement agencies. Well, that was not perfectly true. Ponderosa counted, too. She was my lover. I killed her boyfriend. She was living with Stan when he died, and she was the last person to see him alive. So her thinking and statements were important as it related to the authorities.

When I finally asked her if she had spoken to the FBI and if so why hadn't she mentioned it to me, she said she'd forgotten all about it because she thought I wasn't worried about the investigation. That was hard to believe, but certainly logical given my nonstop performance of pretending to be uninterested and aloof. I did not know if she really believed my theatrics, probably not, but what was I going to do? Get upset with her for playing along with me? I had nothing to hide, and I didn't care, right? Everything, of course, was unspoken and evolving, and to certain degree intangible, but the net result, in my thinking, was that our positions toward each other had fundamentally changed. Where I once thought I was the one in control with my secrets, plotting and romanticizing, I now firmly believed that she was the one in control. And she wasn't doing a damn thing but accepting my lead, sitting in the rear of the canoe holding a sun umbrella while I paddled.

*

About two weeks after my irritating and educational FBI visit, Jonathan called. I hadn't spoken to him for some time. As usual, he was full of confidence and candor, and he told me he was keeping up with the Tyler death extravaganza and had instructed his undergraduate contemporary history class at Harvard to come up with a convincing theory of what happened—or, as far as I was concerned, what was still very much happening.

He would have called sooner, he said, but he was waiting for their results. I could hear him crack open a can of beer as he plopped down on the couch. Evidently, the couch continued to be a serious place for him, because he then became very serious: "Listen," he said, "and listen good. You didn't heed my advice. That's always a mistake."

"What are you talking about?"

"Hank Tyler."

"Hank's no longer a concern. I'm President of Prostitute Eclectic Records. I'm taking over the music. It's a done deal."

"Well, of course you are, *now*," he frowned through the phone.

"What do you mean?"

"Did they tap your phone yet?"

I never thought of that. "Can they?" I asked.

"They can do anything they want with aviation. I thought you would have realized that before—"

He stopped himself, probably thinking the phone could be tapped. I made a split-second decision to pretend I didn't care.

"Jonathan, I'm getting the feeling you think I had something to do with all this mess."

"A feeling? Interesting terminology."

"If you do, you're being ridiculous."

"Is it true about his fiancée?"

"True?"

"Are you with her?"

"Yes."

"That was probably your best move. It appears too obvious. What about sister?"

"Sister?"

"The Scarlet Letter sister."

He remembers everything, I thought. "Megan died all by herself," I said.

"You're sure about that?"

"Pretty sure. We became friends. She was tired of struggling, Jonathan."

"So Hank Tyler had nothing to do with it?"

"Not that I know of."

"Then he thinks you did."

If I was reading Jonathan correctly, he was saying that Hank and I were the only ones capable of killing Tylers.

"You may be underestimating some of my half siblings," I said.

"They lack discipline."

"Joseph Tyler is cloning people. Paying off surrogate mothers who risk their lives. That's pretty disciplined. Wouldn't you say?"

When I revealed this, I was hoping the phone was tapped. Being a murderer and a habitual liar did not lessen my contempt of Joseph's obsession. There was a pause from the other end of the line, which was unusual, then: "Is he really cloning humans?" he asked.

"Yes, he really is, Jonathan," I said, feeling proud I knew something he didn't.

"Then he's probably cloning Ben Tyler."

That never occurred to me. But it rang true. I remembered how tickled Joseph's slobbering partner Sascha was over my resemblance to Ben.

"What did your class come up with?" I asked, trying to steer away from his brilliance, which was depressingly accurate.

"The most interesting theory was that Megan Tyler arranged for her half-brother Stan Tyler's demise and then killed herself from drug-addicted self-loathing. The most boring: Joseph and Jessica Tyler are working together."

"Anybody wink my way?" I asked.

"Two."

"Two out of what?"

"Twenty-two."

"You have a bright class."

"No, I take that back. Three."

"I see."

"You might want to keep in mind one thing, my friend."

"What?"

"Relationships."

"What about them?"

"They can be untidy. Even if everything else is in place."

"Yeah?"

"Yeah. Got to go, but call me if you need to."

"Okay," I said, and hung up the phone.

With Jonathan, one always has to read between the lines. My interpretation of our conversation: He believed that I killed Stan (he was the third person in class), and it could have been avoided had I listened to him and handled the situation better. He also shed light on why Hank did not delay my Prostitute contract upon hearing the news of the criminal investigation. According to Jonathan, Hank, too, believed that I had killed Stan and maybe Megan. He respected murder and was rewarding me, or perhaps he was afraid the same could happen to him. Either way, if Jonathan was correct, Hank believed I was guilty.

That night, Marge visited the Prostitute Eclectic store for the first time. I was told she wondered around trance-like before she revealed her identity and was directed into my office, where I watched her look around some more before volunteering that she preferred the old place. I explained that we could only sustain one store in the Detroit area, and given my new responsibilities, I had to make a tough decision. "I hope we can keep this one open," I added.

"It's sad," she responded. "Going out and buying records has always been such a fun thing to do."

The reason for her existential visit, which became more reflective and obscure as the moments lingered on: one of her clients came into the salon and showed her a new board game she bought online called *Tyler Estate*. It was similar in concept to the board game *Clue*, and the object of the game was to be the first player to devise a Tyler murder plot.

Players pick from two decks of cards, one deck has cartoon drawings of all the possible villains, mostly Tylers, and the second deck singles out specific events. By choosing from both decks, one can sequence out a theory. So, for instance, depending on the luck of the draw, a player could promulgate that Claire and Jessica worked together as a team with the goal of splitting the Tyler estate between them. They did this by sabotaging Stan's hot air balloon and killing Joseph in his Newcastle lab with nitroglycerin.

The prediction part (Joseph, at this point, was alive and well and attempting to clone human beings) was what made *Tyler Estate* a little more fun and sick. Just think of how marvelous it would be if things turned out just that way!

The game was developed by a pair of Princeton undergraduate freshmen and, according to Marge's client, would soon be available for purchase at large retail chains like Target and Kmart. Marge was particularly offended by the unflattering caricature of yours truly stamped on the game's playing cards. As portrayed by the teenage freshmen, both through the drawings and background data, I was a loser-type Detroit slum bastard who was living in the stacks of my seedy little mom-and-pop secondhand record shop, trying to score the big one by manipulating my way into my biological father's recording business.

There was no consideration given to my college years at Michigan, nor to the stellar reputation of Eclectic Emporium, which Prostitute Records copied. What was included, however (and not only by the nerdy, money-grabbing, privileged, spoiled Princeton brats, but by the media and others as well), was my relationship to my former employer, the incarcerated counterfeiter Sledge Parker. Even though I was a part-time employee of his and away at college during most of his spree, a sinister connection was implied which, ironically, was not taken seriously by the authorities or anyone that mattered. The beautiful fact that I actually took advantage of his talent was further evidence of how convoluted everything was becoming.

Regardless, as mentioned, any negative or false portrayal had little real effect. The FBI was my only concern, and everybody else could go climb a tree.

"It's horrible people can be so amused by all this," Marge said sadly as she opened up the board game and showed me the two decks of cards.

"It's a bunch of nonsense," I replied, trying not to chuckle at the cartoon depictions of my half siblings. I particularly liked the Josh card on which his head is shaped like a guitar and ablaze with fire. Jessica's was fairly amusing, too. On hers she holds up a giant carving knife dripping with blood all ready to carve up the Tyler estate pie shaped like a gondola balloon.

"Stu mentioned you're going to be moving to Los Angeles soon," Marge said, forcing me to put away the cards.

"That's the way it's looking, Mom. I was going to tell you when I was certain about the dates."

"I'm happy for you. I just wish all this other stuff would go away."

"It will at some point," I said.

Marge was not in agreement. "I have a feeling it won't, dear," she said with a little too much authority. "You know them by now. Would they really go so far as to kill one another?"

This was a conversation I desperately wanted to avoid. I did not want to drag Marge down the sewer with me and start lying to her, too. It so depressed me. I will now have to remember which lies I told her and which ones I didn't. There was no real choice, though. If she found out the truth, she would be shattered for life. "I don't know, Mom," I replied, "maybe."

After she left, I had a late-night meeting with Tom Hamilton, one of Hank's vice presidents in charge of the record label, who arrived from Los Angeles that evening. Tom gave me a rundown of the major artists we had under contract. He also discussed in detail Prostitute's basic strategy for the immediate future. None of it was ambitious and was further evidence that Hank was pulling back on music and focusing on diversifying.

My first order of business on the label side, I told him, would be to start up a new mini-label under the Prostitute banner that would focus exclusively on digital garage bands. I wanted to market them in a way that would be both digital-friendly and profitable without requiring us to spend huge sums.

"Use the technology and freedom to our advantage," I remembered hearing myself say, although I wasn't sure what that meant and how it would manifest into solid dollars and cents for us. But it sounded good, and I sort of meant it.

He, like everyone else, saw the future as uncertain, and therefore was open to anything that would bring in revenue. But I could tell his strong suit was not brainstorming ideas. He was a Hank yes man. He was echoing Hank when he told me I should start thinking about making the move to Los Angeles if I was serious about taking over; more proof that Hank had accepted the new arrangement and perhaps was beginning to see the advantage of having someone like me around.

*

From this point on, there is much to tell that transpired in such a short period of time that it still makes me dizzy. The first month of the New Year went smoothly for me. I learned my new responsibilities, implemented the new national retail plan, and consolidated the two Eclectic stores. By early February, I was ready to make the transition to Los Angeles, but decided at the last moment to spend a week in Wyoming with Ponderosa. I needed a break, and this would be my last chance for some real R & R before my life became very busy. Or so I thought.

As we all know, Ponderosa loved horses and she and I went riding quite a bit during this visit. But each time we walked over to the barn to saddle up, we would see Stan's hot air balloon platform. It had degenerated considerably since my last visit, or rather, since Stan stopped using it, and it now looked more like an ice coated cargo pallet left behind from a traveling carnival. More importantly, though, it served as a harsh reminder that someone had been snooping around the grounds and plotting against Stan, if we were to believe the findings of the NTSB (and that Stan did not kill himself).

Ponderosa and I had never discussed Stan's death in depth, nor the subsequent revelation of a possible sabotage. Ever. Our conversations never lasted that long. But we were always reminded of how unresolved everything was under the surface by the sight of the balloon platform. At those times, when we were trying not to stare at the platform, I had the chance to come clean with her and determine where she really stood. I could have easily introduced the subject as a hypothetical, lightly disguising the facts to protect ourselves against implicating each other. Such as, for instance, "What if I knew the person who was guilty of sabotaging Stan's balloon...?" But I never did, and by not doing so, I never gave her the opportunity to either forgive me or not forgive me, or at least to get a clue of which way she would fall if push came to shove. After I left the ranch that February, I never had the opportunity again.

The other incident at the KO Corral during this February week that bears mentioning was the timing of another inquiry by the FBI. One day after taking a particularly beautiful and long horse ride through the snowy plains and getting lost in the magic of the winter landscape, I returned to the ranch to discover a message on my cell from the Detroit office that agents Agee and Hunter called and requested I contact them. I never told anyone at the Detroit store where I was vacationing (the days were gone when I would explain my whereabouts to anyone as long as I could be reached), but I did check with Ponderosa to see if she had been talking to the FBI lately, say within the last two weeks or so, since she had a tendency to forget to tell me those little details. She said she had not, and I believed her, so I walked outside to be alone and called the agents.

To my displeasure, the federal agents wanted to review the first Wyoming trip I made to solicit Stan to join forces with me against Hank. We had discussed this in length during the first interrogation, and I reminded them of that, pretending to be irritated by the intrusion and fully aware of the irony of my present location. They were insistent, regardless, and I had no choice.

"Did you ever go back to Wyoming after Stan shunned you?" Agent Agee asked me.

"No—I mean, yes, I went back in December sometime."

"Why?" the other one asked, they were on speaker phone.

"To see Ponderosa. It was right after I got back from Europe. I thought I told you that. Or maybe I didn't. I forget." And that was true, I couldn't remember.

"But you didn't go back a second time when Stan was alive?"

"No. It was weeks after his funeral."

This of course was the big lie and the key to my survival. I practiced it in my sleep.

"Did you go straight back to Detroit when you left that first time?"

"When I went out to talk to Stan?"

"Yes."

"Yes, I think I did."

"You flew back, right?"

"Right."

"Once you returned to Detroit, did you leave town again for any reason prior to the time of Stan's death on November 8th?"

"That would be a time frame of about three weeks," the other one volunteered, making sure I completely understood the question.

"Not that I remember," I said. "I'm not sure."

There was a pause, and then, "We need you to be sure, Mr. Reilly," Agent Huter said. "Please think about it carefully. Take your time. Did you leave Detroit at all during those three weeks or so after you flew back from Wyoming and before November 8th, the day Stan Tyler died?"

I did think about it, carefully, like they suggested, wondering if they stumbled upon something. I was positive that I had covered my tracks during Wyoming 2. The cheap Denver motel, the Chicago sporting goods store, and the few places I stopped for gas could not be traced to me unless there were cameras present. But even then, Hunter and Agee would have had to assume a pattern, a schedule and a routine and then check literally tens of thousands of retail establishments between Detroit and Jackson, Wyoming—that is, if they believed I drove and didn't fly or take a train, or what have you.

I seriously doubted they could demand that kind of manpower for this relatively minor investigation, despite whatever publicity it was generating. This was not an al-Qaida operation involving jumbo aircraft and political terrorism, it was Stan Tyler's little red, white, and blue balloon, and if there was an angle, it was nothing more than simple, old-fashioned greed. I decided to stick with the overwhelming Vegas odds: they were fishing. Besides, if I told them I left town, I would have to lie about where I had gone and foolishly provide them with proof of my deceit. Again, there was no decision here.

"No," I said. "I did not leave town."

More silence, then: "You're sure?"

"I'm sure. Is there anything else?"

"We understand you're about to relocate to Los Angeles for your new position at Prostitute Records," Agee said.

I wasn't certain if that was a question, so I said, "The new company name is going to be Prostitute-Eclectic Records."

"You must be excited?"

"Thrilled."

"Taking a little time off before the big move?" Hunter asked.

"Yes, I am," I answered. "And now I have to go," and clicked off the phone, hoping my rudeness would be interpreted as agitation and wondering what the hell motivated them to contact me in the first place. They were fishing alright, but their timing suggested something new, otherwise it made no sense—unless they simply wanted me to know that they knew I was in Wyoming with Ponderosa, a dead issue at that point. And if so, I massively overestimated them. I reminded myself that the FBI can be remarkably fucking stupid, and their case studies prove it over and over, which I took time out to review at the old library on Woodward. Still, Hunter and Agee did not seem to be dull-witted. They may have believed I had sufficient motive. They, more than others, understood the significance of what I had gained and then lost after Isabella died and how I could have been pushed over the edge by Stan's snub, playing me or not. But motive without proof doesn't mean a thing. And I was quite certain they didn't have a shred of proof. If they did, I would not have received a courtesy phone call. I would have been graced with a visit.

*

After Wyoming, I made the transition to Los Angeles and took my rightful place in the sun. The biggest perk, among many, was that I inherited bio-Dad's office in the Prostitute building. That was how I chose to look at it—an inheritance—even though I had earned every square inch of that office space.

The person most happy for me, outside of myself, and possibly Ponderosa, was Vicky, who, I found out, knew from the first moment she set eyes on me that I was a disenfranchised Tyler. She welcomed me with open arms and showered me with suggestions about everything Los Angeles, like where to live, what gym to join, restaurants to frequent, etc. I think, also, her exuberance was motivated by the fact that there would now be another Tyler to challenge Hank's hegemony.

On my third night in Los Angeles, Hank threw a party for me at a little club on Wilcox Street in old Hollywood. I had the pleasure to meet many of our recording and performing artists, most of whom had the courtesy to approach me and introduce themselves. Needless to say, it was more dreams coming true, and I had to pinch myself to make sure this was happening. On the other hand, I was more than ready, and most of these people recognized the Tyler blood in me and felt at ease. It was a very uplifting experience and thoughtful of Hank to arrange it. I wanted Ponderosa to be there with me, but she refused on the grounds that she had met Hank Tyler once before as Stan's girlfriend and did not want to do a repeat performance as my girlfriend. Not yet anyway. I understood, but kept pressuring her to move to Los Angeles.

As the L.A. days ticked on, things kept getting busier and better, as I knew they would. One particularly special moment occurred when I read about my professional advancement in the Hollywood trades. That was a new sensation and much more preferable than reading about myself in the Detroit newspapers as someone loosely connected to the Tyler death scandal. When the reporters called the office for details, I put together a resume that highlighted my Eclectic Emporium days and included a sizable plug for Sledge and his almost thirty years as an innovator of retail music in the Detroit market. I also took the opportunity to formalize the new Prostitute-Eclectic Records name. Hank offered no resistance and I think he actually liked it without admitting so. He also understood well, as I did, that he should pick his battles, and the new name was not a big deal as long the word Prostitute came first.

As President of the company, I began receiving a salary of $390,000 per year plus expenses and was in charge of all music-related operations. Those were the basic terms of the contract, even though the document went on for twelve pages. The salary was nice, but the real money, the wealth, would come with ownership once probate was over. When that would actually happen, I had no idea. Until then, Hank was really in control, and I was not yet a rich man.

In the meantime, the state-appointed executor, a lawyer from Sacramento, was managing bio-Dad's portion of the estate and Isabella's lawyers were taking care of Isabella's portion. Hank had to consult both of them before offering me the contract, and they of course welcomed it since I was scheduled to inherit from both sides of the estate now that I owned Joseph's pending interest. My agreement with Jessica was still in place, and as a team we would soon control 26 percent of the company. I asked Stu if he could put out some feelers about Jessica in the event she was having second thoughts. He reported back that Jessica's lawyers gave no indication of any change. I'd had no contact at all with Jessica since Megan's memorial, and I was hoping she would regain her senses so we could be on speaking terms.

A few days after I signed the contract, and about three weeks after I moved to Los Angeles, I checked out of my hotel and settled into a rented duplex apartment above Sunset near Horn Avenue. Coincidentally, it was not too far from where the old El Matador used to stand. That was the hotel I stayed at during my maiden L.A. journey as a teenage and which had since been demolished and replaced by a Hertz rental car lot.

I immediately fell in love with my new apartment building. It was old Hollywood Spanish Revival and smothered with eucalyptus and palm trees. Inside, high ceilings, strategic skylights, and about 2,000 square feet of oak floor. Upstairs, on the deck, a sauna and whirlpool connected to the master bedroom. The heated pool of course was in the secluded yard below. I loved every inch of it.

Vicky hired a decorator to help me furnish, and as soon as there was something to sit on and utensils with which to cook and eat, I invited Claire over to dinner to celebrate. When she arrived, I presented her with an elegant gold watch that I recklessly purchased with phony money at an expensive Beverly Hills jewelry store. It was both stupid and arrogant of me to do that at this stage, but my confidence was returning and my fear of the FBI diminishing. Besides, that was the only way I could afford to buy it outright. I couldn't use my Prostitute expense account for a personal gift, and my salary advance was already swallowed up from the deposit on the apartment, furniture, and decorator. So I used a portion of what was left of Sledge's currency.

That evening, I had never seen Claire look more beautiful or relaxed. One explanation was the setting. For a change, we were not sitting in a dark, somber church staring at an urn of ashes or a coffin with our hearts ripped out. Another reason was she began seeing someone, "a nice gentleman who plays the violin." She met him at the Santa Monica farmers market, and he invited her to the Disney Concert Hall to watch the L.A. Philharmonic perform. They had a wonderful time and quickly became companions. I was very happy for her. I remembered how lonely she appeared after Isabella died.

For dinner, I made my best four-hour attempt at Irish stew. I also bought some good wine and fresh Italian bread from the overpriced gourmet grocery store on Sunset. About midway through the meal, I had to stop from almost crying. I became overwhelmed by my good fortune. It wasn't too long before when I was dead broke and on the verge of humiliation and collapse. I now, somehow, was living my dream beyond dreams. Most of this had to do with Isabella and Claire, along with some reprehensible behavior on my part. Behavior that was driven by the unholy trinity of fear, revenge, and greed. Unfortunately, for me, that seemed to work best for motivation and not the parochial school prescribed virtue, faith, and honesty. The ancient Stoics believed virtue will yield happiness, but it just didn't seem to apply in today's world, or rather my world. I'd only be lying to myself, like I was lying to everyone else, if I tried to convince myself otherwise.

I told Claire of my plans to start a new label and my decision to include Josh. She was surprised, remembering well what Josh had done to me. But she was happy for him if I could work it out.

"I knew you would make a difference," she said. "So did Isabella."

The next morning, I walked to work, down Horn to Sunset, past the Hertz rental lot that used to be the El Matador Hotel, past the cafes and boutiques on the West Hollywood strip, and entered my elegant Prostitute building and my handsome office suite to a smiling cast of beautiful, exotic women who worked for me. It was a good way to start the day and a big change from the old Detroit shuffle in the bitter cold.

I checked to see if Hank was in, he was not. I wanted to talk to him about Josh. I chatted with my staff while somebody made me a cappuccino and then retreated to my office and began planning the day.

I had a meeting set up later that morning with Tom Hamilton to go over the figures for the royalties of our music publishing. Publishing was a steady flow of income and probably the only reason Hank hadn't already abandoned ship with the music and turned the place into a gas station. My job—a job Hank did not want anymore, another reason why, I believe, he capitulated—was to boost the other side of the label business, the music recording and retail side, in this unrelenting, metamorphosed digital era.

I also wanted Tom to look over my plans for the new label and get feedback about how separate the two labels should be in terms of accounting and publicity. Later that afternoon, I had meetings scheduled with two of our established recording artists, both of whom were in discussions to renew their contracts with us. Neither one was selling too many CDs, either, and that was a problem. This would be my first time negotiating a contract. I was looking forward to the challenge. Afterward, we were all going to a club to listen to a young new band one of our clients was recommending. Secretly, I was hoping this band would be as good as advertised and I would sign them to the new EE Label. But I was jumping ahead of myself. One thing at a time.

I buzzed Vicky and asked if she could set up an appointment with Josh Tyler. She was familiar with Josh and the problems he had caused both Ben and Hank, and expressed those concerns to me. I told her not to worry. She didn't believe me and said so. She was looking after my interests. I appreciated that, but insisted that she do so anyway. I knew it wouldn't be long before I promoted her to vice president. I needed a good one. She was more than capable. I had plans. Big plans.

Five minutes later, the phone buzzed and I thought it might be Josh, but it was Sonia, the receptionist, telling me that a woman who did not have an appointment was here to see me.

"What's her name?" I asked.

"Karolina Torgustive."

This caught me by complete surprise.

"She should talk to Hank," I said.

"Hank still isn't here yet."

"Tell her to come back when he is. Or call."

I had nothing to say to Karolina. She was Hank's monster, not mine. Two minutes later, the phone buzzed again.

"She won't leave," Sonia said in a frustrated whisper. "And she doesn't want to talk to Hank. She wants to talk to you."

"Well, I don't want to talk to her."

"Should I call security?" she asked. And when she did, a cold chill shot through my spine. I realized that I had seen this movie before, only with me being in Karolina's role. Hank agreed to see me that time I dropped in on him unexpectedly. Should I do the same with Karo?

"No, don't do that," I said (like he probably did).

"What do you want me to do?"

"I'll see her."

"Are you sure?"

"Have Vicky bring her back."

I hung up the phone, thinking what in hell did this duplicitous predator want with me now? I fired her twice. Why can't she take a hint?

33
THE UGLY PAST

As usual, she looked stunning. She was wearing a short skirt and a purple silk blouse. Her teeth were glowing bright between thick, spongy lips covered with purple paste. She sat down without waiting for the invitation and lit up a cigarette. I could see her crotch. It was covered with purple panties. Purple was the color of the day.

"You have thirty minutes, not a second more," I said, checking my watch at the same time.

She laughed out loud like she didn't believe me. Then she looked around. "Was this Ben Tyler's office?"

"Yes."

"I underestimated you," she said, but not in an apologetic way. She was admonishing herself.

"That's yesterday's news, Karo. This is the present. What can I do for you?"

"Quite a bit, I think."

"You'll have to be more specific."

"I had a talk with the FBI," she said.

"So? Who hasn't talked to the FBI? These days, it's like ordering lunch."

"They asked me a lot of questions about you."

"There's an investigation. I'm a Tyler."

"I'm thinking about talking to them again. Only this time with the truth in mind."

"You mean you didn't tell the truth the first time? Shame on you."

"I thought I did, but I didn't. I know that now."

"Karo, it's none of my business what you talk to the FBI about or how true or untrue it is. That's between you and them."

"No, you have that wrong, Nic. It's very much your business, too."

I looked at my watch to indicate that precious time was ticking away. I had a ton of things to do. I lit up a cigarette to help me with my patience. "Okay. What is it?" I asked.

I waited. We looked at each other. It was about control with her. In the beginning, there was harmony, respect and reciprocity. I tried to remember when it began to change, when she wanted to be the boss. Maybe I shouldn't have turned over the store to her. But then again, she did such a great job. No easy answers here.

After proving her point, she finally proceeded: "The FBI agents asked me about your activities after you came home from visiting Stan and Ponderosa in Wyoming. I told them you pretended to be sick and went off to meet up with Ponderosa without Stan. That's what I believed happened. We talked about it in your office before you and Ponderosa were set to go to Paris but didn't go. When Megan died."

"I don't remember it like that," I said, purposely lying and trying to be noncompliant. The truth was I remembered it exactly like that.

"Well, I do," she said, "because that's what happened. Now this is the part you need to understand, Nic. I thought you went off to see Ponderosa, but as it turns out you didn't go see her. I know because I talked to Ponderosa two days ago, and she told me you didn't. She said after you left the ranch she didn't talk to you again or see you again until after Stan Tyler died—excuse me—was killed."

"So you got it wrong, huh?" I said, raising my eyebrows to suggest irony, disbelief, and I don't care.

"You didn't go to see Ponderosa," she continued, "and that's what Ponderosa told the FBI, too, but you did go somewhere. I can prove you went somewhere. So where did you go, Nic?"

I was almost disappointed. This was all she had? She came all this way to ask me, "Where did you go?"

"None of your goddamn business," I shot back. "And by the way, what were you doing breaking into my house, anyway? Is there anything else, Karo?"

"You did it, I know you did."

She was pathetic. Desperate. Bitter. Even stupid. Then I thought: There has to be more to it. "Are you carrying a microphone?" I asked.

She didn't respond.

"Who sent you, Karo? Those FBI agents? Or maybe my partner, Hank? Your old pal?"

I could see the hatred in her eyes growing. Her purple lips began to quiver. If she had a revolver, she'd blow my brains out, but she didn't, and that's why I kept it up: "Look what it got you for being his patsy. You lost everything. You should be sitting next door in his office as my partner, running the whole operation. And look at you. You're crawling in here like a two-bit slut with a hangover and cum stains on your face."

"Nic?" she said softly, coolly.

"What?"

"I don't need a microphone, you asshole."

"Yeah, well, we're entitled to our opinions. But just for the record—and then you have to go—the way I remember it was you were with me in the shop with those high-school kids when we got word that Stan died 1,700 miles away. Do you remember that part?"

"That's what threw me off," she retorted. "But when I talked to Ponderosa two days ago, she told me Stan left town for three weeks right after you went back to Detroit. And nobody flew the balloon for those three weeks since the day you left."

"So?"

"That's why you were in Detroit when it happened."

"Your time is up."

"I can prove it."

"You can't prove shit except that you broke into my house." I stood up to emphasize my point. "Now get the fuck out of here. I don't want to call security. But I will."

"You don't have to call security, Nic, because you called me."

"What?"

"Remember? You called the store. Twice. Both times to tell me you weren't coming in that day. You left messages."

My heart stopped.

"So?"

Her eyes were focused, sensor mode, ready to instantly record the tiniest reaction. "Yeah, so?" she said back.

She put out her cigarette and stood up. "Maybe you're right. It is time for me to go now. I'll be in touch."

And she walked out of the room.

*

A few minutes after she was gone, I buzzed Vicky and told her to hold the calls and cancel all my meetings. I had to think. I shut the office door and locked it. I walked over to bio-Dad's couch and sat down. I had to go back over everything in my head. Obviously, I took no notes during the time in question, so it was all about memory. My recollection. I needed to be clear about where I stood with Karolina and what my options were, if any. Those cell phone calls she referred to were not saved, but obviously they were geographically traceable by cell towers. It was careless of me. Stupid, even. Stupid beyond belief if considered in a certain light. In my defense, however, there is an explanation. When I was feverishly planning Stan Tyler's farewell, many adversaries came to mind, including all the siblings, Hank Tyler, the various local and state police forces, the FBI and FAA, and even Ponderosa. But never once, at that time, did I think of Karolina as an enemy.

In the pre-Hindenburg 2 days, Karolina was grouped with Stu and Marge. She was family. Newly disgruntled family perhaps, at that particular point, but family nonetheless. I never, ever thought she would betray me, nor did I ever imagine a future scenario in which she would become a principal adversary, threatening to eliminate the fruits of the much-earned and much-deserved bio-quest. When I moved forward with my passionate balloon mission, I left messages for her because I did not want her checking up on me—just in case. She believed that I was ill. She was used to running the store by herself and might have even preferred it that way. She knew I'd come back to work when I was healthy.

My calling was a precaution, not essential. But then Stu called the store, and she wanted to relay that to me. When I failed to respond, she did what anyone else would have done in her position and stopped by my house on her way home from work. Having found the place empty, she returned a second time the next night, late, and I was still not there. This is what convinced her that I had a girlfriend. A logical but erroneous conclusion (and may have helped to induce her to switch sides). This is what she must have told the FBI when questioned, even though my relationship with Ponderosa had not begun until months later.

Apparently, that misguided hypothesis stood firm until just two days ago when Ponderosa nullified it with the truth and provided the basis for Karolina's new and much more incriminating theory: that I pretended to be sick and traveled back to Wyoming and sabotaged Stan's balloon.

*

In my rush to satisfy my survival instincts and destroy Hank Tyler, I lacked diligence and foresight in orchestrating my disappearance to Karolina—a treasonous infidel left for dead twice, who once again had come back to life. She, herself, as I examined the facts, did not have physical proof. Nor did she have the ability to subpoena records and trace the origins of my calls to obscure cell towers in Wyoming. But the FBI did. And if alerted, they could get those records in a heartbeat. I believe that is why she left my office when she did, to give me time to make the next move. If she had the physical proof, she would have said so.

This left me with some choices, none of them very good. The first would be to tell her to go fuck herself when she got back "in touch" with me. Those phone calls might easily be traced to a cell tower next to an all-night grocery store a few blocks from my house or some little love nest upriver. Or anyplace in the world except Wyoming. She was guessing, despite her conviction and instincts. She didn't know for certain. So in a sense, I would be calling her bluff. "Go on, tell the FBI, I could care less." She might then realize the futility of her actions and not bother to take it any further and drop it. The risk, of course, was she had nothing to lose by contacting them anyway except maybe her credibility, which at that moment in time meant nothing to her or anyone else. She was unemployed, desperate, beaten, humiliated, hysterical, and possibly fucking crazy. And it would be no big deal for the agents to routinely follow up and discover (1) that I had lied to them, point blank, and (2) that I was within striking distance of Stan's balloon craft during the crucial three-week period when Stan was away from the ranch. Not a very hopeful or prudent choice.

Another choice would be to tell her—after she contacted me and not the other way around, because I would not want to appear anxious—that I was not afraid of the phone calls because they had nothing to do with Stan Tyler or his balloon, but her coming to Los Angeles made me rethink things and maybe we should try to settle our differences after all. Many of her good ideas were now being used in all the Prostitute Eclectic stores, and it was a mistake for me to push her away. Perhaps it's time we join forces again and conquer the world. She could move out here to Los Angeles where she belongs and take one of the offices down the hall from me. In essence, there would be no admission of guilt, just "a change of heart" on my part.

After two hours of uninterrupted thinking, those were my only real choices, except to simply ignore her if she called, which would essentially equate to calling her bluff. Of the two, the "change of heart" strategy became my best bet because I knew she would accept it. That was what she really wanted—to get back in the game. To have a future. But as usual there was a catch. A big one. And that was: there would be no guarantee that she would not contact the FBI *anyway*. If not immediately, somewhere down the line. In fact, by bringing her back in, I may be inviting more danger on myself because there would be a new incentive for her to get rid of me and take over. This was something she proved she was more than capable of doing.

Thus, regardless of what could be said, promised, agreed to, or signed between the two of us, she would retain the ability to use those phone calls against me. As far as I understood, first or second-degree murder is a criminal offense and takes legal precedence over any contractual agreement our lawyers could draw up. She could sign with her blood and swear on the life of her future children and still have the option to tip off the feds if she wanted. This is what separated her threat from other forms of coercive ransom.

For instance, with kidnapping, you return the Mcguffin in exchange for payoff, but in my situation, you hold on to the Mcguffin, even though you get the payoff. Karolina gets her job, her future, but she still maintains the ability to destroy me. So, ultimately, it comes down to: Do I trust her? Not only do I trust her, but do I trust her with my life? And the answer to that was a big "fuck no." Karolina could have a bad clothing day, and I'd wind up in San Quentin with my ass perched in the air. She had been in bed with Hank and Jam, my archenemies, spying on me during my most vulnerable days.

Thus, as it then appeared to me, in that moment in time, any kind of "change of heart" strategy would not cut it because it would involve trusting Karolina. Nor would any deal that involved a payoff, whether I admitted guilt or not. Hiring Karolina was nothing more than a form of bribery anyway. Yet it would always boil down to her still having the means to destroy me if so desired. The only possible advantage it would render would be to buy time until I could figure something else out. Keep her close to me and take it one baby step at a time until something better came along. But ultimately—as I calculated in the sanctum of my office with no feedback from anyone—any compromises to Karolina would ultimately make her more dangerous. At least now, as it then stood, she was still on the outside looking in.

34
WHAT'S LEFT?

I could kill her. I could kill the diehard bitch. In the post-Hindenburg 2 era, murder was a legitimate default. I had already done it once—which she was so counting on for her future—so why not do it again? To her! Maybe Jessica wasn't too far off the mark about me, after all.

It would not be too difficult to accomplish, either. I would contract out this one. It would go down in Detroit, not Los Angeles. In Detroit, people were dropping like flies. It had the highest crime rate of all American cities. She'd just be one more statistic. With her great looks, she was an easy target. It was a no-brainer.

I would be discreet. I would use shopping mall pay phones, disguise myself, hand over cash, drugs, whatever, in Walmart bags. And the cash would be real, just in case. I wouldn't want to ignite the wrath of a hired gangbanger with phony bills after he killed somebody for me. Nor would I want him getting caught circulating counterfeit money. He could easily talk and I could be traced.

After that was all arranged, I would call up Karolina and placate her, tell her what she wanted to hear, promise her anything, including a big job here in L.A., and then suggest that she return to Detroit and pack. And when she did, she would be randomly killed by a desperate, tweaked-out, half-conscious, drug-addict thief. He wouldn't be allowed to rape her, just kill her. Rape would look better to the ensuing investigation, but I wouldn't want that for personal reasons. Obviously, I would have no way to enforce that particular instruction. Perhaps I could promise a bonus if the attacker did not rape and provided proof? Either way, Karolina would fall victim to urban crime just like the tens of thousands who preceded her. And with Karo gone, so would go my troubles. Right?

Wrong. Dead wrong. And for a bunch of good reasons, too. This time, I wrote them down in black and white on the back side of a blank envelope so I could study them and not allow myself to do anything stupid. (I later burned the envelope.) To begin with, killing Karolina would create more problems than it would eliminate. She had come to Los Angeles with the sole purpose of meeting up with me. It was documented that she had entered the Prostitute suite and would not leave until she was allowed to see me. Eventually, she was allowed and we talked, and then she left. This was public knowledge. Her death would bring to light this episode and raise questions about what she so passionately wanted to talk to me about.

Secondly, she had to be in contact with others. Others in whom she confided. I already knew about Ponderosa because she told me. There had to be more. At the very least, her death would almost certainly make these people reexamine her accusations. So even if Karolina expired by her own doing, or of natural causes, in front of a stadium full of people, and I had a foolproof alibi, her fatality would eventually draw negative attention to me from the people who counted. And this, possibly, perhaps undoubtedly, would lead to the exposure of her damaging information against me, because the subject matter would come up upon investigation and interviews. So by killing her, I would, in fact, be risking exposure of those phone calls to the authorities and likewise make myself a suspect for a second murder rap. As it stood now, with Karolina breathing, I was still in the clear and there was time to maneuver. Or so I thought.

Finally—and I'm proud to say this was my predominant concern—killing Karolina, or arranging for her demise, would make me a multiple murderer, a title I could not and would not allow or endure. In my heart, I still believed, rightly or wrongly, probably wrongly, that I was not a true murderer, despite Stan. As a somewhat incongruent and meaningless comparison, some men, and now women, go to war and are constitutionally granted license to kill and do so, willingly and efficiently. And if they don't kill, they maim, another vulgarism taken to new heights with the growing medical technology. I consider those soldiers, along with the men who create those war situations, on all sides, to be much more murderous than myself. For me, Stan was a wicked aberration, a fluke, and executed almost in a trance. Thus, murdering a second time, even in the post-Hindenburg 2 era, was never going to happen. Enough was enough. My murdering days were over. So after briefly entertaining this fantasy, I shelved it forever.

*

Given the above, I was forced to prepare myself for the possibility of an FBI onslaught. Maybe those phone calls could be minimized? I made the first call from the city of Denver early on a Wednesday morning during my journey to Jackson from Detroit. Denver, Colorado, is about 500 miles away from Jackson, Wyoming—not exactly a stone's throw. I could have been skiing. Or drinking. Or anything else I could dream up that could not be disproved.

The second call, however, was more of a problem. It was made somewhere between Pinedale and Boulder, Wyoming, on Highway 191, the same road that leads to Jackson from Rock Springs, Wyoming. That call was made at about 7:15 on Thursday morning, Mountain Time, about two hours after I began my journey back to Detroit after sabotaging Stan's propane tank. Again, Pinedale, Wyoming, is not Jackson, Wyoming, so there was no absolute definitive proof that I was in Jackson at Stan's ranch, but it did leave open the question of what the hell I was doing out in western Wyoming that early in the morning, and where else could I possibly be coming from or going to if not the KO Corral, a little more than 150 miles away. This was exacerbated by the separate issue of my lying to the FBI, which by then would already have been firmly established. One does not "not recall" driving over 1,500 miles—half a continent—from where you said you were. It was not a "sleeping pill episode."

This also occurred directly after I had returned to Detroit from Wyoming, having flown back. So why did I suddenly turn around and journey back to Wyoming? And why was I now driving? And where? And why did I purposefully and consciously lie about it? The two agents were quite specific with their questioning. Given my jackrabbit pace, what could I have possibly been doing in such a short period of time except maybe sabotaging Stan's balloon? But still, despite all that, despite the lying and the proximity factors, those phone calls were circumstantial and not hard physical evidence.

Furthermore, the tampering could have occurred at any point during Stan's three-week absence. It could have occurred the day he left the ranch or on the day he returned to the ranch or anytime in between. My subsequent Wyoming coordinates, and the documented time and dates associated with those coordinates, made it physically possible for me to have committed the crime, but it also left open the possibility that many other people, tens of thousands of people, could have also done so. Even if they attached motive—Stan's harsh rejection of my Prostitute offer—it would still be a stretch for them to indict me. Furthermore, if they did charge me with murder and sabotage, I would still have to be convicted in a court of law by a jury of my peers. That was not an easy thing to do with circumstantial evidence. Especially in our O.J. Simpson/ Robert Blake jury mentality school of justice era when obscenely guilty persons get acquitted by a twelve-member jury.

I would have to invent a couple of really lame excuses for my whereabouts and actions and why I had lied to the FBI and of course hire a team of gifted distortionists and pay them a hell of a lot of real money, but I could do that and very possibly sway a few dimwitted jurists to conclude reasonable doubt and then exonerate me. The big downside would be the public humiliation I would have to endure in what would turn out to be a grossly spectacular, media-obsessed trial. But my chances were decent that I would walk away a free man and a rich man. That is, if everything stayed the same. But that was the big problem. There was no guarantee that anything at all would stay the same.

In fact, once the FBI discovered that I had purposely lied to them—which they would do in this scenario—they would shelve their other suspects and theories and go strictly after my ass. This would mean that I would become the subject of a forensic witch hunt, something that I had been spared thus far. These agents would subpoena my vehicle and clothing; they would engage in embarrassing searches that would include Prostitute Eclectic Detroit and Marge's house; and they would DNA-test everything to death until they found something linking me to that balloon site.

From what I knew about these digital crusades (will the digital curse ever go away?!), the evidence could turn out to be something like cock perspiration that dripped out of my pants and was preserved underneath a pile of frozen horse shit next to the platform. Thus, without being sure about any future evidence used against me, I likewise could not be sure that the vulnerable jury system would provide me with a reasonable doubt and the ability to walk out of a courtroom unescorted by an army of federal officers. If I was not careful about simple phone calls, the odds were fair to middling that something else more incriminating would be unearthed sooner or later. The more I thought about everything, the more I did not like my chances in the long run.

35
DECISION

We always get help. It may not turn out to be the best help or the right help, but we get it, and many times it comes from the most unexpected sources. As I camped out on bio-Dad's couch with the door locked and the phone muzzled in an effort to fully comprehend the implications of Karolina's attempted reentry into my world, I heard Sonia's sweetly accented voice emanating into the airspace. "I know you don't want to be disturbed, but there's another unscheduled visitor wanting to see you."

I was forced to get up from bio-Dad's couch and walk over to my desk, "Who?" I asked.

"Josh Tyler."

"Didn't Vicky call him?"

"She never reached him. He just showed up."

"He won't go away?"

"Are you kidding?"

I wanted to talk with Josh, but not then. Hank needed to be included.

"Where's Hank?"

"He won't be in today. He has meetings all day." She then whispered, "I'm surprised he didn't just barge in. That's what he usually does."

"Let him in."

When he entered my office, he flopped down on the couch, like he probably had done many times before when Ben was alive. He appeared sober but deeply agitated. That was a big difference from *not* sober and deeply agitated.

"What's wrong?" I asked.

"Wrong? Have you any fucking idea what I put up with every

day? What's wrong? Everything's fucking wrong!"

He did have it rough, I thought. His face was becoming a regular item in the gossip tabloids. He was always portrayed as the disinherited plotting mad-man/child brat, main suspect, house-burning, gambling murderer. His lawyers were working overtime to keep him in the inheritance game, but the overwhelming odds were that he was going to come in short. Had he not been inked into his mother's conditional trust funds, the judge would probably be more sympathetic with regard to his father's stated demands.

"Are you here about the label?" I asked.

"No. Not really. I mean, yeah I am, but there's something else that comes first."

"What do you mean?"

"I think you're in trouble, dude."

This was not news. It was just a question of which trouble. "I'm listening," I said.

He lit up a cigarette, thinking about how best to proceed. "I called Jessica to see about a loan," he said. "She told me somebody who used to work for you can prove you killed Stan."

"Oh yeah?"

"Yeah."

"Karolina?"

"Right, that's the name."

Karo had access to all my contact information when she worked for me. It would be easy for her to call Jessica. It made we wonder about how many other people she could be talking to and why she wasn't being discreet if she was attempting to blackmail me. But maybe that was part of the overall strategy.

"It's just cheap talk," I said, lying. "She was spying for Hank at my other shop, and I had him get rid of her before I took over here. She's desperate."

"There's more."

"Oh?"

"Jessica still thinks we don't like each other, you and me. She doesn't know anything about the new label stuff. So she wasn't worried about this getting back to you. Got it?"

"Yeah."

"Jessica said Karolina was going to blackmail you to get herself back in here at Prostitute, but Jessica told her to go directly to the FBI with her information and she'll talk to Hank."

"She did, huh?"

"Yeah."

It made sense. Jessica mistakenly believed that I had killed Megan and probably Stan, too, but had no proof so she was playing it safe by not rocking the boat and collecting her scheduled windfall—thanks to me. But now with Karolina's so-called proof, she no longer had to do that.

"When did you talk to Jessica?" I asked.

"About an hour ago. This affects me, too," he continued.

"How?"

"My situation may not change for five years, and I want in here with the new label. But without you around, that won't happen. So, once again, I get screwed. Just like I get screwed all the time."

I lit up a cigarette. It kept getting worse. "You're jumping the gun," I told him.

"Let me ask you something, and I want the fucking truth."

"I didn't kill him," I said, saving him the question. Never admit it to anyone. Never. Besides, he might be wired.

"Who the fuck killed him then?" he asked bewilderedly. "Somebody did. And it wasn't me or any of my friends."

"It's not proven that he was killed."

"Fuck that. Stan wouldn't kill himself. That's just bullshit my lawyers came up with."

"Did you ask Joseph?"

He became thoughtful. "He says, no," he replied.

"He's the one with all that Frankenstein stuff going on. He'd do anything to keep it going."

"I know."

"What about Jessica?"

"Jessica? I don't know about that."

"Why not? She gets just as much booty as Joseph with Stan dead. And now she's trying to get rid of me. Right?"

"She's got it in her," he conceded softly. "That's for sure."

"Did she agree to the loan?"

"She said I'm going to have to wait. I already tapped Joseph."

"Maybe I can help out with the lawyer fees."

"Yeah?"

"Yeah. And don't worry about here. You're in. And when you get in, we'll figure out a way to get rid of Uncle Hank."

"Promise?"

"Promise."

"Fucking A, dude."

He stood up, energized, smiling. "Yeah, I'm going to bet on you. You beat Hank. You're going to win out. I know it. Fuck the bunch of them. And you got Ponderosa, too."

"Oh, you like her?"

"She was too good for Stan. Any idiot could see that. She was probably cashing in. But so what? I'd do the same."

"Thanks for the information."

"It's cool. Just hurry up with the label. I got some good ideas."

"I'll call you when we're ready."

He walked to the door, stopped, and looked around. He turned back to me. "You know," he said, "I'm a little jealous about you getting this office."

"Forget it. This one's mine. I earned it."

"Yeah, I guess you did."

"What about Hank's?"

"Hank's?" he said, not having thought of it before.

"Not right away," I replied cooly, "but it's something to work for."

When he left five excruciating seconds later, I locked the door, returned to the couch, and thought deeply about Josh's timely visit. He was a messenger. I needed to act. That was the message. Jessica and Karolina as a team was a frightening prospect. Between them, they had enough venom to melt a city. And then there was all that money Jessica was going to inherit. The possibility that Karolina would go to the FBI anyway, or first, had now become more of a possibility, thereby eliminating most of my choices. But maybe messenger Josh also provided me with a solution: Ponderosa. She may have been too good for Stan, like he said, but she was loyal to him, regardless. Perhaps the time had come to test that loyalty for myself.

As I now viewed it, my romance with her and my visits to the KO Corral following the hot air balloon mission could be a positive thing. Every time I was there, I was also leaving bits and pieces of me all over the place. In the event the FBI should become suspicious and dig up further evidence at the ranch, I could always say: "Yeah, you found (this or that), but that's because I was at that spot two months later when I visiting Ponderosa." I had also visited the one time prior to his death, a well-documented visit. Thus, given the brief time span and the multiple dates, it would be almost impossible for the investigators to state unequivocally that I left evidence of myself on one of those few days when I drove back into the state of Wyoming when Stan was out of town.

There were, of course, limits to how far I could play this. For instance, if felonious evidence with my name on it was discovered, the above would not apply. That is, if the FBI found the atomic equivalent of a stick of dynamite attached to a surviving piece of balloon craft with my fingerprints on it, I would still be held responsible. Or, if they found felonious evidence away from the KO ranch, like in the Chicago store where I bought the propane, then I would still be culpable. But that was less likely to happen the less they investigated me, which leads to the second and more critical possibility as it related to Ponderosa: What if I were able to proclaim to the FBI—if questioned again—that I had traveled into Wyoming during Stan's absence to meet up with Ponderosa? What then? It would account for why I had purposely lied to the FBI and the proximity factor of my Wyoming-traced phone call during that period. I'd still have to be creative about why I drove instead of flew to Wyoming and things of that nature, but it would explain my secrecy. I was attempting to prevent the public exposure of an illicit relationship.

There was a huge downside, however. Ponderosa would have to perjure herself if questioned to corroborate the untruth and admit to prenuptial infidelity; something which she was most definitely not guilty of doing. I suppose, too, there was a remote chance that she could be tagged a co-conspirator in the event that I was convicted.

Overall, though, the Josh-inspired, Ponderosa alternative strategy might solve my problems. It would almost, if not completely, wash out Karolina's digital evidence; it would keep Karolina out of Prostitute (or whatever the terms of her ransom); and it would bring Ponderosa and I closer together because I would, in fact, be admitting my fault to her. By accepting my confession, she would be forgiving me. She, more than anyone, knew the extent of Stan's cruelty. In my heart I knew she was aware of the truth anyway, dating back to our walk in the park.

*

I decided to test the waters with Ponderosa. First, I would ask her about her recent conversation with Karolina. Depending on how that went, I would inch my way into the more delicate issue at hand.

I called the ranch, there was no answer. I then called her cell. She answered. She was in Dallas on real estate business. This was basically what she said when questioned:

Two days earlier, Karolina called her for help. Karolina was despondent about the recent turn of events and wanted to see if Ponderosa could help patch things up between herself and Prostitute Records. She admitted her espionage—which Ponderosa brought up—and said at the time she felt alone, abandoned and frustrated, and was seduced over to Prostitute by Hank himself. This was also the time she became aware of what she thought was my new romance—with Ponderosa, as it turned out—which only made her feel worse since Karolina and I had been off-and-on lovers. Ponderosa then corrected her about her dates, because the two of us had not become intimate until months after Stan died.

"Didn't he go back out to see you again?" Karolina asked her a couple of times. Ponderosa reiterated her timetable, and eventually the conversation ended with Ponderosa saying that she would speak to me on her behalf.

"It wasn't a high priority," she said.

"That was it?" I asked her.

"Pretty much."

"She came to visit me today in Los Angeles. She thinks I'm

responsible for Stan's balloon crash."

"She is?"

"Yeah. She said she can prove it."

"Well, can she?" Ponderosa asked, matter-of-factly.

I was about to answer her when I remembered Jonathan's warning about the phones being tapped and asked her if I could fly out to Dallas to be with her. She agreed and gave me the hotel where she was staying. I checked my watch, it was already after 3 pm. Time was vanishing. I made the flight arrangements myself. If Karolina did team up with Jessica, I wanted to leave town before I was questioned by the FBI.

I neglected to ask Josh if he knew when Jessica had conspired with Karolina. I was guessing that it was after Karo had come into my office this morning with her threat, otherwise why would she even bother coming in? But who knows? Maybe she thought she could get more by blackmailing me? Although, it was hard to believe that she did not prefer to see me behind bars, and with Jessica maybe she could have her cake and eat it, too. But then again, maybe she was planning to do that anyway, down the line.

And what about Hank? What the hell was he up to all day, and who was he meeting with? Most likely, if Karolina did already contact the FBI, they would still need time to investigate those phone calls, which should give me a little breathing room, but not much. Hopefully enough time to arrive in Dallas and talk with Ponderosa. I wasn't sure if lying to the FBI and being within striking distance of the balloon craft during that crucial time period was enough for them to arrest me. Wouldn't they need more concrete evidence? And if I did get arrested, what would the charges be and what kind of bail could I expect? At some point, I needed to talk discreetly with a good criminal lawyer, but I did not want to think in those terms yet. Ponderosa first. The Ponderosa alternative could still deflect most if not all of this.

I collected a few belongings and told Vicky that I'd call her in the morning to see what tomorrow looked like. She was frustrated by the schedule changes since there was so much going on for us. I asked her to please bear with me, without being specific.

I arrived at LAX. While publicly undressing to clear the new security screening, I received a call from Ponderosa. She explained that she had to take an unscheduled meeting and if I arrived at the hotel before she returned, I should check with the front desk and let myself in.

"I can't wait to see you," I said.

"Me, too," she said. "Got to run."

After clearing security, I hustled to the airport gate only to discover my flight had been delayed and the aircraft had not yet landed. So I had to wait again.

While sitting there, helplessly, I made a mental note never to fly when running from justice. Video surveillance is ubiquitous, security personnel are at every turn, and the infrastructure is equivalent to Sledge's prison, where all areas are quarantined and sectioned off. And in my particular case—an alleged aviation saboteur—I could easily be computer-tagged as "terrorist," the crème de la crème of modern-day bad guys, and my silly face would flash across every airport security computer screen in the universe in half a nanosecond. What then? AK47s pointed at my head? Angry groups of buff men in fatigue uniforms, wrestling me to the ground, handcuffing my hands behind my back, as the innocent public gasped and watched in horror?

Fortunately, I arrived in Dallas without incident and taxied to the hotel. Because of the delays, I was hoping Ponderosa would be in her hotel room. She was not. I was forced to return to the hotel lobby and secure the card key from the front desk. Once inside the hotel room, I proceeded to wait again. I was tempted to call her, but I knew she had a big meeting and decided against it. I sat down on the bed, stretched out, and allowed my eyes to close. I should be safe until morning. I purposely told no one where in Dallas I was going, and I was not a registered guest. Ponderosa did, however, leave my name at the front desk.

I opened my eyes again. There was no way I could sleep. On the night table, I noticed one of those small hotel notepads. A phone number was scribbled on the pad. The number had a Detroit area code. I immediately deduced that it must be Karolina's number. Ponderosa said Karo called, and she probably recorded the number. I no longer kept Karolina's phone information, but I knew she had gotten new numbers since I excommunicated her. Maybe it would not be such a terrible idea to set up a meeting just in case? If she took the meeting, it would suggest that she had not yet talked to the FBI and had not followed Jessica's advice. She and I both knew she was not absolutely certain about the origin of my phone calls. She may have told people like Jessica that she was sure, but she was not. Until those calls were traced, I was the only human being who knew from where they originated.

Furthermore, if she contacted the FBI before waiting for me, and the phone calls turned out to be nothing, then her game was over, practically before it began. I would bury her. But if she gave me a chance first, her odds were much better that something might materialize for her. I decided to call the number. If she took the meeting, I could safely bet that she had not contacted the FBI. If she did not take the meeting, then she probably did contact them.

I pushed the numbers on my cell, she answered on the fourth ring. "Hi, Nic," she said, obviously recognizing my number.

"Hi, Karo. How are you doing?"

"So-so."

"Where are you staying in Los Angeles?"

"Some little place on Sunset."

"I was thinking about what you said this morning, and I decided not to wait until you contacted me. I'd like to set up another meeting so the two of us can talk. I'm out of town right now, but I'll be back on Friday. Do you still want to meet?"

There was a slight pause, and then: "Okay."

"Would Friday work? That's the soonest I can do it."

"Friday works."

"How about 10 am at my office?"

"Okay, at 10."

"It will give you time to look around. Are you enjoying your stay in Los Angeles?"

"Yes, I am. I'll see you on Friday, Nic."

"See you then."

We both clicked off. So far, so good, I thought, although she got off rather quickly. But that could be a tactic. Karo was clever. My gut, which was rotting and probably could not be trusted, said she had not yet contacted the feds. She was calling people who knew my business and crying wolf, but that may be part of the overall blackmail. I had to remember that she was desperate and throwing everything she had at me.

After thinking about it some more, I began to feel better. I walked over to the little hotel refrigerator and cracked open a bottle of Guinness. Guinness was my favorite. I did not know if the hotel already had it stocked or if Ponderosa ordered it knowing I was coming. As I was sucking down my second one, Ponderosa entered. She apologized for the delay but said the meeting turned into a big sale of a large commercial property in the Duncanville section of Dallas. I congratulated her good fortune. I was happy that she was happy. It would make it that much easier for me. She was tired, and we undressed and went to bed and made love for a long time. Afterward, we fell asleep in each other's arms.

I awoke sometime after 3 am, forced myself out of bed, and drank another Guinness. I wanted to review again what we were surely going to talk about in the morning. I would ask her to corroborate a felonious reason why I was in Wyoming, and by doing so, I would be admitting my responsibility for the death of her fiancée and my half-brother. As it turned out, the conversation—or the initial conversation, rather—didn't have to wait until daylight. She awoke and saw me sitting by the window.

"What is it, Darling?" she asked, still half asleep.

I did not respond.

"Are you alright?" she continued.

"Not really," I said.

"What is it?"

"I'm scared."

She sat up in bed, "About what?" she asked.

"About Karo."

"Oh, that's right, Karolina," she said, as if to confirm the inconvenience and worry she was causing me.

"I need your help," I said.

"What kind of help?"

"Karo thinks she has information that could place me in a vulnerable position. As it turns out, it can."

"What kind of information?"

"One time, I made a phone call when I was driving through Wyoming."

"A phone call?"

"Yes. A phone call. I told the FBI I wasn't in Wyoming during this time period. The phone call can prove I was."

"When did this happen?"

"It was around the time Stan went to Denver for his business."

There was a long moment of silent confirmation.

"They could draw conclusions," I continued carefully. "It could get ugly, especially with all the publicity surrounding Stan's death."

"So what are you asking, Nic?"

"I need a reason why I was in Wyoming."

"I'm your reason?"

"Yes."

She looked at me deeply, her eyes almost squinting. She whispered, "Nic?"

"I know. It's terrible. I'm sorry."

"Come back to bed. We'll talk about it in the morning."

"Yeah?"

"Come on. Let's go back to sleep."

I put the bottle of beer on the floor, crawled back underneath the covers, snuggled up against her warm, lovely body, and moments later drifted back into the dream world.

36
AWAKENINGS

When I woke up again, Ponderosa was in the bathroom with the door shut. Moments later, I heard the toilet flush, and she came out naked carrying her pocket book. She put the bag on the chair by the bed, walked over to the little bar kitchen area, and switched on the coffee maker. She stood staring down at the machine and waited until the coffee began to drip. She filled her cup with black coffee and walked back to the bed and sat on the edge, facing me. "You're asking a lot, Nic," she said, as she sipped her coffee.

"I know."

"I already told the FBI we got together in Chicago after Stan died."

"That's what happened."

"It makes me look like a tramp and a gold digger."

"I know."

"And maybe even a suspect."

"I think you're covered there. Why would you jeopardize your pending fortune?"

"Got it all figured out, huh?"

"Apparently not. This is the last thing I wanted."

"I need something from you."

"What?"

"Tell me why."

"Why?"

"Yes, why?" she repeated.

"Because I was scared," I answered. "Just like I am now."

"You were scared, that's why you killed him?"

"Yes."

"It doesn't seem like much of a reason. I get scared all the time. I got scared when he died—when you killed him."

"I know. I'm sorry. I'm trying to make it up to you. I just have to get through this one snag, and it will be over."

"Snag?"

"Call it what you want. It's only if they ask you again. They may not."

She thought more. I was now bracing myself for a "no" or worse. But it didn't happen.

She said: "Okay. If they ask me again, I'll tell them what you want."

"Thank you."

"But don't ever ask me to do something like this again. Ever. Promise."

"I promise."

*

I had no way to adequately express my gratitude to Ponderosa. She accepted me for the murderous liar that I was. And it was not without risk, either. Obstruction of justice and abetting a murderer were serious crimes. We agreed that if she were questioned again, she would amend her statement and reveal that she and I did in fact meet up again prior to Stan's death, in Jackson, Wyoming.

"Where in Jackson?" she asked.

"Anyplace you choose, preferably where people don't know you.

She thought for a second and said, "The Horseshoe, I never go in that place."

"Fine, the parking lot of The Horseshoe," I said. "We never went into the restaurant. Then we took a long drive together in my car and talked. We spent the day together talking. I never went to the ranch. Then I drove back to Detroit."

"Is that it?"

"Yeah. You can tell them it was my idea to meet. That's all they need to know. The less the better."

"Won't they be curious why you drove and didn't fly?"

"Because I just flew out of Jackson a couple of days earlier, and I didn't want to be seen returning. By the cab drivers, people like that.

It's a small airport. Stan just left town."

"Okay. That makes sense."

Before parting, I asked her again to come and live in Los Angeles and stay at my new apartment. She refused for the same old reasons. She was also uneasy about our new complicity and thought it would be better to be apart if questioned again. Her logic was irrefutable. I reminded her that she should not discuss any of this over the phone or in e-mails but I would appreciate a text message letting me know if the FBI or Karolina or anyone like that contacted her again. She agreed.

I arrived back in Los Angeles around noon feeling more at ease than when I left the day before. I now had Ponderosa's alibi if need be. But I was not out of the woods by any stretch, and I would take one more precautionary measure before returning to the office—an extremely vulnerable location where anyone could find me. Thus, I called Vicky and told her I would not be available for meetings until the following day, Friday, and to pencil in Karolina for 10.

"We're getting backed-up here," she said as a reminder, trying to conceal her frustration.

"I'll be free by tomorrow."

"Hank wants to talk to you."

"Is he there now?"

"He just left for lunch."

"Tell him I'll call him this evening. I'm tied up for the rest of the after-noon."

I clicked off, thinking I had to be cautious with Hank. Whatever he wanted to talk about would need to be deciphered. Karolina and Jessica were actively plotting against me, and the chances were excellent that he was in contact with one or both of them. Never a dull moment at the office.

I walked to the airport parking lot, slipped into my company car, and headed south toward San Pedro. Once in San Pedro, I climbed over the Vincent Thomas Bridge and seeped into the industrial turmoil of Terminal Island. It was time to consult the master again and bring him up to date. This would mark my first visit to Sledge since making the move to Los Angeles.

*

Sledge kept on looking younger, better, healthier each time I saw him. He was now braiding his hair and beard, and he reminded me of Paramahansa Yogananda, or one of those meditation gurus you see on posters in overpriced spiritual bookstores, where beautiful women tend to gravitate on lonely holidays. From the sparkle in his eyes, I sensed a little pride, too, like I was his pupil, and I had returned to the summit having learned much from my worldly travels.

"I've been reading about you, young man," he said with a smile, "and not all of it good, either."

"Did you read I'm now President of Prostitute Eclectic Records?"

"Yes, I did. Congratulations."

"It was the best I could do with the name."

"You did good with the name. I like it."

"I had to close down the old Woodward store and combine it with the Prostitute store in Detroit."

"I probably would have done the same."

"I'm starting a new Eclectic music label."

"Sounds like you're doing a hell of a job."

"I had some help along the way."

"Oh yeah?"

"I stumbled on some unexpected resources."

"Where did you stumble on them?"

"Deep down."

He nodded his head, "Yeah, that's always the place to look first—deep down. So how we doing now? Right now?"

"We're struggling again, Sledge."

"Struggling is a part of it."

"This time, the stakes are higher. You might even say it's life or death."

He thought about what I said and then tactfully replied, "That's what happens when we make certain choices. Am I right?"

"Yes, you're right," I replied, and when I did, I watched his eyes freeze, registering what he might have already suspected.

"We're responsible for our choices," he said calmly.

"I know."

"It's tough."

"Confusing, too."

"Maybe you're having problems keeping up?"

"Yeah. That's it."

"Maybe it keeps changing, the people keep changing?"

"All of that."

"That's to be expected. That's why you always need a Plan B."

"Plan B?"

"Yeah, Plan B. And maybe even a Plan C, too, but a Plan B for sure."

"What are Plan Bs like?"

"Well, I'll put it this way: I'm living my Plan B right now. But this wouldn't be everyone's Plan B. This wouldn't be *most* people's Plan B. Do you understand?"

"Yes, I understand."

"Everyone has to find his own Plan B, but you don't want to wait too long, because you never know when you'll need to use it. You don't want to wait."

"Of course."

When I left the Terminal Island Federal Correctional Institution, I had one thing on my mind: a Plan B.

On the way back to Los Angeles, I stopped at a large automobile dealership on the banks of the 405 Freeway to purchase a new vehicle. My old car, I left with Marge in Detroit. That was the vehicle I drove to Wyoming, and I should have destroyed it. Another mistake. Since arriving in Los Angeles, I was using a company car. But now I had the strong urge to own one again. A brand new one.

The freeway dealership that I chose possessed a circus atmosphere. There were swarms of pantomime salesmen, bright stadium lighting, and dozens of colored balloons and Samurai banners flapping away in the highway breeze. I wasted no time and told the fourth or fifth salesperson who approached me that I wanted something with great gas mileage that wasn't too flashy, something that would blend in. He directed me to a white fully loaded Toyota Prius, a hybrid, which was available to be driven away on the spot. I immediately accepted the deal, not caring too much how I was getting taken.

After arranging for the purchase using my new credit, I paid the salesman 300 dollars real cash to drive my new car to my house. He jumped at the offer and followed me back to West Hollywood, where I instructed him to park the car down the street from where I lived, near Sunset. I then gave him another 50 bucks for a taxi back to his dealership.

I returned to my apartment and called Hank. There was no answer. I left a message for him to call back or else I'd see him in the morning at the office. I then took a chance and called Stu in Detroit, hoping he'd be up late. He was. I expressed my regrets about not being close to Marge anymore.

"Not to worry," he replied, "she's taken care of."

I was glad he said that. He then informed me we were two, maybe three weeks away from a decision.

"Wow, that close?" I replied, thinking it would go on forever.

He explained that without a criminal indictment or concrete proof implicating one of the beneficiaries, the judge had no choice but to move forward regardless. I thanked Stu for everything he had done for me and bade him good-night. I clicked off and called Ponderosa. I wanted to speak to her again, to hear her poised, calm voice and tell her how much I loved her. But her cell was off and she didn't pick up on the land line, so I was forced to leave a digital recording. That disappointed me.

I then went online and spent the next four hours or so researching and implementing my Plan B. The process exhausted me after a long day, and I passed out around 3 am. When I awoke, it was already 9, and I had to hurry for my 10 o'clock meeting with Karolina. As I was preparing to leave the apartment, I took a moment. There were so many things pending, so many variables, uncertainties, and miscellaneous intrigues to sort out. What was I going to do with Karolina? What did Hank want to talk about? How long would I have to endure the risk of being discovered? Would Ponderosa be questioned again by the FBI, and if so, when? What about me? And then there was all the legitimate stuff, like the business, the new label, the clients, Vicky and all the backed up meetings...

I drove the company car to work and parked underneath our building. It was ten minutes after 10 when I got there, making me ten minutes late. In the parking underground, I noticed professional movers carting in new furniture through the service elevator. I wondered if any of it was for me. I knew Vicky ordered a new widescreen monitor and a conference table for my office. I decided to wait and see and took the lobby elevator up to the Prostitute suites. When the doors opened, I walked through our offices, acknowledging my employees. The last person I said good morning to was Vicky. The first thing out of her mouth was, "Karolina canceled."

"When did she call?" I asked.

"She didn't. When she didn't show up, I called her. She said she wasn't feeling well and forgot to call."

"Okay," I said, showing no emotion. "Why don't you give me fifteen minutes, and then we'll go over the schedule. Is Hank here?"

"Yes."

I walked into my office, realizing that I had gotten Karo dead wrong. That seemed to be happening more and more lately—me getting it wrong. Evidently, she had already spewed to the FBI, otherwise she would have been perched on a lobby chair with her eyes glued to the elevator doors. Thankfully, I was one step ahead of all of them with the Ponderosa alternative. Her corroboration should keep me out of harm's way and provide sufficient alibi for my unexpected trip into Wyoming. If the feds wanted to take it further, they would need more. I was not the only person in Wyoming during those three weeks in question. It would be up to them to produce the burden of proof. I was going to win this. I was going to prevail.

In the unlikely event they made a case against me anyway, we—me and my defense team—would simply opt for the Simpson-Blake retarded jury strategy, knowing full well that almost anything they dug up on the ranch could also be attributed to my prior or subsequent visits. We're talking weeks and months at most. Not centuries. Hence, carbon dating would not apply.

I poured myself a cup of coffee, feeling more confident by the second. Perhaps it was best this way. I would never have to spar with Karolina again. It was finally "over, over," a phrase I picked up from Megan. Karolina had nothing else, because there was nothing else.

I walked out of my office and down the hall and knocked on Hank's open door. He was behind his desk, yapping on the phone. He looked up and waved me in. He gestured for me to shut the door. I did as I was instructed, sat down, and waited for him to get off the phone.

In the short time Hank and I had been working together, we were developing a mutual understanding and acceptance. My entrance was viewed by the Prostitute investors and employees as a favorable change, and Hank looked good for allowing it to happen. This served to strengthen both of our positions. Hank was also glad to be focusing on other areas, with the music marketplace becoming complex and infuriating. I, on the other hand, looked forward to the challenge and quickly became accustomed to the deep pockets of the corporate structure. So even though it was perceived by outsiders that he and I were not on the best of terms, in reality we had a very codependent relationship, and it was deepening.

When he was finished with his phone call, he turned to me, "Where the hell you been?"

"I was out of town."

He ignored the explanation and got right into it: "Jessica keeps calling me."

"That doesn't surprise me."

"She keeps waving her Prostitute inheritance flag in front of my nose. She wants me to help your old employee, Karolina."

"*Your* old employee."

"Whatever. What do you say to that?"

"Jessica can go fuck herself."

He lit up a smoke, took a deep breath, exhaled, "Yeah, that's what I thought you'd say. I can't blame you, either. So I told her the same not using those words. I mean, I figured as long as me and you are on the same page, she can do all the bitching she wants. Right?"

"Right."

"I was going to leave it at that, but then something happened this morning."

"The FBI?"

"No. Jessica again. She called me at my house right before I came in here. She told me she just flew into town from Europe to meet with me."

"You're kidding?"

"Have you ever seen me kid?"

"No."

"She said she was going to bring someone with her."

"Karolina?" I suggested.

"No, someone else."

"But it's about the same thing, helping Karolina?"

"Yeah, right, so maybe Karolina would be there, too, I don't know."

"Okay?"

"Okay what?"

"Who's the other person?"

"Ponderosa."

"Ponderosa?"

"Yeah. Now, as I understand it, that's your girlfriend, the one you stole from Stan. Right?"

I lit up a cigarette, took a deep breath, exhaled. This was going to take a few heartbeats to mull over. What he was saying could not be accurate, or else there was more to it. Ponderosa coming here with Jessica to see Hank about Karolina was an absurdity.

"Go on," I said halfheartedly, choosing not to dispute the stealing Ponderosa from Stan part because it was not important.

"Well, what's your girlfriend doing with those two? Because, let me tell you, they want to cut your balls off."

"I don't know," I replied. "Maybe Jessica's lying to you. Or maybe Ponderosa's going along with them for my sake. What did you say to her?"

"I told her I didn't give a rat's ass if she brought the Pope or the King of Spain or wherever the fuck she's coming from. Until she legally inherits her father's vested interest in my company, I'm not interested in her opinions about how I should run things and who should help me run them."

"Good for you."

"Yeah, thanks, but then she said something else. And I think it was her temper talking, because I don't think she wanted to say it."

"What did she say, Hank?"

"She said you're—that's you—you're going to be arrested and your interest in Prostitute nullified by the probate court and she will likely wind up getting most of it herself and so I better talk to her now or else she might not want to talk to me later. Can you believe that?"

"I can believe anything at this point."

"I asked her how she knew you were going to be arrested and even if you do get arrested, it doesn't mean you're guilty and maybe nothing's going to change in probate court except it will take a little more time. And you know what she said?"

"She said she could prove it?"

"Yeah, that's what she said."

I relaxed again. We were back to square one. Hank saw in my face that I was no longer concerned.

"You think she's bluffing?" he asked.

"Don't you?"

"I asked you first."

"Karolina thinks she has proof. Granted, she does have some embarrassing information, but she doesn't have proof. So you're making the right choice by not talking to her, because nothing's going to change, I can almost guarantee it."

"That's not where the proof is coming from."

"What?" I asked.

"The proof is not coming from Karolina."

"Who's it coming from?"

"Ponderosa. That's why she's coming with her."

My heart dropped. I heard it crash. "She said that?" I asked, using all my strength to utter those three words.

"Yeah. The proof is coming from your girlfriend."

We both lit up new cigarettes.

"Should I be worried?" he exhaled, hoping for a negative response. I said nothing. We both sat there in silence. He understood.

"Listen," he started up again, almost paternally, "there are times in our lives when we do things we think we have to do. I don't know if we really have to do them, but we think we do—at the time. I did some stuff I thought I had to do when I was around your age. Just about your age in fact. I'm not proud of what I did, but I did it because I thought I had to do it. I got in trouble for it, too. Luckily for me, the timing was right and my kid brother scored big and helped me out. He turned my life around. I owe him everything. When I look at you now, sitting there, fucking speechless, I see me.

"Now, I know I'm probably part of the reason you felt you had to do certain things. I'm sorry about that. I fought you in the past because I didn't know you, I didn't trust you, and maybe I was just a little fucking confused by all of Ben's other kids. And I'm a prick to begin with. Ask anybody. But you proved yourself. And I want to help you if I can. Now I'm going to ask you a question, and I want an answer. I want you to tell me the fucking truth."

"The truth?" I asked, barely managing to whisper it.

"Is Ponderosa a problem?"

I crushed out my cigarette and told him the truth as I knew it: "Yeah, a big problem."

He stayed poised, thinking. "Okay," he said. "This is what I can do. I can hook you up with a good criminal attorney, and you can find out where you stand. You're probably going to need a new line of credit, and I can help you out there, too. I can also protect your position here and keep you on salary, whether you come in or not. I'll stall Jessica as long as I can. We'll just have to take it one step at a time. Okay?"

"Okay," I muttered.

"It's a goddamn shame that damn probate didn't end already. You'd be in a lot better shape if you had those assets."

"I know. I'm going back to my office. Tell Vicky to hold all my calls and postpone all my meetings."

"Sure."

"Thanks."

"Hang in there, kid."

I walked out of his office, down the hallway to the lounge bathroom in the rear of the suite. I locked the door behind me. In the bathroom, I unzipped my pants and whipped out my cock, but I could not urinate. My body had instantly dehydrated. No moisture, no piss, no fluidity, no saliva. I was as dry as a fucking museum bone from antiquity. No wonder Ponderosa never called back last night, I thought. She probably was with Jessica and Karolina planning my arrest.

I pushed open the window for some air. In my panic, in my haste, in my fear, I made the one mistake that I swore I would never make: I told somebody I committed murder. A fatal error, no matter what the circumstances were or how twisted the situation had become. She was clever, too, in how she phrased her crucial question, "why" instead of "if." It could, once again I suppose, boil down to my word against hers in a dreaded court of law. Or rather, since my lawyers would never allow me to take the stand in a last-resort, retarded-jury trial, it could rest on her credibility as a witness.

Yet, despite that, her reversal (if that's what it was) was particularly damaging because without her alibi, I would retreat back to my earlier position of: "What was I doing in Wyoming?" and "Why did I lie to the FBI?" And that, tragically, would then be compounded with: "Why did I ask Ponderosa to lie for me about being in Wyoming?" and "Why would she lie under oath and say that I told her I killed Stan Tyler if I didn't tell her that?"

My defense team would try to soil her and her testimony by painting her as a sugar doll who tried to cash in on Stan's good fortune, which would not be entirely incorrect. They might also emphasize that she was screwing around with me right after Stan died, and what does that tell you about her? And, in fact, only the two of us, she and I, really knew for sure what we said to each other, and her motives may very well be rooted in revenge and bitterness based on personal animosity or jealousy, or other unknown lascivious, convoluted thinking, and therefore nobody should believe a word she says.

On the other hand, Ponderosa was a model citizen with no history of wrongdoing and supported herself independently of Stan, and whatever character flaws she might possess did not negate my false statements and suspect whereabouts or my motives and the circumstantial evidence that was starting to snowball into an avalanche.

I gave up trying to pee but continued to stare down into the urinal, deeply contemplating my circumstances. It was then I had a minor epiphany. An authentic revelation. I *knew* it was the truth, too, the moment it came to my mind. And that was: *They already have all the evidence they need.* I remembered well the previous morning in the Dallas hotel room, when I woke up and Ponderosa was in the bathroom. She came out naked, carrying her pocketbook. What was the pocketbook all about? What if it contained a little digital recorder that she had just turned on? What if she recorded my confession? Maybe that was why she waited until the morning to talk to me about Karolina—the recorder was not turned on in the middle of the night. Maybe that was one of the activities that caused her delay the previous evening: to purchase or be given a digital recorder. If so, it had FBI written all over it. After Josh's and now Hank's information, to assume anything but the most pessimistic and disheartening scenario would be schoolboy naivety.

As I stood there, with my limp cock still in hand, I began to realize my limitations. There was no way on earth I could endure a highly publicized trial; not with Marge alive, watching it play out in the macabre media; not with Molly knowing that I had killed her son (and maybe her daughter—mistakenly); not with Claire realizing that she had been made a fool of; and not with the brutal, unrelenting, nonstop negative attention that would plague me every step of the way as the prosecution presented sworn testimonies and digital recordings, and me with no alibis and plenty of false statements to the FBI. No, a trial, even in this retarded jury age, was now out, as was a plea bargain, because that was essentially more of the same, only a little less public. I'd still be crucified.

This decision, in the bathroom some fourteen flights above sea level, was corroborated about twenty seconds after I made it. As I watched below me from my bathroom window, nine or ten automobiles quietly stopped and double-parked in front of the Prostitute building. Even from that distance, I immediately spotted FBI agents Agee and Hunter—Hunter's medium length hair bouncing nicely from her aerobic, jerky motions—as they leaped out of their shared vehicle and hustled across the sidewalk and through the front doors. They were followed by twenty-or-so men, some in special blue jumpsuits, some not, but all of them carrying shotguns and rifles. They were on a serious, no-nonsense mission to apprehend a dangerous suspect, and that had to be me.

Once again: What to do? It was becoming an old, tiresome question of late, and my batting average was sinking. Fortunately, I had already made the key decision: I was not going to prison for the rest of my life. So, right or wrong, smart or dumb, I decided to fucking run.

I dashed out of the bathroom, into the hallway, and over to the cargo elevator in the rear of the building. There was no stairwell exit at that location otherwise I would have taken the stairs. I drumbeat the elevator button and waited. I looked behind me and saw one of the student interns from USC staring at me. He saw me run out of the bathroom. I waved to him, trying to conceal my apprehension. He waved back.

"I'm getting my new plasma delivered for my office," I said, loud enough for him to hear.

"Cool," he said, nodding his head in agreement.

"I like your hat." He had one of the rapper ski hats pulled beneath his ears. I wanted it.

"Thanks."

"Do you mind if I wear it?"

He had no problem with that. He may have even been flattered, you know, the President of the company requesting to wear something of his. He walked over to me, yanked the hat off his head, and handed it over as the elevator door opened.

"I'll give it back to you later," I said. But I lied.

"Take your time, man."

"Thanks."

I walked into the elevator and pressed the underground parking level button. I put on his hat and pulled it beneath my ears as the door shut, leaving the intern standing there. I wondered if I should have asked him not to mention my departure to anyone if questioned, but I figured his hat was more than enough contribution.

As the elevator descended, I stripped down to my T-shirt. When the doors opened again, I walked out, stuffed my shirt in the trash, and grabbed the first oversized box that I saw in the loading area. I think it was a Downy box, filled with folded, dispenser paper towels. It was not too heavy, but it was not too light either, maybe 30 pounds or so. I carried it on my shoulder with the side of my head helping to balance it. I walked up the driveway and out of the garage onto the surface level in the rear of the building.

Government cars were parked back there, too. I could not see them before from my elevated bathroom window. Fortunately nobody batted an eyelash. There were other movers present, and I blended in. I assumed, too, since this was a surprise sting, the FBI was not expecting to see me flee at that early point, if at all. It was a white-collar arrest in that respect—although, make no mistake about the authenticity of the military caliber weapons. They were everywhere, loaded, and ready to be tested at will.

I walked around to the side of the building, seemingly headed to one of the parked trucks, but kept walking past the trucks and onto Sunset, where I boldly turned west into the maze of flesh and steel. A remarkably gutsy move, but time was of the essence and I had to take the chance. A congregation of passersby was beginning to form in front of our building as they noticed the obstructing vehicles and jump-suited agents standing about, carrying arms, and yapping into walkie-talkies. I slithered right through this budding, curious crowd, past the no-nonsense law-enforcement personnel (I knew Agee and Hunter were upstairs), and kept going due west, crossing the intersecting side streets, trying to wait for the green, but not always able to do so.

When it felt safe, I detoured to the north side of Sunset and chanced a quick peek sideways at the commotion behind me. I noticed there were new bursts of energy, new movement, as FBI agents began running back onto the sidewalk and street from the building, looking in all directions, panicking to some degree. I picked up my pace. Once I reached Horn, I turned north and climbed about 10 yards up the street and stopped in front of my new Prius. I flipped open the back hatch using my remote and placed the paper towel box in the rear section of the car.

As I made my way around to the driver's-side door, I spotted three Los Angeles County Sheriff police cars parked in front of my apartment building much further up the street. I assumed Sheriff's Officers were inside the vehicles, but I could not be sure. Either way, nothing happened. I settled behind the wheel of my new car, turned her over, listened to the virgin hybrid motor purr, and then carefully maneuvered onto Sunset, turning west again. I proceeded to drive through Beverly Hills, past UCLA and Bel Air, and back onto the 405 Freeway heading south. This time, I drove all the way to the Mexican border.

37
MEXICO

I know many people take refuge in bathrooms, public or private, when they need a moment to themselves, to get away from the gossip, maybe, or the lies or the misconceptions, or perhaps to cry about something stupid or not so stupid. Whatever the case may be, we're fortunate to have them, especially if they're ventilated properly and provide a view of the neighborhood.

On my way to Mexico, I used another bathroom, this time a public one at a highway rest area, to shave my head and eyebrows. I thought the clean, cerebral, bespectacled look would go well with the smart new hybrid as I prepared to drive into Mexico.

For the record, to get into Tijuana from California, by car or by foot, you don't need to show ID unless they request it. The chances are greater the Border Patrol will stop you and ask questions if you drive, as opposed to parking your car and walking across, as most people do, but not that much greater unless you're dragging something like a trailer or a camper. (It's a much different story if you're traveling the other way into the United States, where a passport is required.)

My decision to drive instead of walk—I had 185 minutes to think about this—was based upon the following: (1) I did not want to leave the car at the Mexican border, because eventually it would be discovered and traced, and the feds would know for sure that I fled to Mexico; (2) the car was loaded with Plan B accessories, including what was left of my phony money, and I still had quite a distance to travel after I crossed into Mexico; and (3) there was a decent chance the Border Patrol were alerted of my Houdini escape, and I was better off folded up in a little automobile with the tinted windows zipped up and a shiny robotic head, my most salient feature, than walking around in full view.

Fortunately, it was a good decision (the second one in a row, in fact). I had no close calls crossing. From Tijuana, I drove east off the Baja peninsula to Nogales, and then headed straight south again all the way into the southern part of Sinaloa. I remembered that Sinaloa was the Mexican state in which Isabella crashed her plane, and in the spirit of motorized heresy, I drove the car off a cliff into an obscure and isolated ravine. To have held onto it any longer would have been risky no matter how far south I chartered into the continent. It made me feel sad to waste such a fine vehicle, and I would have preferred to give it away to, say, some nice peasant farmer with a big family, somebody who could use it, but it would have stuck out like a sore thumb in those parts—you know, with the chickens and the kids sitting on the hybrid solar panels—and it was best not to take the risk.

Before ditching it, I purchased a 30-year-old beater pickup from a goat breeder in the small town of Novolata. I gave him 1,000 phony gringo dollars, and he was thrilled. The fact they were fake no longer had any significance, because everything seemed fake in Mexico. Or not real. And I had a feeling the Mexican banks felt the same. From there, I inched my way down to the Pacific coast and camped out on the beach, eating fresh fish that I caught with my own hands and drinking warm *cerveza* that I purchased from a tiny grocery hut near the coastline.

After three days, I felt rejuvenated, physically strong enough to continue my journey, but I was still hesitant. On one level, I felt anesthetized from living in such coastal splendor and cleanliness and so utterly grateful for my freedom and to be alive. Yet I was plagued by my quixotic circumstances whenever I looked back, which I could not help but do. Everything had happened so quickly. Incomprehensibly quickly. In a period of less than a few weeks, I had achieved my bio-dream of being at the top of the Tyler musical fiefdom and taking my rightful place in the sun as Ben's oldest. I also believed I had found my soul mate, my wife-to-be, in Ponderosa, and I was falling in love.

And then, without warning, my entire universe flipped like a banana pancake. Not only did I lose my magical musical fiefdom, I lost my soul mate, and, inconceivably, my soul mate turned out to be the one responsible for the loss of my fiefdom. I then nearly lost my life, too, if not for an unscheduled bathroom breather following my conversation with Hank. Yes, going to maximum-security state prison for the rest of my life equated to loss of life. I saw no difference.

Perhaps the most disheartening of all was the helplessness I felt about Marge. I knew she must have been shattered to the core by the news, and my fleeing only confirmed my guilt.

My only solace, with regard to her coping, was my preferred fugitive status as opposed to a captured criminal, especially with the frenzied media on twenty-four-hour world duty. Mercifully, she would see no footage of my apprehension and my later being shuttled from one cage to another, day after day, hand-cuffed, unwashed and unshaven. Nor would she see or read about any preliminaries, trials, verdicts, or plea bargains. Hopefully, at some point the ruckus would die down and the world would soon forget about me. Jonathan always said the American people have poor memories, and I was now hoping, once again, to prove him right.

During my isolated stay on the Sinaloan coast, I had no news of what the North American authorities were up to or how their manhunt was coming along. I possessed no TV, radio, newspapers, laptop, Internet, or information of any kind. I spent each day thinking, meditating, fishing, cooking, sleeping, and reading Ralph Ellison's *Invisible Man*, a book that I included in the Plan B reading material.

After eight full days of this routine, the book had ended and it was time to go, time to leave my temporary sanctuary. I gathered my humble belongings and returned to my beater pickup truck and began driving south again. I drove straight through Nayarit and Jalisco into Michoacán, where I turned to the east and climbed into the central mountains.

When I was high enough, almost 8,000 feet, I followed a trail of monarch butterflies into the Oyamel forests. It was early March, and the butterflies were still in seasonal bloom, having migrated down from New England and Canada for the winter. There were millions and millions of butterflies munching on the cool fir trees, and it was amazing to watch them flap their lithe wings in harmonious fusion, which sounded like soft rain on a sweet summer day. They were so beautiful and yet so carnivorous, as they devoured the trees and forest that desperately and naturally needed to be replenished. The process reminded me of my situation, only the butterflies were Ponderosa, Karolina, and Jessica—gnawing away at me, eating my bark, sucking the life out of me.

It was up to me to replenish myself, to keep my eyes in front of me and not look back and become bitter, lest I wither away like the dwindling Michoacán forest. I kept telling myself to remember the story in the Bible about Lot's wife. If I did not look back, I would make it.

After two full days of butterflies, I decided the time had come to take the last leg of my journey, or rather my immediate journey, and I packed up and drove southwest down the central mountains and across the plateaus and lowlands, past Morelia and Uruapan and into the Sierras. In Aguililla, I stopped to get directions using my broken Spanish and fake money, and a couple of *campos* drew me a map on the back of a paper placemat, which I used to navigate along a series of unpaved roads, through canyons and valleys and up to a mountain ranch nestled in the hinterland.

On the ranch grounds, I saw a lot of plush green and scaling slopes that kept going on and on, and animals scattered about, and fruit and pine trees and agricultural growth in the near and distant fields. I saw avocados and macadamias and sesame, and perhaps some other growth farther out, such as hemp and sorghum.

No one was present on the grounds, not that I could tell, so I dropped out of my dirty truck and walked to the old Spanish Colonial house and knocked on the front door. Shortly later, the door opened and a small, dark, middle-aged woman appeared wearing a light-gray work dress and a red apron. She looked surprised, not expecting to see a young gringo.

"Puedo ayudarle?

"Estoy buscando el señor Vasquelez?

She thought about it for a moment and decided I was no danger.

"Entrar, señor."

I entered, and she shut the door behind me.

"Un momento, por favor," she said.

She walked into the other rooms, and I waited as I always did. Half my life was spent waiting, I thought. Maybe even more than half my life. Sometime later, Isabella's father strolled into the room, slowly at first, unsure of his unexpected anonymous visitor. As he got closer, I could see the recognition in his face gradually materialize, but it took almost the entire walk, the length of the room. The last time I saw him, he had been drinking heavily, mourning the loss of his daughter. This time, his eyes were clear and there was much strength in his demeanor, his presence. Here was the proud, brave entrepreneur; here was the man Isabella loved and would turn to in times of need; here was the man immortalized in her cherished photographs.

"So, you have come to talk?" he said in broken English.

"Yes. I have come to talk."

"You are welcome, my friend."

"Thank you."

Señor Vasquelez was well informed of my escape from Los Angeles, although he was interested in the details leading up to the point of my attempted arrest. He was interested in knowing the things only I knew about. He asked me if I had sabotaged the balloon, and I told him that I had. He made it apparent that he did not approve, but I felt no severe judgment, either. Nor did he ask why I did it. Perhaps he did not want to know those details. He, more than most, was aware of how challenging bio-Dad's kids were from talking with Isabella and from knowing a few of them personally—not that that was an excuse. But I'm sure it was taken into consideration as he assessed my predicament.

He also understood what it was like to be an outlaw, having been a marijuana exporter and illegal labor contractor with big clients in both markets up and down the state of California. But those days are gone, and he is now retired and poses no threat to whichever group happens to be in power in Mexico City or in the state capital of Morelia. He prefers a low profile and spends most of his time as a part-time farmer and rancher. After Isabella died, he slowed down even more and began taking siestas after lunch that often last into the early evening.

He told me I could stay with him as long as I needed and pretty much guaranteed my safety, even if the Mexican authorities find out about me, which he hinted may happen anyway, depending on the length of my stay. Once things cool down, he offered to set me up with a new identity and suggested Argentina, Australia, or Europe, but advised I first research the extradition treaties of the United States. I might be better off in China, where no extradition treaty exists between the two countries. He told me there were "plenty of gringos in Shanghai" and I could blend in.

His cooperation and assistance, I believe, has much to do with Isabella's kind words about me. Once again, Isabella, dead or alive, proves to be the difference in my life. If I start adding up all the differences she made, she could easily be upgraded to my guardian angel as opposed to "friend," or bio-Dad's second wife. I have no idea why my life was blessed with her, and it leads me to think about the bigger question of how and why people choose one another. In retrospect, it is shocking and ironic that many of the people who I thought were allies turned out to be enemies, and many of my enemies, allies.

At the end of the long, long day, the previously loathed and dangerous Hank, Josh, and to some degree Joseph supported me; whereas Ponderosa, Jessica, and Karolina became my executioners, after starting out as friends, lovers, or both. I'm not sure if this is a true reflection of who I really am—my essence—and, if ultimately, I belong in the first group rather than the second, or it's simply proof that things change and people change and one should not look any further. Still, they were stunning reversals, and the only more dramatic turnaround I can think of would be if Stan himself came back from the dead to exonerate me because he knew I was in a tough spot and wanted to help out.

Another bio-curiosity in terms of my fate is my sister, Megan. When I met her in Florida and we unexpectedly bonded, I said to myself that I would do anything for her and in a way I very much did. When she died shortly after my visit, Jessica blamed me and mobilized against me. She petitioned Ponderosa and then later actively supported Karolina and her cause, and the combination proved almost fatal for me. This is not to suggest that Ponderosa would not have double-crossed me anyway—that I'll never know—but with Jessica pounding away at her, she might have come to believe that I assisted in Megan's suicide, and that, along with knowledge of my role in Stan's sabotage, could have made the difference for her. So I may have gotten what I wished for but at a big price.

Ponderosa continues to take up a lot of real estate in my head. I keep wondering: Why not just a little bit of courtesy? Why so vicious? First she sleeps with me, and then she secretly records a confession with full intent to send me to prison or worse. There was no middle ground or the slightest breath of compassion. Not to my face, anyway. Maybe she was afraid of me like some of the others. Obviously, she had not forgiven me for killing Stan or for stealing her pot of gold like the Nazis never forgave the French for Versailles. I remember when we were in the Dallas hotel; she told me that being afraid was not a good reason to kill. And she was right, it's not, but it's the only reason that makes sense, and it's the best answer anyone could possibly give. I thought that would make a difference. I was mistaken.

She liked Karolina, too, and that did not help. Karolina has a way with people. And Ponderosa and Jessica had been friendly since the Stan days. So in addition to everything else, there was a sisterly bond among the three of them. Ironically, that same bond is what saved me from getting caught and was cause for their only mistake, if you can make the argument that they made one. After I confessed to Ponderosa in Dallas, the authorities did not attempt to apprehend me until the next day in Los Angeles, a full twenty-four hours later.

I was on Terminal Island, in prison of all places, for most of that confessional day, but they could have easily waited for me to return home that night and then surprised me. I believe the delay was the result of Jessica trying to strike a deal with Hank about Karolina. Jessica wanted Hank to agree to bring Karo into Prostitute before the litigation began to decide what to do with my pending ownership, after I was arrested, and Ponderosa must have gone along with it. That ties into what Hank told me, too. But when Hank balked, they figured correctly they would get nowhere with him (he is probably still less regarded than me although at that point I'd say we were about neck and neck), and Ponderosa then turned over her evidence to the FBI, and they charged ahead. But by that time, I had already gone to work, talked with Hank, learned about Ponderosa, and taken an inspirational bathroom break.

Probably the best thing about fleeing into Mexico and drifting aimlessly for a while until I got my bearings was the 100 percent news and media blackout, which I highly recommend to anyone breathing. For over three weeks, I was completely out of touch with the rest of the world, but that ended abruptly with señor Vasquelez's nifty TV satellite system and Internet. When that moment came, it was culture shock for many reasons, but I'm going to stick to the Tyler news.

To begin with, I was more than surprised to discover that I am portrayed as a bit of a folk hero, and Ponderosa is tagged a villain of sorts, or more accurately a whorish gold-digger (ironically, her stated fear if she held to her word and supported me), who slept with both me and Stan, and then turned on me when it looked like I was succeeding and she was not. It makes absolutely no sense to someone who knows the facts, and it is not fair either, but that's the way it goes in the mysterious and unintelligible media-generated fairyland of perception.

What may have helped with my favorable public image, however misguided, is the story of my humble Detroit upbringing, coupled with my disappearing act while virtually in the grasp of the bloodthirsty FBI. People seem to love it. I have become a kind of myth—a bastard, rags-to-riches-back-to-rags myth. It's strange how murder can be tolerated in our society, because I don't think anyone doubts my guilt at this stage. I did it. I rigged the balloon. But it does not matter. Had I been caught, I would have been human and responsible. But I was not caught. I vanished like the gods.

Hank apparently did nothing to dispel this theory or this image with his one and only public statement: "Everyone is innocent until proven guilty." Quite a statement and more evidence of the remarkable reversals, although in my heart I know he is sympathetic because we are both murderers. And as much as I appreciate what he did for me at the end, it still unnerves me to acknowledge that my longtime nemesis—whom I once equated with Satan himself—is now a pal and a paternal figure. In many ways, I have become just like him.

True to character, though, Hank made no apologies to anyone for anything or anyone's behavior at Prostitute-Eclectic Records (he did not change back the name), and from what I can read between the lines, he is not giving in to Jessica's pressure, Karolina has not been re-hired, and he is preparing to weather out the mind-boggling probate process that will now go on indefinitely. He also continues to diversify his assets outside the music entertainment industry.

Josh, too, is getting better press because, as it turns out, he is not guilty. Segments of the public are becoming sympathetic to his cause and his legal struggle, now that my Prostitute inheritance will revert back to his mother's side, except for the portion I bought from Joseph, which I assume will go to the state of California because technically I would have owned it once Joseph inherited it. (It's getting complicated again, but I no longer have the inclination to keep up.) I, for one, am rooting for Josh to get my stake and hoping he will start up the new EE label.

Four days ago, I began code e-mailing Jonathan through his student-faculty e-mail address. He immediately tuned in, probably expecting it, and we are able to converse freely in our own codex based on our Michigan college days. He has assured me that at some point he will go to Detroit and visit Marge and Stu and tell them that I am okay. I asked him to convey how sorry I am about how things turned out. I left it up to him to devise a way for them to go through him to communicate to me if need be, but I did not request it, not wanting to push the envelope or endanger anyone.

Jonathan is another person who refrains from judging me. He is understandably disappointed, yet holds no reservations about my escape. It was the only thing to do. Interestingly, he parenthetically noted that the few students who pegged me as the villain come from low-income families and are subsidized by scholastic or athletic scholarships. As a whole, though, the Harvard students, he wrote, are consistent with the public reaction, and categorize me as a victim pushed to the extreme and do not think the odious stigma of planned murder is all that terrible if the circumstances warrant it.

This widespread public amnesty sentiment continues to baffle me. In my mind, I should be condemned and treated like a murderer. I killed Stan because he was about to screw up my fortune, my bio-quest. Yes, had he not been such a supreme jerk I may not have axed him, but nobody knows the true extent of his horrid behavior except Ponderosa and me (although his disagreeable personality has been duly noted by those who knew him and reported to the public-at-large). In addition, he had half the same blood pumping through his veins as I do, which I thought would post-stamp me as Jack-the-Ripper's lover. But no. It proves, once again, how utterly out of touch I am in relation to this media-sick planet, and how foolish I was to ever think I could get away with anything.

Jonathan proves to be an excellent link to the world I left behind, but there are a couple of loose ends. My biggest regret is that I cannot express my remorse to Claire and Molly. Claire is friends with señor Vasquelez, and I suppose if she ever chooses to visit down here, I can do something then. It grieves me to think that she might believe that I played her the whole time and that I, astonishingly, have turned out to be the worst Tyler of all. In my heart, I have always cared for Claire and cherish her friendship, a cup of tea or no cup of tea. I pair her with her longtime companion Isabella.

Molly's case is worse. How do you apologize to a mother for killing her only son? I read her drinking has landed her in rehab, and I feel horribly responsible, but there is nothing I can do without endangering myself or others. I don't know what I'd say to her, if given the chance, but at least I could try, just to rid myself of the darkness. Maybe I could convince her that Megan and I had become friends and that I tried to help her. I'm hoping Preacher Jane has put in a good word for me about Megan, since she, in my thinking, was cognizant of most of the truth all along. Regardless, I remain tormented by the fact that I can love one sibling so purely and despise the other one just as purely—to the point of execution. This warped dichotomy, this illness, this bipolar blasphemy will live with me for the rest of my days.

Last but not least, there is Sledge, my mentor. I desperately want to thank him for his Plan B advice. It saved my life. Unlike the others, though, I fully believe that he and I will meet up again down the line. I forget how old he is and the year he is set to be released, but he continues to grow healthier and more spiritually fit as the years roll on. He will long survive, and perhaps his prison sabbatical was a wise decision after all.

One final note. The USC intern—I never found out his name—who lent me his hat when I escaped my office building, never let on to the FBI that he gave me the hat, or that he watched me exit via the freight elevator. Maybe he was afraid of the consequences, or maybe he just liked me; either way, it is our little secret. I still have his hat, and occasionally I put it on at night to cover my shaved head when the mountain air becomes brisk and the coyotes howl and the birds never stop.